JournalStone's 2011
Warped Words

90 Minutes
to Live

Compiled By
Joel Kirkpatrick

JournalStone
San Francisco

JournalStone books may be ordered through booksellers or by contacting:

JournalStone
199 State Street
San Mateo, CA 94401
www.journalstone.com

The views expressed in this work are solely those of the authors and do not necessarily reflect the views of the publisher, and the publisher hereby disclaims any responsibility for them.

ISBN: 978-1-936564-33-0   (sc)
ISBN: 978-1-936564-34-7   (dsj)
ISBN: 978-1-936564-35-4   (ebook)

Library of Congress Control Number: 2011943918

Printed in the United States of America
JournalStone rev. date:

Cover Design: Denis Daniel
Cover Art: Philip Renne

Edited By: Elizabeth Reuter

Dedication

To Rocky Wood

Additional titles from JournalStone:

Shaman's Blood
Anne C. Petty

The Traiteur's Ring
Jeffrey Wilson

Jokers Club
Gregory Bastianelli

Ghosts of Coronado Bay
J.G. Faherty

Imperial Hostage,
Book 1 of the Destruction Series
Phil Cantrill

That Which Should Not Be
Brett J. Talley

Reign of the Nightmare Prince
Mike Phillips

Available through your local and online bookseller or at
www.journalstone.com

Contents

Dead Already
(Science Fiction)

By

John La Rue

Smitty's a good kid.

He ducks through the hatchways ahead of me; pops a corner, pretty good for anybody born after the war. A little over-eager maybe but I let him do it. There's no need; this ship is dead already and so is everyone on it.

If anyone is still here.

"Anything doing?" Captain Jaz buzzes us from back aboard the *Lancer*.

"No ma'am," I report. "Empty hallways."

It's creepy. Dead ships always are and I've never gotten used to the big ones, even when they're filled with people. A spaceship, to me, is a snug thing, wrapped as tightly around a spaceman as a phone around a battery.

But that was before. Back when dead ships stayed dead.

These days, the nanobots just keep chugging away till they run out of slag. Microscopic, mindless drones working from a schematic of the ship's original layout, swarming invisibly over the hull to fill in dents and scratches, bridge gaps and repair systems. They'll repair the ship all right—right back to mint condition even. Only question is whether you're still alive when the fail-safes reset and life support kicks back on.

They market these boats as unsinkable. Indestructible. Set it and forget it—the ship that repairs itself! Sounds great in a pamphlet I guess.

Fate repays us with ships like this one, the *Hannah Lee*, adrift in space with all its machinery ticking over. But somewhere in here I know there are bodies on the deck, rigid as they fell. Silence rings through the ship, end to end, with the click of our boots.

I keep expecting Linda to come around the corner. Keep hoping that she'll tell me how glad she is to see me. That she's sorry she ever left.

The *Hannah Lee's* a luxury cruiser. A party boat. Two people can run it; two hundred could ride. Full-gravity decks, real showers, an inflatable ballroom puffed out of one side, that sort of thing. Gravity decks, can you believe it? Hell of an engine in here somewhere, to support all that.

Now it's just empty, one hallway after another, gentle machines humming in the background, doors hissing open in front of us with perfect automation.

"What the-" Smitty's too sweet of a kid to swear in front of me, thinks I'm some kind of hero from the war. Like we *never* swore.... He stops just through the ballroom door. Any marine I ever met could've killed him from his right side, easy—he never looked and the blind spot on these pressure suits is like...an acre, even with the visor rolled back. I let it slide and duck past him into the ballroom.

The ballroom's pretty swank, if you ask me. Some kind of chandelier with prisms and the walls, though I know they're some light polymer, look a hell of a lot like polished marble.

But it's a ship that's got Smitty's attention. Shit, it's a Betty, parked right there on the dance floor. Jesus H.P. Christ, a whole goddamn Betty, all in one piece.

"Didn't you fly one of these, sir?" Smitty asks me, eyes shining.

A Betty's the least ship a man can take into the sky. Two men, strapped back-to-back around a fuel core—gunner and pilot. You have no life support in there, just you and your suit. No gravity, no air and no eject button.

I went to battle in a Betty a half-dozen times, before me and Randy got promoted past the point of flying—promotion by virtue of survival we figured, cause we never met anybody else who brought back a whole Betty more than four times in a row.

But this one is intact, with the low-libido hull still wrapped in its black matte finish, stealth pinholes as unblemished as the day she was made. Believe me, we stopped making those damned machines before the war even ended.

"What gives?" Captain Jaz buzzes again.

"You won't believe us," Smitty says, "But there's a Betty down here in the ballroom."

"How many pieces?"

That's the way they always came back. Pieces.

"Just the one," said Smitty, "Shipshape, by the look of it. God, what a beauty."

Something *is* wrong with this ship though. Something more than the echo of a pre-flight knot in my stomach. She's uncanny, this one, unearthly, like she's watching me. Ready to put her BB stinger through my pressure suit.

I shake it off.

"Let's cut the chatter," I snap—harder than I meant to, "Smitty, the lifeboats?"

He double-times downstairs, guilty, runs round the Betty to the far wall—the one that's hull plating when the ballroom's not inflated. "Both here," he shouts up.

Well shit.

"Cap'n, is that all of 'em?" I buzz Jaz, but I know the answer already.

"Yeah," she says. "That's all." Jaz keeps the sympathy out of her voice but she has to know it's a blow. No survivors then. No chance Linda got out before whatever happened here took down the ship and everybody on it.

"Now what?" says Smitty, coming back up the ladder.

"Look for bodies," I say.

"Where?"

I just look him in the eye. Make him work it out himself. He plays with the open visor on his helmet as he thinks.

"I guess if my ship were busting up...I'd go for the life support first."

I follow him back out of the ballroom, looking back at that damned Betty.

Now I'm glad Smitty's going through hatches first. There are some things I don't want to see.

It doesn't take long.

"Got one Sir," he calls back.

I can see the legs through the hatch. Can't help but hold my breath. *Anyone but Linda....*

It's Taylor. Bent awkwardly, lying on his face.

"He died in null-G," I observe.

"How you reckon?"

"Bend in the elbow," I point. "Only rigor-mortis in Z-G gives you that twist. He died first and came down after, when our invisible friends got grav going again. A while after or he wouldn't be stiff when he came down."

Smitty nods. "Suffocation," he says. I raise an eyebrow. His turn to explain. He only points. A facemask and a canister lie in the corner, gauge upturned and orange.

Both of us glance at our own gauges. Can't help it.

Suffocation's not a way I want to go, watching the minutes tick down while you struggle harder and harder to draw enough breath.

I figure the first hour is fine. You try to solve whatever problem has you in a bind. You count on the bots to pull through with a repair, patch things up enough to save your sorry ass. Maybe you pray, if that's your thing. After an hour, you start to worry. You tick into yellow on your gauge and start to panic. Then you hit orange. Then you die.

I shudder.

"Think it was a blowout?" Smitty asks.

"Possible," I say. I pause a minute, thinking over whether I want to ask what's on my mind. Oh hell. We came this far. "Your guys bring a forty-four?"

"A what?"

"An N-44," I say but he doesn't get it until I pantomime the hat.

"Oh!" says Smitty, "Oh sure! But ours is a 260. It's *way* better-"

"Run get it, will you?" I cut him off.

"Bring it here, sir?" he asks.

"It's where the stiff is, no?"

He goes.

The forty-four is a thing our guys cooked up during the war, back when we were still learning how to have a real good knockdown up here among the stars. The trouble was, you mostly had whole ships alive or whole ships dead. Never had wounded to tell you how things went bad, so a lot of our trouble-shooting schemes were entirely theoretical.

I turn Taylor over with my foot. His eyes stare up past me, gray.

I reach down and shut them, pull a clump of hair from his head. Funny how much you can tell from hair. It's like a little chemical printout of the last month of a man's life. The air he breathed, the water he drank, the food he ate—it's all bound up in keratin and melanin and oil, laid down line by line as it creeps out of his scalp. They used to use the print to work out where a man had been, Earth or Mars or one of the stations. Wasn't till the war that somebody worked out you could cross-reference the readout with a scan of his cortex and the ship's logs and get a good read on his state of mind in the closing moments.

Good enough to run a simulation. A resurrection, we mostly called it.

You'd see the MP's sitting there with their headphones on, talking, asking questions, watching teletype scrawl across a little green screen, fifty characters at a time and listening close for that thin, flat voice, crackling through static from somewhere beyond.

I did a fair number of exit interviews myself. "Tell Sally I love her," they'd say at the end. Or "Tell Mom I'm sorry." It sticks with you, the idea everybody dies with something left unsaid.

Taylor—I'm not sure I want to do Taylor. I never met the man, when he was alive. Just heard Linda talk about him. About his boat—this boat. About his plans for ion harvesters in the Beltway. About his damned haircut. It's enough to know I resent him. His expiration doesn't change that.

I hear something move in the hallway and fight back the unreasonable surge of hope it might be Linda, climbing out of some unknown safe room. *She's dead, somewhere in here.*

The noise is Smitty, hauling something that looks like a beige cabinet, balanced across a four-wheeled cart half its size and trailing a power cord down the hall.

"What the holy hell is that?" I ask.

"The 260," he says. "It's kind of a wall unit but you said to bring it over...."

If I'd known, I would've had him haul Taylor over to the *Lancer*. It would've been easier.

"Why's it so damned big?"

The N-44 was a thin thing, like a skullcap made of plastic with copper lacework. It had a jack for the processor and another for the headset and that was about the whole deal. You plugged it into the ship's data feed and the computer did the rest.

"It's an all-in-one unit," says Smitty, like a salesman. "You put the hair in there, the head and the hand," he points to the different-sized holes in the thing.

"The hand?"

"Well, sure," says Smitty, but he doesn't look sure. "It gauges conductivity I think. And blood type. All that stuff."

I shake my head. "Wouldn't've worked in my day."

"Sure it would've," he says, "Works anywhere, any time."

"Not if he doesn't have a hand."

I've seen a fair number of those in my day. Back in the first year of the war, the theory was that, in case of a blowout—when your ship's got a hole in it and you're losing air—the best thing to do was to sound an alarm, then roll the bulkheads slowly shut. Give people time to evacuate.

But people didn't evacuate. Not spacemen anyway, brave cusses that we were. We found all kinds of bodies mangled in the doorways or freeze-dried in the blown out room and it didn't get any better when they slowed the roll to give a little more evacuation time.

Not till we had the forty-fours up and running did we work out that men were running towards danger, instead of away from it. Ducking through the doors with the idea they could seal up the hole and save the ship, be a hero. Jamming shoulders into hatchways to hold them open so one more man could come through. You never heard a story where that kind of courage *didn't* end badly mangled.

All the newer ships came with snap doors. Loaded them with pressurized pistons that slammed the buggers shut in a couple of milliseconds. Slice right through you if you were unlucky enough to step through the door at just the wrong instant.

But it worked. Fatalities dropped ten percent and all of us stepped a little quicker through our hatchways. Fleet hop, they call it.

But I don't weigh Smitty down with all that. He'll see enough messes in his day without hearing all mine.

"You ever run that thing?" I ask.

"Just the once," he grins.

"Then by all means." I hold out the lock of hair for him. He takes it gravely from me, drops it in a slot and covers it with a cap.

He lifts Taylor by the shoulders and drags him around until his head slides neatly into a cavity in the cabinet, chattering to me while he works.

"Cap'n says not to worry if you feel a shudder or two—there's a thruster misfiring, so we've got a little spin she's going to dampen out. Hope you don't mind if we drift a bit."

I shrug. I tore into Jaz more than once over the last week to keep the slop out of her search pattern but now we've tracked down the *Hannah Lee*, I don't have any reason to be precise. At least the thruster would give Jaz something to think about, instead of buzzing us every two minutes.

"Ready?" Smitty asks.

I nod; he hits the button.

Taylor's eyes fly open. His jaw snaps, tongue lolling.

"Jesus God Almighty-" I can't help myself. The dead man twitches all over, lightly, rippling under his skin.

"Oh, sorry, sir," says Smitty, "Don't mind the jitters. It's just calibrating."

"What the-?"

"All the nerves fire off," says Smitty, "Maps the pathways through the extremities, the gut. Lots of nerves in the gut."

No shit. I can feel all of mine.

The twitching stops.

"Here we go!" says Smitty, and the screen lights up. There's Taylor's face, in full 3D.

I still hate the guy.

"Boy, am I glad to see you!" he says, "I thought I was *done*."

"It's all right now," I say. It's dangerous, letting a simulation—a resurrection—dwell on his own well-being. Once he realizes he's dead, it's anybody's guess what he'll do. There's no way accurately to simulate that kind of event, so it throws off all the parameters and the program can't handle it. The personality crumples and you get no information at all.

"Where's Linda?" he asks.

I can see Smitty shoot me a look but I keep cool. I've handled interviews before. Worse ones even.

"She's safe," I lie. "We'll take care of her." I've got to change the subject. Get him to focus. Move back in his memory so he can run up on death from the front end, instead of working backwards.

"Was that a Betty I saw down in the ballroom?" Resurrections go best if you can give them something specific to latch onto. A nice, tactile memory that lights up a couple parts of the brain the forty-four can locate and use as a baseline. Objects. Places. People. Sex.

He grins. "Hell yeah! Can you believe it? Museum-quality. Totally intact." his face changes. "But it's mine, you hear? We found it."

"Not here for the salvage," I reassure him. A Betty like that's worth a good ten, eleven figures. Only natural he'd be wary. Especially a guy like Taylor.

"Where'd you find her?"

"Pretty much right here," he says. "We sort of stumbled on her—a distress call, real weak. Matched speeds and brought her on board. Slid her into the ballroom—that was Linda's idea. Is she ok?"

"She's safe," I nod. "What'd you do after you brought her in? Open her up?"

"Damned skippy," he says, "You think I'm going to haul her home with a couple of forty-year-old corpses still inside?"

Forty years. Has it been so long?

"Besides," says Taylor, "I'm as agnostic as the next guy but a man deserves a funeral."

I respect that. Grudgingly but there it is. It's more than I would've expected from a guy like Taylor. I guess I should do the same for him.

"Poor guys must have been freeze-dried," I say. Better than the alternative. Bacteria takes a while to get at you in zero-G but when they do, it's a mess. Taylor shakes his head—the simulated one.

"That was the weirdest thing. We cracked her open and she had full pressure—you could hear the hiss and smell the dust when we opened her up—but there wasn't anyone inside. I've never seen anything like it. Three-quarter fuel, slag topped off, Hopper full of BB's, safety still on; but nobody home. Linda figured it must've been blasted straight out of a hangar, in a blowout or something."

That doesn't sit right with me. A Betty at three-quarter fuel? Unlikely. On deck, she's full, empty or latched onto a pump. And slag? For nanobots? Betties didn't have bots. Weren't even standard issue till the end of the war and by then we'd given up on Betties.

"Hang on," I say, "You had pressure on the Betty? Air inside?"

"Sure," says Taylor, "She out-gassed when we cracked her open."

"Fuck." I swore. I left him there. Left Smitty. Started running. "Smitty go back to the ship," I shout over my shoulder. I hit the intercom. "Fire her up, Jaz, We gotta clear out." Nothing. "Jaz, you hear me?" Never mind. Smitty will tell her. Me, I'm bolting for the ballroom, my head ringing with a stupid story I heard in a bar a while back. A story about a set of goddamned Betties.

We stopped building them near the end of the war, it's true, cause too many men inside never came back out. But it didn't mean our boys didn't come up with new uses for the ones we already had.

I take the ballroom stairs three at a time, swing around the Betty to her handholds.

Our weapons crews stocked empty Bettys with all kind of surprises. Sent them out, dead in the water after a battle, usually one we were losing, cause that's pretty much all we did for the first three-quarters of the war. Set them up to trigger after we all left, maybe when the enemy comes along looking to salvage and BOOM, there's a nuke or a neutron or grav-warp or some such.

Here are the handholds, giant staples up her spine. Three, four, and circle left for the gunner's hatch.

But the one story that gave all of us at the bar the willies, was the swarm. A nano-weapon that ate ships alive. Load up a Betty with a slag tank and a swarm of bots that are swapped from repair to consume. Pressurize the cockpit, so when their techs come along to take a look at her guts—puff! A little breath of air carries a microscopic army out and spews them all over your deck, or your hull or wherever you are. You don't see a thing. Don't even notice. But silently, methodically, they start chewing through your ship's systems one by one until *nothing* is left.

Comms go down, so you can't cry out. Alarm systems go offline, so you never know it's coming. So your own bots never even activate. Power shuts off, so you can't fight back. Thrust and grav so you can't maneuver. Life support at the very last.

You can't shoot 'em and you can't stop 'em. Your only hope—so they said at the bar—was to board the Betty and find the control box, shut the swarm down from its command center.

I come through the hatch and see it. A flat black thing no bigger than a toaster, six green lights and bolted to the floor where the pilot ought to stand. No buttons, no switches and no inputs I can see.

God damn, God damn!

My hand flies to my belt but I don't carry a sidearm anymore. But here, yes, above the door, the pry-bar, standard issue as an engineer's concession the machine would probably be busted all to hell, before we landed it and wanted to get out.

Thank God.

I plunge the pry-bar down between my feet—no room in here for a decent swing at the thing. One-two. Three-four. I-have. To-kill. This-God. Damn-box.

I stop, sweating, breathing hard. Bits of electronics lie scattered around the tiny cabin. The six little lights are dark.

I sigh and lean back against the fuel column, tipping my helmet back into the familiar cradle, letting relief wash through me. God, it's just as sweet as it used to be. Coming away alive and kicking.

"Like old times, hey Randy?" I say to no one in particular. Randy hated it when I did that. When we'd pulled out of a battle that was mostly over and I'd lean back, relax my intensity while he drove us home.

"God damn it, Pepper," he used to say, "Fat lady ain't singing till we hit the deck!"

And I'd close my eyes and just float off, while Randy juked us back to the carrier. Drove him nuts.

I can't help but look over at the mirror—the only sightline between gunner and pilot, just a small thing, size of a credit card.

Eyes stare back at me. I freeze. My breath catches in my throat and my mind reels off in six directions.

Taylor said the cockpits were empty; I know those eyes; the pilot's dead; get out, get out; the pilot's dead—*it's Linda.*

I twist round to look but that's dumb. There's no better way to see the pilot's side than the mirror. She's still staring at me. She'll stare forever. She's dead.

The thought slides around my mind like an ice cube in an empty tumbler; I feel its touch but it won't sink in. It's not real.

I guess I've known for a while now that I'd find her body somewhere aboard. But here she is, looking at me. Me, I just look back. I think about the way her hair tosses when she runs. Tossed when she ran.

I have to go around. Come at her through the pilot's hatch.

I shake off her gaze, push through the hatch and swing around. I'm not sure what I'm going to do. Take her away I guess. Put her to rest.

I open the door and there she is.

She's buckled the harness across her chest; her head leans against the cradle. What's left of it anyway. Linda never was the type to wait around for suffocation to set in and I don't have to look for a pistol on the floor to know what happened here.

The world blurs for a while as I cling to the handholds outside the pilot's hatch.

A million half-regrets flit through my head.

If only I'd kept her happier.

If only we hadn't fought.

If only that goddamned Taylor-

If only-

But all that slides away and my eyes run dry as they catch sight of the floor at Linda's fleet.

Six green lights blink away atop a small flat box that shouldn't be there.

My God.

The pistol's there too, and a wax pencil, and the pilot's crowbar, chipped and a little bent from hard use.

God damn.

I look up again at Linda, at her light brown eyes with nothing behind them.

Something is written on her arm, big letters in red wax pencil.

They regrow, it says.

God damn, God damn. How long have I wasted? I'm such an idiot. A lazy, sentimental fool. Fat lady ain't singing. If there are two control boxes, there could just as easily be three or four. I could hunt all day and never find them all.

I drop down from the Betty's side and dash for the stairs. God damn, God damn. Randy always told me this would happen one day. I let my guard down too early and the enemy kept moving. Probably by now, the one I killed has respawned.

I'm up the ladder and slinging down the hall, hollering into my Comms. "Jaz! You there? Smitty?" The empty ship echoes, a clatter of shouts and my own sharp footfalls but nobody chatters back.

And now here's Smitty, jogging up to meet me.

"We got to *go!*" I shout, waving at him to turn around.

"No good," he says, "Hatch is locked, and I can't raise Jaz."

I shoulder past him without explaining. Round the corner and bang on the hatch with my fists. "JAAAAZ!"

"Shhh!" says Smitty, "What's that?"

There's a clank. Another.

"No, no *no no*," I say. "We're right here, Jaz, just open the door. *Open the door!*" But there's the hiss, the rumble and that little jolt severing one ship from another.

I swing over to the nearest window. God damn. There she goes, drifting away. Did she know?

"Suit up," I snap at Smitty, pulling my visor down. It's not too far, between the *Lancer* and us yet. Our suits will stand up to the vacuum; Jaz can swing around and pick us up. It might even be better this way; less chance the weaponized bots will leap the distance, from the *Hannah Lee* to the *Lancer*.

But then the running lights flicker and I see a touch of tumble in her flight path. That's not Jaz's hand at the controls. The lights wink out. I can hardly see the ship at all, lit by nothing but stars and the backwash of the *Hannah Lee's* windows. A ghost of a ship.

"Well shit-" says Smitty, his voice small and tinny through the speakers.

"C'mon," I say, snapping the seals back off my helmet again. "We got to finish talking with Taylor."

There's nothing else to do.

Taylor's still awake on the screen when we get back. He's quiet, till he sees us.

"I'm dead, aren't I?" he says, straight off. It's not really a question, so I nod.

"Linda, too?"

I nod again. He bites his lip.

"You remember?" I ask.

"Yeah."

I wait.

"It was awful," he says. "Me and Linda were so excited. So happy. We found the Betty," he smiles, bitter. "We were rich," he shakes his head. "We went upstairs to celebrate. Had a few drinks. A shower. Had a good time."

I don't meet Smitty's eye.

"We didn't even know anything was wrong, till Linda went back up to the controls. Nothing worked. No thrust. No attitude. Nothing.

"Figured it was a fuse," Taylor's resurrection shakes its head again. "I started down to look and I—I just stepped through the door here when the blowout sounded, the doors clapped shut."

"I put on my mask. Ninety minutes I figured, plenty of time. We'd be fine." Taylor breaks off for a minute. I wait him out. "I tried to fix it. God, I tried. I rebooted everything. Soft, hard, all of it. I couldn't get a damned thing working."

There's something he isn't saying. He's looking at me now. Deciding.

"I think I might've killed us," he says, "Cause every time I tried to fix something, it only got worse."

He wants me to tell him it's not his fault. But it is. It's his fault she was here at all. I didn't want her to go. God, we fought about that.

"Linda said she thought it was the bots. That they'd turned against us."

I nod. "She fought back."

"That's Linda." Taylor bites his lip. Neither one of us says anything.

Behind the forty-four I can see Smitty's eyes get big. His hand goes up to his mouth and I can see the nickel drop as he works it all out: the bots, the failures and the *Lancer*. He leans back against the bulkhead. Doesn't say anything. A good kid, Smitty.

"There was nothing I could do," says Taylor, almost begging. "I tried everything. Hard reboots. Manuals. The shit just didn't work. Didn't even respond after a while."

He's hit a groove; he can't stop talking. I can see sweat standing out on his simulated skin.

"The air went out. The grav turned off. The power went down. Then the backup. I was just floating in the dark. Just floating. Till you came. Just floating in the dark and wondering if Linda was going to make it, if she got down to the lifeboats, if she got away."

I can't look at him. Can't look at Smitty. I stare at the orange gauge on Taylor's empty air tank. Usually by now a resurrection's gone off kilter, got so wrapped up in its own thoughts it can't function and goes silent for a final time. I wonder if that might be better.

"We were going to get married you know."

"I know." I say. It shuts him up. I force myself to meet his gaze.

Taylor looks at me for a while.

"You're her father," he says.

I nod.

"I'm sorry," he says. There's nothing more to say.

The lights go down. His face flickers out.

"It's okay." I say, to the empty space in the forty-four.

I flip down my faceplate and check my gauge.

Less than two hours left.

"So now what," says Smitty, "We're just going to sit here and wait to die?"

I turn and start to unclip.

"Here," I say, pulling the hose free from my air can. "Take it."

"That's yours Sir," Smitty says.

"I don't want it." I say. Everything I love is dead already. Without the tank connected, it's already getting hot and stuffy in my suit. It's much better this way. Better than waiting all that time.

Smitty will have twice as long now. Maybe long enough to outlast the attack. Maybe long enough someone will come by and rescue him.

"Fuck you sir." Smitty says. He's shoving the hose back on the can.

"Come on Smitty," I say, but I'm too lightheaded to fight him.

"Respectfully, sir, I don't intend to outlive you," he says. Somewhere in my suit, a valve opens and I can feel the cool air rush up past my face. "You want me to live; you gotta save both our asses."

Smitty stands up and strides out into the hall, leaving me sitting alone, watching the spots in front of my eyes. I follow him, jogging to catch up.

"Feeling better sir," he says. It's not a question. I don't answer. He moves on. "Lemme get this right: the nanobots are bad."

"Yes."

"They're killing the ship."

"Yes."

"And we can't fight 'em."

"No."

Smitty nods, once.

"Then we'll run."

"Taylor and Linda played this game once already," I say.

"Yeah, but we're gonna win." He's headed for the ballroom.

"Lifeboats won't go," I remind him.

"Not taking them." We bust through the doors. "We're taking *that.*"

The Betty.

Smitty pulls up his visor, seals in.

"Can you fly this thing?" he asks.

"Yeah," I say, hesitating. He cocks his head, asking *what gives*. I flick my chin toward the ship. "Linda's in there."

He nods. Climbs up to the pilot's hatch. My stomach flip-flops, watching him lean in and haul her body out. It's not till she floats out into the room and hangs in the air that I realize the gravity's gone out, engines cut. We're all freewheeling now, my feet whispering up off the deck unbidden.

I hold the banister and watch her drift—Linda—revolving slowly in the air, her long hair wrapping carelessly across the cavity at the back of her head. Peaceful.

"You coming?" Smitty calls back, voice distant through the faceplate.

I sling out across the ballroom, muscle memory taking over. I twist in the air and wheel one hand to swing my feet around and I slide past Smitty right into the cockpit.

He grins and shakes his head, muttering something too low for me to hear.

"Gunner's back there," I hock my thumb. "Back door only."

Again, he gives me that grin and hauls hand over hand back to the other hatch.

"Hey Smitty," I shout as he goes, "You thought about how to get out of here?" The doors aren't open and I'd bet those were the first systems the nanobots shut down. Betties aren't loaded with explosives—it was always pure ballistics, basically ball bearings at high enough speeds to melt through hull plating.

"What," says Smitty, "Don't the Navy teach you kids how to punch your way out of a paper bag?"

It's obvious then what he's going to do. I don't need to hear the whir of the turrets warming up.

The inflatable walls aren't meant for any kind of impact; you're expected to deflate and shut the lid when there's trouble, rely on the plated stuff and fold up the polymer walls behind a couple of bulkheads.

Smitty rakes down the length of the wall with his first salvo. A second won't be needed—it's tearing open under the interior pressure. It looks like one of those slow-motion clips of bursting water balloons, with polymer strands rippling back from the slash Smitty's opened.

Air surges forward into the vacuum and it crystallizes, hurling Linda's body out past us into the night, and sweeping us with it in a swirling, screaming snowstorm.

I punch the engine once, hard and get us clear of the debris. Outside sounds fall away and all we're left with is Smitty's hollering, "Oh *hell* yeah! I *like* them apples!"

I let him whoop for a moment but now I know how Randy felt—we're far from safe just yet.

"Ok kid, bring it back for a sec," I say, "You see a box on the floor? Six green lights?"

"Yeah," says Smitty. "So?"

"That's the brains for the bots. I killed it once but found another over here, so that one grew back."

"Can we kill them both at once?"

"That's the idea," I say, "But I want to get away from the other ships first."

"There are other boxes on them?"

Smart kid, Smitty.

"Sir?" he says, "Is that the Lancer?"

"Where?"

"Forward, three-five?"

Shit, it is. All dark still, a shadow passing before the stars, with just a hint of an ion glow at her tail. And she's moving towards us—exactly towards us, on an intercept course. It doesn't make any sense, unless—

"Jaz?" I punch up the hailing frequencies. "Jaz, you in there?" Maybe she's made it after all. Maybe she fought back the bots, retook the *Lancer*.

"Sir, if it's not her-"

"Don't shoot!" I snap, "Jaz, you read me? Gimme a waggle." I shake our tail as the *Lancer* looms closer, still right on track to cross our path. "Waggle dammit-"

Smitty opens up with everything he's got. It isn't much, just bright little blips hurled out along our path.

"Sorry Jaz," I whisper.

I can see the *Lancer* shudder with the first impacts. Her nose drifts down as gasses vent somewhere forward and I pull up hard and edge over her, close enough to feel the tug of her gravity plates.

Smitty swings the guns around as we pass.

"Engines," I shout, "Get the engines!" Shit, if these bots are flying our boats...God, I wish it were me in the gunner's pit and Randy at the stick. I've made that shot a hundred times and it's killing me to hear the guns clatter without knowing where they're pointed.

But I see the blue arc aft, a plasma breach in at least one tube and Smitty's shouting, "Punch it, punch it!"

I don't need to be told. We're already gone.

"Shit, shit, shit," he says, "The *Hannah Lee*."

She's lumbering around to follow us now too, already coming abreast of the crippled *Lancer*.

"How the hell are they following us?" I ask. The Betty's only form of armor is her low-libido hull, which is supposed to baffle any kind of automated tracking, on the theory you can't shoot what you can't see. Well, forty years ago anyway.

"You said these boxes broadcast, yeah?"

Shit, of course they do. I grab my pry-bar and talk Smitty through to his.

"One, two, THREE."

The crowbar shakes and stings my hands through my gloves as I hammer away at my box and I relish every shockwave as another tiny taste of vengeance.

"Got mine," says Smitty.

I don't wait to confirm, I just yank the stick around and angle my mirrors to watch the *Hannah Lee* come up behind us. She sails on by, course unchanged.

Smitty laughs.

At first, I figure it's just nerves but he just keeps going.

"Something funny?"

"I just realized," he says, "We beat 'em, but we're gonna die anyway," he shakes his head. "I got two hours of air in here and we're in the middle of fucking nowhere."

He's right.

I've got less air than him. Maybe ninety minutes. The nearest station is Freemason's and that's six days away by any reasonable burn. The only chance is... "Hey Smitty," I say, and now I'm the one laughing like a maniac. "How you feel about eight G's?"

It's about as much acceleration as Betty can crank out at full throttle. I don't know how long she can do it; I don't think anybody knows.

"I feel like I'd pass out," says Smitty.

He's right. The blood rushes down from your brain to your feet and pools there—a pressure suit does a lot to keep circulation normal but at eight G's you have to expect you'll cut down oxygen flow to the brain and then it's goodnight for at least a while.

"I feel like I use less O2 when I'm blacked out," he says.

Good enough. I'm already pulling the Betty's nose around, letting her drift and correct. If I'm off by even a tenth of a degree at this distance—if there's even a touch of tumble on her—we'll miss Freemason's by thirty-five million miles. Nobody's going to be awake to correct the course and we don't even have time to decelerate properly.

This will only work if the aim is perfect. We have to come in on an impact path—or at least closely enough the computers will flag the trajectory and somebody will come out to find us.

"Smitty," I say, "You're a good kid."

I punch it.

THE END

Godforsaken
(Horror)

By

Brad Carpenter

Death didn't knock; He rang the doorbell. He hovered over my front porch with a scythe in one hand and a bouquet of freshly cut roses in the other. I opened the door in my skivvies, sipping a cup of coffee as black as the apparition before me. "Ronald Scanlan," Death wailed, rattling concealed chains hidden in the depths of his robe. "You have lived far, far too long." I emphatically agreed. He handed me the roses, I inhaled their ethereal fragrance and then, as usual, I woke up.

The pain in my hip throbbed, my arthritis-ridden joints ached, my bladder was full, my heart empty. A few days ago, I turned eighty. That's eight-zero. At this rate of decay Death was all I had left.

I live by my lonesome in the magical land of Hollywood, where anything and everything is possible; unless you're an eighty-year-old washout like me. In this city, in my line of work, I'm an ancient ruin. A fucking Mayan temple. In my former life—my life before my kids forced me into assisted living—I was a hotshot in the field of special effects. If a film needed monster makeup or any type of animatronics, my partner and I were always the first to get the call. But these crackerjacks running the industry today wanted nothing to do with the likes of me; they cared *nothing* about my work ethic, nor my expertise. To them, I was just another fossil, stuck in the tar pits of La Brea.

Never mind that I have more film credits than I have socks.

And I have a lot of socks.

I picked out a pair, got out of bed and showered. Today was election day. The year was 1984, the time of hot summers and cold wars. I called my son with the faint hope he'd give me a ride to the county courthouse. He said he had to work—but at least he answered my call. That's more than I could say for my daughter; I got the distinct impression she was ignoring me completely. *Guess you're walking today Ronald, you sorry-ass-sack-of-shit.* Luckily my hip was feeling very medicated at the moment but I knew, by the time *Charles in Charge* started at eight o'clock, it would be throbbing something awful.

I voted for Walter Mondale but Reagan would win, of course...again. Everyone knew it. If you ask me, democracy doesn't work.

I didn't even watch the results. I didn't care. Instead I took advantage of my VCR, which, by the way, was the best invention to come along since air conditioning. Tonight was some B movie starring people I've never heard of. The special effects were atrocious—something any asshole could do in their backyard—but I kept watching because the girl in it had wonderful tits. In a funny coincidence, it happened to be about Death. *Hey, stranger...I was just thinking 'bout you.*

My mind wandered off then, as it so often does. I started thinking about creative ways to kill myself. Not that I'd actually do it mind you. Just a way to pass the time. *I could suffocate myself wearing a silicone monster mask,* I thought, grinning so wide the wrinkles on my forehead became folds. *Yes! A monster mask, preferably something with fangs!* I imagined my ghost floating in the rafters, watching the police find my body stretched out on my piss-yellow couch wearing the grotesque face of a gargoyle. That'd be a great way to go. It'd be like leaving behind a calling card of my work.

A scream ripped me from my daydream. The well-endowed brunette was naked, running through a very smoky graveyard. Behind her came Death: tall, lean, with bleached, boney fingers always reaching outward. I sighed deeply, trying to riddle out why Death hadn't found his way to my front porch yet. I was beginning to think he'd never find me. Then, on a sweltering hot morning in mid-August, the doorbell rang.

* * *

Alas, it wasn't the Grim Reaper. But it was close enough. It was a Hollywood executive who probably wanted the same thing as Death: to take whatever's left of my soul.

He wore a manicured gray suit with a gaudy red bowtie, a risky bit of fashion that would have made a less confident man look foolish but this man appeared regal, sleek and even elegant. On the other hand, I was still in my bathrobe, the one with the Tabasco stain on it. Also, my socks were mismatched: one black with a red stripe, one solid white with no stripe.

"Don't act like you aren't happy to see me Scanlan," said Bernie Heller. He smiled a fiendish smile, revealing a solid gold tooth. I swear it sparkled, just like in a goddamn cartoon. He didn't wait for an invitation; he waltzed into the living room, took off his coat and laid it over the couch. He paused when he saw the oval mirror on the wall; straightened his bowtie.

Bernie Heller was a Jew with a real cocky attitude—what I like to call 'Jewitude'. He had wealth, he had power and he lived to flaunt his authority. "My dad would be furious to see you rotting away in a dump like this."

His father was my former partner. Joel Heller worked his way through the ranks, beginning as my partner in the fifties and then he dabbled in set design. Next, sometime in the mid-sixties, he moved on to producing and directing. Then, due to his considerable wealth, he formed his own production company; by the time Bernie was born his dad had his own studio. It's no surprise his son picked up where Joel left off. The Hellers were like hot air balloons, they kept on rising and rising, until the entire world stretched below them.

"Get dressed," he snapped his fingers at me. "Maybe take a shower. We gotta be downtown in..." he paused, glanced at his wristwatch. "*Ah* Christ-on-a-pogo-stick, we're gonna be late. Better skip the shower Scanlan, just put on a tie and let's hit the road. If ya don't have a tie you can borrow one of mine. I gotta few spares."

I frowned, momentarily speechless. "I have a tie," I said, stupidly.

"Well, giddyup."

When I didn't move he placed a hand on my shoulder, looked me square in the eyes. "Jesus, are you going to make me say it? Look, we need you to give us your opinion on something."

"A movie?" It was the last thing I expected to hear. Could it be? Was it possible, one of these young assholes valued my professional opinion?

"Yeah, some B-movie horror picture called *Godforsaken*." Bernie scratched the stubble under his chin. "This one's got us big-shots perplexed. I mean, it's brilliant. But we don't know what to do with it. We don't have a clue how the director achieved some of these shots. The effects...well...shit...it's something we've never seen before. I mentioned your name to some of the others, showed 'em some of your work, plus I remembered you and my dad were buddy-buddy...thought you could give us some insight."

"I'm...I'm honored."

"Don't get all sentimental on me, Sally Field. It's just some low-budget Grind-house flick."

"Well, I'm still honored."

He smiled at me again. But this time the smile was genuine. For a brief moment I saw beyond the silly bowtie and gold tooth; I saw his father, the man I grew to love all those years ago.

I was about to say something reminiscent about his old man, when Bernie's face suddenly turned serious. "Scanlan, that movie..." his voice trailed away; stopped short in his throat. "That goddamn movie...I can't get it out of my head. *Godforsaken* is an apt title indeed. It's the most terrifying thing I've seen...*ever.*"

* * *

Four silhouettes gathered around a ticking projector; their shadows were faceless giants in neatly tailored suits, arguing amongst themselves, grumbling, flailing hands, flapping gums, smoking like chimneys. I had to take a step back to let my tired eyes really drink in the situation. An hour ago, I was inventing clever ways to kill myself and now, here I stood, in the presence of some of the biggest players in Hollywood—at least on the business end of things.

They hardly noticed me.

Not a one bothered to shake my hand or took the time to introduce themselves. For a good ten minutes I stood there feeling like a turd in a field of roses; until, finally, a man with gargantuan gold rings on each of his ten fingers handed me a freshly cut cigar, then gave a second one to Bernie. I don't really like to smoke, (the smell gets stuck in my mustache, I end up smelling it all day and night) but I took the cigar anyway. It tasted wonderful, made me wonder if I'd been smoking Average Joe cigars my whole life and these were some high-end, ultra-swanky cigars only available to millionaires and fascist dictators.

"Most movie directors are vain people Mr. Scanlan, as I'm sure you're aware," said Ring Man, pacing. "So, why then do we have *no* idea who made this film?"

The other two nameless men didn't bother to turn around. Both were seated in the second row of the viewing area. The first man—a skinny fellow, built like an upside down broom with an extra-pointy nose reminding me of a pyramid—doodled on a napkin impatiently. Every few seconds he'd look at his watch and sigh. The other man was a huge, lumpy grizzly bear who puffed on a cigarette instead of a cigar. Not once did he look me in the eyes.

Bernie Heller continued where Ring Man left off. "We have absolutely nothing to go on. There's no opening credits. There's no closing credits. In fact, the only credit throughout the entire movie is the title crawl, which you will see here in just a second...it's very disturbing."

I cleared my throat, doing my best to sound as if I actually belonged in this room. "How did you...um...how did you come across this film in the first place?"

"It was a gift...of sorts," said Bernie. He passed a manila envelope to me, addressed to him and to three others, already ripped open. In the center, written in tiny, perfect calligraphy was a single word: *Godforsaken*. "Two weeks ago I found this on my front porch. Just laying there, pink bow and all. Little did I know each one of these cocksuckers got the same gift on their doorsteps."

"This isn't summer camp for us, Mr. Scanlan. We don't necessarily like each other. In fact, just last year my studio about went bankrupt thanks to George," explained Ring Man, using his cigar as a pointer. The corpulent man with his back to me waved, pleased with himself. I couldn't see his face but I could tell he was smiling.

Pyramid Nose decided now was a great time to break his vow of silence. Years of sucking tar made his voice sound more robotic than human—gruff, coarse, like a goose honking at a predator. "You fellas missed the bulls-eye on this one. The question isn't *who* made this picture, it's *how*...Now I've seen some shit in movies that falls short of actual magic but this film...this film makes my eyes want to bleed."

Ring Man took this as his cue to start the movie. He flipped a switch on the projector, which gave a loud pop. The warm, welcoming aroma of burnt celluloid tickled my nostrils; before I'd fully prepared myself, the movie began.

Words scrolled up like in the beginning of *Star Wars*:

Five people. One simple rule.

Get out of the house.

Get out of the house before the movie is over. Before THE END.

Ready? Let's begin....

Lights.

Camera.

Action....

Godforsaken.

FADES IN: Dandelions sway back and forth; a few whiskers rip apart from their brothers and glide in the gentle breeze. A scene of serenity. Yet the music tells a different story. Bold, brass, bellicose horns foreshadow the horror to come; high-pitched violins erupt in a storm of strings. The camera pans across the field of dandelions, slowly, with no apparent rush. Buzzing flies are heard before they are seen. A large man drags a cow's carcass through the mud, leaving behind a trail of blood. The man's face is never seen, camera stays on the cow.

Eventually, the camera pans up, revealing a dilapidated two-story house complete with a wraparound porch and a slanted, brick chimney. All the windows are missing; the front door is sideways, hanging by a single hinge. In an upstairs window, screams can be heard—shouts for help....

At the bottom left corner of the screen, black numbers appear. Starts at 00:00, and begins to count up. 00:01, 00:02....

I took my eyes away from the screen for only a second, tapped Bernie on the shoulder. He wasn't blinking. "Those numbers," I asked, "is that some sort of new time code you guys put in post production?"

Bernie shook his head. "No. It's part of the film. It's a countdown...to the end."

My heart raced inside my chest and I then realized; I was terrified. "How long's the film?"

"Standard industry length," said Bernie. "Ninety minutes."

The cow is now being pulled up the front porch stairs. The head slaps each step. Thump. Thump. Thump. *Something dressed in stained overalls sits on a rocking chair petting a cat—at first you think it is human but then you see the rat-like snout and pointed whiskers. It dangles a wooden marionette over the purring kitten. The camera moves past the creature—only showing it for half a second—it's neither explained nor seen again. In fact, a heartbeat later, the rocking chair is empty and the marionette is in crumbles on the floorboards; crows peck at the crumbs, cawing, barking, flapping.*

The cow is hurled suddenly—rather violently—inside the house. It bounces slightly upon impact. Black things, too tall and too slender to be human, emerge from the shadows. They can't be properly seen in such low light. But they are fast. In a flash, they have attached themselves to the corpse, stripping what's left of the flesh, tearing cartilage, sucking marrow, devouring her whole.

CUTS TO: UPSTAIRS ROOM. Five people are nailed to the wall: Two males, three females. Both sexes are bleeding, filthy, screaming for help. Someone has dressed them up in animal costumes. The clock is ticking. 08:30, 08:31, 08:32...

A voice calls out from behind the camera. "Time for roll call!" says the voice.

"Dog," says a slender man, dressed in floppy ears and blood-caked fur. Over a dozen nails keep him plastered to the wall.

"Cat," sobs the next victim, a girl, only a teenager, no older than sixteen. She is dressed in a cat costume, with her face painted black with whiskers. There is a hole in the costume, exposing her left breast. She tries to scream for help but the camera cuts quickly to the next person.

"Bird," says the other male, a black man. He has a huge wound going down his side. Long peacock feathers of every color of the rainbow have been tarred to his

arms and his exposed back. An extra layer of barbed wire is stretched across his bare chest, making certain he is nice and snug.

"Tiger," says a blonde.

"Monkey," a girl with glasses.

The camera cuts to a wide shot; shows all five writhing in pain, clinging to the wall. "ACTION!" shouts the voice behind the camera. All five, one by one, slowly, painfully, rip themselves free of the nails and the barbwire.

I turned my head during this scene. I admit...I was feeling pretty squeamish. Every few seconds I'd peek at the screen to check on their progress. Once they all got down from the wall, for a good five minutes, all they did was scream at each other. Finally, the man in the bird costume got them working together. They did their best to stop each other's bleeding. In a desperate attempt to make weapons, Dog began ripping floorboards.

Twenty minutes and counting...19:99, 20:00, 20:01....

Cautiously, they make their way outside the room into the hallway. Figures are stirring; encroaching ever closer. Peculiar shadows float above the ground, closing in from all directions. They are round as beach balls with water-hose arms scooting against the floor as they float past; long necks sprout up from their swollen torsos leading to an elongated cow-shaped head, with rotten flesh and exposed serrated teeth. They hiss at the people, spitting black tar. Dog and Bird swing their boards at the creatures but the brittle wood shatters against their bulbous, round hides. Monkey takes one good look at the hovering menaces and finds she can't move. An eruption of tar covers her legs and hips. Instantly, she hits the floor—face first—screaming, burning and fizzing. The skin around her leg is reduced to a flakey, gooey paste. Tiger runs to help her, pulls Monkey to her feet; but the skin peels off like a banana, revealing bone. She passes out in Tiger's arms.

They have no choice but to leave Monkey behind. Rubbery hands grope her clothing, ripping it to shreds. Their tongues unravel and roll across her body, coating her in a thick lacquer of saliva. Sometime around the 23:00 minute mark, they grow bored of her. A dozen hands pluck her from the ground and, with tremendous force, they slam her head into the wall. Her nose shatters, her glasses split in half; her skull cracks; and they leave her there, twitching, as blood pools over the floor's wooden slats.

"CUT!" says the off screen voice. Finally, the Director walks out from behind the camera. He stands over the body of Monkey, grinning a smile too big for a human face. The Director has dark eyes with hair the color of wheat, his facial features are simple, as if they were merely painted on; he wears a pinstriped suit, with brown penny loafers, complete with a tiny copper penny. He bends down, kisses her forehead at the exact spot of the gash. Methodically, building tension, the Director reaches

inside his coat pocket, produces a tiny pair of scissors and cuts a lock of her hair. He smells it. He kisses it. Then, he pins it to his shirt. He shows the camera. *"Four to go!" he shouts, giddy.*
      31:19, 31:20, 31:21....

At this point, I'd had enough. Something seemed too realistic about it...it never felt like I was watching a movie. I asked for a drink of water but nobody moved. I got up, found the bathroom on my own, splashed water on my face, and gave my heart a minute to slow down. When I came back, *something*—the cross between a praying mantis and a petrified, gnarled tree—carried the head of the man in the dog costume in his hands...and only the head! The body was left inside some bizarre torture device with spikes and wheels and bloody pieces of hemp rope. I was instantly glad I'd missed that part.

    "You gonna puke, Scanlan?" Bernie asked me.

    "Maybe."

    "So, howdoya think he did it? How were those effects possible? Computer graphics, you think?"

    I shook my head, lost in thought. *How did they do this?* I wondered. *How was this movie even possible? Did he super-impose these monsters? No, couldn't be.* I was almost a hundred percent certain it wasn't any kind of layer or a composite; I have a good eye for that kind of thing. And these monsters were seamless! *Computers*? I supposed it was possible but as far as I knew, there wasn't a computer on the planet that could generate something so realistic. It definitely wasn't prosthetics or wirework of any kind. I mean, the monsters didn't even have a humanistic base...this was something else entirely.

    "What if it's real?" I heard myself say. As soon as I said it, I wished I could take it back. However, surprisingly, no one laughed.

    "You just gave the director the ultimate compliment Ronald," said Pyramid Nose, his gruff voice echoed above the screams of the girl dressed as a tiger. She was being burned alive on some kind of gigantic oven; her hands bound, her feet dangling over an eye of a stove. The flames were so intense her costume melted and then her skin began to catch fire. A group of weasel-like atrocities sat around a picnic table, naked, save for plastic bibs; they beat forks and knives on the table like impatient children.

    But before they were allowed to dig in, the same man with blonde curly locks stepped out from behind the camera, yielding a very familiar pair of scissors. Again, the Director clipped out a chunk of her charred, well-done hair, then pinned the clump next to the first one. He was getting quite the collection.

44:58, 44:59, 45:00....

"Should I be impressed? Or should I be horrified?" I asked.

"Show him the letter," barked the corpulent man in the front row.

Bernie did as he was told. He handed me a letter, handwritten, on thick yellowed paper.

Dear Sirs,

I am pleased you have taken an interest in my films. And, I am told, you have taken quite the interest in me as well. This is understandable considering my mysterious nature. Please, allow me to explain: movies to me, are more than moving, talking pictures. They are a gateway into the human soul. No matter how perverse or how graphic, anything you see on the screen lives within all of our hearts.

A director is a god of his own universe. Just as the God above our heads needs no recognition, neither do I. All I want to do is tell a story. A story of death, of survival and of fear. Humanity at its most naked.

After reading these words, if you still wish to meet with me, I'd be honored for you to visit my home in Bouldergreen, Kentucky. Address is on the envelope. I do not have a phone but you can call the local grocery store and leave a message with the grocer if you plan on making a visit. Sorry in advance for any inconvenience but I will never step foot in Hollywood. You must come to me.

Wink, wink.

-The Director-

I looked up from the letter, baffled. "He's just some nutter living in the woods of Kentucky?"

"So it would seem."

"Impossible. How'd he get the money to do this?" I pointed at the screen. At the moment, the black man in the bird costume was being pecked to death by a murder of carrion crows. How ironic. Blood dripped from their beaks, splashing on the lens of the camera. 71:40, 71:41, 71:42....

"That's one of the questions I'm going to ask him."

"Bernie, no. You can't. This guy...he's a creeper. I mean, who in their right mind closes their letters with *wink, wink*?"

We watched the rest of the movie in relative silence, save for the nervous patter of tapping feet and the occasional awkward cough. At the climax, somewhere around the 82:00 minute mark, the house had completely melted away, revealing to the audience they were, in fact, in

Hell. The only human left alive was Cat. She waited by a large iron gate guarded by a beast with three heads. The Director emerged from the shadows, four fresh locks of hair dangled from his lapel. He handed Cat something—some odd package. I asked Bernie what was in the package but he didn't have a clue. It was another one of things that's never explained or even mentioned again.

"Run, now, Kitty." says the Director. The gates open. Through walls of bleeding, burning souls, she runs; through brimstone and ruin; past reaching hands, beyond cackling, faceless demons; ever onward she runs, faster, faster. 89:58, 89:59....

Then...Hell vanishes. Cat is alone in a field of dandelions with the house to her back. She runs. FADE TO BLACK.

I looked at Bernie unsure of what to say. His gold tooth winked at me. "The studio is letting me use their private plane. There's plenty of room for you, Ronald." He called me Ronald. That's how I knew he was serious. "Whoever this freak-show turns out to be, just look what he has done for cinema. He's just pushed film forward twenty years! This is the equivalent of seeing *King Kong* for the first time! I've gotta know how he did it; I could *really* use your expertise."

"Bernie, I'm too...."

"Old?" he rolled his eyes. "Yeah, you're right. Maybe I should just take you back to assisted living, so you can veg out on your couch and watch low-budget porno movies on your VCR until you eventually die."

I opened my mouth to argue but nothing came out. The little shit had a point. A damned good point. Somewhere down the hall, people cheered. I was offended. I thought, *what in the hell is worth cheering about?* Then I remembered. The election. Reagan must have won. I'd completely forgotten.

* * *

I hated flying. Or rather, my stomach hated flying. So did my hip. It throbbed, humming relentlessly, harmonizing with the roar of the plane's tiny engines. This was the first time I hadn't flown commercial. Hell, I'd never even flown first class before; now here I was, reclining in a posh leather seat, drinking a very expensive bottle of wine, in a studio-provided jet. I looked out my window at the cotton candy clouds and wondered what would happen if I died at 35,000 feet. Would Death still find me? Would He still bring flowers?

Bernie talked nonstop throughout the flight, only pausing to sip his mimosa. He was one of those pinky-straight-out kind of sippers. At one point he lit up a bloated joint of marijuana, puffed. breathed in, and then handed it to me. It was tempting but I declined. He called me a pussy and made squishy noises with his mouth.

We landed about thirty miles east of Fort Knox, on a strip of land once a storing ground for decommissioned train carts. We took a taxi out of the city; civilization disappeared like the tide.

The town of Bouldergreen seemed frozen in time, as if they hadn't heard everyone else in the world had moved on. We met the grocer—the man mentioned in the Director's letter—and he gave us directions to the address on the envelope.

Trees and grassland stretched the entire panorama; there were no buildings, no water towers and no smoke in the air. The only inkling of human interference was a small gravel road, dissecting the hill in half. Bernie swore the house wasn't too far. He also swore if my hip broke, he'd carry me the rest of the way.

We saw it for the first time when we came over the ridge: The house—the same house from the movie. I don't know what we were expecting. We should have known. Maybe we did know on some uncharted level of our subconscious. Then we saw him—the Director—sitting in a rocking chair on the front porch, fanning away the southern heat, dressed in the same pinstriped suit as he wore in the film. The sun reflected off his golden hair; he waved to us, beckoning us closer.

"So, dreams do come true," he shouted to us. "Hollywood actually does come a-knock'n."

"We do when we see a film like *Godforsaken*," said Bernie, trying to match the Director's wide grin.

His handshake surprised me: limp, lightweight, harmless. "What do we call you?" I asked. "What is your name?"

"The Director."

"I hope you'll not be this mysterious when it comes to the tricks of your trade," I said, exuding my excitement. "Can't wait to see how you achieved these effects! Really quite mind-boggling!"

"The devil's in the details my friend," he winked at me, twice. Wink, wink. He led us into his home, humming the tune from *Green Acres* under his breath.

Sunlight drenched the opening foyer in rich, beams of light. Production equipment of all shapes and sizes filled the room, leaving no wall untouched. Halogen lights, cameras, tracks, dollies, even a makeshift crane for the high shots. "I use all my own equipment," he boasted proudly. His wild eyes rolled like marbles in his skull, a sling of saliva foamed at the corners of his mouth. He clapped his hands together happily. "Wonderful! The full cast is here now, absolutely, positivity wonderful!"

"Cast?" Bernie asked.

"Yeah, that's what I said silly, cast. The other three are upstairs...waiting. Some have been waiting a while. Waiting for you two silly-willies. This time around we'll go bigger. More monsters, more carnage! Yes! Moviegoers do love their carnage. At least, I sure do."

Steadily, I moved back for the door. Bernie didn't seem to understand what was about to happen. "Sorry? I'm confused?"

"A sequel dear boy!" he shouted; his words filled the vast, open room. "I'm making a sequel."

The front door slammed shut. A wave of shadows swallowed the light, leaving the room in total darkness. Bernie turned on the balls of his feet and launched himself at the front door, using his shoulder as a battering ram. When the door didn't give, Bernie switched strategies; he kicked it, once, twice, three times, swearing, screaming and muttering a prayer in Hebrew. I, on the other hand, froze in place; my bladder let go.

"Places, people! Places!" The Director clapped his hands again. Sparks ignited each time his palm found its counterpart. Then, abruptly, the production lights switched on, popping in unbridled harmony.

A dozen oblong shapes—forms—materialized out of thin air. Colorless, pale to the verge of translucence, their flesh drooped from their bones, wilting like the skin of warm fried chicken; a glob of wrinkles amassed under their eye sockets which contained the reddest, deadest eyes I'd ever witnessed; they blazed with an inferno of bioluminescence, assessing me, assessing Bernie, waiting for permission to strike. A yawning black maw existed where a mouth should have been, filled with pink, soft tissue and jagged teeth. The only thing comparable would be the underbelly of a squid.

"Okay, first on the agenda for you lot...." he turned to us. "We've got to get you to makeup and wardrobe." The Director snapped his fingers at a pair of the monsters. "Take the talent upstairs to meet the others. No talking," he wagged his finger at Bernie and me. "Stay professional. I want to get things rolling in, oh...." he looked at his wrist, at a nonexistent watch, "Let's say ten minutes, shall we? Then, I'll start the clock.

"And both of you know what that means...don't worry friends. Same rules apply. Ninety minutes of pure elation—well, elation for me, certain death for you—but, hey, chin up! I'll wager you silly-willies will fare better than the last two boys who were in my movie." A glass of wine suddenly appeared in his hand—at least I hoped it was wine. He toasted us. "Cheers, here's to the Jew-boy and Mr. Pee-Pee-Pants-Man! Wink, wink."

* * *

Everything in life was a lie. From the day I was born, to this day—the day I will surely die—it has all been a lie. But that was the biggest lie of them all, the whopper of all whoppers: Death. Death does not exist. Neither do I.

I opened my eyes.

Gradually, things came into focus. A nail protruded out of both my wrists, rope held my body upright. I felt no pain, because pain was a lie.

I couldn't remember how I got here—on this wall—or why I was dressed in a dog costume. For the life of me, I couldn't figure out why a blinking, digital clock was connected to the costume, tied around my wrist. Numbers flashed at me: 09:04, 0:9:05, 09:06....

I looked to my left. A girl in a monkey suit thrashed inside a tomb of barbed wire. To my right, another girl, this one covered in glued feathers, had just freed her arms from the nails. She fell to the floor.

"Ronald!" I heard Bernie scream at me from below. *No,* I thought, *that can't be Bernie, because Bernie is a lie.* He was dressed as a tiger. "We're gonna get you outta there Ronald!"

Reality came back in a rush. The pain hit me like a sucker punch. I felt the nail inside my skin. I felt it tearing me, ripping my eighty-year-old skin. I screamed. *What am I doing here? I should be in my little apartment, ordering the nurse to fetch me another doughnut.* In panicked struggle, I whipped and flailed my legs, which only made things worse. Bernie shouted at me to stop moving but the pain had taken over my sense of hearing.

I thought of the family I'd never see again: my son, my daughter and my four grandkids. It made me sick to think about all the time I wasted sitting on my piss-yellow couch, wishing I were dead, when I should have been living!

What a fool I am. What a selfish fucking idiot. I suppose I deserved to die. Well, I'd soon get my chance...

Then, once again, I passed out.

I woke up with my head in Bernie's lap. He smiled when he saw my eyes flutter open. I saw his gold tooth and I wished that were a lie. But it wasn't. This was all real: the nails, the pain, the blood and the monsters...every last fucking detail.

-And the devil's in the details-

Monkey and Bird helped me to my feet while Cat checked me for any more cuts. My wounds had been wrapped with various strands of cloth. Some of it came from the polo shirt I had worn here. That's when I realized, I was completely naked under this damned dog outfit. It smelled of piss and bile; I had a suspicion this was the same outfit worn in the first film, which made me want to vomit. So I did. I puked up all the crackers and beer I'd had on the plane.

18:59, 19:00, 19:01....

"Where is the Director?" I asked, scanning the room for any sign of him. I knew he was there somewhere, I knew he was filming us that very moment.

He appeared, magically, only a few yards away from us. He hid behind a large camera on a tripod. "Cut! The fourth wall, Dog! Don't break the fourth wall!"

Then, he disappeared back into the shadows.

* * *

We did our best to bring the three girls—Cat, Bird and Monkey— up to speed. We told them as much as we could about *Godforsaken;* we prepared them for the bloated, long-tongued monsters that could be waiting for us right outside that door. However, we soon discovered *Godforsaken II* was going to be very different from the original.

Bernie kicked opened the door. We stepped into a circular dungeon made of ancient, mismatched bricks; bones of all shapes and sizes littered the floor, clumped together in tidy heaps; to our right was a strange, ornamental limestone archway, with decorations depicting the story of Satan falling from Heaven. At the far end of the room, several yards away, a winding staircase coiled into an abyss of absolute darkness.

A pair of fawns, colossal in scale and mass, emerged from the archway. Their beards were afire—turbulent fingers of bright, orange flame blazed under their chins—in their hands, they clutched two mighty maces, barbed and spiked, which they wielded effortlessly, as if they were feather pillows. With weapons raised, they charged us; their human upper-halves scraped against the ceiling, their hooves shook the ground.

Whatever plan of teamwork we might have had before the fawns appeared was quickly lost in the chaos. We dispersed in every direction, every costumed animal for themselves. I was the last to move. For a heartbeat or two, I didn't see a point in running. One fawn chased after Bernie and the girls, the other spotted me. It must have singled me out as the weakest. It attacked quickly, slammed down the mace as hard as it could. The tsunami of wind blew back my floppy dog ears.

Then, suddenly, my feet moved before my brain could catch up.

The spiked, metal meteorite pounded the ground—inches behind me—leaving behind a crater in its wake. The beast roared in anger; I ran; my hip was on the verge of breaking. Any second now, it would snap...I could feel it. The second fawn spotted me. It pivoted on cloven hoofs and again, brought its mace down upon me. This time it landed ahead of me. I tried to slow down but at my speed, halting suddenly would have been against the laws of physics. I slammed into the mace at full force, splitting open my mouth.

The pain kept me awake, kept me alive. I spit out a mouthful of blood and teeth, pushed off the mace and kept the stairs in my sights. The others were already making their way down. Only Bernie slowed to see if I lived or died. I could feel the heat of both fawns. The ground quaked violently beneath my feet; I could barely stand. So, the only thing I could think to do—was jump. For a good couple of seconds I tumbled down the stairs, until, quite literally, I fell on top of the others. I slammed into Bird, knocking her off her feet. Bernie tripped over her and fell too. We scrambled, all of us clawing, shoving, pushing. Powerful hands held me against the ground. Someone else stepped on my face. Fighting back, I reached up and grabbed Cat by the hair, and yanked her to the ground.

I thought: *When darkness falls, when the ground threatens to collapse out from under you, we're all beasts, cloven hooves or not.*

Cat fought back. Suddenly the stairs were gone. The air sucked itself from my lungs. She had kicked me off the side of the stairs and I was falling; falling into an abyss, into ultimate darkness. I closed my eyes expecting my skull to crack open on a floor of bricks. To my relief, it wasn't bricks waiting for me at the bottom...it was water. However, water was just as brutal as bricks; the only difference being instead of bouncing when I landed, I was engulfed. My hip shattered upon impact.

I resurfaced gasping for breath. A high-pitched wail echoed in all directions. I figured it was the fawns about to pounce on me from above but then, as my mind cleared, I realized it was my own screams making all the racket.

"I got you, I'm coming Ronald. Hold on!" Bernie splashed into the lake from above, he wrapped his arm around me—my own personal life preserver—and we swam to where the water wasn't so deep. "Can you stand?"

I knew I couldn't. I tried to speak but all that came out were anguish-soaked yelps.

"He's dead!" said Cat. She hovered over me, shaking her head. She refused to look me in the eyes, only looking at Bernie. "Sorry, man, I know he's your friend but-"

"Fuck you!" Bernie yelled. Ah, Bernie...what a guy. I wanted to give him a bloody, toothless kiss but resisted.

"All he's gonna do is slow us down!" shouted Cat, angrily. "We can't take him with us." Water geysered outward; a worm, the color of dirt, exploded from the inky depths. Before Cat had time to scream, the eel attached itself to her, tearing out her throat. Blood sprayed everywhere, showering both Bernie and me. Quick on his feet, Bernie scooped me up just as the eel swiveled in our direction; fresh Cat blood oozed from crooked daggers inside its mouth.

Suddenly, production lights flashed all around us. Ozone filled my nostrils. My eyes were used to the darkness and the sudden intrusiveness stung. The Director stood in the exact spot where Cat had been slaughtered. He siphoned through the water until he brought up her corpse. The laceration in her neck ran so deep, her head limped backwards, dangling just shy of her butt. It swung back and forth like a pendulum. The Director stopped it from swaying, scissored out a chunk of her slick, brown hair, then pinned it—where else?—to his coat.

With me in tow, Bernie forced his way through the shallows, hobbling clumsily through the waves. Bernie asked me for a time check. Red numbers flashed down the seconds from the stopwatch tied to my wrist.

30:02, 30:03, 30:04....
"Time's a-flying past, boys and girls! Tick, tick!"

* * *

Bernie held me in his arms like I was his bride. The pain in my hip shot up my spinal cord every time he took a step. But how could I complain? I was alive, thanks to this man, this hero, this larger-than-life Hollywood executive.

It turned out, two heads are better than one after all. Every new room we entered, we would split the room in half, he'd scan right and I'd scan left, looking for any inkling of the next door that would take us deeper into the Director's twisted maze. We tried our best to keep the girls with us—honestly, we tried. But they entered each room in a kamikaze death run—it's a wonder they made it as far as they did.

A few rooms later, we came to a well-lit dining room where the walls were bleeding; a slow, steady congealment of blood seeped from the crown molding. A large banquet table spread out before us, filled with a smorgasbord of food ranging from decadent, to more decadent, to extremely, scrumptiously decadent. The beef tips and lobster tails tempted me the most. Although...the salmon-wrapped sea scallops, I must confess, made me salivate like a dog begging for scraps.

Four chairs sat around the table. One for each of us. As we got closer, we realized the chairs were already occupied...with us. At least different versions of us, completely oblivious of our presence. I can't relate the dizziness I felt seeing myself sitting next to a different Bernie, sharing a plate of crab cakes.

What happened next was hard to explain. None of us saw Monkey disappear. We were all too busy watching ourselves stuff our faces. We don't know how she ended up on the table; it just happened. One second she was standing next to us, the next...she was on the menu.

Suddenly, the contents of the table shifted. Gone were the platters of chicken cutlets and veal skewers, replaced by the vivisected corpse of our former cast mater. Somehow, despite her severe wounds, Monkey was alive, screaming for us to intervene.

She should have already been dead.

All we could do was watch.

Four sets of greedy, grubby fingers entered her open chest cavity-ripping, tearing, splitting, sharing, and pulling out organs of all shapes and sizes. In a ravenous fit of cannibalism, Bird and Bernie fought over the large intestines, while I devoured a kidney; the parallel version of Monkey shoveled handfuls of her own flesh inside her own red-stained mouth.

I closed my eyes, sealed them tight. However, hearing the sounds of the gluttonous orgy was just as bad as seeing it. The Director appeared on top of the table towering over Monkey's corpse. She had been picked clean.

"Don't fret my pets," cackled the maniacal man with scissors. "Hair keeps growing long after you're dead. It'll grow back. Snip, snip!"

58:21, 58:22, 58:23....

Where had all the time gone? *Jesus*, how long were we watching ourselves eat? We took off, running into a hallway of molded, knotty wood. Behind us, Bird lost her footing. It was so tempting to keep moving, not even look back. (That's probably what I would have done if I'd been able to use my legs.) Bernie, however, slowed, waited for her to catch up.

A low, guttural rumble rattled the walls and vibrated under our feet. Two eyes blinked to life inside the knots in the wood. The floor opened revealing rows of splintery teeth; a tongue of pink insulation shot out and coiled around Bird's leg. She didn't scream; she didn't try to fight it. The tongue retracted back into the mouth, swallowing Bird in a single gulp. *At least the Director won't get her hair as a trophy,* I thought.

"Only two left, oh me oh my!" said the face in the floor with the voice of the Director. The face twitched, spasmed, and morphed until the wood and drywall became skin and blonde hair. "You two silly-willies are blowing through my house in record time! You're almost there...only one more place to show you...and oh what a place it is!"

We vanished—the Director, Bernie and me—we reappeared in Hell.

An enormous black iron gate blocked any further passage. People, so many people...every dead person from every dead age of Earth's history were sewn into the ancient walls, woven together in writhing honeycombs. They called the names of their loved ones, they shouted for help and for water. I never knew what the phrase *gnashing of teeth* meant until that very moment. I thought my ears were going to explode.

67:00, 67:01, 67:02....

For the first time, Bernie faltered. He dropped me on the harsh stone, my hip exploded in an orgasm of pain. He fell to his knees with his hands over his ears. That was when I accepted my fate. It was time to die. Hell...that time had long passed.

"Are you the Devil?" asked Bernie, wincing.

"No you fool. I'm God. And you are the forsaken," said the Director. He reached inside his jacket and pulled out a package. On the top of the package were three addresses, in the center, in big, bold letters were the words: *Godforsaken II*.

Bernie shook his head. "I don't want it."

"You don't have a choice. This is how it works. One person leaves. Never two. One person always survives. Someone has to deliver the package. And it is sure not going to be this old fuck!"

"What if I refuse?"

The Director seemed unfazed. "Sure, sure, Bernie the Jew. That's an option. But you won't like it," he took a breath, paced around us like a drill instructor. "It'd be a shame for you to have to watch the wrinkled skin of your mother, Miriam Heller, being pulled apart by one of my imps. Also, I'd be forced to take care of poor Mr. Scanlan's family as well. His son, his daughter, his four sweet grandbabies!"

He snatched the package from the Director's hands. "Okay," he said, defeated. "Ronald. What happens to Ronald?"

"When the clock reaches ninety, he dies."

Bernie Heller looked down at me with tears in his eyes. "I'm sorry."

I nodded. I didn't think there was anything left to say. But then again there was a lot to say. I just didn't know how to say it. So a nod would have to suffice.

The black iron gates opened slightly, enough of a sliver for Bernie to slip through. I didn't turn around to watch him leave. It would've been too hard. I didn't want to be blubbering like a baby in one of my final acts of life. I knew he was gone when I heard metal scrap against metal and heard the sound of a key turning inside an ancient lock. This was the sound of finality. The sound of the end.

77:44, 77:45, 77:46....

I had time. Not much time, but enough.

Sprawled on the cool caves of Hell, I raised my head to look the Director in the eyes. He was next to me, close enough to kiss my lips or bite my neck, yet, still, he moved closer; his sulfuric breath puffed into my ear. "You've lived a long time Mr. Scanlan. I think someone wants to meet you. Wink, wink."

High above my head Death descended, gradually; inch by delicate inch, he floated like a glacier in black tattered cloth; His hood covered His face; He carried a large wooden scythe that pointed downward, directly at me.

I smiled at Him, unafraid.

He didn't have flowers.

Damn.

87:01, 87:02, 87:03....

The Director, once again behind his camera, zoomed in as close as he could to my face, trying to capture my fear. But I wasn't going to give him the satisfaction. If I had to die, I'd die with dignity, on my feet, looking Death in the eyes. I used the last ounce of my remaining strength to lift up from the rocks. My hipbone punctured nerve endings but I pushed through it.

Standing, I waited.

88:29, 88:30, 88:31....

I pictured my son, my daughter, all four of my grandchildren; I even pictured the face of the wife I'd neglected for years until she finally gave up and left me. Each one of those important relationships I had single-handily sabotaged in one way or another. I hoped they knew how much I loved them, how much I wished I could fix things.

The numbers were counting down long before I came to this house; I just never saw them until it was too late.

89:50, 89:51, 89:52....

Suddenly, it all seemed to make sense—both life and death. In the end, it's all dust in an hourglass. What a tragic waste, I got to live so long but actually *lived* so little.

I thought of the day my son was born, the day of my daughter's fifth birthday party; I thought of my honeymoon. Those were the moments that mattered—the real moments, the genuine moments.

Everything else was just special effects.

THE END

3rd Place

Acapulco Blue
(Science Fiction)

By

Bruce Golden

He could hear the tune, he could almost see its lyrics written capriciously across a saffron-tinted sky, but he couldn't remember its title. It distressed him that he couldn't remember. It *nagged* at him. Try as he might, he couldn't concentrate. His recollection was an empty slate.

Then, as imperceptibly as it had deserted him, consciousness reasserted itself. The vivid kaleidoscope that was his dream and the song that scored it both expired. Yet with consciousness came only darkness and silence.

No chirping birds or barking dogs greeted him. He felt the early morning sunlight splash across his face but he couldn't see it. The dull ache of his polyethylene, chrome-cobalt alloy knees and the dryness of his throat alerted him to the new day's arrival. It had been that way for years; waking not with a bang but with a creak and a whimper, discomfort the daily reminder of his continued existence. Still, he'd never grown accustomed to regaining consciousness blind and deaf.

As he disengaged from the cobwebs of slumber, awareness gradually returned and he recalled his place in the universe. For Benjamin Edward Glucorde, that awareness was not wholly gratifying. Though half-forgotten decades had dulled its razor sharpness and diminished its capacity to conceive—his mind was still his. Whether that was a curse or a blessing was a debate his inner voice never fully resolved.

His fingers inched across the cool Lycra sheet until they brushed the familiar texture of the rubberized control pad. The head of the bed began to elevate.

With the first upward movement, his optic array activated, revealing daylight in progressively brighter increments. There was, however, nothing incremental about the stiffness in his back. It carped grievously against the change of position, drawing attention away from the complaint emanating from his titanium-plated hips. The pain came and went at its own discretion.

He had few body parts that didn't whine and squawk from time to time. He ignored the pain as best he could. He could do little else, since he refused to dull his senses with drugs.

When the bed reached a forty-three degree angle, his cochlear implants became fully operative. As was often the case, the first sound he heard came from a passing aerocar. *Damned flying gewgaws*, he thought. They were always swooping over his place as if they were on some kind of bloody bombing run. He was almost glad his ears shut down when he slept. Lately though, the volume control was all over the place. One moment he could hardly hear a thing, the next he was listening to a gnat walk up the wall.

At exactly seventy-six degrees, the bed halted. With a technique honed by repetition he slowly shifted his legs over the side and planted his feet on the carpeted floor. He took a deep breath and started to rub his eyes. He checked himself. There was something about rubbing his eyes he was supposed to remember–something about fracturing the lenses.

Standing required greater effort but once his weight was equally distributed, what he liked to call his "bionic knees" made walking easy, if not pain free.

He had a sullen agreement with his body–at least what there was left of the original equipment. If it could go about its business without making him look like Mr. Roboto he would resist the temptation to do the Highland fling.

He hobbled into the kitchen to see if he could find anything other than the Easy-Digest Nutrients swill he'd tried the day before but the phone chime diverted him. He triggered the display and saw a stern-faced old man dressed in a dark suit. Of course, *old* was a relative term.

"Grandfather, it's me, William. Can you see me? Can you hear me okay?"

It took a few moments before he recognized the face. "I can see and hear just fine, Billy. What do you want?"

"I know you don't want to hear this but if you're going to insist on living in that place all alone, I should have some SecureVision cameras installed. That way, if anything happened to–"

"You're not spying on me with no cameras!"

"Not spying, Grandfather. They just alert the medtechs if you fall or..."

"I don't need anyone to babysit me."

"Well, anyway, that's not why I called. I wanted to remind you that Amber is coming to visit you tomorrow."

"Amber? Is that one of my grandkids?"

"No Grandfather, *I'm* your grandson." There was impatience in William's tone, only somewhat disguised by a look of concern. "Amber is *my* granddaughter. She's your great-great-granddaughter."

"Oh," Ben muttered, chagrined. "So you say she's coming to visit?"

"Yes, don't you remember? She's coming to see you tomorrow. And I wish you'd try to talk to her."

"About what?"

"Her mother says she's been spending time with some university extremists, reading prohibited books, that sort of thing."

"Prohibited books?"

"We thought maybe she might listen to you. She's always liked you. She won't listen to her mother or me. Will you do that? Will you talk some sense into her?"

"I'll take her for a ride in my car."

"Your car? Grandfather, that automobile's almost as old as you are. You shouldn't be driving that thing."

"What are you talking about Billy?" Outrage fortified his voice. "Driving my car's the only thing I got left in this miserable life!"

"That antique is dangerous. You should get rid of it."

"Maybe then you ought to get rid of me too."

"Grandfather, don't be ridiculous."

"Then don't be a dickhead, boy. I was driving that car before you were toilet-trained. So don't be telling me to trash her like she was some worn-out old shoe."

"All right, we'll talk about it some other time. *Just remember*, Amber will be there tomorrow."

"I'll remember."

"And, Grandfather, I'm seventy-six years old. Nobody calls me 'Billy' any more. My name's William."

Ben was still staring at the phone display as it went black. "You're still little snot-nosed Billy to me," he said to the blank screen.

Grumbling, he made his way with some effort to the side door. "Thinks he can tell me what to do just because he's an old fart now. Let's see how bossy he is when he's a hundred." The door dilated at his approach.

"Talking like a crazy man–get rid of my car. Sure, something's old, so it must be useless. Just dump it, replace it, get some newfangled flying *thingamajig*." He stepped into the garage and the lights came on.

The sight of it calmed him. He stood steadfast, staring. It was a dazzling blue vision, trimmed in shimmering chrome and carved with sleek dynamic lines that conveyed the quality of motion even while stationary. Just seeing the old Ford was enough to alleviate the grumpy aftertaste left by the conversation with his grandson.

He limped around to the driver's side, inhaling the lingering scent of oil and exhaust. His fingers trailed across the hood, relishing the cool, soothing metal. So many years together; so many memories. How could his grandson understand? How could anyone understand when they made such a ritual of replacing the old with the new? It didn't matter if the oven still cooked properly, the stereo still sounded great or the clothes weren't worn. What mattered was that there was always more money to spend–fresh styles, novel gadgets–toss out the used, buy the up-to-date.

He peered through the driver's window. A strange face stared back at him.

It took a moment to recognize his own reflection, disguised as it was by ruckled rows of mottled skin and wispy, wild strands of white hair. His face reminded him of a shirt that had been left in the hamper too long.

How different he'd looked the first time he'd gazed through that glass. He'd been a dashing young rogue of forty-something. He could have bought a brand-new car but he chose this one instead. Already a classic, it had been on the road more than three decades. He picked it because it was like his first car, the one he'd bought with his own money as a teenager. He'd loved that car too, until he was drafted into the Army and had to sell it. When he got this one, he vowed never to part with it.

He grasped the chrome handle and pressed the button that opened the door. Not a console pad or touch-screen but a real mechanical button. The immaculate white vinyl beckoned him, but bending down and sliding into the seat was tricky. He managed it though, resting his hands on the steering wheel. The hard resin finish was smooth as a woman's thigh. He stroked it lovingly, his hands coming to rest on its chrome centerpiece, where a silver horse galloped ever-in-place across a red, white and blue field.

He pumped the accelerator once, twice, three times and released it–a routine ingrained in him by his own father more than a century ago. He turned the key and felt the eight-cylinder beast rear up, its 289 cubic-inch engine roaring through dual exhaust. Twice more he pumped fuel into the four-barrel carburetor. She pulled at the reins but hushed as he lifted his foot, routinely checking the gauges. He needed to order more gas.

The garage door activated and he drove out into the sunshine.

He could still handle her, as long as he didn't push it, his reflexes not being as prompt as they once were. He drove past Cecilia's place. She was outside messing with her plants. She smiled and waved. He gave her a cursory wave back.

The woman had designs on him—he was sure. It didn't seem to matter to her that she was young enough to be his granddaughter. Hell, twenty or thirty years ago he might have taken her up on it and given her the thrill of her life. Now he just humored her because her son was some fancy engineer who liked *antiques*. He was the only person Ben knew who could work on the old Ford when some part needed replacing.

He took his usual route, an old paved road running down by the sea cliffs and getting little use these days. He was glad he lived far from the city proper, teeming as it was with what they called *people-movers* and *urban-cycles*—not to mention all the crazy flying contraptions taking off and landing all over the place. He didn't want to maneuver through those streets. He'd tried it once. It was like being a potato bug in a swarm of bees. No, he was content to cruise his back roads, reveling in the stares he provoked.

She still drove like a dream, that car—smooth, steady, yet she had the get-up-and-go when he felt like testing her. He was sure she could outrun any of those flying cars—that was, if they stayed grounded.

"Yes sir, they don't make 'em like this anymore," he said aloud, smiling at his own inanity. "Hold it together Benny, don't start talking to yourself."

He glanced at his rearview mirror and thought for a moment he saw something. He looked again but nothing was there. Nothing but an empty road and the hundreds of thousands of miles he had left behind. That's the way life was, always trailing behind…memories always back there a ways, just beyond the vanishing point.

He reached over, opened the console and pulled out a small, clear plastic baggie. Sealed inside it was a lock of light red hair—her hair—still as soft looking as the first day he'd laid eyes on it so many years before. He kept it in the car for good luck. Maybe that's why the old engine had lasted so long. He put the baggie back.

Off to his left now, far down from the cliff wall, was the ocean. It was a balmy day and the waters were tranquil. He couldn't see a whitecap or a single vessel all the way to the horizon. The only thing marring the view was a phalanx of rusted old wind power turbines, plumbing the depths offshore.

When he decided to turn around and drive home, he noticed the engine was running hot. Worried she might overheat he babied her the rest of the way. As he approached Cecilia's house steam sprayed up from under the hood. He stopped, turned off the engine and got out.

It was a struggle to open the hood and he cursed himself for the decrepit old cripple he was. When he finally pushed it up, a cloud of steam billowed out, scalding his face and forcing him back. He cursed some more until he tired of it and started walking. Fortunately his place was just up the road a bit from Cecilia's. He saw her as he rounded the corner and tried to call out. But when he opened his mouth nothing but a gurgle came out. He became dizzy, then uncomfortably warm. His optic array began to malfunction; everything grew blurry.

Panic gripped him. A chill raced through his body. Was this it? Was it finally going to end? Conflicting emotions cascaded and collided. Fright—dread of the unknown—regret—acceptance...relief. He'd wished for it more times than he could count. Now that it seemed near, he both feared and welcomed it.

He couldn't breathe. His chest was on fire. He felt himself falling and heard Cecilia scream.

"Benjamin!"

* * *

He opened his eyes. He didn't know where he was but he knew he was alive. He knew because he could feel his body—his old, worn out body. Anger surged through him. He'd been so close, so ready. Why wasn't he dead? Why wouldn't they let him die?

"Why did you do this to me?" he asked, his voice a hoarse whisper.

"Did you say something Mr. Glucorde?"

He turned his head and found himself staring up at his doctor—Dr. Hooten, a woman with the bedside manner of a servodroid.

"How are you feeling Mr. Glucorde?" she asked without taking her eyes off the various monitors she surveyed. "Can you hear me all right?"

"Why does everyone want to know if I can hear them? Of *course* I hear you. You don't have to yell."

"I'm not yelling Mr. Glucorde, but sometimes when the body shuts down like that, it can affect certain implants."

"Shuts down?"

"Yes," she said, turning to look at him for the first time. "That's what happened. One of your artificial kidneys malfunctioned and when your nano sensors discovered they couldn't correct the problem, they shut everything down. The trouble is, some of your artificial organs are so old their technology doesn't interface properly with the nanites that regulate your system. It's like sticking a self-heat packet into an old microwave. They both have the same function but together they're counterproductive."

"What if I'd been driving? Those damned nano bugs could've got me killed."

A nurse walked in, smiled her nurse-smile at him and handed the doctor a pad.

"Those *bugs*, as you say, saved your life Mr. Glucorde," the doctor said as she read the pad. "Besides, you shouldn't be flying. Your medical-"

"I said driving, *not* flying! Are you deaf?"

"You shouldn't be driving either Mr. Glucorde." The doctor stood. "Now we've given you a new kidney, one which will exchange information if you will, with the dominant nanites. As for your remaining, outdated organs, I hesitate to-"

"So when can I go home?"

"Why, you can go home right now Mr. Glucorde. Your hearing and vision seem fine, but if you experience any problems with those implants have someone bring you back in. Just promise me, no jitterbugging for a week."

"You're a funny lady, Doc," he said as she walked out. "Except the jitterbug was already extinct when I was born."

* * *

He detested flying—especially the takeoffs and landings—but as the Medvan descended he caught a glimpse of her. The sight relaxed him. She was parked out front, looking as resplendent as the day he bought her. *Now, when exactly was that?* He couldn't remember what year it had been, though somehow he could still picture the place. Too bad they didn't have an implant to boost his memory.

He ignored the medtech's dry insistence that they wheel him up to his front door like a sack of potatoes. Instead, he made his own way slowly over to the car. By the time he reached it the Medvan had taken off.

"She's as good as new." It was Cecilia's boy, Steve. "Glad to see you are too," he opened the hood and Ben felt a prick of jealousy. "The problem was your water pump, Ben. I don't know how long it was in there but it was rusted through. Don't worry though; I fabricated a new one—one that won't rust. I altered the design a little so it should–"

"I don't want some fancy new pump. I just want the same old kind I've been using for years."

"Sorry Ben but they don't make pumps like that anymore. They probably haven't for decades. I don't know where you managed to find the last one."

"Junkyard," Ben replied gruffly.

"Well, anyway, she should drive fine now," Steve said, closing the hood.

"Didn't mean to sound ungrateful. I appreciate all the work you do helping me keep her in shape."

"Don't worry about it. I know she's more to you than just wires and pistons. But I'm afraid I've got some bad news. I've been transferred to our corporate headquarters in Osaka, so I won't be around to help you anymore. I'll miss it. I love working on this old relic. It's probably the only one of its kind still running."

"Yeah," said Ben, "we relics have to stick together."

Steve chuckled and said, "Looks like you've got company."

Ben turned and saw a hovering aerocar.

"I'm going to get going. Best of luck to you, Ben."

"Thanks for all your help Steve."

The aerocar landed and both hatches lifted. Out one side popped a little pixie of a girl. She had on a pink and white T-shirt and white shorts revealing skinny legs.

"Grampa Ben!" she screeched and threw her arms around him.

He held on just to keep his balance as she hugged him with puppy-like zeal. She smelled of lilacs, or some kind of flower he thought. He felt the silky smooth skin of her arms and the soft pressure of her breasts against his stomach. She was a tiny thing, not more than five-two or five-three he figured.

Truthfully, he didn't recognize her. *Something* was familiar about her—that light red hair, the slightly upturned nose. He was sure she looked like someone he had once known.

"Amber?"

"It's so swanking to see you again Grampa Ben."

Someone else emerged from the aerocar—a young fellow carrying two small bags. He was neat-and-clean and oddly serious-looking, except half his head was shaved nearly bald, with a tattoo of a featureless mask under the stubble. The other half had a full shock of wavy blond hair. The odd-looking young man stopped a few feet behind Amber.

"Grampa Ben, this is Shon. Shon, this is my great-great-grandfather, Grampa Ben."

"Jell to face with you Mr. Glucorde," the boy said formally. But even as he spoke his eyes were drawn to the car. "Scan this, Am. This is swanking," he said, as he circled it. "Must be at least fifty years old–a real museum piece."

"Hmmph! It's a lot older than that boy. This is a 1965 Ford Mustang."

"You're jacking me? Did you file that Am? This ob is more than a hundred years old."

"Sure, Grampa Ben's had that forever. I swoon for the color."

"Acapulco Blue," Ben said, and as the words left his mouth he was brushed by a vivid recollection. The woman with the red hair. He remembered now. She'd looked like Amber. How could he have ever forgotten her? The lapse angered him. Through the disgust with his faulty memory he saw her clearly now. He recalled the time he'd taken the car to have it painted and how she'd insisted on that color because its designation reminded her of their trip to Mexico. From then on, it was never just *blue*. It was the blue-blue of the clear blue water off the beaches of Acapulco.

"Does it actually pow'up?" Shon reached out and tentatively touched the car as if its metal skin might come to life.

"If you mean does she go–damn straight!" Ben growled; his fragile reminiscence shattered. "She'll blow the Turtle Wax off that contraption of yours."

"Turtle wax?"

"Yeah, Turtle–*oh never mind*. It's fast, boy, real fast."

"You'll have to take us for a ride Grampa."

"Sure, sure. But right now I've got to go inside and take a nap. Just got myself a brand-new kidney you know."

* * *

From the senseless void where he slept, consciousness returned and he groped for the control pad. As the bed elevated and his vision and hearing returned on cue, he recalled fragments of a lingering dream.

He was young again. He was running—running as fast as he could. Not chasing or being chased, just running; the sheer freedom of it was exhilarating. The dream shifted and he was driving his car, a young beauty in the passenger seat, her red hair flying wildly from the air stream of the open window. He couldn't see her face but remembered her laugh and the engine's sound as it accelerated. He had felt a chill. A familiar, disturbing sensation of being overcome by cold. It had driven him from his dream and back to reality.

Now he heard another sound–not from the dream–a real sound. The sound of lovemaking. Unmistakable moans of pleasure, labored breathing, a rapturous cry–sounds he had not heard in...he couldn't remember how long it had been. He realized it must be Amber and her fellow.

Why not? They were young, full of life. He wished he still could but he hadn't been able to for a long time. The drugs were *incompatible* with his nano bugs and he refused an implant. He imagined it would be as much fun as poking somebody with a stick. Yet he still had the inclination–dry and dusty as it was.

He waited a while after the sounds of passion ceased, then made plenty of noise of his own before he came out. He found Amber and Shon sitting at his dining table. They'd made a meal out of what they'd found in his fridge and were going at it with youthful exuberance.

"Hi, sleepyhead." Amber jumped up from her seat and kissed him on the cheek. She was all aglow, bubbling over with enthusiasm. She almost made him feel guilty about being such an old curmudgeon. Almost.

"Are you hungry?" she asked. "I hope you don't mind–we helped ourselves. We were fammed."

"I told you to make yourselves at home, girl and I meant it."

"It's swank and plenty Mr. Glucorde," spoke up Shon. "Ease-on and face."

"You kids *are* speaking English, aren't you?"

They both laughed.

"I'll eat later. I'm just going to have some juice. You two go ahead and finish, then I'll take you for that ride I promised."

"Are you sure, Grampa Ben? You'd better eat something."

"Don't be trying to mother me girl," he said, admonishing her with his finger. "You don't have the wrinkles for it."

The refrigerator door slid open at his touch and he chose a plastic container. He steadied himself as his vision blurred momentarily. *Must not be awake yet*, he thought.

"How long you two planning on staying?" he asked as he filled a glass.

"I don't know Grampa," Amber replied hesitantly. She glanced at Shon with a look that said there was a disagreement. "We haven't decided. We don't want to impose for too long."

"Hell, girl, I don't hardly ever get any visitors. You both stay as long as you like. I'm sure you'll get bored with an old fossil like me long before I get fed up with you," he took a drink from his glass, frowned, and made a noise as if to spit out what he'd swallowed. "Damn! Tastes like metal. They can put a man on Mars but they can't make a decent glass of lemonade. I don't envy you kids–having to live in this screwed-up world."

"Screwed-up?" asked Amber.

"You know," Ben replied, "*messed up*, made into a mess, disgusting, like that juice."

"Some of us won't input the mess," Shon said. "We're going to change things."

"*Shon*," said Amber, censuring him.

"Good for you." Ben poured the remaining juice into the sink. "I was all fired up to change the world when I was your age too. Yeah, we thought we could stop a war by singing songs and handing out flowers. We found out the hard way the world didn't want to change. Maybe you can do a better job of it."

* * *

"This is swanking Grampa Ben." With the wind playing through her hair and a big smile on her face, she reminded him again of someone. Though at the moment he couldn't remember who. "I've never gone so fast this close to the ground."

"After all these years, she can still move. It's starting to get a bit chilly though, we'd better roll up the windows."

"Roll up?"

"Yeah, like this," he cranked the handle on his side until the window closed. Amber followed suit.

"You control this automobile real jell," Shon said from the backseat.

"You mean for an old man don't you? Well this car and me, we've been together a long time. I can remember driving her to the Grand Canyon with my son when he was still little, crossing the Hoover Dam late at night when no one was around. It was eerie–like we were the only people left alive in the whole world. It's funny how I can remember that, when I can't even recall what I had for dinner last night," he glanced to the side momentarily, trying to remember and then capitulated with a shake of his head. "You've heard of the Grand Canyon and Hoover Dam I suppose?"

"Sure, Grampa, we input a virtual trip last summer."

"Virtual? That's not the same as being there. You need to see it firsthand." Ben paused, lost in thought. "Now what was I talking about? Oh yeah. We've got a connection, this car and me," he clutched the gearshift as if to demonstrate. "I can feel by the vibrations of the tires and the surge of the accelerator if everything isn't just right. There's a rhythm to driving her, an awareness. It's like making love. Yes sir. She's an ode unto herself and every street's another stanza. Heck, when it's my time to go, I want to be buried in her."

"You're jacking us, aren't you Mr. Glucorde?"

"I'm as serious as a heart attack."

"Bizarrama."

"Bizarrama? You mean like that half-a-head of hair you're wearing?"

"That's a political statement," Shon replied quickly, as if the comparison wasn't valid.

"Just what are your politics?" asked Ben, slowing to take a sharp turn.

"We're SADIR, Grampa Ben."

"Sadder than who?"

"No, *SADIR*," Amber replied. "S-A-D-I-R; students against digital image recognition."

"What the hell is that?"

"The Face Recognition System," Shon said. When Ben gave no sign he understood, Shon continued. "They've got SecureCams everywhere–haven't you seen them?"

"I...don't remember. I don't think so. I don't get to the city much. The only camera I've seen is the one the doctor stuck up my ass."

"But you've seen casts, haven't you Grampa?"

"I don't watch the news anymore. It's a bunch of illiterate, pre-programmed smiley faces spouting politically correct platitudes. Can't stand to listen to it."

"They scan you wherever you go," Shon said, the emotion evident in his voice. "The cameras upload your image, the system contrasts and compares, selects and categorizes. Once you're identified, your movements are codified, your tendencies profiled."

"Big Brother's watching huh?"

"Privacy deleted," added Amber.

"We're not citizens anymore," said Shon, "we're potential security risks."

"Well, if there's one thing I've learned," said Ben, "it's that complaining about it won't change anything."

"We're going to do more than complain." Shon started to say more, but a look from Amber shut him up. Something passed between them, so Ben didn't pursue it. Instead, he focused on the road ahead. The steady hum of the engine was the only sound they heard for the next few miles.

Soon Ben found he was having trouble seeing. He thought his vision was blurring again. He eased off the accelerator and noticed the windshield was beginning to fog up. He flipped on the defroster.

"You know Grampa," Amber said, breaking the silence, "I think it's swank you want to be buried in your Mustang."

* * *

"You kids get yourselves something to eat if you want."

He walked to the bathroom to relieve the bloated walnut that was his bladder. As he did, he heard the muffled sounds of an argument. Futilely he shook his head, trying to kick his implants into a higher gear. Damned super hearing never worked when he needed it.

When he came out Amber didn't seem too happy.

"Mr. Glucorde," Shon said, "a friend from the city wants to pow'down and face with us. Is that jell?"

Ben looked at Amber but she'd turned away. "Sure, you kids have a party if you want–God knows it's been years since I've been to one of those."

"No parties Grampa Ben, just one friend. That reminds me though; I need to face with Grandfather. He's in a swoon for me to come to Grandmother's birthday party."

"Yeah, the old sourpuss told me the same thing."

"He thinks 'cause my father's dead he can edit me and that I'll just input it. He's certain he files what's jell for me."

"You're not the Lone Ranger girl. He treats me the same. As if I wasn't already a man of the world when he was just an itch in his daddy's pants. Well, enough rambling. There's the phone over there."

"The phone?"

"Yeah, the telephone. The *whatchamacallit*—the Com display. I'm going to lie down and rest for a while."

He turned for the bedroom but his left leg didn't turn with him. He almost collapsed.

"Grampa Ben! Are you okay?"

"I'm fine, I'm fine. Sometimes I just move too quick. The old muscles get cranky and freeze up on me. I forget I'm not a young buck of fifty anymore. I'll be okay."

He closed the door behind himself and maneuvered onto the bed. Before he could lower it, his ears popped and he heard voices from the next room like they were right next to him.

". . . doing fine, Grandfather. He's jell. He even took us for a ride in his old car."

"What do you mean 'us'?"

"A friend's with me."

"Who's this friend?"

"Does it matter, Grandfather?"

"Well you two better not be bothering your Grampa Ben. He shouldn't be out driving that old piece of junk."

"The drive was his idea. And you should know—he wants to be buried in his car when he dies."

"Buried in it? That's crazy."

"I don't think it's so crazy. It's what he wants."

"Do you know what it could cost to buy a plot that large? I don't even know if such a thing would be legal. And even if it was, what would people say? The truth is I should put him in a full-care facility where-"

Then, as suddenly as his implants had picked up the voices, they were gone, leaving the anger to sour in him like moldy scraps in a drainpipe.

He's the one who's crazy if he thinks he's putting me in some kind of home.

He didn't care if snot-nosed Billy *was* in his seventies. He was going to take him over his artificial knee the next time he saw him and paddle his ass raw.

* * *

When he woke from his nap he was hungry, so he ambled into the kitchen to make a sandwich. Not your ordinary everyday sandwich. He was going to pile on as much crap as he could find that was suitable for sandwiching. It was going to be festival of pre-processed meats, pseudo cheeses and vinegar-soaked garnishes, the likes of which would give his doctor a stroke.

As he worked on his grand design he heard voices from the living room. Amber and Shon and another voice he didn't recognize. He continued to put together his meal but the eavesdropping slowed him.

". . . downloaded into the system in under an hour." That was Shon. "Even with backups where the worm can't mode, it'll take days for a system rinse."

"I still say we blow the whole Security Center into microts," said the new voice.

"That's more wank than swank," his great-great-granddaughter replied. "This is supposed to be a non-violent, symbolic protest. If we start blasting everything, no one will input our message."

"I file. I'm just swooning for an upmode."

"This won't delete it," said Shon. "It'll take multi-tasking to input any real change. For that to click, we have to avoid confinement. That's what's faulty with this plan. Your employ codes can get us in but even if we get out before auto-security locks down the building, alert mode will have the gops tracking the power signatures of every aerocar in range."

"We can walk it," the other voice replied. "I know a hackshack a few miles from the Security Center where we could pausemode, till the gops sign off."

"Miles?" Shon didn't sound hopeful. "The gops are going to wall it off quicktime. We wouldn't make it."

So his great-great-granddaughter was up to her pretty neck in some revolutionary scheme was she? He didn't know much about this *face recognition* system but he didn't like the idea of the government spying on its own people. Hell, he'd been incensed when they forced national ID cards on everyone. He'd railed against that, for all the good it had done.

Now little Amber was trying to throw a monkey wrench into the works. Well good for her. What was a monkey wrench anyway? He tried but couldn't remember. It didn't matter. What mattered was what Amber was doing.

He had an idea. He would help them with their little plot. He found the notion invigorating. It had been a long time since he'd done anything really foolish–had any real fun. He was long overdue.

Ben walked into the living room carrying his three-inch thick sandwich on a plate. "I've got the answer to your problem," he said, sitting gingerly in his favorite seat. Amber, Shon and another young fellow, coiffured with the same *political statement* as Shon, stared at him with various degrees of surprise.

"I hope we didn't wake you Grampa Ben."

"Nope. I was in the kitchen making myself this Dagwood and I overheard you."

"What did you hear?" Shon asked, apprehension tainting his voice.

"You're planning on breaking in somewhere, planting some kind of computer virus and then breaking out. I assume it has something to do with this SADIR thing of yours and those cameras you told me about. Am I right?"

"That deletes it!" The newcomer shot out of his chair.

"I think it's great what you're doing. At least what you're trying to do. It won't do any good in the long run you know. Despite their unflagging acclaim for freedom, most people don't have the gumption to stand up for it–to accept the risks, to do what it takes to be free." Ben took a bite of his sandwich. "But that doesn't mean I won't help you," he added with his mouth full.

"How can *you* help?" Shon asked.

Amber stood. "Grampa Ben is *not* getting involved!"

"Ease-on a microt Am. Input what he has to say first."

Amber glared at Shon but Ben continued.

"As I understand it, the glitch in your plan is the escape. Well I've got three hundred horsepower of getaway car and no power signature that the... *gops*, as you call them, can trace."

"He's right," Shon said. "We could use the museum piece and there'd be no way for them to track us."

"I don't file," the other fellow said.

"Mr. Glucorde here has this old gasoline-burning automobile that's still operational."

"*Jesus*, boy, you make it sound like a toaster. It's a 1965 Mustang with a high performance V8 engine. And if we're going to be co-conspirators, don't call me Mr. Glucorde. I'm Ben or Benny."

"Grampa Ben, you're not going to do this," Amber said firmly. She turned to Shon. "We'll find another way."

"I program this cell and I say we let him help." Shon tried to sound authoritative but Ben noticed how quickly he mellowed when he made eye contact with Amber. "There's no other way Am."

"He shouldn't be involved."

"Dammit girl, I sit in this house every day, doing nothing of any substance, stagnating in a swamp of decrepitude and boredom. I'm a hundred and nineteen years old and my dance card is blank. You think I want to live another ninety years? I'd rather have ninety minutes to live and do something purposeful with them. I don't just want to do this, I *need* to do this."

"It's a swank idea Am," Shon said. "And with...*Ben's* help, it should be jell for me to file how to operate the ob."

"Whoa there! I didn't say anything about that. Nobody drives that car but me. This isn't amateur hour boy. You're going to need a good wheelman. Hell, you don't think I'm letting you kids have all the fun while I stay home do you?"

"Grampa Ben, you–"

"Amber, you hush now. You're not talking me out of this, so save your breath. Now what's the plan? I want to see if this little cabal knows what it's doing."

* * *

It had been a gray day, given life only by intermittent drizzle. Periodically moonlight stole through the clouds and everything glistened. When it did, one slender beam of soft white light managed to find its way through the city spires and onto the car's hood. Ben noticed how the water still beaded up in little Acapulco Blue droplets.

He'd been waiting for more than twenty minutes. His hip ached and a new, sharper pain ran down his left leg. He needed to get up and move around but he was afraid to. They'd said it would be less than half an hour when they left him there, wearing their rubber masks. He'd thought it was a nice touch, wearing facsimiles of the Homeland Security director's face. However, the longer he waited, the more he began to doubt the whole scheme. What if something happened to Amber? He'd never hear the end of it from his snot-nosed grandson. But hell, she would have gone and done it anyway—or something equally as rash. He convinced himself, at least this way he was here to help.

He looked out the side window and, as he did, caught a glimpse of something that rankled his nerves. Was that a chip in the paint—right next to the mirror? In the dim light he couldn't tell for sure but it looked like a scratch. How the hell did that get there? He was about to open the door to take a better look, when out of the raw silence an alarm shrieked. His heart battered his chest. He reached for the ignition key but didn't turn it. He thought he saw something. Was that them? His eyes blurred. For a moment, he couldn't see a thing. The alarm continued to blare. He started to sweat. His vision cleared but he still couldn't see them. Where were they? Were they caught? Were they-?

A shadow opened and closed and three figures hurried towards him. They pulled off their masks as they threw open the passenger door and climbed in.

"Let's mode!" cried Shon.

"Go Grampa Ben, go!" encouraged Amber.

He started the engine, racing the motor in his anxiety and pulled it into drive. Again he hit the pedal too hard and the rear wheels spun and screeched against the wet pavement, until they grabbed hold and took off.

"Did you do it? Did it work?" Ben asked.

"The worm is served," replied Shon.

"Watch out!" Amber yelled.

Ben swerved to miss a street-cleaning droid.

"You almost deleted us old man!" the nameless subversive carped.

"Oh, don't mess your diapers sonny. I'll get you there."

"Just be careful Grampa."

Careful wasn't what he was feeling. He felt robust, simultaneously fearless and fearful. He sensed his nano bugs working overtime, pumping out the adrenaline. For the first time in a long time, he felt alive. *Careful* didn't have a chance.

"There's where we get out!" Shon called.

Ben pulled up next to the designated building.

"Okay, we're just kids out having a swank time now," Shon said, winking at Ben.

They piled out and Amber ran around to the driver's side.

"Thanks Grampa," she said, kissing him on the cheek. "I won't ever forget what you did for us."

"Ever's a long time," replied Ben. "Even longer for some. You just keep marching to the beat of your own drummer, you hear? Don't take any guff from no one–that includes Shon boy," he paused, studying her face. It was a face he remembered from long ago. A face he had known so well once upon a time. "You know, standing there, your cheeks flushed with excitement, you look just like your great-great-grandmother. *Exactly* like her."

He saw Amber smile but hoped she couldn't see the tears welling up in his eyes.

A light passed over them. Ben looked up to see a pair of airborne searchlights.

"Get going now. I'll distract them."

He turned the wheel and his tires screamed for traction. Amber called to him but he couldn't hear what she said.

He had to get going—get that flying bloodhound to follow him. When the searchlight settled on the Ford he hit the accelerator. He figured if he drove like a madman it would stay with him. But he didn't plan on letting it stay with him for long. He had a few fancy moves left in him, and he grinned. It was glorious to be thumbing his nose at *the man* again.

Tires screeched as he turned sharply—first left, then right. Maneuvering under an overpass he figured he'd evaded his pursuer. Then he saw another light up ahead. They'd called in reinforcements—good! The more attention he attracted the less likely they'd bother with Amber. He turned another corner and accelerated again, hoping to lose the aerocars in the dark of a smaller street. But they didn't shake that easily. They were tracking him somehow.

Amidst the swirl of excitement he felt something in his chest–a flutter. For a moment he had trouble breathing. His vision blurred. *Not now*, he thought, *not yet.*

He glanced in the mirror. There were even more of them. He'd never lose them all. They swarmed above and all around him like mutant fireflies, targeting him with their pallid, probing lights. He approached a turn. He had to decide; he had to make up his mind now. He could stop. They'd question him. Probably fine him. Maybe even arrest him for speeding. But they couldn't connect him to the break-in...to the kids. Could they?

Or he could keep going. Take the turnoff and head for the ocean. Ignore the flock of federales overhead. Drive straight to sunrise.

He slowed to make the turn. Gripping the wheel a little too tightly, he accelerated and as the Mustang roared off, chasing the light of its headlamps, a mish-mash of old song lyrics bobbed through the murk of his memory. Something about taking the highway to the end of the night, riding a snake to the lake and a blue bus. Yes, he remembered now. *The blue bus is calling us. Driver, where you taking us?*

He glanced down at the green glow of the dashboard instruments. The speedometer's toothy grin and the unwinking orbs of the fuel and temp gauges smiled back at him. Then, as if sensing his awareness, a red warning—the oil light. She'd blown a gasket or worse. He was pushing the old girl too hard. Just a little longer—he coaxed her—just a little farther.

Through the windshield the first hint of dawn flaunted itself along the horizon and beneath the illumination, he saw the ocean's dark expanse. He could even make out the wind-tossed whitecaps playing along its surface and the gulls soaring above.

He was where he wanted to be. He was also afraid. That familiar chill coursed through his veins. It reminded him of the pain, the aching complaints and the sameness of the days. He didn't belong anymore. What was left? Let them put him in a home and junk his car? He welcomed the chill. He embraced it. As he did, he dropped the hammer—pressed the accelerator to the floor and rolled down the window feeling the rushing wind. He'd take her with him. Drive into eternity. Let the gods watch with envious eyes as he cruised by.

Downward he drove. Down towards the rocky cliffs. Down a bumpy incline of shallow gullies, through parched weeds, racing towards the precipice. In one awkward instant the old steel horse was airborne, graceful as a zephyr.

Once a demon of cerulean speed, it began its descent in slow motion, as if resigned to its fate but still not wanting to go. In that split-second of soaring exhilaration Ben felt something clutch his heart—a burning, ripping pain. As consciousness faded, he heard the engine die— its last piston thrust withering to a conclusive silence, before man and car drove through the surface and disappeared into the sea.

The End

The Writer
(Horror)

By

Jeffrey Wilson

I don't know how to start. That may not seem strange to you, but it is weird as hell to me. I have been a writer all of my life or at least all of it I can remember. You wouldn't recognize me at the Food Lion or anything but I have had the good fortune to make a healthy living at it these last ten years. In all that time I have never had a problem with my opening sentences.

When I wrote *Flesh Donor*, the first paragraph poured out of me into my computer and then it was off to the races. I wrote the whole damned thing in about seven weeks, working like a man possessed, which is really kind of how it always was. Stories just got into my head, appearing there at the most bizarre times, like in the middle of a conversation or once while making love to a girlfriend. Then I just sit at the computer and the story writes itself. It's been that way since I wrote my very first one—*Freedom* it was called—in the seventh grade. *God*, how I miss that feeling—the feeling when a story possesses you and you are just the pitcher that holds the tall drink you hope it might become. But that's over now.

I haven't written a word, that I can remember, in seven months, not so much as a post-it note. I have been far away, alone in a cabana on a small island near Crete, no computers, no typewriters. But I am home now and *the calling* is back. Soon it will be dark and I need to get out of here before then. I am writing this long hand, on a legal pad and I'll send it to my sister to be typed. Don't know what she'll do with it and I don't really care. I think I have to write it— it's different from the writing that slipped out beyond control, but not completely different…maybe.

And I know this will be the last thing I ever write, one way or another. I can't help but tell this story though. I am terrified by it, mostly because it is true but, God, it is a hell of a story. I wish like hell it had been born in the slightly psychotic part of my brain that has made me a good deal of money over the years instead of *whatever* levels of Hell it actually sprung from. As a story it could be a real gold mine—a great follow up to my last book—the one my agent has been asking for. Still, I am afraid, so bear with me and I will try to get this out without hurting anyone.

I met Barbara (Babs to her college friends but as God is my witness, I swear I never, ever called her that) about six years ago. *Flesh Donor* had been a great success, financially anyway, and I had just moved to Clearwater Beach. *Fade* was sitting on the chopping block (my affectionate term for my agent/editor Dan Howard's desk, the sight of many a great and bloody revisions) and I had just cashed the first of three installments on my advance of three more books.

I was drying up from a two-year party binge, a long time to celebrate publishing a book most people have never heard of but having money—even the modestly comfortable amount I enjoyed as a fairly unknown pulp writer—takes some getting used to. I had cut down to hitting the clubs only twice a week (well, more during the Clearwater spring break hot chick parade....I was twenty-eight and only human) and had finally settled into a work routine. I would sit diligently at my computer hacking away, at least four hours a day.

Now I know those of you with real jobs will roll your eyes at this but trust me when I tell you that four hours is a long time to write, especially every day. I put out a lot of work, mostly novel ideas that collapsed into short stories and novellas but my real project, *Night Light,* was taking shape and more importantly, I enjoyed writing again.

After my first book, the fear I would be discovered for the fraud I believed I was had made writing a real chore. Honestly, I never really thought that *Fade* was all that great (I still cashed the checks though—I know I am no artist). The point is, I was happy and enjoying work, which I think most writers will agree is the key to producing a story that is worth a shit.

Anyway, Barbara came along at the right time, when I was ready to settle down and have some stability in my life. She was sitting at the bar on the pool deck, at Adam's Mark on the beach. I used to go by for a beer after walking on the beach (it was supposed to be a run but almost never was) and I noticed her immediately. Barb had the kind of looks that made you notice her, even in a crowd, and then watch her from afar. I guess I was feeling exuberant that day, feeling like a bit of a success, and the beers didn't hurt.

After about a half hour of watching her laugh (a quiet but pretty laugh that started with her eyes) and chat with her grad school friends, I picked up my beer and walked over. I just sat down next to her. I've never had any kind of gift with opening lines, despite how easily they came in my writing. I just sort of smiled and said, "Hi."

Barb looked at me curiously, *sized me up* is how it felt, and I guess I passed some inner litmus test because she gave a, "Hi," back, and then, well, like the stories—off to the races. She had moved to Tampa, about forty minutes away when the tourist traffic didn't slow the bridge to a crawl, and worked for some investment company named after a bunch of rich partners. Her friends from graduate school at UVA had come down for the week and she was hanging out with them, reliving some simpler days from school.

My guess is, had I met her out with her work friends, she wouldn't have given me a second glance, but life kind of happens that way sometimes. With her number and a promise to have dinner later in the week, I left the resort feeling like a stud. And…damn if I didn't call her later that same night and every night, until Thursday when I picked her up for a fancy dinner at Ruth's Chris steak house, on her side of the bridge. I didn't make it back to Clearwater until Sunday.

I could tell you a lot about the next two years but writing is such a struggle now and I am honestly terrified, so suffice it to say, she filled a need I thought I had. I pursued her like a man on a Great Crusade and said all the things she wanted to hear. I treated her the way I knew, in her mind, she needed to be treated.

We married only eight months later; a haughty affair in her hometown of Alexandria, Virginia (where the few friends I had were almost as uncomfortable as I was.…*that should have been a hint*) and then I bought a house I couldn't afford down on the beach in the Indian Rocks area of St. Petersburg.

Those first two years were good. Can't say I was deliriously happy but I was content. I worked hard and put out some good stuff. It wasn't that we didn't get along. We shared company and that was enough. We took some nice trips, laughed a little, had satisfying (though certainly not mind blowing) sex. We rarely went out, except to dinner or a movie and then usually just the two of us. I didn't have a lot of friends and the ones I had were sacrificed. She never really cared for any of them. I found her friends boring and self-absorbed. I didn't like who she was when she was with them (pretentious, always talking about money and bragging about my income in ways that weren't actually true) but I suffered through a night out with them, or parties at their big houses now and again.

I began to notice she talked a lot about money and my contracts but never really about my work. I am not sure she ever read any of my stuff, although she claimed she did but it wasn't really her genre. She excelled at spending the goddamn proceeds however. In retrospect, I can't remember a deep or memorable conversation we had about anything. Like I said, we just kind of shared company.

I received my three-year contract for three books and *Blood Games* actually spent a short time on the bestseller list. Dan negotiated a better contract (*Real* money Barbara called it) with a different publisher and I guess I felt too good about myself professionally to notice how our marriage changed. When Barbara started going out more with her friends from work, it wasn't even on my radar screen but I sure as fuck noticed the first time she stayed out all night. I accepted her explanation—not really even an apology— that she had stayed at her friends after drinking too much. I pouted for a few days but then shrugged it off and I got back to work.

His named turned out to be Chad, a perfect name for a materialistic shithead, who I later found out, had been banging my wife for the better part of that year. She cried a little, blamed me a lot. Apparently all I cared about was my work…I guess I was supposed to care more about money and clothes like her Porsche-driving asshole. Without ever saying she was sorry, she promised to be true. Yeah—right. Six months later I signed the divorce papers which arrived by certified mail while she and Chad laughed and fucked at his big house on Harbour Island in Tampa.

Holy shit I was bitter. I think I knew then and definitely know now, I wasn't really in love with her but nobody likes to look like an idiot. What really burned my ass was the smug look on Chad's face when she came in a rented truck to get *her* stuff. *Her* stuff included most of the furniture from *our* house. I really hated him, with a passionate hate those of you who have been there know and those of you who haven't, can't really imagine. Writing the kind of stuff I do, I let my imagination run wild, drank heavily at home and pictured a lot of horrible deaths for that guy. All were graphic and painful. Then I wrote the story that started it all.

Or *something* wrote it.

Not having worked in any real way, in almost a month, I wanted to knock out a quick story centered on a terrible death for my friend Chad, so I would feel better. Maybe at the same time get my creative juices flowing again. Sitting at my computer at about 1:30 in the morning, a cool buzz from too much Sapphire gin, I just let it pour out of me. My stories write themselves, but not like *this*. This was different. Hard to describe but it's almost as if the story controlled me. It most definitely possessed me.

I wrote like a mad man and finished exhausted. Not tired like you would expect because it was four o'clock in the morning and I had sucked down more than a third of a bottle of gin. *Exhausted*, like a marathon runner feels after the high is gone and he is left with just a body-wide achy pain.

I collapsed in my bed, almost unable to move. My dry throat burned and I panted uncontrollably. The strangest part is I couldn't remember what I had just written—not a word. I knew Chad had died in the story (that was not the name I had used but it was most definitely him in every way) but I couldn't remember a thing about how my story had done him in. Frustrated, but more than that—scared—for reasons I couldn't get a grip on, I had no memory of any of it. I briefly entertained that in my drunken stupor nothing had been written. I was sober enough to know that wasn't true. I had the sense I was more like a tool for some other force or power. It sounds crazy but that was how I felt.

I'd passed out rather than slept and…dreamed—horrible things. No real plot, just fragmented terrible images of Chad's screams as something— some unseen creature—literally tore him apart in the dark corner of my mind. I suspect that many people assume horror writers like me have nightmares all the time. Not me, not once that I remember. My stories are just that—just stories. They don't get inside me and they sure as hell don't haunt me.

That night, Chad's screams woke me up and those screams definitely haunted me the next morning. Chilling, visceral screams of terror and horrible pain. Waking in my bed the screams were still there, off in the distance, fading slowly but real. I swear to God. And there was something else—a presence in my room. I know how that sounds too, believe me. It sounds like something from one of my books. I accept that if anyone ever reads this they will think I am either full of shit or a raving lunatic (You know the kinds of things he would write? I mean this was no surprise…) I'm fine with it actually. I am telling you what happened because I have to and frankly, *what you do with it?*…well, I could really care less.

There *was* something there, something powerful and evil. Maybe it felt temporarily satiated from the blood I fed to it but a *hunger* still filled my room. I got out of bed and ran from the presence. The presence that sat belching in the corner of my bedroom, bloated from Chad's flesh.

I sat down slowly in front of my office computer, sweating; the sound of my pulse loud in my temples, a coppery taste in my dry mouth. The computer was on, my screen saver (the cover from *The Donor*—how fucking vain is that?) floating about eerily. I sat in my chair, the chair from which I made a living, and reached out a shaking hand to the mouse. The moment I moved it the story appeared, the last page sitting there with my editor program box asking me if I wanted to save it. I came very close to clicking *no*, turning the goddamn thing off and having a Gin and Tonic for breakfast. It scared me shitless, but at the same time, I had to know.

What I had written all night—what had unchained the thing slumbering hungrily in the dark? I clicked *yes* and watched the little boxes scroll to the bottom of my screen. The story saved to my desktop. I then forced myself not to read what was on the last page (why ruin the ending?) I scrolled to the top. Only twenty-eight pages, double-spaced. Less than ten thousand words—give or take.

I read.

It essentially revolved around Chad getting hit by a car, with a morbid description of his injuries. The bulk took place in *his* mind, awake but paralyzed, both by devastating head and spinal injuries and the medicine given to him when they snaked a breathing tube down his throat. It was a classic terror story; maybe more trite than classic. It centered on his unimaginable pain and terror at knowing his life was slipping away, unable to move or speak or stop the cycle of his death. It was the kind of thing I *would* write. I admit that. But what scared me was my certainty that I did *not* write it.

Every writer has a distinctive voice. If you are an avid reader, you know what I am talking about. You can read just a few paragraphs from the middle of a book and tell right away whether it was written by John Le Carre or Robert Ludlum. It's not the context or even the plot. It is the voice.

This was not my voice. Not even close. More importantly, it didn't all come together for me as I read. Instead, it seemed I heard this story for the very first time—there is no doubt in my mind about that. A lot of things I am telling you I have come to believe over time and to be fair, they are my interpretations of things I in no way understand, but this one thing is certain fact. I had never written, read, or thought up the story I was now reading— not in my entire life.

That thought chilled me as I sat there. When I closed the file, *"save changes?"* the computer asked me. "No thank-you" I answered with a click. The screen went black instead of flipping back over to the menu or even to my floating vanity of a screen saver. It just faded to black, like an old diode tube TV, flashing light for a moment, then rapidly disappearing to a single white dot in the middle. It hung there for a second then disappeared with a nearly audible *pop*. Lingering in the center was a red dot. Blood red.

I stared at it for a moment in surprise.

Fade to Black, right, man? Just like your second, crappy novel.

I pressed my eyes firmly into the palms of my hands, until white spots exploded in my vision like fireworks. When I opened them, the screen looked normal, back to the menu bar. Surprise made me shift backwards reflexively, nearly knocking over my chair. My hand darted out, grasping for the wall and I violently jerked the plug to the power-strip surge protector out of the socket. Without knowing why, I was suddenly terrified of my computer. I pulled the plug to kill it and the story written by some stranger, but it didn't work.

The cord lay on the floor but the screen was the same, set to my menu bar. And then the screen changed. The mouse arrow moved slowly across the blank monitor—moved by an unseen force. I looked without thinking at the mouse sitting on the *Grateful Dead* pad beside the key board but it lay perfectly still. Yet the arrow continued until it arrived where I knew it was headed, paused a moment, then clicked on the big blue *W* for my word program. The screen fluttered, the way a road seems to flutter when the sun has been baking it all day and then a blank page appeared. A little black rectangle was blinking in the left upper corner. It was calling to me.

Come on and sit down. Let's go again.

I ran from the room—all the way out of my fucking house, out the back door and onto the beach. Barefoot, which wasn't weird where I live but in my boxers, not unheard of in my neighborhood but a little out of the ordinary. I didn't give a shit. I just wanted to be as far away from the computer as possible and the creature who owned it. You should know, at this point I knew Chad was dead. Knew it in the calm way you know the sun will come up again tomorrow. Afraid of what his death meant, I am ashamed to admit feeling no *remorse* for my role in it, whatever the hell that was.

I sat on the beach for a long time. It started getting hot out and the glaring late morning sun reflecting off the water made me wish for my sunglasses. I don't smoke but I would have smoked then. I needed *something* and really wanted a drink. But the drink was made less appealing by my haunting hope that this was all some sort of alcohol-induced hallucination.

Sitting on the hot sand, my knees hugged tightly to my chest, pulse still pounding in my temples, I could hear the phone ringing in my house through the open door. No fucking way I was going in there at that moment. It would ring and ring and then stop, then my cell-phone would chirp a while and stop, then my phone would start again. My mind groped desperately for any explanation that would make the terrible fear, the churning in my stomach, disappear. Sitting there, I slowly rationalized my way to a truce with my nagging terror. No more gin, I had decided. Time to clean my ass up and get back to work. That would keep this nightmare from recurring…right?

If only.

As I headed into the kitchen from my deck the cell phone chirped again and I looked at the caller ID. Jason Drake, the husband of one of Barb's coworkers and probably the only one from that crowd I ever really liked. Jason was an ER doc at the big hospital in Tampa and his wife was gorgeous, but a lot like Barb.

Unlike me I suppose, Jason had done a good job at remaining content with his decision to trade a deep relationship for nightly access to her tight body. He and I would often hang out, off by ourselves, when the accounting gang would get together. He was a good guy. I flipped open my phone.

"Hello?"

"Hey guy. Where have you been? I've been trying to catch you for over an hour." The heaviness in his voice bothered me. Something was definitely wrong and of course, I knew what it was.

"Out running," I lied. "What's up?"

"It's Chad, man. Did you hear?" his voice was tense.

I felt my stomach flip and my heart renewed its pounding. I reached a trembling hand out towards the blue bottle of Sapphire on the counter, then thought better of it and pushed it away. I closed my eyes and steadied myself on the counter.

"No, what happened?"

There was a long pause. Then he spoke calmly, as if putting on his doctor hat.

"It's bad, man. Hit by a car. He is really fucked up."

"Dead?" I asked, trembling.

"Not yet, but he won't make it. Bad closed head injury, spinal injury. He's on a ventilator in the ICU. No way he's going to make it. I was on duty in the ER," he paused again, maybe waiting for me to say something. I said nothing, and after an awkward moment, he continued.

"I've never seen anything like it. Hit and run. Whatever the guy was driving it tore him apart. Bad…I've never seen anything like it," his voice had a tremor in it.

Terrified, I didn't answer but thought of my nightmares, of Chad torn apart in the shadows by some unseen creature. I thought of those horrible visceral screams and of the presence felt in my room. I said nothing.

"Are you there?" Jason asked; his voice more controlled.

"Yeah, I uh…." not knowing what the hell to say. "I just don't know what the hell to say. I don't know how to feel about this."

"I hear you man," he seemed satisfied with my answer.

Then the doorbell rang, which nearly made me shit myself.

"Someone at the door, Jase. Can I call you later?"

"Sure, sure—call any time," and he was gone. I went to the door with some trepidation, imagining some other person from my life with Barb coming to give me the bad news.

It wasn't.

Two officers stood uncomfortably on my doorstep, no doubt hot in their dark uniforms. Their eyes scanned my porch and yard as I watched them through the peephole. I don't know what made me panic, *shit*, I didn't really do anything wrong…right? I only wrote a fucking story. I had even deleted it from my desktop. Then I thought of something else—the wastebasket on my computer, a repository of discarded files. I had not emptied it, so the story would still be there.

My pulse quickened and my mouth became drier than my moderate hangover had already left it. I don't know what the hell made me think these two cops were gonna search through my computer or what it would mean to them to find that story.

Ah Ha! A story about a car accident! Just as we thought! Place your hands on top of your head, palms up sir, and drop to your knees!

Ridiculous, right? Yeah, well, I was still nervous as hell but I opened the door.

"Mr. Reynolds?"

"Yes," as casually as possible.

"May we come in sir?" I could feel their eyes dissecting me and felt my right knee shaking. I tried to stop it, certain they would notice. They were sizing me up but why? What the hell would bring them here? No way I was going to let them in the house. They would see right through my anxiety and guilt and they would be sure I had killed Chad. No fucking way they could come in.

"Sure, come on in," I opened the door further for them.

They stepped into my foyer and stood politely as I closed the door behind them, hand convulsing. I jammed my hands into my pockets, knowing they would notice. That was when I realized I was standing in my foyer in my fucking underwear, with two of St. Petersburg's finest.

Perfect.

"Uh, you guys mind if I pull on some clothes?"

"Not at all, sir. We'll wait right here."

I started for the stairs but stopped. I couldn't possibly go up there. That was the scene of the crime, wasn't it? Plus, in spite of my rationalization on the beach, I still had the terrifying feeling something really horrible hid in the corner of my room—a creature who, even as I spoke to these fine officers, dozed and quietly digested Chad's flesh. It would probably be getting hungry for breakfast. I turned abruptly and headed to my laundry room where I grabbed a clean T-shirt and some marginally clean running shorts.

"Late night sir?" asked one of the officers. Loaded question?

"Up late working," I answered, rejoining them in the foyer. "I'm a writer," I said, then immediately regretted it for some reason.

"Yes sir," the older cop opened a notebook. Then he looked at me again and I felt his gaze boring through me, inside to where my guilt lay smoldering. His younger partner just looked bored. "Where were you last night, sir?"

"Right here," I answered uncomfortably, glad I finally had some pockets to shove my hands in. "What is this all about?" I already knew of course.

"There's been an accident sir," the younger cop said.

"Do you know a guy named Chad Keller?" the older cop asked.

"Oh, yeah," I said and rolled my eyes. "He's shacking up with my wife." My knee quivered again.

The older cop looked at me for a moment, his lips pursed.

"Ex-wife, right?"

"Yeah, right," I agreed. "Ex-wife."

"May we have a look at your car sir?" The younger cop again.

"Sure," I tried to appear nonchalant. "Can you tell me what the hell is going on?"

"Hit and run sir," the older cop said. He watched me carefully, looking for my reaction. I tried to give him none. "Mr. Keller is dead."

"That's horrible," I said and tried to appear genuinely surprised. "What does it have to do with me?"

"Well," the older cop put his little notebook back in his shirt pocket. I hadn't seen him actually write anything in it. "We're just trying to piece everything together. Just need a quick look at your vehicle. You haven't been involved in any accidents recently, have you sir?"

"No," but now my mind really started to screw with me. What if my car was in the garage, banged to shit and covered in blood? What might it mean—other than I was completely crazy? Hell, I couldn't remember writing that damned story, even after I read it in my office, in my home, on my computer. What else didn't I remember? I was a gnat's hymen away from telling those guys to piss off and get a warrant and then going in the garage for a preview by myself. But the script was kind of written by that point, so I figured well, might as well see the show. Plus, if my car was the weapon used in Chad's execution, I think at that moment I would have preferred to be in a jail cell and away from the bloated thing in the corner of my room.

It didn't occur to me I might just be nuts (not at that point). If the car was beat up and glistening with ol' Chad's blood and gray matter, it might just mean I had murdered him. Nothing from one of my books; no hidden creatures or supernatural forces—just a depressed and angry guy, screwed up on expensive gin, running that dipshit down with his M3 BMW convertible.

It didn't seem possible to me that I could have such rage. Hell, I live in Clearwater Florida and I don't even fish. Feel too bad for the damned fish—brains the size of a cashew. No way it would have occurred to me that I could run a guy down in cold blood and then back over him a time or two, from what Jason had described on the phone. Then drive home, write a quick short story for *Weird Tales* and crawl into bed. To me, it was still about something more evil and powerful and the feeling I was just a witless pawn. Only one way to get some answers and I had become a little fatalistic at that point, so, my hand already on the knob, I twisted it and opened the door to the garage.

We went in together, down the two short steps, the light coming on automatically when it sensed our movement. I stopped and the younger cop bumped into me. Larry, Moe, and Curly. He grunted an apology and we all stood there, looking at it together.

A pristine, charcoal gray M3 BMW convertible with tan leather seats, the top down, was beckoning us. *Let's cruise!* Well, not pristine. I don't wash it like I should, especially since the bitch who made me buy it had left me. So there was dust and dirt around the wheel wells and a few of the billion Florida bugs stuck to the trophy wall the fancy grill had become. But no dents. No blood or brains. Nothing suggesting my car had knocked Chad down on a Tampa street and then somehow torn him apart alive. Just an infrequently cleaned, poorly maintained yuppie's status mobile.

Crockett and Tubbs walked around it for a few moments and the older guy looked underneath for some damned reason (Maybe I had just dropped my car on top of poor Chad?) then stepped back over to me by the door. This time he really did scribble something in his little book, then slipped it back into his pocket. They looked at each other and nodded, the younger cop apparently disappointed I wasn't a killer.

"Anything else you want to tell us?"

"About what?" I asked, the perfect angel, the lid on the cookie jar and the crumbs on my chin apparently invisible. The older cop pursed his lips again and paused. Then he stuck out his hand.

"We appreciate your cooperation, Mr. Reynolds." I shook his outstretched hand and then followed them back to the front door.

"Have a nice day sir," the younger cop said on his way out, placing his bus driver hat back on his head.

"You too, guys," I said, then pointlessly added "Good luck." And they were gone. I stood in the foyer for a while, unsure what else to do, then felt an uncontrollable urge to get out of the house. I grabbed my wallet and cell phone and headed out the back door for the beach, still barefoot and in my gym clothes.

I walked for a long time, lost in thought. The morning became a bit more unrealistic to me and it felt good actually. My mind rationalized the night away, insulating itself from my fear and guilt. So I had written a bad story in some kind of drunken stupor about Chad's death and now he was dead. Disturbing, of course, but hardly evidence some evil force had moved into my bedroom or a powerful murderous creature controlled my computer. My feelings in the morning were doubtlessly leftover fear from my terrible nightmare, a remnant of the horror that it had created. As I said, I never really had any nightmares before this, so how in the hell would I know how it left you. Less drinking and more working and I would be fine.

I ended up at a little outdoor bar and grill I went to sometimes and realized I was starving. I sat under a little umbrella at a plastic table, had a great blackened-grouper sandwich with fries and chased it down with a cold beer. By the time I got home it was mid-afternoon and I was actually thinking about my next writing project, which had gotten off to a rocky start. I had some ideas about how to fix it and figured sitting at my desk, tapping out some real work might erase what was left of my fear. Maybe it would make me feel more normal again.

Feeling a twinge of anxiety I headed up the stairs, momentarily considering sitting on the couch to watch a little TV but forced myself to climb anyway. My bedroom looked completely normal, no bloodthirsty creatures in my closet when I pulled out some clean jeans and a shirt. I actually laughed at myself a bit. I took a long hot shower, put on my clean clothes and walked into my office.

The computer sat on my desk, the screen dark, normal. I sat down, tried to turn it on and was momentarily confused when nothing happened. Then I remembered I had unplugged it. I popped the cord back into the wall, pushed the power button and sat patiently through the start-up. I stared a moment at my normal appearing task bar. Before opening my word program, I clicked my trash bin, clicked on *empty trash* and watched the files disappear.

The end.

It seems funny to me now but I felt very normal, despite the fact my ex-wife was just across the bridge, mourning the horrible and bloody death of her boyfriend. I am sure I didn't think about her or Chad at all the rest of the day. I'm not sure that's normal but it's the truth. I opened up my project file and in a very short time I was lost in my work, tapping away, writing out new ideas as I always did. As usual, the one hour turned out to be more like three hours and when I stretched out the ache in my back from hunching over my key board, the sky outside my office window was a reddish orange. The wall clock, a neon job with martini glasses for hands, said it was nearly seven-thirty. I saved my work in my *new stories* file and then watched the floating book cover screen-saver pop on. Everything felt normal and I sighed, content.

I wasn't really hungry but walked a block down the road to a little pizza joint I like, got a white pizza with chicken and artichokes to go and carried it home. I was feeling pretty pleased. Under the circumstances, *that* may not be normal, no matter how satisfied I felt.

When I got home there were a few messages on my machine but I chose not to listen to them (why ruin my good mood?). I grabbed a Heineken from the 'fridge and poured it into a frosted pilsner mug from the freezer. I joined my pizza in the living room and sat on the couch to flip through the TV channels while I ate.

I found a favorite movie on the Sci-Fi channel (*Blade Runner*, with a very young Harrison Ford) and settled into my mindless evening. I fell asleep on the couch about half way through a re-run of the *Dennis Miller Live* show on HBO. Half a pizza was hardening in the box on my coffee table and the other half a bowling ball in my stomach.

Then another dream came. At least if felt like a dream, even as it happened. I woke up on the couch with the TV still on. I can't really explain the feeling (a real weakness for a writer I admit but hey I'm no T.H. Lawrence) but it was rather surreal. Dreamlike, which I know is a cop-out.

I remember comforting myself with the knowledge that it wasn't real. The pull I felt was like a calling, for lack of a better term. I want you to understand, I had a deep need to go upstairs. I didn't decide to go, just knew there was no choice; I had to go and did. The house was dark and I went slowly, frightened, but in the way you get scared watching a slasher movie. It is an exhilarating fear. Exciting because it's fun to be scared (thank God or I would have to get a real job), as long as you are secure in knowledge it is make believe, just a thrill ride. That was how I felt.

My office was lit by the soft glow of my computer screen, a soft white luminescent aura. The word program was open, the page blank and the little rectangle blinked in the upper left corner, softly calling to me. It wasn't an invitation, more of a demand.

Feed me Seymour, feed me!

I sat down in my chair and placed my hands on the keyboard. The rectangle still blinked, faster it seemed; it was no longer black but a crimson red.

Now! It said, *get going! Let's ride!*

My fingers started tapping away, slowly at first and then building faster and faster, like Ravel's *Bolero*. I sat there with the sensation my fingers were not mine own. I didn't even look at the screen, afraid of what I would see. They worked furiously and my wrists started to ache. I had no idea what I wrote and still don't. I worked like that for hours it seemed, my back burning, my arms aching. Sweat ran down my face and stung my eyes.

At times I would pull my hand away from the keys, with what seemed like incredible difficulty, to wipe the sweat from my face. They would then be violently yanked back to the keyboard. I was aware that I breathed heavily and my dry throat had become sore. I was desperate to get up from the chair, to get a drink of water—or better, gin—but couldn't break the hold. The force kept me in the chair, hunched over, using my hands to write its horrible tale.

When I finished I sat panting, my skin cool and glistening with perspiration. My shirt stuck uncomfortably to my back and I remember a burning in my crotch, like the chafe you get after running on a blistering hot day. My hands sat limply in my lap and I felt overwhelmingly exhausted. I looked with trepidation at the blinking light on the screen of my computer where a box flashed.

Save?

I wanted to get up, to ignore the computers question or better yet to press the delete key. Instead my hand raised slowly, moved the mouse to place the arrow over the *yes* box and without any help from me, my trembling finger pressed the mouse. The story collapsed to the bottom of the screen, turning into a benign marker.

I got up from the chair and walked slowly to the door. I felt my stomach heave and tasted bile in the back of my throat. I dashed down the hall to the bathroom and dropped to my knees in front of my beckoning porcelain friend.

I vomited violently, heard the splashing in the toilet in the dark, trying desperately to suck air into my lungs between each heave of my stomach. When I was empty, to the point I felt I might actually collapse into myself, dry and brittle, I leaned forward relishing the coolness of the toilet rim on my forehead.

I didn't try to figure out what I had written as I sat hunched over the stench of my own vomit. In fact, I struggled with all my will not to think about it. After a few minutes I shakily got to my feet, my stomach settling an uneasy truce with the rest of my body and staggered towards my bedroom. I paused at my office door just long enough to see the computer screen was again black. That was when I remembered, it had all been a dream. I wobbled towards the bedroom but stopped in the doorway.

The corner of the room, the dark corner beside my closet door, pulsed with a subtle but definite glow. Not orange like when a campfire is simmering its last breath of heat but a deep crimson red, the same red as the cursor had turned on the screen as I wrote. And a sound. I had never heard a sound like it but I will never forget it.

There is no glow in present time for me (not that I would see it, I sleep with all the lights on these days) but my mind can still hear that horrible sound—a wet crunching, behind a low throaty growl. It was the sound of something horrible. And it was feeding. Feeding on the bones and flesh of whomever was sacrificed. I heard a rustling, like it settled into a more comfortable position and then a terrible crack followed by a tearing—the sound of a body being torn apart between strong jaws and sharp teeth.

I dashed down the stairs, aware of a child like cry emanating from my own throat. I was intent on making it to the back door, of dashing into the moonlight on the beach, of running crying on the sand to the first light and comfort of people I could find. But I didn't make it. Instead, I made it to the bottom of the steps, engulfed by a near exhaustion and the couch called to me in a sweet low voice.

I collapsed onto it heavily, almost paralyzed with fatigue. I was able to get my arms up enough to press my hands against my ears, to block out the now distant but distinct slobbering growl of the creature upstairs. It swallowed the last chunks of flesh from our victim, then licked spilled crumbs and blood from my carpet. I passed out, pulled deeply into the darkness of a dreamless sleep.

My bladder jolted me awake. Since I had turned to gin, a few beers is not enough to give me a buzz but still goes through my plumbing with relative ease. I was uncomfortably full and dashed to the downstairs bathroom. I felt haunted by my nightmare and was afraid to go upstairs but knew I had to—to search for my sanity.

I glanced into my office in passing, then headed instead to the upstairs bathroom. The upstairs bathroom reeked of vomit, the un-flushed toilet full of little chunks of undigested white pizza floating in a pool of puke. I listened intently for sounds from my bedroom, heard none. I flushed my dinner and walked slowly to my office, dreading what I might find.

It was as I remembered it, the computer screen dark. It took me a moment to find the strength to move my legs and walk to my desk. I moved slowly, trembling. A nervous sweat beaded again on my face. I sat down stiffly and reached out with a trembling hand to move the mouse, bringing the screen to life. I saw my floating book cover briefly, then it disappeared, leaving multiple icons down the left side. I glanced at the strip at the bottom of the screen and there it was; a blue rectangle with a big *W* in a white square and written next to it was a title, *Whore's Death – Microsoft…*

Barb was dead. I knew it immediately. What was left of her was digesting in the belly of the beast that now called the corner of my bedroom home. It was sleeping again, until nightfall, when I would be called to serve up another dish to its voracious appetite for blood.

I felt my stomach contract. Tears welled up in my eyes. I had no love for that woman who had used me and then traded up for a more expensive model but I'm no killer either, not of my own volition anyway. I had shared a bed with her for several years, had enjoyed some good times and then had fed her to the creature possessing my computer, my soul.

With fear and disgust, I moved my mouse viciously on the rock and roll pad and placed the white arrow over the blue rectangle. For a moment, I hesitated, torn by a sudden need to know how we had killed her but then, knowing the knowledge would drive me insane, I clicked the right button. The cursor scrolled down to the delete prompt. I clicked it so hard it made my finger hurt.

"Are you sure you want to delete file Whores Death-Microsoft Word *to the trash bin?"* my accomplice asked.

Fuck yes! I answered by clicking the *yes* icon and the file disappeared. I clicked on the little trash can on the left of the screen, then on the *empty trash bin* icon and it was done. I had disposed of the murder weapon.

That was when I realized the shit I was in. They would definitely come calling again. They would be sure I had done it—the scorned ex-husband. First Chad and now Barb. What would they find at her house? I saw them in my mind, taking pictures of the blood-spattered walls, picking up what was left of my former lover and dropping the pieces into bags to be analyzed later. I shook my head violently, tossing the images out of my mind.

And now what? I was out of enemies. Whom would I slice up and serve in the sushi bar of my mind and computer now? Would it be friends or strangers? I knew for sure it wouldn't stop, that the creature in my room would demand feeding, again and again and again. I had to stop it somehow. I had to make it stop now. I wasn't just horrified, I was terrified. I don't even fish for Christ's sake and now I had a role in the deaths of two people. Not even strangers or people trying to kill me, like in war. These were people I knew, one of whom I had once loved.

It was unbearable but more unbearable was the thought that when darkness came, I would be unable to fight the beast's possession and another person would die. I had to go, but where? I realized the when was more important than where and that I needed to be gone before nightfall. Far away, *somewhere* where the beast in the corner and the computer in my office could not reach out and find me.

The knock on the door didn't bother me, didn't make me jump. I knew it was coming. My friends in blue would be on my front porch, here to tell me the news and study my face for reaction. I wasn't frightened this time because I knew there couldn't possibly be any physical evidence tying me to the crime and all I had to do was hold to my story—I was here working all night—not too tricky since it was actually the truth. I had no evidence of it, save my beer bottles and pizza box but fuck 'em. They had the burden of proof, right? Just be polite, act surprised and horrified, tell them my story, and usher them out.

By tomorrow I would be long gone. Tomorrow I would be far, far away. I have no idea how I would make a living as part of this master plan but with the cops at my door and my ex-wife's corpse still warm, I really wasn't worrying about it yet. I had a fair amount of money stashed away and a couple of advances still coming on my contract but not a lifetime's worth. I am a young man and have proven in many ways to have no skills other than my twisted (my mother's word) imagination but all I was thinking about was getting the hell out of there.

I answered the door and it was indeed my two friends. But the news they brought was not expected.

"Good morning sir,"

"Good morning," I answered and waited without asking them in.

"Sir," the older cop said, "We were wondering if your ex-wife might be here?"

Well that was a bit of a surprise. Especially since I knew whatever was left of her was indeed here, upstairs in the hot belly of my beast, being broken down into her molecular components.

"Uh, no..." I answered, confounded. "Why on earth would she be here?"

"Just checking everywhere sir. Seems she has gone missing."

Gone missing. What in the hell did that mean? She was missing alright, working her way slowly through the gut of my insatiable roommate, getting converted from a self-centered bitch into what would doubtlessly be one hellish shit. My surprise was genuine is the point. We spoke only a few minutes more, me answering questions about my whereabouts the evening before, assuring them I had not spoken to her in quite a while and certainly not in the last twenty-four hours. They were polite and didn't seem too concerned for her safety. I resisted the urge to ask them if they had any news on Chad's death, afraid that looking curious might make me look guilty of something. They thanked me and left.

At no point did I entertain the possibility Barb was still alive. I knew she was dead, knew we had killed her just as we had killed Chad. And I still knew that I had to go. It would not stop until I did. It did occur to me leaving would make me look like I had done something wrong of course but that was hardly a concern then. I had to go or I would help the beast kill again.

The rest of the morning was not worth telling. I packed a large suitcase, called a travel agent and arranged a flight and a place to stay. I called my mom and my sister, told them the recent events were too unbearable. I couldn't work and was going away for a while to Greece, to a little place where I could get back to my writing in relative quiet. I recall crying during both calls. Not for the reasons they thought of course but my grief was real, bloodied as it was by guilt.

I called my agent and friend Dan and asked him to take care of my business affairs while I was away, working on my new book. I had even called the number on the card the police officer had given me, telling them I had to get away. I gave them a number where I could be reached, on a remote island near Crete, should they have any other questions.

By early afternoon I was on a plane, out over the Atlantic Ocean, alone with my thoughts. I felt weak, having so readily run away, leaving the beast to possess my home and my computer but what else could I have done? I had no real plans for when and if I would ever return and I believed I would never come back.

Well, I am back. The months in Greece are surreal. I feel like I just awoke from a pleasant dream. I drank a lot of beer while I was there, laid on the beach, hung out in clubs. I got laid a few times, mostly tourist girls—always drunk and never memorable. I found a little place to hang out, a seaside restaurant-bar a short walk from my villa, on a cliff looking out over the blue sea. The owner and I became friends of sorts, filling my need for someone to be familiar with and his need to add some U.S. dollars to his till.

We talked about nothing, but at length, almost every night. No one knew me, though to be honest, even in the States I rarely run into a *fan* and no one ever recognizes me. Occasionally in conversation it will come out I am a writer and I will name some of my books when asked, only to be greeted with "oh, you're that guy".

I did get a few phone calls. I had no phone in my room, which was fine by me but would sometimes get summoned to front the desk. Most were from my mother, one from my sister. I got a few from the St. Petersburg Police. They continued looking for some more ideas on where my ex-wife might have gone, questions about what else I might know, when I was coming back, that type of thing. They never found her. They were working on the assumption she had disappeared in grief and continued to look for her, but assumed she had left the area. Might I know where she would go? Did she have friends out of town? A favorite vacation spot? Never an accusation outright but I surely remained a suspect for them.

I know where she went of course.

I said before, this is the first thing I remember writing in seven months and that's true. I didn't even keep pens or stationary in my little cabana. I felt nervous and frightened even signing my name on a credit card receipt for Christ's sake. But I know now, I did write while away. I wrote a lot in fact, as I learned just hours ago and perhaps that was why I had to come back. It was only yesterday that I heard the horrifying news and even writing it down now fills me with terror.

I had asked my sister to pick up my mail once a week from the floor of my foyer where it falls through my mail slot. She forwarded it to Dan Howard, business looking stuff—bills and the like. I guess he would do about anything I asked, if he thought it would help me get him another manuscript sometime soon. I am way behind my deadlines now but have lived comfortably on my advances without much guilt. The other stuff, junk mail and such, she had been putting on my desk for my return, which they had expected much sooner than now and I had hoped would never come.

I found out about the letters by mistake. I had gone to the desk to pay the cute young girl who worked there every day. Her English was poor but after a few confusing moments I realized she was asking about letters I had sent and wondering if I had one to go out. The impact of what she asked grabbed me tightly by the throat. I tasted bile in my mouth.

"Your letters—for the mailing in America," she tried to explain.

"What letters?"

"For mailing in America," she smiled again; confused by my look, no doubt thinking I didn't understand her. But I did, all too well. Then she reached under the counter and produced an envelope.

The letter had no return address but the addressee was me, at my home in Florida. The handwriting was mine but the letters more block like. I didn't open it, couldn't possibly open it. I stared at it in horror for a moment, then looked up at the girl. My face must have been easy to read because she looked uncomfortable, maybe even a little scared.

"How many?" I choked out.

She shook her head nervously, not understanding.

"How many?" I asked again, waving the letter in front of her. "Many? One-two-three-four-five...." My voice grew louder because we all know the louder you talk, the easier it is to understand a raving lunatic. But she did understand and nodded quickly to let me know.

"Yes, yes...Manny! Wery, wery manny!" she started flashing up fingers, ten at a time, over and over. I felt dizzy, my head pounding. I finally relented to the heaving of my stomach and dropped the letter to the floor, bolting to the small lobby washroom. I spit up my poorly digested late-night snack and beer into the sink, my head swimming and dizzy, sweat pouring down my body. I have absolutely no recollection of writing anything—much less writing regularly—what I can only assume to be more horrible death stories to feed my pet back home.

But I had—written them and then put them in envelopes, addressed them to myself, charged postage to my room I suppose and asked them to be mailed. How was that possible? How could a beast that controlled my mind and computer over three thousand miles away, reach out across the distance, and use me as a weapon even there, in my sanctuary? But there it was. Could it mean the creature was inside me? Or worse, the creature *was* me, my mind, my rage? Was it some force in *me* which used my words to kill, horribly and hungrily, from the quiet of my little office at home and now my paradise on the other side of the earth?

I didn't think so—I still don't think so. I had heard the beast in the corner of my room. I had heard his powerful jaws, tearing flesh from my ex-wife and licking blood from my carpet. I had heard his growling snore as he digested Chad in the dark. I had felt the heat, smelled the stench. And what about the glow—that horrible blood-red glow I had seen twice?

That was real, right?

I cleaned up the mess in the sink as best I could, running the tap water and using a paper towel to sweep the chunks of meat into the little metal trash can. I felt guilty that the cutie at the desk would probably be cleaning up my mess, aerating out the smell later.

I walked quickly through the lobby without stopping or acknowledging my hostess, stepping over the letter on the floor like it was a bloody arm at the scene of an accident. I headed straight to my room and started throwing my wrinkled things into my suitcase.

I hadn't run away at all you see? My cowardly escape had stopped nothing. The creature in my house still ate blood and I still fed it. Now it just ordered out. I have no idea how many stories I wrote in a drunken haze, sitting in the lobby in the middle of the night but apparently, it was "wery, wery manny".

I wonder how I looked to the night clerk, an older man who spoke *no* English. I was another crazy American, writing furiously on stationary, a wild and crazed look on his face, then stuffing the stories into envelopes and dropping them at his desk. I wondered who had been our victims. It couldn't have been people I knew. I mean, the cops might have mentioned it if all of

Barb and Chad's friends had started disappearing or been found dead on roadways and in alleys, torn apart alive.

I couldn't be a suspect of course. They talked to me several times and knew, full well, I was far away, in the Mediterranean, a coward hiding in luxury by the sea. But they would have had to mention it. Would not have been able to contain themselves, even if they had no thoughts of me as a mass murderer.

So it couldn't be people I knew. Who then? Just innocent people going about their lives, no bother to me or my Demon. Were they mothers and fathers? Children? Oh, my God, could they have been children? And how had we killed them? I knew from my limited experience with Chad's death and the horror of my own imagination, the imagination that had made me a very comfortable living, that they were terrible deaths. Painful, bloody deaths. I cried uncontrollably as I zipped my suitcase, then sat on the floor, sobbing.

Those same thoughts haunted me on my cab ride to the airport, as I stood in line to pay (a shitload of money) for the first available flight home and as I drank my way across Europe and the Atlantic ocean.

Now I am home or what use to be my home. Well, technically not IN my home. When I got here a while ago, before I started writing this, I was struck as I came through the door by the horrible smell. It lingers even out here on my deck, as I tell my last story. Even as I have acclimated to it, I'm still nauseated by the aroma of death.

Writing about it now is making me more aware of the stench and I feel the same bile rising as I did when I first walked in. It sent me out here, where I sit cross-legged in a corner of my cedar patio. It is a smell of hot death, like if you were to burn blood in a barrel somehow. It is mixed with a sulfur smell and something much more foul, like flesh rotting in the sun. I have twice come across the rotting corpse of a dolphin on the beach, baking in the Florida heat and the smell was horrible. It was nothing compared to this.

So now, all I have left is to tell you how this story ends. That is the struggle for young writers but comes to me effortlessly. I'm not saying I necessarily know the ending when I start writing but it is always obvious to me when I get there.

It's like that today. When I sat down to write this, huddled uncomfortably in the corner of my deck with my legal pad and two pens.

I know.

I knew in my heart when I left Greece and still know now. I am not a killer. Despite my thoughts, I know the power at work here is not inside my mind. I guess I needed you to know it too and so I scribbled this story. The beast is real but it's not me. I'm the weapon it chose, for whatever reason (perhaps it read some of my work and appreciated my twisted imagination). Does it matter? It was me and now here I am.

Did my mind in some way create this blood hungry beast? Maybe, but I don't think so. I get the feeling it has been around a long, long time. It doesn't really matter. What difference could it possibly make where it came from? I can't escape its reach, not even across the globe and I can't resist its call for flesh.

I really don't have a lot of fucking choices do I? Maybe it will still be around for a long time after I am gone but I don't have to be a part of it. The sun is nearly down. Tonight is a full moon and it is almost time. The blood-red square will be blinking in the corner of my already-opened but blank, Word document and I'll need to feed it. Apparently I can't do anything else.

Wery, wery manny times before. But I can make this its last meal, maybe. It will definitely be the last time it feeds at my hand.

Hey, if you were a fan, thanks for the ride. It was fun. I hope you liked my last story.

It is all true.

Brad walked down the darkened beach, just a short distance from his beachfront home where he wrote his horror stories. He was unaware of the killer who waited for him, hiding in the shadows, just out of view. As he approached, the metal blade in the killer's hand gleamed in the full moon…

THE END

An Eye For An Eye
(Horror)

By

Brett J. Talley

When Lewis awoke, the darkness was so thick he thought it might be a real thing and his first inclination was to scream. When the truth became apparent, when he realized why not even a single shard of light lifted the gloom, he did scream. And he didn't stop screaming for a very long time.

Lewis had been dreaming, right before his flickering eyes opened to darkness. A simple dream but not one he would have left willingly. He was in a park, with his daughter. With his Julia. It was a kite that had brought them there. A great, big butterfly kite Julia had seen and fallen in love with immediately. She hadn't begged him for it. She hadn't needed to. She looked up at him with those sparkling blue eyes and he saw it in her face. He'd never been able to resist that look, the one of pure joy, pure hope and a pure, unending innocence. He remembered rubbing his hand through her strawberry blond hair that smelled of peppermint and vanilla. He had opened his wallet and brought out the flimsy piece of plastic without a second thought. The drive out to the park in the middle of a little nondescript town they had never been to, just to see how her new toy flew, was serene.

The park was little more than an empty field and a few rusty, metal benches. A lifeless and desolate one at that, as too much summer heat and too little rain had turned the blades of grass a dead brown that crackled and collapsed beneath their footsteps. The constant breeze kicked up the dust left behind, stinging Lewis's eyes and leaving grit in his teeth. But the kite flew high and Julia didn't seem to mind. So Lewis didn't mind either.

How long did they stay there? Hours it seemed, until the sun began to set in the western sky and Lewis started worrying they wouldn't make it back to Denver until late in the evening. He didn't remember leaving though. In his dream, it was as if they would linger in that place forever. He thought that was not an altogether unpleasant fate.

It was strange. He was dreaming and he knew that. Or thought he knew it, at least. It had that unreal feeling, that floating-outside-of-yourself-sensation he had come to expect from the sleeping world. In other ways, it seemed less like a fantasy. Too real. Too solid. More like a memory, but one that was hazy and heavy. It felt like he couldn't quite see through the gloom that weighed on his vision. But yes, much more like a shrouded memory than a dream.

He even remembered how they had come to that place. They had been driving back to Denver, back from a trip to somewhere he couldn't recall. And they had stopped for lunch. That was when they saw the little toy store with the butterfly kite she wanted. He couldn't refuse her even before she could ask. He remembered all of that. And he remembered the man. The older guy in the brown duster and hat, the man that looked familiar to him. The one he had seen in other places, though the memories were obscured in a tangled web of confusion.

It had not been an easy passage from the dream world to the one of reality. Sleep had been thick and unrelenting. He had to fight through it. It reminded him of a time from his childhood. He had almost drowned back then on a camping trip with his Boy Scout troop. His canoe had flipped in rough water and when he sought the surface, he found himself trapped underneath the boat. He had seen the end, in the midst of that struggle. Seen his life spread out before him. Not only where he had been but also where he might have gone. And that vision had inspired him to fight. This waking sensation was not unlike the struggle against the surface of the water he had nearly succumbed to, all those years ago. Just as he had eventually broken through to fresh air, so too did he wake from his stupor. He knew immediately he was somewhere he shouldn't be. Not yet at least.

It wasn't just the darkness; it was the cold silence that hung over him. He had never heard absence of sound like that, complete and utter stillness. Had he been anywhere else, he would have sat up in shock. He knew such a reaction would be a mistake. Through some preternatural sense, he felt the thick darkness surrounding him hid something solid only a few inches from his face. He reached up and touched it. He felt the coarse bite of unplanned wood and screamed.

He might never have stopped screaming. He might have continued till the air was gone and he passed into oblivion. But as he cried out, beating upon the cold, pine roof above him with his frail hands, dirt filtered onto his face. Some lodged in his mouth leaving him spitting the substance back into the enveloping blackness. Something about the acrid taste of the soil brought him back, made him stop and think. "Get a hold of yourself," he said out loud. "Think this through." If he didn't, he would never accept where he was, and without acceptance, there could be no solution and no escape. Now, here, in that wooden tomb, some unknown distance beneath the surface of the earth, acceptance came easily. He was sure if he could not figure this out—if he could not reason it through—he would die there.

A couple of thoughts came to him, half-remembered bits of trivia he recalled from something he had seen on television once, one of those survivor shows that had tackled this very unlikely scenario—oh the irony of that now—of being buried alive. He probably had sixty minutes, maybe an hour and a half worth of oxygen, less if he struggled or panicked. That was ninety minutes, tops, that he had left to live. The standard grave is eight feet deep, eight feet so the coffin can rest comfortably with six feet of dirt on top of it. But most people don't know that. Most people think graves are six feet deep, which meant, whoever dug this one probably would have left at the most four feet of dirt above him. And if they were lazy or incompetent, maybe even less. Likely even less, especially if they didn't have the right equipment, and something told him he wasn't dealing with professionals. He rubbed his hands along the pine roof and pushed it gently. It gave a little and more dirt rained down on his face.

"Can't be four feet," he said to himself. Four feet of dirt probably weighed a lot, enough to crush the flimsy box in which he lay. If there were four feet of dirt above him, he'd be dead already. So that was a start.

He had very little space to move. He couldn't turn over even if he wanted to. The cold grip of claustrophobia fell over him and he was paralyzed by it as much as if the wooden planks had held him fast on all sides. When he was ten years old, his cousin had locked him in a storage space underneath the stairs in his parents' home. It had been all in fun, a game his cousin had meant to last only a few minutes. But when he tried to open the closet, the door would not budge; it had jammed. Lewis spent an hour in there, in the darkness. With the rats and the bugs and the shadows. Screaming and beating against the door as they tried to free him. He heard things that day in the little space beneath the stairs, saw things in the darkness he couldn't explain. He had been afraid of tight spaces ever since.

The fear of death was greater. To lose control now was to surrender to that fate. So he lay there, fumbling over in his mind how this had happened, hoping that finding the answer to that question would also present an escape. He thought back to the dream, the fantasy world that had seemed so real. That vision would not be silenced, as inconsequential as he told himself it must be. But the memories came flooding back and in the deluge he found the truth: it had been no dream. It was Sunday. They had spent the weekend at the Hoover Dam. They were supposed to have been home Sunday night but they never made it. There had been a detour. They *had* been in that park, he and Julia, somewhere in southern Utah. The elderly man had been there too. The old man in the hat and the duster. It wasn't the first time Lewis had seen him. No, there had been other instances along that journey. He had been at the diner where they stopped for breakfast. He had been in the mall where they bought the kite. Never too close, always at a distance. Lewis cursed himself for not noticing him earlier. Back then, before he came to be buried in what he hoped was a shallow grave, Lewis had only considered it in the back of his mind, in that reptilian part of the brain left over from an age when such observations were the difference between life and death.

What role had the man played, if any? His presence could not be a coincidence. He had been following them. He was Lewis's last, true memory. Between then and now, somehow he had come to this, left to die, entombed within the earth.

Suddenly he noticed a tingling on his lips, an unusual taste he couldn't quite place. But it wasn't the soil. No, it was too acidic, too metallic...too chemical. He had never experienced chloroform before but it was no matter. Lewis was sure he had been drugged. Only then did he feel the presence; he was suddenly aware there was something in the coffin with him. The electromagnetic hum tripped some sixth sense and caused him to rub his hands along the wooden sides as far as he could, until he felt the sterile, artificial touch of plastic. He grabbed the walkie-talkie and pulled it towards him just as the man began to speak.

"You awake yet, boy?"

The man spoke almost in a whisper but the sudden sound split the silence as booming thunder.

Lewis fumbled with the machine in the darkness, dropping it once. He found his bearings and clicked the button on the side.

"Who the hell is this?" he shrieked. "What the hell is going on?"

The man laughed, chuckled really. "Now, now there son. I've got no use for such language. If you're gonna talk like that I might just have to leave you alone to your own devices. We'll see how things work out for you then."

"No, no, no," Lewis begged as he felt the panic and fear overcome his anger. "No, I'm sorry. I'm sorry." And as he said it he felt stupid and small. Inept and truthfully, just flat out scared. "Look, look you gotta help me."

"Me? Help you? How do you think you got where you are boy? Who do you think put you there?"

"It doesn't matter. Nobody's ever gotta know about that. Nobody's ever gotta know. You just get me out of here and I'll pay you whatever you want. I'll do whatever you want. Just don't leave me here."

"Oh, you'll pay me, will you? You'll pay me? Pay me for my labor of digging you up. Is that right?"

"Yes," Lewis said, "yes. Whatever you ask. Whatever you want!"

The man laughed again. There was no joy there, no humor. The laugh terrified Lewis. It was a sound he had never heard before. It was a laugh of hatred, of pain, and it was a laugh of anger. There was no soul in that voice, no heart. There was only death.

"Ohhhh my boy. If only you knew. That's the thing about money, isn't it? It's only worth what you can buy with it. Got no value of its own. Only what you can purchase. Fact is, I got a house, and I got food and I got a car. Which means, the only thing I need to spend money on is entertainment. And let me tell you Lewis, right now, I am entertained."

Lewis pounded his fist against the coffin lid. It cracked slightly and another rain of dirt fell on him. His anger masked the pain in his hand. "What the hell is this you sick son of a bitch! What the hell is this!"

"Is entertainment not enough? Do I need another reason? Maybe I just enjoy listening to you squirm."

Lewis flew from one emotion to another, from fear to anger to desperation and back to fear. "I've got a family," he cried. "I got people who are waiting on me! They'll know I'm missing. They'll know I'm missing and they'll find you!"

"You think so? Here, a hundred miles from where you are supposed to be? I don't think you're correct Lewis. But, just for the sake of argument, let's say you're right. So what if they do? You'll be long dead by then. Long dead. And do you think anything they do to me will be as bad as what you'll suffer? As the air grows thin and you breathe in your own waste. As your throat and your lungs burn from lack of oxygen. As your brain cells die, one by one. As you slowly, painfully, slip away? Do you think anything they do to me will be worse than that?

"Hell, it'll take them fifteen years to kill me. Even if they do find me, even if they do prove I did this to you. And even if they do, they'll send me off on a nice, white cloud. I'll go to sleep and never wake up. You know, I always said I wanted to die in my sleep. Seems to me I get the better end of this bargain. You'll die in pain Lewis. I'll just be taking a nap."

Lewis had always believed you could reason with anyone. He was a businessman. It was his job to negotiate. People always want something. If you have it and are willing to give it away, two people could always reach an agreement. But as he listened to the man cackle on the other end of the line, somewhere above him, somewhere beyond him, he began to realize maybe, maybe that wasn't always true.

"There must be *something* you want," he whimpered.

The man laughed.

"This is what I want. *This is what I want.* And you are giving it to me Lewis. Oh yes...you are doing a fine job."

"You'll burn in Hell for this," Lewis spat. "God will judge you for this."

"Ahhh, now you want to bring God into it. Is that it Lewis? Is that it? God. Yes, I do believe God will judge me. But God judges us for the things we do that are wrong Lewis. And God condemns us when we do evil *Lewis*. God gives justice when injustice is done. But he rewards the righteous. He honors those who punish evil. And I tell you this, there is no greater good than a man who rights a wrong. Did you know that Lewis? Or maybe I should call you Adam."

Lewis felt a shiver run from the top of his head to the bottom of his feet. His blood ran cold at the sound of that name. The name he had not uttered for some time. The name he hoped he would never hear again.

"Oh, are you surprised?" the man asked, reading Lewis's thoughts. "Did you think no one remembered? I remembered. I never forgot. You could run Adam, you could run for the rest of your life. But I would have found you eventually. I would have found you one day."

Lewis now knew why the man was familiar. He had lied to himself, almost convinced himself it was all because he had seen him in other places those past few days, because the man had been following him. That was the story he had told himself but now he was painfully aware that no, Lewis had known him much longer than that.

* * *

Malinda Jackson called herself Lindy and that's how her friends had always known her. She was a cute girl, not beautiful, but pretty enough that the boys always noticed. Her teachers in high school commented amongst themselves, she was a particularly clever young lady and with time she would find a nice man to marry, one who would take care of her and build a world for her, in which to raise her children. And that, in the little town she called home, was the highest aspiration for a middle class girl such as herself.

College came and it came fast. In it, far from the little town where her daddy was the pastor at the local Church of God, she found herself in a world she did not understand and it scared her. She made friends slowly and at times she was desperate in her loneliness. So when an older boy she had met in her Calculus class asked her to a party at his fraternity, she accepted without question or qualification.

He was to pick her up at 7:00 p.m. sharp, though he was early. He patiently waited in the lobby of the all-girls dorm, the severe-faced matriarch of the place never ceasing to scowl at him over her reading glasses. He smiled when he saw Lindy, told her she was lovely in her light pink dress with a matching bow in her hair. He even held the door open for her, like a gentleman should.

He had picked a place on the river for dinner. However, it was crowded, and he was foolish and the waiting list was long for a couple without a reservation. His fears evaporated as she just smiled when he told her about the wait. For the next hour they fed the ducks bread and watched the barges float coal down the sluggish, brown water of the Choctawhatchee River, laughing at each other's awkwardness. When dinner finally came, the two of them sat outside and watched as the sun dipped into the flowing water. They were both too young to drink but he knew the waiter and for a cool twenty he brought them a bottle of sweet, bubbling Prosecco. She had only had alcohol once before—at her cousin's wedding when she was twelve—and then only for a singular toast that she was permitted to give. Lindy didn't tell him that now. It was funny, she had known him only for a few hours but she was terrified this new boy would find her boring or naïve. To prevent that, she would do anything.

So she smiled and sipped her wine, though she was surprised by what she found. It was not as harsh and bitter as she remembered. It did not burn her tongue or make her scrunch up her nose in disgust. Instead it simply tickled a little, while different flavors seemed to dance like fire on her tongue. As it sat in her stomach, warming her from the inside, the sensation of the subtle flames was complete. Everything was going so well.

The party was different.

The fraternity house sat on a hill overlooking the main boulevard. The pure white columns and ornate brick façade conveyed a message of wealth and power, of future influence and past glory. Not that night, though. That night the very structure seemed to be alive and it pulsated with energy and sound. The house breathed in the young and stole their youth. And when Lindy left the porch and stepped through the front door, she felt an overwhelming sense she should flee, that turning and running was the best thing, perhaps the only thing, to do. Back to the romance of the night's beginning, away from the debauchery of its end.

She told herself that was foolish and when Lewis offered her a beer she took it. It was the first of several, though she promised herself she would stay in control, that she wouldn't let the liquor's influence take hold of her. She probably would have succeeded but in the end, it wasn't the alcohol she had to fear.

Lewis would later swear he wasn't the one who slipped the pill into Lindy's drink. Lindy didn't notice, not really. She simply felt herself float away but not like she was falling asleep, not that peaceful. It was a total collapse of her mind and her will. She fought against it but her struggle was futile. She disappeared and whoever replaced her, whoever peered out from her eyes and took control of her body, it was no longer Lindy.

Lewis really didn't care who she was or who was responsible when Lindy fell into his arms and looked up at him dreamily, before pulling his head down into an open mouth kiss. He just accepted it and counted his good fortune. When he looked in her eyes, he saw only desire.

What happened next was a frenzy of activity and energy, all directed at one goal. They stumbled up the winding steps of the house, past amused coeds and their dates, up to a place where they would not be bothered. A semblance of privacy. By the time they fell into one of the senior's rooms and collapsed into the bed, her shirt was on the floor and her bra unclasped.

Then something happened, something that changed what should have been merely one of many drunken mistakes made that night, into a far more terrible thing. In the back of Lindy's mind, something snapped. A voice emerged from under the drug-induced shroud and it said one word: "No." And then Lindy said it too. Mumbled at first and then said it louder and more clearly. It grew to a word and finally a scream.

Lewis didn't hear it. He was too drunk and too high to notice. That's what he told himself in the weeks and years that followed. The thing he would repeat in his mind on most days. But in the darker moments of the many nights to come, he would know differently. When it was over, he sat on the side of the bed and she cried.

Lewis had just pulled on his jeans when there was a knock on the door. It was a senior, someone he recognized only from the tortures of Hell week. The boy looked over his shoulder and smiled.

"You mind?"

The combination of the alcohol and the adrenaline and the look in the other boy's eyes made Lewis sick.

"No, man. She's my date."

The boy cursed and pushed Lewis out of the way. He would have fought him; Lewis had made the decision. He wouldn't have let it happen, as much for his own sake as for hers. But when he turned around the other boy was just standing there, staring out towards the small balcony jutting from the side of the house. Lindy was crouched on the railing, most of her body over it but with her face turned back towards the boys inside. The catcalls of the people below, who saw nothing more than a naked girl, trickled in on the breeze as it whipped the curtain up in the air, alternately obscuring and revealing the terrified child beyond.

"Lindy!" Lewis cried. "Lindy, come back baby," he held out his hand to her and crept forward, though she seemed to inch closer to the edge with every step he took. Lewis was afraid, for in her eyes he saw a wildness, a lack of reason or rationality, brought on by alcohol and drugs and fear and pain. He started talking to her but even at the time he wasn't entirely sure what he was saying. Perhaps he was merely telling her it would be OK, that he was sorry. He had crept to only ten feet away from her but every step seemed like a mile as she leaned farther and farther—impossibly far—out over the ground below.

He was almost to her when his world ended in a crescendo of tragedy. Another second and he would have been there. All it would have taken was a few more steps. But it was a few steps too far. The police investigators could never be sure exactly what had happened. Whether she slipped. Or whether she jumped. In that last moment Lewis lunged forward and grabbed. For one singular instant he held something and in that isolated moment Lindy's fall was halted. But it was only for a second. Then she gave way and Lewis was left with only a clump of her brown hair and a bloody bit of scalp in his hands.

The trial was a sensational affair. The district attorney wanted blood, while the judge smelled fame and Lewis faced a life sentence for second degree murder and rape. Truth was, the actual evidence against him was thin at best. Nobody could prove he drugged Lindy's drink and a dozen different witnesses testified she was throwing herself at him during the party. There was no one to testify about the rape, no one alive at least. The path to his freedom was clear and Lewis took it. He watched as his attorney painted a picture for the seven women and five men who sat in judgment of him, a picture of a lost girl. He listened as Lindy was described as little more than a sorority harlot, an immoral seductress who dressed provocatively and got exactly what she was asking for. Hell, she probably took the drugs herself, just another delinquent chasing a high and losing her life. Why compound the tragedy by stripping Lewis's future away from him as well? The lawyer talked and the jury nodded. Even the judge seemed convinced. It had almost worked. But there was one witness they hadn't counted on. One witness who would not be denied.

By the time Lindy's father had left the witness stand, Lewis thought he was going to jail for sure. The old preacher poured his passion, his fire and his love for his little girl into the testimony. The fact he never took his eyes off the boy he swore had killed his daughter was simply unbearable. Lewis could not match that gaze, even though he knew to look away from it was to admit guilt. Lindy's father damned Lewis and when he had finished, the easy path to freedom no longer seemed so assured.

But the prejudices Lewis had counted on were too much to overcome. Most of the jury was swayed by the old man's vehemence, but there were three who weren't. Three who were not convinced or perhaps even blamed Lindy's father for what had happened, for the disappointment his daughter had surely become. The jury hung and the television cameras and newspapers moved on. The D.A. didn't have the heart to retry Lewis and Lewis didn't have the stomach to fight any more. He never wanted to feel those eyes upon him again. Lewis agreed to plead guilty to involuntary manslaughter. He served less than a year.

Lewis did his time. He had a bit of an epiphany between the cold gray walls of the penitentiary and he swore he would atone for what he had done. He promised Lindy, as he hid his tears from the men who surrounded him—he would live his life in her honor. And in the years that followed, he liked to think he had kept his word. After nine months, he was a free man. Then he disappeared. Or maybe it was more accurate to say Lewis was born that day, in front of an Alabama prison. He changed his name and his parents paid to enroll him at a small college in the mountains, where no one had ever heard of Adam Langston. It was there he met Sophia and it was there he made a promise, to himself and to his new wife, he would leave the past behind. But every night when he turned out the lights, he still saw the image of Lindy on the concrete below, her neck broken and her open eyes empty of life.

* * *

"Please," Lewis said, "please."

"Ohhhh, so now you're begging me? No more talk of right and wrong, huh? No more talk of God and my damnation. Now you want mercy? The truth is—you've had mercy. You've had a reprieve. All these years, you've been living on borrowed time.

"I waited for you, you know. I had it all planned out. The day you walked out of that prison I was going to be there. The day you tasted freedom, I was going to take it away from you. I bought a gun and I waited. Do you know why you lived? A stupid thing really. A simple twist of fate. They publicized your release date wrong and you got out a week early. By the time I realized it, you were gone. You covered your tracks well and it took a long time to find you. But I didn't give up. And now here we are. Together."

"Mr. Jackson, please…"

"That's what I like to hear, son. Now you know who I am. And I know exactly who you are. You're the man who killed my daughter."

"Mr. Jackson I promise you I did not kill your daughter. I did not kill your daughter. It was an accident. It was an accident. *It was an accident!* I wish I could take it back every day. I wish I could stop it. I wish I could trade places with her. I'd do it gladly if I could."

"Well that's just the problem isn't it? You can't trade places with her and you can't go back. You might as well join her. Cause I tell you what, you did kill her. You killed her as much as if you had pushed her out of that window."

Neither man spoke then. Thomas Jackson, standing over a mound of dirt, staring down at it with a walkie-talkie in his hand. And Lewis Freeman, in a coffin beneath him. Lewis Freeman—who had been Adam Langston many years before. Both men thought back on that night, the night that had come to define their lives. The night that now threatened to end the life of one and the night that had, for all practical purposes, killed the other. When Lewis spoke again, Thomas could hear him sobbing and the sound of it made him smile.

"Please, Mr. Jackson, this is not justice. Killing me is not justice for your daughter."

Thomas stopped smiling. It was time to end this.

"Justice?" he said through clenched teeth. "You speak of justice? Funny Adam, I guess we can agree on something can't we? On this one thing. Killing you is not justice. Do you know your scripture Mr. Langston? Have you read your Bible?" Lewis didn't answer and Thomas didn't wait. "No, I don't guess you would have. Well there's one verse I'm sure even you are familiar with. 'You shall give life for life, eye for eye, tooth for tooth, hand for hand, foot for foot, burn for burn, wound for wound, stripe for stripe.' You've heard that one, haven't you Adam? Haven't you? An eye for an eye? You didn't just kill my daughter that night all those years ago. You killed me too, just as sure as if you shot me in the heart. No…justice for you requires something more."

Thomas paused for a second and let his words wash over Lewis. He felt it, in his bones, when it all came together for him.

"You found the walkie talkie," Thomas said. "Did you find anything else?"

Lewis hadn't waited on Thomas to speak. He had already started feeling around the coffin again, franticly searching for something. What, he couldn't say. He only hoped he didn't find anything. Then he felt it. Soft but coarse all at once. Solid and separate, thick and thin all the same. His hand started to shake as he breathed in peppermint and vanilla when he brought the thick lock of hair to his face, the one he knew was strawberry blond, even in the darkness smothering him. Lewis lost it then, started screaming and beating against the pine walls enclosing him. He would do so until the air ran out and the final darkness took him.

He didn't hear the last thing Thomas said, before he dropped the walkie talkie and left Lewis to his fate. But he didn't need to hear it, for he already knew.

"No Lewis. Two lives were lost that night. Two lives. An eye for an eye Lewis. *That* is justice."

The End

House of Roses
(Horror)

By

Jasmine Cabanaw

The crimson sun was sitting low by the time Kevin Archer and Justine Francis pulled into the driveway of their new home. The hemlock trees lining the driveway looked jagged and scraggly against the flaming hues of the evening sky. The house loomed at the end of the drive like the silhouette of some sleeping giant, with its roof sagging in the middle and its rickety stairs leading up the porch like rows of teeth into a gaping mouth. Like lids closed tightly over glassy eyes, the windows were boarded shut against the outside world.

Kevin and Justine were weary from the long drive from South Carolina to Gravenstein, New Hampshire. They had started out at eleven o'clock the night before and had driven straight through, anxious to begin their new life in this tiny town nestled against New Hampshire's White Mountain National Forest. A month before, the town and the house had seemed dreamy and alluring, like something out of a romantic fairytale. However, stepping out of the car and surveying the overgrown property in the chill of the autumn air, Justine was no longer feeling so enchanted.

Kevin, on the other hand, was practically bouncing up and down with excitement. "Justine!" he cried, as he picked her up and twirled her around in a dizzying embrace. "This place is so incredible! The air is so crisp! And look at these gorgeous trees!" he sighed. "We're going to love it here."

Justine stood back for a moment and watched her boyfriend start to unload the car. He looked a bit like a scarecrow right then, in his ripped jeans and plaid shirt and with wisps of curly hair sticking out from under his cap.

He was tall and gangly, like a scarecrow. It was amusing how he already seemed to fit in with the place.

Justine grabbed a few boxes and followed him up the porch stairs. He fumbled with the lock for a moment but then the heavy, oak door opened with a groan to reveal a large parlor room. A round table brooded in the center, a wrought iron chandelier hanging above it. A staircase rose up against the west wall to the second level, a living room was through a door to the east and the kitchen and dining room were in the back, at the end of a short hallway. Three bedrooms and a bathroom occupied the second floor, with a large attic above. The house wasn't enormous but it was certainly much larger than the two-bedroom apartment they had left in South Carolina.

The other bonus was that the house came fully furnished. While it did seem a little odd the previous owners had left their furniture and appliances, Kevin and Justine hadn't pushed the realtor for details. They hadn't wanted to jinx their good luck. With the money they saved from not having to hire movers, plus the money they made from selling all their furniture, they had been able to stash away some cash for an engagement ring. Kevin had yet to buy the ring, as Justine wanted to wait until she found the perfect one, but it was reassuring to know they would have the money available. The tide finally seemed to be turning for them. Kevin had gotten a job at the local high school, they had found this house and she was almost in the right frame of mind to start writing again.

Kevin was like a whirlwind, grabbing luggage from the car, running it inside and racing back out again. Justine had put her first load of boxes on top of the parlor table and sat down on the porch, watching the spectacle that was her boyfriend. She still felt tired from everything that had happened. In fact, she was suddenly feeling like she could barely keep her eyes open.

Noticing her slumped against the porch fence, Kevin took a break from running boxes and sat down beside her. "Hey," he said, lightly brushing a hand through her short, blonde hair. "Why don't you get to bed and I'll finish unloading the car?" his brown eyes searched her blue ones with concern. "Darling, you look exhausted."

She sighed. "Yes but I can't possibly let you finish unpacking the car by yourself."

He smiled. She was so stubborn sometimes. "Yes, you can. Besides, I have all this energy right now and if I don't do something with it, I'll be bouncing off the walls. Go upstairs and climb into bed and I'll meet you in a little bit."

Justine reluctantly agreed. "Thank you," she gave him a kiss. "I owe you one."

She trudged up the stairs and into the master bedroom, flicking on the light to find a large poster bed in the middle of the room, with end tables on either side. A dresser with a large mirror stood against the wall, across from the foot of the bed. Justine shuddered. She hated sleeping across from a mirror but was too tired to be bothered with rearranging any furniture.

The whole room had a darkness about it, with wine-colored curtains covering the only window and furniture carved out of dark mahogany. Even the comforter on the bed was a deep red. She would have preferred stripping it, sleeping in her own sheets, but she barely had enough energy to pull back the blankets and crawl in before she was fast asleep.

* * *

The next few days were spent unpacking, rearranging furniture, driving the mile into town to get supplies and settling into their new home. The fatigue she felt on their first night had disappeared after waking the following morning. She still felt the sadness that had plagued her for months but the move had spurred a new hopefulness in her. She and Kevin were behaving like ants rebuilding a colony. So much work had to be done. The porch steps had to be fixed, the boards had to be pried off the windows, all the carpets and floors needed cleaning. The structure of the house was in such neglect but Justine could tell it once felt love. She kept finding little details, like a single tile, patterned with roses amongst all the beige tiles on the kitchen floor, throughout the house. There were also roses carved into the fireplace mantel and a stained glass window with roses, in the upstairs bathroom. The roses had a romance about them, as if someone had put them there as a gift for their lover.

Justine was sitting at the table in the kitchen, sipping coffee, when she heard Kevin calling her from the attic. A smile lit her face. Something in his voice suddenly made her heart race with excitement. She put down her mug and sprinted up the stairs.

He was standing in the attic beside a bay window. The view was of the back of the property, studded with old maple, oak and chestnut trees, alight in autumn colors and stretching on for over an acre, until it gave way to the edge of the forest. White-tipped mountain peaks stood like sentinels on the horizon. However, the view of his love, breathless and face flushed as she entered the room, was more alluring to Kevin than any natural wonder. He had known she was the girl he wanted to marry since their first date.

Justine rushed over to his side. "Well, what's got you so excited?"

He took her hand. "Here, have a seat," he said, motioning for her to sit on the bench in front of the window.

"I know we planned to pick this out together but this somehow seems like the perfect ring for you."

Justine's eyes widened as she watched Kevin get down on one knee and open his fingers to reveal a gold ring with a stunning diamond in the middle. He placed the ring in her palm so she could examine it in detail. Tiny, intricately carved leaves decorated the band and the diamond was set within a tiny, gold rose.

Justine managed to pry her eyes away from it to look at Kevin. "It's absolutely perfect," she breathed.

He grinned and slipped the ring on her finger. A chill, like an electric shock, went down Justine's spine.

"A little jumpy, are we?"

She shook her head. "Just excited," she held up her hand to admire how the ring looked on her finger; it was a perfect fit. "Where did you get this?"

"It was in the top drawer of that desk over there," he pointed to a large desk crammed up against several other pieces of furniture. "I was attempting to straighten out the attic. There is such a great view from up here; it would be a shame to let this room go to waste."

He lowered his eyes and then brought them up again to meet hers. "So, what do you think? I know this ring is unexpected but it's so perfect," he paused. "Will you marry me?"

"Absolutely!" she cried and threw her arms around him.

Kevin sighed. It was so good to see her happy again. "Justine, I think we really can start over in this place. We'll settle into this home and make new friends and no one will even have to know about our past and what we went through with the baby."

Her eyes darkened. "Why would you even mention that right now?" she pulled away from him. "Why would you do that?"

"Honey, I'm so sorry. It just came out. I love you. Please don't be upset. Everything is so beautiful right now. Let's just be happy," he pulled her back to him.

"Okay," she conceded, but the sadness had already returned in her voice.

* * *

The house felt empty and eerily quiet with Kevin away at work. She was sitting on her bed, trying to motivate herself to unpack her last few boxes. It was exciting for Kevin to be starting the new job teaching history at the high school but she was sad not to have her fiancé by her side during the day. *Fiancé*, she thought. She was looking forward to using that word, yet the title was bittersweet. In a way, she hated that being engaged and married mattered so much to people, particularly her former friends and family. When the baby died, just ninety minutes after it was born, her *supposed* loved ones blamed the death on her and Kevin's *sinful* lifestyle. Her own mother had said, "This is what happens to people who don't abide by God's rules."

Justine hadn't planned on getting pregnant; she and Kevin had only been dating for two months. She couldn't deny that aborting the baby had crossed her mind but she was raised with enough fire and brimstone to fear the spiritual consequence. And yet, if she had been able to foresee the social consequence—the scorn and disdain of her friends and family throughout her pregnancy—then maybe she would have made a different choice. In the end, her decision to keep the baby hadn't mattered. Within ninety minutes, Justine had gone from witnessing the miracle of God-given life, to the horror that God could not possibly exist. What god would snatch the breath of a newborn baby and turn him a lifeless blue before his mother even had a chance to hold him in her arms? Her child had only been given ninety minutes to live on this Earth. What purpose could there be in that?

She flopped on the bed for a minute and took a few deep breaths to calm her nerves. *A new life*, she told herself. *Kevin and I are starting a new life.* She held up her hand to admire the ring. At first, she thought it was a little weird, wearing a ring that most surely had belonged to someone else, but after just a few days, the ring already felt like it belonged to her.

A door slammed downstairs—interrupting her thoughts. She heard a man's voice call out her name but it didn't sound like Kevin. She looked at the clock. It was only two-thirty; Kevin was not due home from work until four. "Who's there?" she called. The cold shock of fear paralyzed her for just a moment as she heard the heavy thud of footsteps making their way up the stairs and then she was locking the bedroom door, grabbing her cell phone, and frantically dialing 911.

Kevin arrived home to find a cop car in the driveway. Alarmed, he rushed into the house to meet a uniformed officer, seated at the kitchen table with a distraught Justine. She looked so small and frail, sitting hunched over the table, but her eyes lit up as he entered the room. "Kevin!" she cried, and threw herself into his embrace.

"What's going on?" he asked, his brow furrowed in concern and bewilderment.

The officer stood up, extending his hand. "I'm officer Ian Brady. We received an emergency call earlier this afternoon about a possible intruder. I can assure you, me and a fellow officer searched the house and the property grounds thoroughly. If there ever was an intruder here, he's certainly long gone by now. Probably just some local kid, snooping around. This house has been empty for quite some time you know. Wouldn't surprise me if some punk teens had been creeping around in here before you folks moved in."

Kevin looked at Justine. "Was the front door locked? I locked it when I left this morning."

Justine gave him a puzzled look. "I haven't been out and I didn't unlock the door."

"Well," Brady interjected, "There are no signs of forced entry, so you best double check the next time you think you've locked the door."

Kevin shook his head. "I know I locked the door."

Ian Brady shrugged. "It wouldn't be the first time something strange has happened in this house. Just be glad it wasn't as tragic as the last time we were called out here."

Justine gasped, "What do you mean?"

Brady cleared his throat. "Oh, ah, um, nothing you two need to worry about. I best be going," he said, quickly, and gave a tip of his hat. "Call if you need anything else," he said over his shoulder, walking out of the room.

Kevin turned to Justine. "What happened exactly?"

She felt her face flush. "I don't know anymore," she was feeling silly. At the time, she really had thought she had heard something but now she was wondering if her mind was playing tricks on her. The police officers hadn't found a trace of a footprint or anything.

"I thought I heard a man call my name. I heard a door slam. Maybe I'm just stressed from the move and everything that's happened."

He gently kissed her forehead. "I'm here now. We'll go over the house together and tomorrow we'll make sure all the doors and windows are locked before I leave for work," he hugged her tightly. "It'll be okay."

* * *

Justine triple checked all the locks after Kevin left for work the next morning. She was starting to feel better though. If anything, she was embarrassed at having called 911 over what had most likely been her overreacting to being alone in the house.

She decided what she needed that morning was a hot bath to ease her troubled mind. The upstairs bathroom was one of her favorite rooms in the whole house. Justine loved the crown molding, the high ceiling and the blue ceramic tiled floor. There was the stained-glass window with the roses, above the pedestal sink but also beside the claw-foot tub, a large window with the same view of the property as the bay window in the attic. Locked inside the bathroom, Justine felt safe. The hot water felt luxuriously silky as it enveloped her. She eased into the tub with a long sigh. The house was quiet and the scent of vanilla candles perfumed the air. She closed her eyes, had just started to relax when, she felt someone slip into the tub with her.

Her eyes flew open but she was alone. The water was calm and undisturbed. She tried to slow her pounding heart. She really needed to get a grip. As she sat up to grab a washcloth, she suddenly felt something brush her arm. This time she froze.

Justine.

She flinched. The voice was the same as the one she had heard the day before. It was deep and gravelly; a man's voice.

Pick up the razor, Justine.

The voice seemed to be speaking right beside her but no one else was in the room. She wanted to believe this was all in her head, that she was having a mental breakdown from the stress of losing her baby, but there was something too real about what was happening. She looked nervously at the pink Bic razor on the ledge of the tub and found herself wishing she had splurged for the Mach 3 with blade protection.

Pick up the razor, Justine, or I will kill you.

Terrified, she picked up the razor. A rough hand tightened around her wrist and it yanked her, shaking, to her feet. She didn't have time to think. All she could do was gasp as the grip tightened on her wrist. She watched in horror as the razor in her hand slowly lowered onto her inner thigh and the blade pressed down on her delicate skin.

I don't like the way you look at him.

Justine wanted to let go of the razor but at this point, she didn't have a choice. She winced as the blade pressed harder into her skin and the first drops of blood appeared. "Please," she whimpered. Her hand suddenly jerked across her thigh, slicing the blades through her flesh. She screamed and the grip on her wrist faded away.

She dropped the razor and stood in the tub, watching the blood gush down her leg. The pain was sharp and hot. Tears streamed down her face as she tried to collect herself. The room had become silent again, save for her own racking sobs.

* * *

"Well, at least you don't need stitches," the doctor said, as he finished bandaging her leg. He frowned, "But I can't believe you walked here with your leg like this. How far did you say you walked? A mile?"

Justine nodded. "Yes, we're at the old house at the end of Pickard Lane."

House of Roses

"Oh," the doctor said.

She didn't like the look on his face. "Do you know of the place?"

"Yes." He looked into her eyes, as if searching for something. "Did you know the former owners?" he asked.

"Oh, no. We don't know much about the house actually. Just that it was very convenient for us. It even came fully furnished. Do you know anything about the people who lived there before us?"

"Not much. It was a married couple. David and Rose Palmer. But they-"

Justine cut him off. "Rose!" she said, suddenly excited. "That's why there are roses throughout the house!"

The doctor only nodded and took off his gloves. "Well, there's nothing else I can do for you, except to call you a cab. Do try to be more careful the next time you shave. It would help to invest in a better razor," he laughed. "My wife was always stealing mine until I insisted she get her own! Honestly, I don't know why they don't make better razors for women."

Justine shrugged. "Thanks for your help," she went out to sit in the waiting room until the cab arrived.

What was she going to tell Kevin? If she told him what had actually happened, he would think she was mad. Even she was questioning her sanity. Did she have a momentary hallucination? Could stress do that to someone? Already the incident was feeling less real. An invisible man made her cut herself? How could that be possible? Either way, she didn't want to be alone in that house again. In fact, she wanted to move—as soon as possible.

It wasn't until they were undressing for bed that she revealed her injury to Kevin. "It's just a nick," she said.

He stared at her in disbelief. "A nick? A nick that requires bandages? Let me see."

Justine sighed and reluctantly undid the bandage.

"Oh, my God," Kevin gasped. "Justine, that's more than a nick! How did this happen?"

"I just slipped while I was shaving," she avoided meeting his eyes.

He exhaled slowly and his tone became gentle. "Come here," he motioned for her to sit with him on the bed. He kissed the top of her head and looked into her eyes. "Please, be honest with me," he said, slowly. "Are you cutting yourself again?"

"No Kevin, I'm not. Absolutely not!" she pulled away from him, her temper rising. "Look...that was an isolated incident."

"You told me you cut yourself for years, as a teenager."

"*One* year—and it was because my parents were stifling me. I spent five months in an institution. You think I'd risk having to go through that again? I've been fine since then. You know that."

"Except for those two days after the baby died."

Justine stood up and started to pace. "It was just a couple times. That was it. I lost our baby. I didn't even get to meet him. How can you blame me for anything I did after that?" she stopped and looked at her fiancé. She knew she couldn't tell him the truth; he would think she was crazy.

"Really, I just slipped. That's all. You've got to believe me."

Kevin sighed. "All right. I believe you. I wouldn't mind taking a few days off work though, just to be on the safe side."

He expected her to say no, to reassure him she was fine but instead she nodded. "Sure. If that would make you feel better. I miss having you around the house anyway," she frowned. "But what about your new job? Won't they need you?"

"Darling, that's what substitute teachers are for."

A mischievous grin appeared on her face. She pulled off her blouse. "Hey baby. I could be your substitute teacher," she climbed into his lap and looked coyly into his eyes. "We're in biology and I think you need to stay after class. There's more you need to learn about the human anatomy."

Kevin raised his eyebrows. "Yes, ma'am!"

Justine giggled, and then suddenly cried out in pain.

"What is it?"

She looked down at her ring finger. For a second, she had felt searing heat where her ring was, as if someone had suddenly sliced through her finger with a saw. She half-expected to be looking down at a raw, jagged stump.

"It's nothing," she fibbed. "I just twisted the wrong way. We are sitting kind of awkwardly you know."

"Right." Kevin sighed, feeling tired. "Look, let's save the role playing for another night. It's been a long day," he kissed her tenderly and pulled her down beside him. "Let's get some sleep. I love you."

"I love you, too."

Within minutes, he was snoring. Justine felt envious of her husband's restful slumber. She lay wide-awake, despite being exhausted. How was she going to convince him they needed to move? She was already doubting the decision. The house and the town were perfect; it was *she* who was the problem. Maybe she was having some kind of psychological relapse, although she had never hallucinated before. Then again, she had never lost a baby before either. Justine tossed and turned with these thoughts all night, finally falling asleep right before sunrise.

*   *   *

There were no more incidents during the following days. By the time the weekend came, Justine was cheery and hopeful. She loved spending time with Kevin around the house. They painted the living room a sage green and trimmed the rose bushes in the front garden. She was starting to fall back in love with their new home. How could she leave this place? She was convinced she'd had a momentary breakdown. Considering what she had been through, that wasn't too implausible.

They spent the weekend exploring Gravenstein. The town square held a farmer's market on Sunday mornings, with the produce laid out like jewels in the sun. The displays of winter squash made her feel festive and excited. She had always loved Halloween. There was a whole stall dedicated to selling pumpkins. She rushed over and admired the different kinds. She saw the traditional orange pumpkins but there were also white ones, grey ones and ones with bumps all over them.

She turned to Kevin. "Can we buy some pumpkins? Let's branch out this year and get a white one."

"Sure, hon. Whatever you'd like." he smiled. He was happy to see her in a good mood again.

She ran her fingers over the swollen white surface of one and suddenly stopped. Something about the texture, about the firmness of the skin, reminded her of a pregnant belly. She stepped back from the pumpkin. "You know what? Let's buy them when it gets closer to Halloween. We already have so many things to carry today," she motioned to the bags laden with apples, squash and salad greens in his hands.

"Okay. But why don't you get some sunflowers from the last stall before we go."

The bright yellow petals made her smile. Sunflowers were so sunny and hopeful. While Kevin browsed a few stalls down, she grabbed a bunch and went to pay. "How much?" she asked the pretty brunette behind the table.

The woman pushed her glasses up on her nose. She reminded Justine of a cute little mouse. "How many bunches do you have?" the woman asked in a quiet voice.

"Just the one," Justine replied.

"Three dollars, please."

She pulled out a five. "Here you go."

The woman reached to take the money but pulled back, gasping. She looked at Justine in alarm. "Where did you get that ring?"

Justine drew her hand away. "My boyfriend gave it to me. We're engaged."

The woman looked furious. "You need to leave. Now," she stammered.

"What?" Justine said, setting the flowers down.

"Now! Get out of here!"

"Fine," Justine snapped and walked away from the wooden counter. She stormed off, bumping right into Kevin before she recognized him.

"Whoa, slow down there darling." he grinned. "Why the rush?" his smile faded when he saw the look on her face.

"People in this town are weird," she muttered. "That woman freaked out about my ring."

"Well, maybe she knew the former owner. This is a small town." He kissed her reassuringly. "Why don't you wait here and I'll go ask her what the problem is."

She kissed him back. "Okay, but hurry. I'm suddenly not feeling so well."

He nodded, heading back to the vendor. "Excuse me, miss?" he said, approaching the owner.

The woman had tears in her eyes. "Yes?"

He cleared his throat. "My fiancé was just in here. She said you didn't react too kindly to the ring she's wearing."

She nodded. "That was my sister's ring."

"Whoa," Kevin said in surprise. "Um, I'm so sorry," he ran a hand through his hair. "Look, this is really awkward...I can explain. We just moved into a house on Pickard Lane and I found the ring in the attic. The house came fully furnished, so I just assumed anything left was ours to keep. In fact, that might even be in our sales contract," he sighed and threw up his hands. "I'm not sure what else to say."

The woman sobbed. "I don't want that ring. I never wanted to see it again. Don't you know what happened to my sister?"

Kevin shook his head.

She stared off into the distance, shaking, lost in some horrid memory, and started crying uncontrollably. "Look," she said between sobs. "You need to know but this is not the place to talk about it." With a shaky hand, she grabbed a pen and scribbled something down on a sheet of paper.

She thrust it at Kevin. "Here, this is my number. Call me in the next day or two. You *must* call me."

"Thanks," he said, confused. "Hey, are you going to be okay?" he asked, turning to leave.

She nodded.

"Okay then," Kevin said and went out to find Justine.

"Well?" she asked when she saw him.

"The ring was her sister's."

"Oh. Does she want the ring back?" she clutched her hand protectively to her chest.

"No." Kevin put his arm around her. "I think she was just surprised, that's all. She gave me her number. I'll call her tomorrow when she's calmer, to get the whole story."

On Monday, it was back to work for Kevin. Justine felt slightly nervous but aside from the encounter with the woman at the farmer's market, everything had been going smoothly; no more voices, no more pain and no presence of some unseen ghost. She shuddered a bit, thinking about it. However, she much preferred the idea the house was haunted over the realization she was mentally ill. Ghosts she could handle but struggling with her own demons? That seemed much more terrifying. Unfortunately, she was now convinced it was *her* all along. Maybe the trauma from losing the baby had taken her illness to some whole new level?

Still, she was determined to start over. They deserved a good life. Antsy with those thoughts, she decided to tackle the overgrown rose bushes along the side of the house. Justine stood in front of them, surveying the mess. The roses had been left to grow wild, their stems crisscrossing along the house to form a dense hedge. She was just about to grab the shears and get to work when a flash of red caught her eye.

She walked over to the end of the hedge and shook her head in disbelief. A rose? At this time of year? She was reminded of the woman who used to live there before her. Rose Palmer. Justine smiled. She wondered if Rose's lover had planted the garden for her. Had they been happily married? Did they have children? Justine fingered her ring. They certainly had good taste in jewelry.

Sighing, she reached over to pick the rose. The wind picked up a little and a shivering chill went down her spine. And then she stiffened.

Justine.

Scarcely breathing, she stood still, straining to listen. But she heard nothing but the wind whistling through the trees. She felt angry at herself. When was she going to be able to relax and enjoy her new life? She reached out for the rose again and just as she coiled her fingers around the stem, she felt a heavy hand on hers. A body pressed up against her from behind and she felt hot breath on the back of her neck.

It's just my imagination, she tensed. *It's all in my head.*

An unseen arm slipped around her waist and she was held tightly against the presence behind her. "Leave me alone," she said aloud, panic in her voice.

A slut like you doesn't deserve such a pretty flower.

Justine cried out as she felt her thumb being twisted. There was a thorn just below her hand and she saw what was about to happen. "Please," she begged, shaking with fear, like a frail autumn leaf. She helplessly watched her thumb stretch out, over the thorn. It was forced downward slowly. She winced as the tip pierced her skin and then screamed as her flesh was penetrated. She felt it cut through her finger until the tip was pressing against the underside of her thumbnail.

Then suddenly, the pressure was gone and the presence holding her prisoner, had vanished. She stood sobbing, with her thumb stuck to the rose stem, not knowing what to do. Her mind was whirling with thoughts, but none of them made sense. She couldn't possibly have done that to herself, she had felt a *man* standing behind her, with his arm holding her tightly to him, as his hand pushed her thumb down onto the thorn. Yet she hadn't seen anyone.

Carefully, she pulled her thumb away from the stem. The pain was throbbing through her hand, shooting up her arm. *I'm crazy*, she thought. *I am stark raving mad.* She was numb with shock and fear. *I'm going to go into the house, make some mint tea and call Kevin to come home.* If she could just put one foot in front of the other and engage in something as normal as making tea, then maybe everything would be all right. She just needed to get through the next hour or so, until Kevin came home.

* * *

He sat at his desk at school, phone in hand. He glanced down at the sheet of paper from the woman at the market and dialed the number she'd written. It was only a few rings until someone picked up.

"Hello?" a woman answered.

"Hi, um, this is Kevin Archer. We met briefly at the farmer's market on Sunday," he paused, unsure of how to continue. "You were upset about my fiancé's ring...."

The woman inhaled sharply. "Oh, yes," she was quiet for a moment and then she went on. "I'm sorry to have reacted so hysterically."

Kevin fidgeted with the phone cord. "Oh, you don't have to apologize. I'm sure it was a shock seeing your sister's ring on my girlfriend's finger."

"It was indeed."

"Listen, um, I'm sorry, what is your name?"

"Jane."

"Listen Jane, if you want money or some kind of compensation for the ring, I'd be happy to arrange something with you. Justine loves the ring and I know she wouldn't want to part with it."

"She might if she knew what it was made of."

"Excuse me?" Kevin was confused. Was the diamond not real?

"This might make more sense if we start at the beginning. First, you should know David was madly in love with my sister. She couldn't help but be taken in by his romance. He doted on her day and night. The whole family was smitten with him. He treated my sister like a queen and he thought she was as perfect as her name. For a while, his gestures seemed sweet. He planted rose gardens for her and placed rose accents throughout the house. Surely, you have noticed them."

"I have. Justine pointed them out to me actually. She thought they were romantic."

Jane sighed. "They started off that way. But by the time they were married, his fixation with my sister had grown obsessive. Have you heard of Life Gems?"

"Life Gems? Um, no, I haven't."

"It's a company that takes a lock of hair and turns it into a diamond."

Kevin laughed. "What? That's crazy."

"No, it's true. They make diamonds out of cremated remains as well."

Kevin grimaced. "That's kind of creepy."

"Yes, that's what I thought. When Rose told me David had a diamond made for her out of a lock of his hair, I didn't even know what to say. I mean, the ring was beautiful but it seemed a bit over-the-top that she would be wearing his DNA on her finger for the rest of her life. A little much, don't you think?"

"You're telling me that the ring on Justine's finger is made out of this guy's hair? God, that's disturbing."

Jane laughed bitterly. "If you think that's disturbing, wait until you hear the rest."

* * *

Justine stood in front of the stove looking at the pot of water on the burner. They really needed to get a proper kettle. She had been staring at the pot for five minutes, her mind a tumbleweed of thoughts. Bubbles boiling to the surface brought Justine out of her daze for a minute. *So much for a watched pot never boiling,* she thought.

As she reached for the handle, she felt a hand clamp around her arm again. *Oh my God,* she reeled. *this can't be happening!* Nausea hit her stomach and goosebumps popped up along her skin. Her arm was yanked till her hand was directly above the pot, the steam scalding her skin. Before she even had time to react, her hand suddenly plunged into the boiling liquid. After only a few seconds, layers of skin began to peel away. The searing, fiery pain was like nothing she had ever experienced and it took over every fiber of her body.

The guttural screams coming out of Justine's mouth sounded like a wounded animal's. Thirty seconds of total agony passed before Justine's arm was released and she was able to pull her hand out of the water. Those seconds were the longest of her life. She'd screamed her throat raw and had vomited from the pain. The damage was severe. Her skin blistered and peeled—it hung in translucent strips, the absent skin exposing veins and tendons that looked like thin, slimy snakes on the back of her deformed hand.

Sickened and blinded from the torture, Justine managed to run out of the kitchen and up the stairs. She halted, shaking, at the top of the landing to steady herself - her legs almost gave out. Her cell phone was on the bedroom dresser. She could only focus on getting to that phone and calling for help.

* * *

Kevin's mouth hung open in disbelief. "Your sister was what?"

"Rose was murdered," Jane said for the second time. "I'm sorry. I'm jumping too far ahead again. Look, I really want you to know none of us saw it coming. David may have been jealous but we thought he loved her so much. We didn't think that the jealousy would drive him mad."

"David murdered Rose? That's so awful," Kevin could never imagine harming Justine, in any way.

"One day, Rose showed up at my house in tears and with a goose-egg sized knot on her forehead. She said it was an argument with David, he accused her of sleeping around. Then he lost his temper completely and pushed her down the stairs. Then she confessed that wasn't the first time he hurt her. She told me he had also burned her with boiling water, forced her thumb onto the rosebush thorns. And, he sliced her with a razor."

Kevin gasped. "Wait, he sliced her with a razor?" he felt the hair on the back of his neck stand on end.

"Yes," Jane said, emotion creeping into her voice. "She even showed me the scar on her inner thigh."

"Jane, thank you so much for telling me about what happened to Rose. I really think I need to get home to Justine."

"Wait, there's more!" Jane sounded frantic. "Please, you should know what happened."

Kevin looked anxiously at the clock. Justine had already been alone in the house for two hours. "Okay, but please hurry."

"I'll make it quick," Jane agreed. "Rose stayed with me for a few days. I'm not sure what made her go back to the house alone. She had been talking about confronting him but I thought she would have had the good sense to take someone with her. I think she was still in shock and wasn't fully aware of what she was doing. Anyway, when I got home from work and discovered Rose was no longer at my place, I drove straight to her house." Jane's voice broke, "But I was too late - I found my sister...stabbed to death."

"I'm so sorry," Kevin said, his eyes tearing up. "It is a horrible thing to lose a loved one. Jane, I am so sorry to hang up on you like this but I really do need to go. Just tell me one last thing. What happened to David?"

"David was also dead by the time I got there. He had hung himself in the attic."

* * *

Her world was spinning but Justine knew she had to get to her phone. Despite feeling like she was inside a dreidel, she managed to step off the landing and into the hallway. About to take another step, she was suddenly grabbed and thrown roughly against the wall.

You've been sleeping around, haven't you? A voice hissed in her ear. *I have seen the way men look at you, like they've been inside your pants.*

A hand tightened around her throat, choking her, blurring her vision. Her throat was released but she didn't have a chance to catch her breath before she felt herself picked up and hurtled through the air. She fell down the stairs like a life-sized Slinky—head over heels until she landed at the bottom, her forehead slamming into the wall.

She lay in a heap, not wanting to, nor able to move; helpless. She wondered if this was how her baby felt, when his breath was sucked out of him by some unknown force. She could do nothing but lay there and let the events unfold.

She didn't have to wait long. Within moments, *someone* grabbed a fistful of her hair and dragged her across the floor into the kitchen. She was jerked to her feet and pulled toward the kitchen counter. Justine thought, *And now I know what it's like to be a marionette.*

Once again, she was prisoner in the iron-grip of a cruel embrace. A block of knives faced her on the counter like a firing squad and she knew what was next. She felt her arm clutched firmly, forced toward the knives. The glint from the diamond on her ring caught her eye and suddenly...*she knew.* She could sense that *whatever* held her captive—it was connected to the ring.

She was too emotionally numb to care however. Her head was throbbing, her whole body was bruised, aching and the pain from her right hand was agony. Locked in that deadly embrace and with her scalded hand useless, she couldn't have taken the ring off if she tried. She had given up all hope, and then heard Kevin calling her name.

* * *

When he opened the front door, the first thing he saw was a trail of blood leading from the bottom of the stairs to the kitchen. The blood was smeared on the floor, as if someone had been dragged. He closed his eyes for a moment, knowing it had been Justine. He cried out her name and ran into the kitchen.

He stopped in his tracks when he saw her crumpled over the counter, her body mangled and bloody, her arm raised high with a knife clutched in her hand.

"Justine!" he cried, running to her.

His entrance was enough to break the spell for just a moment and she let the knife fall to the floor. Then he was by her side, grabbing her hand and yanking the ring off her finger. Justine was released the second the ring was gone and she immediately had control of her body again. She collapsed into Kevin's arms, sobbing.

He tossed the ring on the counter and looked down at her scalded skin and then at the knots and bruises on her forehead. "Oh, my God," he shook his head in disbelief. "I can't believe this," he muttered crying.

"I'm sorry," she managed to choke out, overcome by the sudden fear he would leave her; he would think she had done all of this to herself. "I didn't do this. You have to believe me," she begged.

Kevin tenderly tilted her face to look at him. "I believe you."

Her eyes widened. "You do?"

"Yes, and we need to get you to a hospital right away."

"So, you're not going to leave me?" Justine persisted. "You don't think I'm crazy?"

He held her close, careful not to hurt her. "I'm here to stay darling. I would never leave you. And," he added. "We'll go shopping for a new engagement ring as soon as you're up for it."

Justine shuddered. "Kevin, we can't get married."

"What? How can you say that?" he searched her eyes.

"Because there is no way in hell that I will ever wear a ring again."

THE END

City of Fire
(Science Fiction)

By

Timothy Miller

The sky above the city was burning.

Colton peered out from under the broken ferrocrete of the half-collapsed bomb shelter, his gaze locked on the storm raging beside the World Wall.

A flash of lighting ignited another of the rolling black clouds gathered near the Wall, transforming the volatile gas into a billowy mass of flame that poured down the side like a blazing waterfall. Across the street from Colton's shelter thinner tendrils of flame lashed at the Maze, scorching the piles of rock and metal to black.

These storms were getting worse.

Colton cursed softly. The pyrotechnics reminded him of erupting lava fields and the waves of molten rock swallowing the hunting grounds of his clan.

"Hell above, Hell below," he muttered. "The whole world is on fire."

Thunder rumbled and another burning cloud burst to life.

Rags tensed, whining softly.

"It's just a storm," Colton said. Laying a hand on the worlhound's bullet-shaped head, he stroked the scaly black hide. "Show some courage."

Rags voiced an offended growl and gazed up at him with narrowed, golden eyes.

Colton chuckled. "Don't be so dramatic."

The worlhound was three-hundred pounds of muscle and razor teeth, a born killer. Colton had raised him from a pup after discovering him in a nest of filthy garments almost six years before.

Another cloud exploded and Rags backed further into the shelter.

Colton rolled his eyes. "Let's have lunch. We're not going anywhere until the storm breaks anyway."

Rags's tongue lolled out in agreement.

Giving a final scratch behind the worlhound's ears, Colton took out his skinning knife and moved to the far back of the shelter where he'd stashed the goat. It was a scrawny specimen, with whitish-pink skin sprouting infrequent tufts of hair, but it was food.

Colton made his first cut just below the ribcage.

Rags had flushed the goat from the Maze and Colton took it as a good omen. He'd not seen so much as a lizard-rat in two weeks and little else since the lava fields erupted two weeks before. Nothing but reavers and those he'd seen in plenty, brought out in their hundreds by the chaos. Those mutants would eat everything and everyone, if they could.

He took heart at finding the goat. If goats still thrived in the shadow of the Wall, perhaps Odin wouldn't object to adding another able scavenger to his den.

Colton frowned, not pleased at the thought of living so near the Maze again. Collapsed spires of glass, crushed machines resembling hollowed eggs, burnt skeletons of metal and men, all jammed together at the foot of the World Wall in a mishmash of twisting corridors and crumbling tunnels. Why Odin would choose to live in such a place was beyond him.

He tossed the goat's innards behind him and Rags tore into the offering with a contented growl.

Colton swiftly butchered the goat. Taking a strip of meat for himself and wrapping the remainder in the hide, patting the bundle down with handfuls of soot to mask the scent. Odin had taught him the trick, one of many, which kept Colton and his den alive the last ten years.

But his den wasn't alive anymore.

"Just me and you now, Rags."

Rags, a half-eaten goat liver in his mouth, didn't reply.

Fixing his meat to one of the blades protruding from either end of his spear, Colton placed the weapon across his knees. Removing a circular tin from his pocket, he peeled off the rumpled foil covering it. The chemical stink of raingrease filled the shelter. He ignited the tin with his flicker and red flames rose from the raingrease inside.

As Colton roasted his dinner over the small fire, the storm's fury began to wane. After eating, he scrubbed his hands with soot. Taking out his canteen, he unscrewed the cap and sniffed the water inside. It smelled rancid.

Removing a silver capsule from a pouch inside his coat, he dropped it into the canteen and swirled the container. Sniffing the water again, he swallowed a mouthful and put the canteen away.

"Three weeks without new water Rags, and all the cisterns are gone," he said. "If Odin doesn't take us in, I'll be drinking raingrease instead of cooking with it."

Rags licked his chops indifferently.

"I'm touched by your concern."

Rags yawned.

Colton leaned against the wall and sank into his thoughts. The lack of water worried him. His den's purifying unit was destroyed in the eruptions and he had no clue how to procure another. He needed water, even more than he needed food.

He glanced at Rags. Like all the city's animals the worlhound took moisture from hardy lichen growing in the ruins. But even the lichen were drying up under the increasingly frequent firestorms. Only the reavers, who drank raingrease, were immune to the drought.

Colton inhaled deeply and closed his eyes.

A small boy stared at him over the shoulder of a grinning reaver.

Colton's eyes snapped open but the haunting image remained in his mind, as real and painful as a fresh burn.

"It wasn't my fault," he said, telling himself it was the truth.

But the words were like ash on his tongue. He didn't close his eyes again until the firestorm ceased to thunder. In the stillness, he again began to edge toward sleep.

Rags's head suddenly came up.

Colton snatched up his spear and moved quickly to the shelter's entrance. "Steady boy," he whispered. "I'll check."

In the aftermath of the storm, the sky was an ashy grey and dim sunlight bathed the city in white sickly haze. Colton scanned the broken structures along the Maze. A hint of movement made him hunker down as a group of hideously deformed men dragged a struggling figure from a building to his left.

"*Reavers,*" Colton hissed, anger and fear tightening his hold on his spear.

There were twenty of the mutants, their skin knotted with scar tissue and weeping blisters. Dressed in soiled rags, they carried crude axes and spears. Their prisoner was a young girl of about sixteen. Her pants and overly thick coat were of a strange greenish hide, a color not often seen in a landscape of blacks and grays. Her dark curls were long, reaching to the center of her back.

Colton touched his scalp, brushing over the quarter-inch bristles. Only an idiot grew long hair in a city that rained fire.

The majority of the reavers fanned out in the street, moving past Colton's hiding place at a loping jog while two spear-wielding guards prodded the girl along from the rear.

Rags crept up beside Colton, his golden eyes shining and alert.

"*They're bringing her to their den,*" Colton whispered. "*They'll butcher her, cutting her up a piece at a time. Unlucky.*"

The memory of the boy rose again in his mind, mocking him for his cowardice, convicting him of his guilt. He banished the image with a growl, concentrating instead on the reavers as those in the front of the group turned a corner up the street, opposite the Maze.

Colton nodded to himself. Once the reavers moved on, he would head into the Maze; no sense giving the pack another chance to pick up his scent. More of the reavers passed his shelter and turned the corner, until only the girl and her guards remained.

Suddenly she tripped and fell, banging her elbows and knees on the soot-covered ferrocrete. Her guards laughed, a sound as harsh as their ravaged skin, and poked her with the tips of their weapons. The girl grimaced but didn't cry out. She started to rise, pushing a stray lock of her absurdly long hair from her face.

And she froze.

With sinking dread Colton realized she was looking right at him.

"*Don't do it,*" he said, his insides curling into a knot. "*Don't you dare.*"

"Help me," the girl said. Then more loudly, "Help me!"

Colton ducked down, but it was too late.

Alerted by the girl's call, one of the guards spotted the furtive movement and voiced a hunting shriek. A spear sliced into his throat, cutting off the shriek as he stumbled back.

Following his attack, Colton charged from the shelter toward the second guard. The reaver met him with a quick stab of sharpened metal but Colton rolled under the assault. Coming up inside the mutant's guard, he hamstrung the reaver with a violent slash of his knife.

The reaver went down, mewling and clutching his leg.

Spinning past it, Colton grabbed the shaft of his spear and jerked it clear of the first guard's throat.

The mutant made a wet gurgling sound and tried to grab him.

Colton cut its legs out from under it and sprinted toward the Maze. An axe-wielding reaver blocked his way but three-hundred pounds of angry worlhound buried it. Silencing the axman with a snap of his jaws, Rags hurried after Colton. Furious shrieking followed them as they ducked between two house-thick durosteel girders and disappeared into the Maze.

Sprinting down a curving passage of blackened metal, Colton reached an oval room linked by a dozen corridors. Choosing at random, he kept running, veering to the left as the corridor split again. At the third such intersection, he abruptly swung around and brought up his spear.

Stiffening his forelegs and dropping to his rear, Rags came to a skidding halt behind him.

"Glad you could keep up," Colton said. "You should work on the stop."

Rags grunted sourly.

A green figure shambled into view, rebounding from the wall in front of Colton.

He nearly skewered the girl before recognizing her as the reavers' prisoner. Lowering the spear, he cursed. Not that he was unhappy the girl escaped...but if *she* had followed him this far, the reavers wouldn't be far behind.

"Why did you run so far ahead?" the girl asked; her face was dripping with sweat and she was breathing heavily. "I almost lost you."

Colton cocked an eyebrow. *Why should he wait for her?* He almost asked. She wasn't even from his den. Instead he said, "You'd run faster if you took off that ridiculous coat."

"Kinda hard to do when you're tied up," she retorted. She held out her hands, exposing the strips of cloth still binding her wrists. "Can you get these off?"

He hesitated—out of pure irritation mostly. Then his spear lashed out and the restraints fell away in fluttering pieces.

The girl yelped, pulling back her fingers as if she expected them to fall off with the bindings.

"You're free," he said flatly. "Now, what are you doing here?"

Rubbing her chaffed wrists, she sagged against the wall. "I got separated from the others, tried to hide in a stairwell." Swallowing thickly, she pulled a water flask from her pocket and took a long drink before adding, "I'm Lina."

"I didn't ask your name," Colton said. "I asked—arghh."

A metal pipe collided with his temple. He staggered, trying to right himself and the reaver who'd dropped from the ceiling to strike him, raised the pipe again.

Lina screamed.

Rags slammed into the reaver like a locomotive, driving it back into a pack of them emerging from around the corner. Rags tore into the group and a mutant screamed as blood spattered the walls.

"Rags!" cried Colton, starting after his friend.

Lina snagged his sleeve. "No," she said. "We have to run!"

He stared at her dumbly and suddenly realized what he'd been about to do; the pipe had scrambled his brains. Rags was giving them a chance. They had to take it.

"This way," he said.

She followed him as they ran to the next intersection and veered left. They'd run only a few hundred meters when a worlhound's howl drew a grimace from Colton.

The howl was a signal. Rags had broken off from the fight.

Minutes later, Rags caught up to them and Colton noted the shallow wounds marking the scaly black hide as his friend came to heel beside him. Fortunately the cuts were minor and Rags seemed unaffected by the injuries.

"You couldn't...have...held...them longer?" he managed between breaths.

Massive chest heaving with his recent exertions, Rags didn't even bother to grunt in reply.

A shriek sounded behind them and Colton willed his legs to move faster. Lina and Rags sped up with him and they kept up the grueling pace until they came to a square chamber, dissected by a deep crevice.

He went to the lip of the chasm and looked down. Far below, glowing lava spit fire into the air. It was too far to jump but a rusted beam, barely a handbreadth across, bridged the divide.

Rags went first, running nimbly over the tiny bridge to the opposite side. Colton followed more cautiously, offering Lina a brief warning as he went. "Don't look down."

But Lina seemed unimpressed by the drop and followed him onto the beam without the slightest hint of hesitation.

"Do you think we lost them?" she asked.

"I don't-"

His foot slipped out from under him. He teetered, his heart in his throat, unable to regain balance. Below, the lava rose up as if in greeting.

Lina grabbed his shoulder, steadying him. "Careful," she said but she was smiling. "It looks hot down there."

Not trusting his voice Colton nodded his thanks and then baby-stepped the rest of the way across.

"So," she said, jumping lightly to the other side, "did we lose them?"

Colton shoved the beam over the edge and it tumbled down into fire and darkness.

"The gap will slow them," he said as he stood, "but they'll find a way around. I have a feeling they'll keep chasing us until the next rain or firestorm washes away our scent."

She stared up at the ceiling and the ashy clouds visible through the wide cracks. "When will that be?"

A reaver's shriek echoed again through the Maze.

Colton's jaw tightened. "Not soon enough."

Several passages branched out from the room and Colton suddenly realized he recognized this place. As Odin's pupil, he used to trap goats in this same room. He glanced back at the chasm, understanding the lava-filled gap had not been present five years ago.

"Come on," he said, moving to the passage furthest to the right. "I have an idea."

They ran down a trash-cluttered corridor for several minutes before Colton stopped next to a thin metal plating resting against the wall. Moving the plate aside, he exposed an opening in the ferrocrete wall, a hole barely wide enough for a man to squeeze inside. He whistled to Rags, and the worlhound obediently ran into the hole.

"Inside," Colton said to her. "Hurry."

She gazed at the dark opening uncertainly. "Where does it lead?"

A distant shriek answered her.

He cursed. "Do you want to die? Get moving or I'll leave you to the reavers!"

Pursing her lips, she dropped to her knees and scrambled into the hole. Grasping the metal plate, Colton backed in after her, covering the opening before moving further into the narrow tunnel. After a dozen meters, the tunnel opened and he was able to stand.

"I can't see," Lina said, sounding very young in the darkness.

"Give me a minute."

Removing his raingrease tin, he ignited it with his flicker. The flame was small but bright enough to illuminate the maintenance shaft. Unlike most of the Maze the ceiling was intact here, which explained the darkness. Rubble blocked the shaft in one direction but the other continued into the black beyond the tin's light.

"What now?" Lina asked.

He crouched down beside the hole in the wall. "The reavers know they're closing in. I'm hoping that means they're overeager and they'll run past us before they realize they've lost our scent."

"And then?"

"We'll head back the way we came. Even if the reavers come back, our new trail will overlap the old. It will be like we disappeared into thin air."

"That makes sense, I guess," she said shortly. "But what if they don't pass us? What if they find the tunnel?"

He nodded down the shaft. "That has to go somewhere. If they come we'll just have to find out where."

She chewed her lip thoughtfully and then shrugged. "Guess so."

Colton smiled. "Take off that coat Lina. It's too heavy and will only slow you down."

"And too hot," she added, shrugging it off, then dropping it to the floor.

Underneath she wore a sleeveless vest of the same green hide. There was a small tattoo on her upper arm of a winged creature with a hooked nose.

His eyes widened. He'd heard of such markings but never seen one himself. "Is that an eagle?"

Lina glanced at the tattoo. "It's our clan mark. Everyone in the scraper has one."

"So you're a skyper," he said. Unlike the street-dwelling scavengers skypers lived in scrapers, the frozen towers of the old world.

Reclusive and aloof, they were rarely seen outside their fortified buildings. He rolled his eyes. "The giant coat, the hair, I should have known the minute I saw you that you were a scraper hugger."

"Well, I knew you were a scavenger right away," she said, pinching her nose and looking at him over her fingers, "from the smell."

Colton laughed. "So what are you doing so close to the Maze? I thought your kind never strayed far from your scrapers."

"We don't, usually," she admitted. "We don't need anything down here."

He patted his canteen. "What about water and food?"

"Our scraper is high," she said, "higher even than the fire clouds. It is cold above but there's rain, clean rain that freezes to ice at the highest levels. We boil it for drinking and use it for our gardens."

His brow furrowed. "Gardens?"

"We grow many things in the inner chambers, vegetables mostly, some fruits." Lina patted her vest. "We even make our clothing from plant fibers."

He could hardly believe what he was hearing. "Food, water, no firestorms or reavers...." he shook his head. "No wonder you stay in your scrapers."

"Yes," she agreed, and then her shoulders sagged. "But skypers can't hide anymore, not now."

"The firestorms can't have affected you that much, not in your scraper," he said. "Even if they have, the lava fields are always spreading. They'll settle down eventually and the clouds will thin out again."

She gave him a curious look. "You don't know where the fire clouds come from do you? Janitor Carlos said that scavengers don't understand about the storms."

"The fields make the clouds. Everyone knows that."

"Then everyone is wrong," Lina said firmly. "The power plant produces the fire clouds and it is the reason the storms are getting worse. The plant has drilled too deep, the crust is failing."

"Is that so?" Colton grinned, amused by the skyper's bizarre superstitions. "Okay, I'll bite. What exactly is a power plant?"

She didn't return his smile. "You think I'm making this up?"

He shrugged, still grinning.

"Well, then let me tell you something else. There is no World Wall."

"Not to call you a liar Lina, but we could see the wall clear enough from the Maze."

"But it's not a wall," she insisted. "It's a cliff, one that circles the entire city."

"A cliff," echoed Colton, with just a touch of sarcasm. "Who knew?"

"I'm telling you the truth. Look."

Brushing the soot around her feet into a pile, she created a small mound.

"This is the city," she said. Putting her finger in the center, she made a small impression. "This is the power plant, right in the center of the lava fields."

Colton rolled his eyes but decided to play along with her little game. At the very least, it kept his mind off the reavers. "Okay. So why doesn't the plant melt?"

"I don't think it can. Janitor Carlos said it was a thing of the old world, made to bring up the heat of the earth to create power for the ancients. No fire can harm it, but it is dying."

"How do you know that?"

"You can see the smokestacks from my scraper," she answered. "Three weeks ago there were seven, all of them wider than my scraper, spitting black fire clouds all day long. After the eruptions two weeks ago, there were only three."

"What happened to the others?"

She pushed two fingers into the soot. "They sank into the clouds, and that's when the fire clouds began to get worse." Drawing up her fingers she made a fist and pushed it into the mound. "After that, scrapers near the fields began to sink, one by one. That's when Carlos realized the plant had finally dug too deep. It has cut a hole so vast and hot the fields are spreading out like water from a tapped spring."

He wanted to laugh but found he couldn't as he remembered his den's hunting grounds sinking slowly into the hot mires of the spreading fields.

"I still don't understand what that has to do with the World Wall. Why do you call it a cliff?"

"The Plant has been digging a long time. Long ago it caused a massive earthquake that dropped the entire city into a vast sinkhole. There is no World Wall Colton. We are living in a hole in the ground, one that's going to get very hot, very soon."

He snorted but was secretly glad to find a flaw in the girl's logic. Lina scowled at him but he raised a hand to forestall any argument.

"No offense Lina, but the World Wall is no cliff. It's a barrier that was built to protect us during the Great War. I have seen the World Gate that leads outside, myself."

"You've see the Gate?" she asked sharply. "What does it look like? Have you opened it?"

"No one has," he replied. He thought of Odin and his many lectures concerning the wastelands beyond the city. "Nothing survives beyond the Gate, not even air. The world is dead."

Undeterred, she leaned closer to him. "Janitor Carlos said after the first great earthquake struck, many of the ancients died. Those who survived created a machine at the foot of the World Wall, a box that could carry people to safety. The box had golden doors, and rises like an eagle to the top of the Wall."

"A golden box that flies people to safety? Do you hear yourself?"

She drew her fist from the soot, gesturing to the impression left behind. "If you were an insect down in that soot, what would you see? Would you see the cliffs all around you? Would you recognize them for what they were?"

He couldn't suppress a shiver. "No," he said softly. "No. I'd see walls."

The shaft trembled and the soot collapsed in on itself, burying the hollow in burnt darkness.

Colton met Lina's eyes, seeing in them the certainty behind her words.

Could it be true? What if Odin, teacher of scavengers and guardian of the World Gate was wrong? What if the Gate wasn't a gate at all?

The trembling ceased and Lina sat down the floor. "Carlos was going to lead us to the machine. But we only just reached the Maze when the reavers found us. We fought but there were so many. Carlos...the reavers...He told everyone to run. I...I...."

"You were separated from the others," Colton said, hearing the pain in her voice and already knowing where her tale would lead. "The reavers caught up with her later."

"In a stairwell," Lina said miserably. "I left the others behind. And the reavers found me anyway."

Guilt cut into him like a dull knife and for a moment, the face of a small boy superimposed itself over Lina's own. He blinked and the apparition faded.

"It wasn't your fault," he said roughly, unsure if he was speaking to her or himself. "There was nothing you could do."

"I should have tried."

Perhaps drawn by her tears, Rags moved closer to Lina and sniffed gently at her greasy long hair. She slapped him on the nose.

"Stop it!"

Rags jerked back and threw Colton an aggrieved look.

"You're not afraid of him. That's rare. Are all skypers so brave?"

"We raised worlhound in the scrapers," she said. "They protected us for as long as they could, when the reavers came," she smiled apologetically and patted Rags's head. "Sorry. I didn't mean to hurt you."

Rags wet her cheek with his long black tongue.

She made a sour face and giggled.

"Alright, I give up," Colton said. "I'll bring you to the Gate. I don't know if it's your machine or not but we'll find out together."

She started to speak but then Rags's ears pricked up and Colton waved her to silence.

A clanking scrape sounded from the hole in the wall. Someone was moving the plate, uncovering the tunnel.

"They've found us." Rising from the floor, he helped Lina top her feet. "We have to go."

They hurried down the shaft, Lina and Rags leading while Colton's tin lit their way from the rear. They hadn't gone far before the sounds of many shuffling feet pursued them.

"Faster," he urged.

The shaft turned and they came to a door, its surface thick with grease and red corrosion. Ducking through the portal, Colton handed her the tin.

"What are you doing?"

"Slowing them down," he replied.

He put his shoulder to the door but the rusted hinges resisted until Rags added his own significant bulk to the task. The door squealed shut and Colton quickly dropped the locking bar in place. No sooner had it clanged down than something struck it hard from the opposite side, denting the rusted metal.

A reaver shrieked and another dent joined the first.

Colton took back the tin. "It won't hold long."

She needed no further prompting and they ran on as reavers struck at the door behind them.

Suddenly, Lina skidded to a stop.

He was about to tell her to keep moving when he spied the oily sheen of raingrease in front of them. The shaft ahead was flooded.

The banging grew louder behind them, followed by the whining screech of tearing metal.

"We're trapped," Lina gasped.

Colton stared hard at the flooded shaft. "No, we're not. I'm not going to die like a cornered lizard rat." Setting down the burning tin well clear of the flammable pool, he stripped off his coat. "We'll swim it."

"We can't. I . . ." her lips began to tremble. "What about Rags?"

"He'll follow us, or he'll fight his way out. Not even reavers want to mess with a cornered worlhound."

Golden eyes fastened on the shaft behind, Rags growled as if in agreement.

"We don't even know how far it goes," she protested shrilly. "We'll drown!"

"No we won't."

"I can't swim, Colton!"

Stepping into the lukewarm pool, he offered her his hand. "I'll help you."

She backed away from him. "I can't."

"Lina!"

"I can't!"

The screech of metal came again, louder than before.

Colton's heart skipped a beat. The door wouldn't hold much longer but clearly Lina wasn't going to enter the raingrease of her own accord and forcing her in would only see them both drowned.

He ground his teeth in frustration. Why was she being so difficult? He wouldn't even be in this mess if not for her. In fact, the longer he stuck with her, the more doom she brought down on him.

If she wanted to stay so badly, let her. He was not going to die for some homeless pup not even from his den.

"I'm sorry Colton," Lina sobbed. "Please don't go."

Turning away, he waded deeper into the raingrease. But then he stopped as that frightened boy rose in his memory. His fingers tightened on his spear and he turned back to Lina.

No. Not again.

"Don't worry Lina," he said, climbing out of the pool. Never again. "I won't."

She stared down at her feet. "I thought....You're not going to leave me?"

His hard expression softened. "You're not the only one who lost their clan. My den was headed for the Wall too. The eruptions destroyed our water purifier and we were going to seek my old teacher, get Odin's help in replacing it. Rags and I were scouting ahead when the reavers attacked. By the time I returned most were already dead. All who remained were a few children the reavers kept alive to bring back to their den." his throat tightened and he cleared it noisily before going on. "A boy I knew spotted me as I watched from hiding. He was only four but he didn't call out. As young and frightened as he was, he was a scavenger and knew not to give away my position."

"Like I did."

"Like you did," Colton agreed without malice. "Had you kept silent I would have remained hiding, as I did then. And I would . . ." his eyes blurred with tears and he dashed them away. "I would have been twice as damned!"

She put a comforting hand on his arm. "I'm sorry."

"Don't be. It was my decision. But I won't leave another pup to the reavers. I'd rather die than live through that again."

Lina glanced at the flooded shaft and licked her lips. "Do you really think we can make it?"

"I don't know," he answered honestly.

She slugged him hard in the shoulder. "You could have lied, you idiot."

Up the shaft, something gave with a loud *clang!* A reaver shrieked.

Rags growl deepened and his golden eyes grew bright.

"Now or never," Colton said to Lina. "Do we swim or fight?"

Reavers rushed from the darkness, scrambling along the walls, floor and ceiling like melted locusts.

Rags charged in, diving into the blistered ranks with a savage howl.

"We'd better not drown," she said weakly.

He grabbed her hand, and together they splashed into the raingrease. "Hang on to my belt. And don't swallow any of it."

Lina seized his belt. "No problem."

He whistled to Rags. "Get in here you mangy lizard!" he shouted, and then dived down into the wet darkness with Lina beside him.

He hit the floor belly-first, nearly expelling the air from his lungs. Tightening his lips, he clawed along the cracked floor, feeling his way through the oily murk. It was slow going and soon his lungs burned. He pushed on, Lina a dragging anchor at his waist. Colors flickered under his eyelids and his pulse pounded in his ears. His muscles grew leaden and his mind wandered to dreams of unseen reavers grabbing at his ankles. The shaft went on and on.

She was right. They were going to drown.

Colton surged up, breaking the surface with a wet scream of denial. Floundering in the muck he gulped down the rank but welcome air. She came up with him. Coughing and spitting, she leaned against his back.

"Told you..." she paused to spit more raingrease from her lips. "Told you we'd make it."

Too exhausted to laugh, Colton examined the alcove around them. The walls, ferrocrete and metal, were marked with drawings of odd-looking beasts with long necks and spotted hides. He knew this place. It was close to the World Wall. A short corridor led away from the pool and the cracked ceiling bled dim sunlight.

Helping Lina out of the pool, he turned back to search the glistening surface for sign of Rags. "Where are you?" he muttered.

A bullet-shaped head broke the surface and Colton nearly swooned in relief. "You had me worried," he scolded as the worlhound doggy paddled to shore. "I thought the reavers got you that time."

Rags grunted as he climbed from the pool and then gave a violent shake, spraying raingrease everywhere.

Colton wiped his face clean and gave the worlhound a hard look. "We're wet enough, thank you," but then added, "glad you made it, Rags."

Dropping to her knees, Lina scratched roughly at the worlhound's ears. "Who's a good worlhound that bites the nasty reavers?" she asked sweetly. "You are! Yes you are!"

Rags's licked her face, replacing raingrease with saliva.

She giggled.

"Yuck," Colton said. He glanced at the sky, noticing the darkening clouds through the cracks in the roof. "Another storm's brewing."

The floor trembled, dislodging soot and gravel from the ceiling in a dusty rain.

The earthquake lasted only moments but Colton frowned at black ripples it left in the pool. The tremors were worsening, growing more frequent, just like the storms.

"We better hurry," he said, scarcely aware he spoke aloud. "Or there'll be nothing by the time we reach your magic machine."

Her eyes lit up. "You believe me?"

"I don't know Lina," he said. He took an empty tin from his pocket and filled it with raingrease. "But something is very wrong. I can feel it in my bones, can taste it in the air. I don't know if the Gate is a savior machine. I doubt it. But I guess it doesn't really matter anymore."

Backing down away from the pool, he dribbled a line of raingrease on the floor behind him.

Lina followed him, squeezing excess muck from her vest as she walked. "What do you mean it doesn't matter?"

"Even if Odin is right and the Gate leads to a wasteland, it's no worse than staying here. The city is dying."

Though she'd pointed out as much herself, Lina shivered at the words. "So we use the Gate?"

He nodded, still trailing raingrease as he walked. "Yes. The only problem is Odin has the key to the Gate."

"Won't he let us use it?"

"I'm not sure. I doubt it." They came to a sharp turn in the passage and he peeked around the corner to make sure the way was clear before leading Lina around it. "But we need that key."

Continuing the line of raingrease around the corner, he discarded the tin and knelt beside Rags. He whispered instructions to the worlhound, wishing he didn't have to ask so much from his old friend.

Rags whined, nuzzling his neck.

"I know," Colton said. Giving the worlhound a fierce hug before he stood. "But it's the only chance we've got, Rags."

With a whining grunt, Rags turned and ran down the hall.

"Where's he going?" Lina eyed the line of raingrease curiously. "And what are you doing?"

"Rags is running an errand." Taking out his flicker, he touched it to the grease and struck the action. Fire licked up, racing back toward the pool. "And I'm making sure the reavers don't follow us this way."

Bright light filled the passage and thunder rolled across the Maze.

* * *

They wove their way through a corridor cluttered with large sections of broken glass.

"Why wouldn't Odin let us use the Gate?" asked Lina for the third time. She ducked beneath a horizon sheet of glass, staying well clear of the razor edge. "I thought you said he used to be your friend."

"Odin was my teacher but he doesn't have friends. He's taught generations of scavengers, orphans like me mostly, showing us how to survive in the city before sending us out to find dens of our own."

"Generations? Just how old is this guy?"

"Old. Very old, but stronger than a worlhound and faster than any man has a right to be." his eyes grew distant and he added softy, "Sometimes I wonder if he's a man at all."

"What was that?"

"Nothing."

The passage abruptly opened up ahead and Colton motioned for her to stay low behind him as he crept to the end of the corridor.

They'd reached the end of the Maze. Outside, a soot-floored clearing nestled at the base of World Wall. Flanked by hillocks of blackened stone, a gentle gravel slope climbed from the clearing to a pair of golden doors twice as tall as a man. The World Gate, pristine despite the passing of a thousand storms, its shining surface glowed with a pale light.

Colton searched for the palm-sized keyhole in the Gate. Though he knew where to look, it was too far to make out.

Lina's face lit with excitement. "The machine," she breathed. "Colton, we found it."

She started to rise but her caught her arm.

"We are not alone," he whispered.

She froze. "Reavers?" she asked fearfully.

His gaze swept the rocks taking only moments to spot movement among the slabs. He sniffed and was unsurprised by the faint odor of treated raingrease.

Well, he hadn't expected Odin to leave the Gate unprotected.

"Odin or his students, I'm guessing. We'll go out to meet them but we have to be careful."

"What do you mean?"

"Odin has been guarding the Gate a long time. If it is your machine, then he knew. He knew but lied about it, lied for years."

"Maybe he didn't know about the machine," she said.

"Odin has the key Lina," he replied grimly. "And he knows more about the ancients than anyone. Believe me, he knew," he handed her his knife. "If it comes to it, don't think, just cut. We need that key and it's going to cost blood. Are you with me?"

She paled but took the knife and tucked it into her belt. "I'm with you."

Colton smiled. "Good girl."

Stepping out from cover they marched out of the Maze together, stopping at the center of the clearing where Colton grounded his spear.

"You might as well come out!" he called. "I can smell the grease on your bowstrings."

He waited for a reply but received only silence.

"Come out Odin! The clouds are gathering and I don't fancy weathering a storm in the open!"

A flicker of silver in his peripheral was his only warning. His spear blurred, knocking the metal shaft from the air before it could plunge into his heart.

Lina yipped as the arrow clanged away, ducking behind Colton but he only scowled at rocks from which it came.

"Is this how you would greet a former student Odin?" he demanded. "Shall I kill the one who shot at me by way of reply?"

"You know the rules," answered a gravelly voice from the rocks. "These lands are for me and my pupils alone. You are one of mine no longer Colton. Go home."

"I didn't come for your food Odin."

"Then why?"

Colton drew a steadying breath. "I want to use the Gate!"

"The Gate is death," Odin roared from hiding.

"To stay in the city is death!" Colton shouted back. "It is dying under our feet!"

A tall man, dressed in dark hides, stepped from the rocks. He was broad of shoulder and lean of waist and his bare arms were thick with corded muscle. His white beard was braided with silver wire and was nearly long enough to cover the wafer-like key held on a chain around his neck. His grin was wide and friendly but his eyes...

Colton felt his throat tighten whenever he met Odin's gaze. The man's eyes were calculating, always calculating and they contained all the emotion of a dead lizard-rat.

"Who says the city is dying?" Odin asked.

"I do," Colton said. He gestured to Lina. "And she does."

"She looks as if she crawled from a sewer. You both do," Odin eyed their greasy clothes. He walked toward them, his spear held loosely at his side. "Who is *she* to convince you of such nonsense?"

"She's Lina, a skyper. The last of her clan, as am I. The reavers have taken everyone else."

"I'm sorry for you both."

Odin approached to within a few steps of them and grounded his spear. "A skyper you say?" he scratched his long whiskers. "It has been a long time indeed since I've spoken to one of the scraper folk. How goes life above the clouds?"

"It doesn't," she answered. "We left our scraper when the power plant sank into the lava fields."

Odin's snowy brows furrowed thoughtfully. "The power plant, you say?"

He sounded confused but Colton wasn't buying it. As she spoke there'd been spark of recognition in the old man's dead eyes.

"You already knew about the power plant," Colton said.

Odin just looked at him.

"Do you know about the Gate too? Is it really a machine that can take us out of the city?" he pressed.

Odin's smile vanished. "Go home Colton. Take the skyper with you."

The ground trembled, sending gravel and rock pattering down from Wall.

"You're lying," Colton stressed, in a voice like beaten iron. "Who are you? Why do you guard the Gate? You owe me the truth!"

"I owe you nothing!" Odin roared. "I...I..." his face twisted as if he was in pain and then he suddenly laughed. "The ancients—how I hate them. Since you ask me a question directly, I am compelled to answer truthfully," he smiled but the expression was thick with malice. "Do you think I wanted to teach every miserable orphan I encountered the last three hundred years? Do you suppose, gifted as I am with near immortality, I would choose to live in this wretched city?" he tapped the key beneath his beard. "I *possess* the means of escape but I *cannot* leave. I am cursed by the very technology that prolongs my life, cursed to remain and aid any survivors I find in ruins."

Lina's hand tightened on Colton's shoulder.

"He's a ky-borg," she whispered. She sounded shocked and afraid. "Colton, he's a ky-borg."

Colton stepped back from the old man. "A what?"

"A ky-borg," she repeated, "a machine-man created by the ancients."

"More machine than man," Odin gave Lina a mocking bow. "It appears the skypers remember something of the old days."

Anger welled up in Colton like molten stone. "I fought to survive every day of my life, I lost my den, all because you said the world outside this Gate was dead."

"You were supposed to bring us to the Gate," Lina said. "The ancients left you here to help the survivors."

"That was their intention," Odin admitted "but their programming doesn't compel it, only that I aid those I find alive and protect myself from damage. They made sure I couldn't even kill myself," he cocked a bushy eyebrow. "And I have aided many. I've shown hundreds how to survive in the desolation. Do you think I would allow *any* to leave here when I cannot? No. We shall face doom *together*. And doom will be coming soon, my old pupil. The clouds are thickening. If I had to guess, I'd say this cesspit will be a nothing but ash and fire in about ninety minutes."

"I've heard enough." Colton jerked his spear from the ground. "Give us the key old man. Or we'll take it from you."

"You forget to whom you are speaking. You forget where you are."

Colton's eyes narrowed dangerously. "You think your pups can stop us?"

"I've had no students for some time," Odin said. "The reavers have seen to that. I entertain a different sort these days—castoffs, murderers and thieves—those whose allegiance is easily bought with the promise of food."

Odin waved his hand in a tight circle. A score of bowmen rose from the rocks, arrows drawn to cheek. An equal number of spearman broke cover as well, jogging into the clearing and quickly surrounding Colton and Lina.

"I gave you a chance to leave but you wouldn't listen."

Colton readied his spear. Lina drew her knife.

Thunder rumbled, and several spearmen shot apprehensive glances at the darkening sky.

Lightning flashed and flames exploded in the sky, painting the clearing in ominous red and yellows. A worlhound howled nearby, as if calling out in greeting to the emerging storm.

"Last chance," Colton said to Odin. "Give us the key or die."

The ground trembled. And waves of fire and rocks began lashing the World Wall in a burning cascade.

The spearmen shifted their feet nervously but a glare from Odin held them in place. His craggily face was demonic in the firelight. "Kill them."

Before the spearman could act, a piercing howl drew all eyes to the Maze. A split-second later, Rags burst the glassy passage from where Colton and Lina had emerged.

A horde of reavers spilled out behind him.

The spearmen cried out and a flight of arrows flew down from the bowmen.

A reaver fell, an arrow through its skull. More took wounds but continued on, despite the metal shafts decorating their blistered flesh. In seconds reavers were among the bowmen, pouncing onto the men like spiders and tearing them apart. More of the mutants ran into the clearing, rushing toward those gathered at its center.

Odin's spearmen swiveled to face the new threat and Colton saw his chance. His spear swept out, cutting two before they knew what was happening. Lina rammed her knife into a third and then the reavers were among them.

Colton blocked a gory axe from cleaving Lina's skull, reversing his spear and impaling her attacker. A reaver rose up behind him and was brought down by Rags.

His dark hide bleeding from a score of cuts the worlhound snapped the mutant's neck with a savage bite and then looked up at Colton.

"Did you have to bring so many?" Colton asked.

Rags grunted roughly.

"Just kidding," Colton pushed Lina toward the worlhound. "Take her to the Gate, Rags. Protect her!"

She began to protest but his glare silenced her. "I can't get the key if I have to worry about you Lina! Go! I'll be right behind you!"

She nodded and turned, running for the slope, Rags close by her side.

Cutting down a reaver who tried to follow the girl, Colton searched the melee for Odin. A fist of flame splashed down on the rocks, engulfing reavers and men alike. Screams filled the air as fire ate to the bone and men and mutants cut and killed.

Lighting flashed and in the glare, a spear stabbed at Colton's chest.

He pivoted aside, taking a glancing slash to his bicep before swinging up his spear to parry Odin's next strike.

"You think reavers can save you?" asked Odin, stabbing at him again with inhuman speed. "You will die with them."

Dancing aside, narrowly avoiding Odin's weapon, "I'm not dead yet," Colton growled, aiming a backhanded slash at the ky-borg's eyes. "Let's go."

Odin defeated the slash with a blurring parry. "As you wish."

The ky-borg rushed in, his spear whirling like a durosteel hurricane.

Spinning and dodging, Colton fought as never before. Despite his bravado a moment before, he realized in the first seconds of the duel he was in trouble. The ky-borg's speed was phenomenal, inhuman. He could barely keep Odin's metal tip from finding his heart, let alone launch a counterattack.

A reaver dove at them from the side. Compared to the lightning-fast ky-borg the mutant appeared to moving in slow motion. Colton cut it down almost negligently as he slid beneath Odin's next attack.

Adrenalin pounded in Colton's veins, making him nearly as fast as the machine-man. But it couldn't last. Soon he would tire and slow. When that happened, he was dead.

Odin came in low, slashing at his legs.

Colton somersaulted back, landing in a crouch with spear extended defensively to prevent Odin from charging in for a quick kill.

Instead of pressing the attack however the ky-borg whirled his spear and laughed.

"I'd forgotten how much fun this is," he said, paying no attention to the struggling group of reavers and spearmen behind him. "You're good Colton. That you survived against me *this long* without augmentation is nothing short of remarkable. It's a shame I have to kill you."

"Yes," Colton taunted him, his gaze flitting over Odin's shoulder. "It's too bad."

With a warrior's bellow, he charged three steps and threw his spear.

Odin moved like a quicksilver, bending his back at an impossible angle, laughing as the spear passed harmlessly over him.

"Foolish scavenger," he mocked as he began to straighten.

Colton's shoulder hit Odin's chest like a battering ram, propelling the off-balance ky-borg into the tangled battle behind him. Two reavers immediately leapt upon the old man, clawing him further into the skirmish.

"Not so foolish," Colton disagreed, lifting up the key he'd snatched from Odin's neck. "Not anymore."

Odin's face purpled with rage. Stabbing a reaver through he flicked the mutant aside. "You think these wretches can stop me?"

A reaver bit into Odin's arm. Pulling it close, he broke its neck with a hammering elbow. Tossing reavers and men alike aside, he moved inexorably toward Colton.

"They are nothing. Nothing!" he stormed. "You are dead!"

In reply, Colton pointed a finger toward the sky. "You first."

Odin's enraged demeanor changed to one of confusion and he looked up.

Fire splashed down from the sky, covering him and all those around him in liquid flame.

Shrieks filled the air but whether they came from the ky-borg or the reavers, Colton didn't know or care. He rushed for the Gate. Scorching fireballs struck the earth around him and he kept one eye on the heavens as he weaved through the flames.

The ground bucked; a crack split the earth before him, spilling thick magma like blood from a wound.

He leapt without slowing. Heat scorched his legs as he soared over the widening crevice. He tucked into a roll to break his fall and then sprang back up and kept running.

At the Gate ahead, Lina shouted encouragements and Rags howled, their voices barely heard over the sounds of the storm and breaking earth.

A wall of flame blistered Colton's arm and face. Ignoring the pain he stumbled the last few steps up the slope.

"I thought you were dead," Lina said. Her cheeks were wet with tears. "I thought he killed you."

"He almost did. Old man was tougher than I thought," he gasped.

A fountain of magma burst up from the Maze, spilling down among the corridors of durosteel and ferrocrete.

"It's happening!" Lina shouted. "The city is sinking."

"We're not sticking around to watch!"

Finding the slot-like keyhole in the Gate's surface, he jammed Odin's key and heard a faint "click."

"I hope you're right about this Lina...."

The doors slid open, revealing an empty box-like room walled in the same golden metal as the Gate.

A woman's voice, gracious and motherly, spoke from thin air. "Emergency elevator engaged. Please enter in an orderly fashion."

Lina and Colton looked at one another, neither of them moving until the next tremor nearly knocked them from their feet.

"You heard her," Colton said, pushing Lina through into the room. "Let's go. You, too, Rags."

The worlhound followed them inside and Colton began searching the featureless interior for some clue as to how to activate the lifting box. But the walls were bare.

"Great," he said. "We're in. Now, how are we supposed to make it go?"

"I don't know." Lina wrung her hangs anxiously. "I thought the key would do it."

The maze erupted again, shooting magma high into the burning clouds and sending a twenty-foot wall of liquid rock racing toward the Gate.

Something chirped and the woman's voice came again. "Are all passengers aboard?"

"Yes!" Lina and Colton shouted as one.

"Closing doors."

Colton breathed a sigh of relief, and turned to Lina. "I think— ackk!"

A blacked arm shot between the doors, seizing Colton's neck in white-hot fingers.

Lina screamed as a scarecrow of a man stuck his smoking head into the room, blocking the doors.

The doors stopped closing.

"Doors obstructed," the woman's voice intoned.

Heat vapor rising from his metallic skull, Odin lifted Colton into the air.

Colton fought against the sizzling hold as his neck blistered but he couldn't break free.

"You are not leaving," Odin hissed.

The fingers tightened on Colton's windpipe and darkness began to close in around Odin's grinning skull.

Rags's growl was like approaching thunder.

There was a flash of scales and blazing golden eyes, and Colton was suddenly free. His legs buckled and he fell to the floor, landing hard on the unforgiving surface. The pain hardly registered and his gaze never wavering from Rags and Odin as they tumbled down the slope outside the Gate, tearing at each other as they approached the rushing wall of lava.

"*Rags!*" Colton breathed. Tears stung his singed cheeks and he looked away a moment before the worlhound disappeared into the unforgiving flames. "Rags!"

The doors closed with a faint hiss and subtle motion touched Colton's belly, taking a backseat to the grief in his soul. Lina hugged him, and he cried unashamedly.

Some minutes later she nudged him gently and pointed at their feet.

"Look."

He glanced down and blinked in surprise. The floor was transparent. The whole of the city, its flaming towers and lava-filled streets stretched out below, growing ever smaller until disappearing completely as the room rose into a black, chemical cloud.

Lightning flashed and fire spread across the floor but there was no heat.

Colton put his arm around Lina as they rose through the fire into a world of startling blue.

"We made it," she looked up, as if trying to gaze beyond the golden ceiling. "What do you suppose it's like up there? Do you think it's safe?"

"I'm not sure," he answered. He doubted anything could be as terrible as the city of fire. But what did he know? He'd spent his entire life in a hole. "I suppose we'll find out."

She snuggled into him and closed her eyes. "I suppose we will."

Colton held the young skyper as she drifted to sleep but his gaze never strayed from the flaming clouds below.

The sky above the city was burning.

THE END

Roque's Requiem
(Science Fiction)

By

Bill Patterson

Milky Way, 2078 AD

The silvery globe had been traveling the void for thousands of years. Hurtling through space at just under the speed of light, wrapped in a time-stopping stasis field, the meter-wide sphere sheltered a core of neutronium massing ten billion metric tons. A leftover projectile from a forgotten interstellar war, the shell was plucked this way and that by the gravitational fields of various stars it passed near. Interstellar magnetic fields induced gradual turns in its path, until it became quite impossible to deduce its original launch point. Like thousands of its brethren, this fired and forgotten projectile would have travelled unchanged, until the heat-death of the universe. Unlike them however, a yellow star seemed to be in the way.

* * *

UNSOC Space Station Roger Chaffee, March 3rd 2082, 0930 EDT

Roque Maximiano Zacarías scowled at the message appearing on his screen. He wanted to see just how long he could make the perfect crystal up here in the microgravity of space. So what if the crystal was the same kind used in solid-state lasers? Yttrium-aluminum garnet, ten centimeters across, drawn slowly out of the crucible. Ah, what a beautiful sight. Two meters long, ten centimeters across and doped with some neodymium. The perfect laser, made entirely from Lunar materials. The fact it could shoot out a bar of infrared light like a sword really didn't matter to him.

Roque was once a fine, able-bodied space hand, all around ladies' man and the top material scientist in the UN Space program. It was he who took common moon soil and developed the processes to break it down into aluminum, iron, oxygen and common sand. When the core of a carbonaceous chrondite meteor was found just under the lunar surface, he assisted McCrary in adding just the right amount of carbon from it to molten iron to form lunar steel. And it was the carbonaceous material, under his magic touch, that formed the budding lunar plastics industry.

The discovery of lunar KREEP material, consisting of potassium (K), rare earth elements and phosphorous, gave Roque all the materials needed to form the neodymium doped yttrium-aluminum-garnet (Nd:YAG) laser. He was now trying to see just how large a crystal could be grown.

"Oh, I suppose that if I really wanted to, we could make a few dozen and terrify the world with an orbital weapons system," he explained to Lisa Daniels, the station commander. "But that would earn us a missile or a hundred. I just want to see if it can be done, that's all."

Lisa smiled as she patted his hand. "Roque, you know that's not the issue at all. The UN Space Operations Command has a mandate to maximize the income generated from the Chaffee. If you take over a manufacturing space just to see how big a crystal you can make, it better be a hunk of diamond."

Roque smiled back. "Even if I did make a diamond, old Subby would saw off a tenth of it for his own piggy bank."

Lisa darted a quick glance towards the hatch. "Now, Roque," she admonished him, "Better watch it. Some of this crew just might report you to UNSOC Director-General Herr Doctor Subraman Venderchanergee for the horrible crime of lèse-majesté. And he's petty enough to order you shipped home."

Roque had been resident in the *Chaffee* for the past twenty years. Normally Roque would never have been allowed to stay aboard the *Chaffee* for so long. But around the halfway point of his first tour, a piece of space junk the size of a rice grain plowed into the back of his spacesuit at a few miles a second. Hot metal droplets sprayed into his spine, paralyzing him from the waist down.

As he once put it, "My legs might be useless but my brain is unhurt." He petitioned for permanent residence on the *Chaffee* and his request was granted. Commanders come and go, UNSOC veterans said, but Roque will stay in space forever.

"Actually," Roque mused, "I have always been of the opinion I will stay here until I die. The Chaffee has become my home."

When the United States abandoned manned space after the closing of the Space Shuttle program, the International Space Station was in limbo. Although it continued to be manned and supplied, no improvements were planned for the station. It represented the only large, habitable volume in Low Earth Orbit, though was woefully underutilized from both a space manufacturing and scientific research point of view.

By the early 2020s, the United States was deep in its own economic troubles. An ardently internationalist president recommended the United States transfer the station to the UN in return for a *paid in full* stamp on their long overdue UN contributions. The press touted the plan as a win-win for both the United States and the United Nations. Congress reluctantly went along. The US Astronaut Corps was completely demoralized.

By then though, the Corps began referring to the ISS as Space Station Roger B. Chaffee, honoring one of their own who had perished at the dawn of the Space Age. Ignoring orders completely, they called it the *Chaffee* relentlessly, ensuring the name would endure no matter what. The name stuck.

Companies wanting to operate a space manufacturing facility realized that it would be far easier to rent space on the *Chaffee* than attempt to launch and operate their own orbital factories. The UN Space Operations Command found itself in the enviable position of picking from a large pool of applicants for a small number of spots. It did what any organization in a similar position does. It took bribes.

It meant—in practice—Subraman Venderchanergee. He was the director-general and absolute despot of the UNSOC. He ensured his *special service fees* were laundered up the chain of command, ensuring zero interference in his fief from without, as well as within. And his serfs knew it. Including Roque.

"Yes Lisa, I will be a good boy," he said sadly. "I remember when space was somewhat pure and unsullied, before the bureaucrats and their fees began encroaching on it."

"You will never lose that romantic streak in you Roque. That's why you're such a pleasure to work with." She straightened up from her floating astronaut crouch and spoke with all the authority of her office.

"Roque, as your commander, I would ask you to limit your crystal growth experiments to just this compartment. Maximum crystal diameter will be three centimeters. And no weapons!"

Roque levered his body upright. "Understood Commander Daniels."

She leaned forward and hugged him briefly, then left the lab, leaving Roque with a lingering smile and a pencil-sized Nd:YAG crystal floating in the air.

* * *

UNSOC Space Station Roger Chaffee, May 23rd 2082, 1400 EDT

Lisa Daniels was performing one of her unannounced station float-arounds. The old ISS structure had been augmented over the years, especially when the Moon Colony *Michael Collins* began mining and shipping up resources from the moon. Aluminum, iron and magnesium, in alloys and pure metal, were flown down from lunar orbit to rendezvous with the *Chaffee*. There, they were molded into new modules, manufacturing spaces, living quarters.

To simplify the engineering, the new spaces were built-out in a linear fashion, similar to the ISS. These two "spikes" as they became known, were connected together by several cross-corridors.

As she moved past a hatch in the cross corridor between the old and new, she met John Hodges, the chief engineer. Nearby, a sign pointing to the Solar Shelters triggered a dormant action item in her memory.

Lisa turned to John as she cleared the hatch combing. "Good morning, John. That sign reminds me—we should conduct a solar shelter drill again. It's been a few months since the last one. Pass the word."

"Good morning Lisa. Gonna cram everyone in the sleds for an hour? We'll have to move some stores out of them to make room. We've had to keep some *Collins* cargo in them."

"Well, I wish you wouldn't. We're never going to get enough warning about a solar storm and I'd hate to have folks out in the halls getting zapped while cases of jock straps get tossed out the hatch."

"Tell the OTVs to speed it up then. Earth is shipping stuff up here faster than we can ship it to the moon." Orbital Transfer Vehicles or OTVs, made the runs between the moon and the *Chaffee*, transferring everything from jock straps to people between the *Collins* and the station. Next generation shuttles made the Chaffee-Earth runs.

"Don't I know it. What about cramming the stuff into MoonCans and storing it outside?"

"Some of those cans aren't airtight apart from the LOX tank. Cargo would get damaged. And we don't have any handy rubber or vinyl to make seals with either."

"Talk to Roque. Remember that tarry stuff the Moon sent down last November? Roque made nylon out of it—maybe he can make you some vinyl."

"Not a bad idea. Hey, I wanted to show you something." John towed her over to the porthole, looking out on the sleds. "Notice anything?"

"You've got something over the sleds."

"Yup! Behold the shields. I took a MoonCan and rolled it flat. Got a couple of sheets of aluminum out of it. I attached it on the top and bottom of the sleds."

"For what purpose?" she asked, intrigued.

"Increased solar shielding. Before, big ions from the Sun would smack into the hull of the sleds, generating a shower of secondary particles, zapping us inside. Now, they hit the aluminum and the secondaries don't get through the hull."

"What about if we have to use them for reentry?"

"I've rigged a jettison switch to the main pilot board. Pop them free at Entry Interface and they fly outward and away. "

"That's wonderful John! What a nice surprise. Speaking of, I better head over to Astronomy. I hear they've got something special for me."

With a wave of her hand, Lisa bounced off the side of the corridor and changed her flight path to head down the new spike to Astronomy. John continued his trek to Engineering.

* * *

Orbit of Mars, Solar System, June 17 2082, 0934 EDT

The projectile flew through the dark. A strange-looking universe surrounded it. Radiation drastically blue-shifted up the spectrum burned into the forward-facing force field. Behind it, the stars guttered a sullen red. All around it stars were colored every shade of the rainbow.

It mattered not to the shell. The occasional bit of dust or speck of gravel would impact the front, in an unseen flare of incandescent plasma. The fuse that would have detected impact with a target from the long-forgotten war was unaffected by these comparatively small pats.

Since solid matter was the exception in space, the odds were literally astronomical against it hitting anything.

But, infinity is a funny thing. In an infinite universe, given enough time, everything will eventually happen. For projectile nine-three-two, having missed its target all those thousands of years ago, that one-in-a-zillion chance came up.

To an observer near the lunar South Pole, a new mote, shining blue-white by reflected sunlight, appeared in the sky. For the next twenty-six minutes, it grew from a speck to a meter-wide sphere just before impact.

Instantly the soil around the impact point was plowed aside by the huge momentum of the object. To the structure of the rock underneath, the impact was an irresistible event, as the force fields broke atomic bonds and forced the shattered debris aside, punching a hole through the rock in its path. The energy of the shell's momentum transferred rapidly to the energy of the motion of the soil and rock. In other words, heat.

Phenomenal, amazing, seemingly unlimited heat. Rock flashed to vapor and vapor to plasma. Ahead of the projectile, the plasma was compressed to a fantastic degree as the shell drilled through kilometers of rock. Eventually the pillar of million-degree, highly compressed plasma began resisting the force of the shell. Its speed slowed as energy bled into the plasma and vaporizing rock. With pressure and heat near the point where atomic reactions were possible, the worst possible event occurred.

The shell's fuse activated.

Designed to detect impact with ship shields, the fuse triggered the collapse of the stasis field keeping the neutronium stable. Ten trillion tons of highly energetic neutrons were sprayed into the million-degree plasma. The impact event, already catastrophic, was transformed into truly horrific proportions as the plasma triggered nuclear fusion.

* * *

UNSOC Space Station Roger Chaffee, June 17 2082, 1000 EDT

Roque was floating effortlessly in the middle of his materials lab, near the manufacturing area of the original spike. He was putting the finishing touches on his latest ND:Yag laser. He patted it fondly.

"Give me a dozen of you and we'll be able to blast space junk, instead of hoping it avoids us."

He felt a sudden wave of heat, which passed almost before it could be felt. A flash of white from a nearby monitor caught his eye while a momentary roar of static erupted from the overhead speaker. A radiation alarm began jangling nearby. The General Quarters alarm sounded moments later. Roque nudged his way over to the lab's central control panel. He pressed his ID bracelet against the reader, registering his presence at his duty station.

On the main monitor screen, a brilliant flare saturated the image of the moon, but it was dying off even as he stared at it. As the glare faded, great masses of debris were seen rising from the point of impact. Roque scarcely noted the silencing of the General Quarters alarm. The speaker above his head clicked on.

"This is Commander Daniels. Something energetic has happened on the moon. I am tying in the feed from the moon to the intercom; you will hear what I hear. I was talking to the *Collins* commander when we were cut off. Ah, he's back." Once again, she looked into the eyes of her friend, Jeng Wo Lee.

"What happened Lisa? You cut off midsentence." A loud voice erupted from the speaker on Lee's desk.

"MAYDAY, MAYDAY! This is McCrary on the surface."

"Lee. Go McCrary."

"The surface of the Earth has brightened at least two magnitudes. Something's going on."

"Collins, this is Chaffee. There's been some kind of flare on the moon. Our radiation meters are off-scale high, and the flare burned out any sensor pointed in your direction."

Roque stared at his monitor, reading the same data as the Bridge. He could add nothing to the ongoing conversation. Celine Greenfield at Astrogation and Commander Lisa Daniels knew their business. A set of ranging circles, centered on the location of the *Collins,* appeared on the screen. Roque noted with apprehension the appearance of a shockwave at the outer edge of the display.

"You've got about twelve minutes until the shockwave hits," said Celine.

In a daze, Roque listened as the McCrary, chief engineer of the station directed disaster operations on the moon. Decontamination and unsuiting procedures took at least a half hour, so McCrary would not be able to get back inside before the shockwave hit.

"This is worse than any disaster scenario ever planned. If the Chaffee can see the shockwave, we may well be done for. But I have faith in all of you. Suit up *now*. Get in a MoonCan *now*. There are enough for everyone.

"The MoonCans are filling with LOX from the main lines. Plug your suits into the fitting inside the MoonCan, just like in the drills. The shockwave will knock you around a lot and some of you may end up under rock or other debris. Do not panic. Remember, a man in a Can will live for at least a week, maybe longer. Help is coming to dig you out. If you feel yourself losing control, you'll find sedatives in the MoonCan. Do not panic. This is McCrary. I will come and get you."

"Commander Daniels, you're next you know," said McCrary.

"Say again," she said. "Next?"

"I suspect that whatever hit the moon was hard enough to throw rock all the way to Earth. The Chaffee will be uninhabitable. Better figure out how to get everyone off."

"Understood. McCrary?" she asked. "Godspeed. You will not be forgotten."

"Commander, I suspect nobody's going to come back here for decades. Too much rock in orbit." With a start, Lisa agreed. If rock could reach Low Earth Orbit, it was going to be around for a long, long time.

"This is McCrary. I can see the debris plume now. It is like a sparkling curtain rising from the south. It is spreading from one source to extend from horizon to horizon."

"Two minutes, McCrary," said Lisa. "Better get inside."

"One last thing," said McCrary. "This is for everyone. Please relay. One hundred and twenty-four years ago on Christmas Eve, three men rounded the moon for the first time and reported back to Earth. They read from Genesis at the dawn of spaceflight. I read from Revelations.

"'I looked when He broke the sixth seal and there was a great earthquake; and the sun became black as sackcloth made of hair and the whole moon became like blood; and the stars of the sky fell to the earth, as a fig tree casts its unripe figs when shaken by a great wind.

"'The sky was split apart like a scroll when it is rolled up and every mountain and island was moved out of their places.

"'Then the kings of the earth and the great men and the commanders and the rich and the strong and every slave and free man hid themselves in the caves and among the rocks of the mountains.'"

McCrary was silent for a second or two.

"And now, our moon is red and we go to hide in our caves. Let this be our final transmission for now: From the crew of the Lunar Colony Collins, we close with good night, good luck and God bless all of you, all of you on the good Earth.

"I bid you farewell." The sound of the MoonCan closing was loud on the speakers. Seconds later, subsonic thumps told of impacts around it. On Roque's main screen, the camera stream from the *Collins* started dropping frames, then stopped completely.

Celine spoke quietly. "All telemetry from the moon has stopped." Chaffee's external cameras showed the shockwave sweep over the small X marking the position of the UNSOC Lunar Colony *Michael Collins*.

* * *

UNSOC Space Station Roger Chaffee, June 17 2082, 1015 EDT

Lisa bowed her head for a moment. She asked Celine for the all-hands channel.

"Attention. This is Commander Daniels. A disaster of unknown origin has engulfed the Collins Lunar Colony. Casualties are unknown. The event that swept over the Collins has thrown a large amount of lunar debris into space. I believe we are in danger from this debris. All personnel are to prepare for immediate evacuation. You will be allowed one standard backpack for personal belongings. Pack now. Department heads, report for conference in five minutes on channel seven. Representatives from all manufacturers are also to join us on channel seven. That is all."

Roque clicked over to channel seven. He floated over to his personal locker. Although he had been originally assigned a spot in the barracks module, he had been babysitting so many lab experiments over the years it just made sense to move his gear into the lab. A ghost of a smile flitted over his face as he opened the locker, withdrawing a small smudged white box.

Floating back to the chair bolted in front of the lab's central command console, he donned a seat restraint to hold him in front of the camera. He idly held the box a quarter meter above the table and watched as the microscopic tidal gravity gently dropped the box to the surface. He lifted the top off the box, withdrew a clear plastic bag with a lock of auburn hair tied in a ribbon. Kissing it gently, he replaced it in the box.

"Soon, Lynn. I will be there all too soon," he whispered to the memento as he wiped a tear from his left eye. The voice of Lisa Daniels brought him back to the present.

"I will be brief, we haven't much time. I've been avoiding UNSOC for the past ten minutes or so, since I believe we have to reach a decision here. We're in deep trouble. When—*whatever* it was—happened on the moon, all of our radiation alarms went off. Medical. Any idea on our radiation dose?"

The young man on the monitor seemed overwhelmed at all the attention. He was a physician's assistant, since the population of the station did not rate a full-time doctor.

"It's a little out of my league, Commander, but here's what I've got. The situation is serious but not immediately fatal. Everyone on board has received between one and two Grays of radiation. Say, ten to twenty thousand chest x-rays. Untreated, there's a good chance about five percent of the folks will die. It's guaranteed about half will be down with nausea and diarrhea in four to six hours. We have to get everyone into a groundside hospital for treatment."

"Four to six hours?"

"Yes Ma'am".

"Astrogation. What's the word on the debris cloud?"

"As things stand now, Commander, we can see the first debris hits as soon as we round the Earth, ten minutes from now." A gasp greeted her words. "But it should be the smallest stuff, dust only. The acceleration needed to move something from the lunar surface to Earth orbit in thirty minutes is certainly enough to powder it. And we're only in real danger when we cross the plane of the moon's rotation, at least in the short term. I think we'll get four to five orbits, say six to nine hours, before our position becomes actively dangerous."

"Thank you, Astrogation. Engineering. Can anything be done to lengthen our time up here?"

John looked mightily unhappy. "No Ma'am. Radar shows objects twenty meters long moving fast enough to escape lunar gravity. Big mountains like that would crush us like a bug fairly soon. Worse, the smaller stuff will be flying along three or four kilometers per second, relative to us. Doesn't take too many golf-ball sized hits to kill everyone on board. We're going to have to evacuate."

"Anyone else? I want everyone to have their say. Roque?"

"I vote to evacuate. We are sitting ducks up here. The laser I have been working on will do nothing against this volume of space debris."

"This is preposterous!" broke in George Cranston, the representative of ZGCFabricam. "I have a major silicon melt going. We've got a large order for the high-Q silicon crystals for the Valley. We can't evacuate now!"

"How much longer do you need?" asked John, leaning forward.

"Thirty-six hours at the earliest." The thumbnail image of Celine was shaking her head mournfully.

"In thirty-six hours, the chances of one or more collision with a ten centimeter object, rises to eighty-seven percent."

"Overruled George. I'd rather be alive and in court on Earth than free but dead up here."

"I've got another two hours until our final production run is up," said Alice Webber of ElectroPore. "We're running an anti-diabetes drug now. Any chance we can wait until then?"

Celine frowned and said, "We'll be taking hits but it will be from sub-millimeter-sized impactors. Risky but doable."

"Celine, to clear the air, at what time does the impact threat for a centimeter-sized object rise to one in a thousand?"

"Six hours."

"Interesting coincidence. Right about that time we'll be woofing up our cookies."

Lisa scanned the images of all the conferees. "Anyone else? OK, here's what I've decided. We evacuate in four hours. We eat *now*. I want the mess hall closed as soon as everyone is through, or in one hour, whichever comes first. No exceptions. And no hoarding. No apple in the pocket. We're going to chuck but I want that to be as content free as possible," she looked around the edges of her conference screen, collecting nods.

"ElectroPore gets their run but all manufacturers will be limited in the product they can ship down."

Kalau Matumbe, head of ExoMat, interrupted. "Excuse me Commander. Ship down in what? There's no shuttle in dock at this time." A chuckle ran around the conference. "What am I missing? George? Alice? You guys know anything?"

Lisa took pity on him. "Ah, sorry, Kalau. Remember those 'solar shelters' we drilled on a few months ago? They are really emergency reentry vehicles. We call them 'sleds.' We're going home in them."

"I never saw anything about such a thing in the UNSOC literature." Kalau looked a little indignant.

"That's because UNSOC doesn't know about them." The rest of the department heads muttered and stirred. "It's time to let the secret out everyone."

Lisa addressed herself to Kalau. "We've been petitioning UNSOC for the sleds for the past twenty-five years. We've always been told no. Once the Collins colony..." Her voice caught and she had to clear her throat to continue, "The colony was able to ship us materials, we decided to build our own reentry craft. They never knew about it."

Kalau looked around his screen. "Are you guys buying this? Risk our life to some hand-built, untested rattletrap?" George and Alice nodded.

"Kalau, I know you haven't been up here long, but there's one thing you have to realize," said Alice earnestly. "UNSOC might be a bunch of corrupt clowns but the astronaut corps is some of the most professional, careful and dedicated people I know. I would absolutely trust my life to them. In fact, we're doing so every day we're in orbit." Kalau subsided, troubled.

"Anything else? Celine and I will set the undock time. Everyone will be in the sleds, strapped down, no less than ten minutes before undock time. Nobody gets left behind. Medical, be prepared. We might have to sedate a couple to get them on board.

"Let's move."

Roque toggled away from channel seven. The off-white box with the lock of Lynn's hair in it caught his eye. He sighed and grasped the box carefully.

"Sorry to disappoint you Commander Daniels," he murmured to himself. "But I won't be aboard."

* * *

UNSOC Space Station Roger Chaffee, June 17 2082, 1100 EDT

Throughout the *Chaffee* people were zipping about, shutting down systems, powering off experiments, gathering records. Anti-static bags of electronic parts and memory chips floated in the air. Engineering was working overtime emptying the sleds of *Collins* supplies to free up room for items that must get to Earth. Medical sent over all of the anti-nausea drugs they had.

And Lisa Daniels found herself with a problem.

"But Roque, you must leave!"

"Ah, my dear Commander, you know that I cannot." his wan smile flashed briefly. "I would be completely helpless on Earth."

"You know you will be killed if you stay," Lisa said.

"My dear," Roque said, "That should have happened eighteen years ago. I figure I just had a little reprieve from the Grim Reaper all these years."

"I could order you sedated and carried aboard you know," she said. "Don't think I won't."

"Ah, Lisa, Lisa. I remember you as a young lieutenant fresh out of UNSOC Ground School. Struggling along here, learning how to swim in the air. But I knew then, as I know now, you were destined to lead people. You do care. That is why I'm not strapped into a sled right now, snoring away. You are allowing me my dignity."

"And I will continue to allow it until it endangers the mission," said Lisa roughly.

"Let me tell you a very brief story. One time, long ago, I was an exchange student to the United States. It was so different from my beloved España. So busy, so alive! My foster family took me to the Outer Banks of North Carolina on their annual vacation. Two weeks of the beach, girls and, even sometimes drinking. I was seventeen and not sure what I wanted to do in life. Then I met Lynn.

"She was eighteen and beautiful, full of life. The second night I was there I went for a walk on the beach near sunset. It was strange. In España, the beaches face west into the setting sun. On the Outer Banks, they face east. The land is so flat you can sometimes see the setting sun through the maze of vacation homes.

"I was walking on the beach towards one of the shafts of sunlight when I saw her. Her hair was a rich auburn, shining like a halo in the reddening light. She had put on a light shirt against the cooling temperatures but she was lithe and slender and to a young boy who was almost a man, irresistibly attractive.

"I somehow got up the nerve to talk to her. Her family had just arrived for their two weeks at the beach and she had also wanted to see the sunset. It was beautiful. I daresay, more beautiful than any I have seen since, yes, even up here."

Roque removed the lid on his smudged white box and retrieved a sealed tube of what looked like green water and sand. Lisa tried not to show her impatience but something must have leaked through her control, and Roque chuckled.

"There is not much left to tell. She was my first love. The two weeks passed both excruciatingly slow and far too fast. She was fascinated by the stars and she spoke often of joining the Astronaut Corps and going to space. I had never considered that and promised I would join too.

"We were each other's first lovers and it was evermore sweet for that. We kept in touch of course. We were trying to figure out how she could visit me in España. Then, for some reason, about eight months later, she stopped writing. My friends all tried to console me, saying I should find another girl, for she must have found another man.

"It was a month later when I received a letter in the mail. Her parents had written to me, enclosing an article from the newspaper. She had been driving home from her job when a drunk driver twice her age plowed into her car, killing her instantly.

"Losing Lynn was the defining moment of my life. I have never had another lover and frankly, never really wanted one. I know others would laugh at me for this, tell me I am wasting my life. But she and I were joined in a way I cannot describe to you, even if I wanted to. I joined UNSOC because of her. I have never regretted it, not even when I lost the use of my legs.

"All I have left of her is this little bottle of seawater from that long ago summer and a lock of her hair." Roque removed the plastic bag with the lock and set it on the table. He straightened up and gripped the worktable firmly.

"I would be totally useless on Earth, Commander Daniels. I have not exercised very much over the years. Even if I survived the journey down, my heart would give out shortly thereafter. Even if I didn't have a heart attack, I would be confined to a flotation bed for weeks as I recovered strength. The work I have done and would have continued to do is all up here. Down there, I would be just another cripple—old, unemployable and half-dead. No, the price of survival is too high. This way it's a fitting end for me. I know Lynn would approve."

Lisa frowned, started to retort, but he overrode her objections.

"You can sedate me if you want but I will curse you forever. But if you let me stay, I will tell those fat-bottoms in UNSOC that I refused your orders. I will protect you Lisa, for I still have friends there. But I will ask a favor of you, in return," he returned the tube of water to its foam recess in the white box.

"What is this favor, Roque?"

"Take this," he said, passing her the white box. "Go to the Dare County Cemetery in North Carolina. The directions are in the box. Tuck that tube in her grave and tell her I never forgot her. Would you do that for me?" Roque gripped her hand hard. "What little I have of Lynn," he patted the lock of hair, "and I, will die together in space."

This time Lisa let her eyes fill with tears, forming floating drops as she shook her head free of them. "Of course, Roque. For you, I will do that."

They held each other for a moment but Lisa's sense of duty rose insistently. "I must go."

Roque released her and formally saluted her. "And I must stay. Tell me how I can be of service as I wait for the end."

"I will. And...thank you Roque," she returned the salute, wiped her eyes and kicked out of his office for the last time, the small box of Roque's memories gripped in her left hand.

* * *

UNSOC Space Station Roger Chaffee, June 17 2082, 1230 EDT

Lisa went from compartment to compartment, chivvying crewmen, solving problems and encouraging the civilians to move faster. Throughout the station, crew and civilians began showing the first signs of radiation sickness. Reports of the spreading illness greeted Lisa upon her return to the Bridge.

"Commander, I recommend we start boarding the shuttles now. Otherwise we'll have too few able spacers to move the sick ones into the sleds," the chief medic said, looking a little green himself.

"Understood. Board the sickest first with enough able-bodied to assist them in the sled."

Clicking to the all-hands channel she announced, "Attention, crew. Begin moving to the sleds. Department heads will direct you to your sled. Man each sled evenly. Move."

"That should keep their minds off the barfs for a while. Doc, make sure you hand out those barf pills to everyone and make sure they take them. Commander's orders."

"Will do. Got a case of whoops bags with me too. See you on the sled." his image faded from her monitor.

Celine popped up on the screen. "Commander, time to drop the bomb on UNSOC."

"Thanks. Time to stop fooling around. Time to talk with the Esteemed Panjandrum himself, Director-General Herr Doctor Subraman Venderchanergee."

Celine initiated the call and was soon speaking to Fred Palowicz, Head Controller of the A, or daytime, shift. He got a quick status report from her.

"Gus is blasting Subby right now, Lisa," Fred said. Gus Blukofski was the head of the C shift. The UNSOC control room had all three shifts in to deal with the emergency, much to Subraman's displeasure.

"You ask about why we have so many shifts in here and I'd love to tell you but I can see Commander Daniels is on the line right now. I think she'd like to tell you herself," he gestured to Fred, who, with a flourish, spun the volume up on the speakers.

"Chaffee, this is CAPCOM A. We have the Director-General Subraman Venderchanergee with us. Please repeat your request."

"Director. The Chaffee crew has sustained serious radiation poisoning from the explosion on the moon. Without treatment, up to five percent of our crew will die within the next two weeks. In addition, we have been monitoring the debris from the event and believe it will intersect our orbit within the next two to four hours. Over the last twenty years, as you know, we have constructed solar shelters from lunar materials. What you don't know is they have been designed to function as emergency reentry vehicles. Lifeboats, if needed.

"In my professional opinion the Chaffee must be abandoned and all crew must return to Earth. To stay aboard will be to risk death from the impact of space debris, the effects of radiation sickness, or both. I request UNSOC assistance for this reentry." On-screen her face was composed and determined.

Subraman's thoughts raced. Abandon the *Chaffee*? What about his deals, his special service fees? Look at the radar; it's clear as a bell! Cowardice! Evacuating all the crew, whether the makeshift 'reentry vehicles' made it or not, meant the *Chaffee* would be out of action for months, as dozens of launches would be needed to ferry a new crew back up to man the station and get operations restarted. The budget would never stand for it.

"Request denied. Frankly, I am surprised at you Commander Daniels, trying to run away like this. Commander Holt would never do anything this drastic. In fact, wasn't there some kind of meteor storm on his watch? Everyone wanted to evacuate the Chaffee then, too. Commander Holt went public, urging calm and declaring he was staying. He lived. So will you. I order you to remain on board and cancel this *evacuation* of yours."

"Sir, with all due respect, the matters are completely different. Meteor storms are one thing; this is a far denser debris cloud. It will spread to all orbits from beyond the moon right down to Low Earth Orbit. If we don't leave in the next four hours our chances of getting hit rise to one in a thousand. The next orbit, ninety minutes later, we will face one in five hundred chances. It gets far worse after that; seven in eight in thirty-six hours."

Subraman looked around at his three chief controllers. "Do we confirm those numbers?" Fred, Gus and Gayatri nodded yes. "From our own data or did it come from the Chaffee?"

All three stared at Subraman. Finally, Fred dropped his eyes and answered. "The Chaffee, sir."

"Well, there you are. Commander Daniels, until we can confirm your radar data and construct our own probability charts, you are ordered not to leave. That is how science works. Independent verification. I am not saying you fudged the numbers but we cannot have you abandoning your post from what could well be some error from your Astrogation section."

Lisa put out her hand to forestall a scathing retort from Celine.

"But our casualties from radiation sickness, sir. They need medical attention."

"Don't you have trained medics? Is this beyond them? Do they need replacement?

Lisa controlled her anger with difficulty. "Two hundred people have been exposed to two Grays of radiation. Half will become incapacitated in another three hours. We have, total, two medics. For one hundred casualties. One person in twenty will die without prompt treatment. You've lost the Collins sir, are you determined to lose the Chaffee too?"

"When the sickest ones become known, we'll send a rescue craft. For the last time Commander Daniels, you are ordered to stay put. Otherwise, the next shuttle will be bringing your replacement." With that, he stalked off to his office and closed the door carefully.

Lisa remained on screen. She knew from her long-ago assignments in the Control Room that Subraman was probably watching her remotely.

"CAPCOM, please advise us as to when you have acquired independent data on our incoming debris."

"Will do Chaffee."

"Our data will be on the sideband."

"No problem Lisa, we have all shifts here."

"It will be radar of the debris plume and radiation measurements."

"Roger Chaffee. Anything else for us?"

"Negative CAPCOM. The channel will remain up but unmanned. Holler and we will hear. Chaffee listening, out."

* * *

UNSOC Space Station Roger Chaffee, June 17 2082, 1315 EDT

"So, we're staying behind?" Celine's eyes were troubled as they sought Lisa's on the Bridge.

"Nope!" snapped Lisa.

"Then we're going on schedule?"

"You bet your sweet ass we are." A quick indrawn breath from Celine caused Lisa to smile. "Sorry. Figure of speech. Patch your panel over to Roque's lab. Then get that aforementioned part down to the sled."

"Aye-aye Commander." Celine dimpled. "I never thought I'd have to chew out my boss about sexual comments."

"Scatter!" Lisa ordered. She floated from station to station, powering them down. In her ready room, she powered down the screen where the background image of her family lingered for seconds afterwards.

"Coming home a bit sooner than you guessed Shep. I hope it's not a disappointment for you," she scanned the room for anything else to take, then shook her head and returned to the Bridge. One final sweep of the space and she left the Bridge for the last time, dogging the door tightly. Maybe Roque would live one more orbit because of that.

The scene around the sled bays was chaotic only to the untrained eye. Lisa could see the staff swiftly handing crew, stowing precious cargo and batting away the unshippable excess. The floating tangle of people, bags, boxes and nets, plus the sheer noise of all this activity made her faintly queasy. Hoping she was not one of the ones affected with radiation sickness, she turned and headed to Roque's laboratory for last minute instructions.

"Ah, Commander Daniels. I was expecting one last appeal."

"Roque my friend, I would not dishonor you so. Unless you are changing your mind?" Peering up at his face, she could tell the answer remained no. "Then we have business."

"Ah, you have found something useful for me to do instead of waiting in dread for Der Tag, eh?"

"Our dear leader, Subraman Venderchanergee has ordered us to stay onboard. Therefore, we are leaving. I need you to delay any inquiries into my whereabouts until retrofire. Then they will have to help us land."

"I think not."

"You won't help me?" Lisa's eyes began to harden.

"Of course I will help you. I just don't think Subraman will help you. He made the announcement in the Control Room, yes?"

"Yeeees…." she admitted.

"Then he cannot back down. It would be an admission he was wrong, and that cannot be borne."

"Wait, let me get this straight. He'd rather see us all die than admit he was wrong?"

"Essentially. Remember, he was born to a high caste. They are taught they are born to rule. Failures are always due to subordinates. That's the theory at least.

"But there's another reason. This station represents the main cash cow for UNSOC. Without it, Subraman's division falls into the red and he'll be removed. Therefore, he must keep this station a going concern."

"You and I both know the Chaffee is doomed."

"Subraman cannot allow himself to believe that. I'll bet he said you were faking the data, true?"

"Yes! How did you know?"

"It fits, it fits. In a nutshell, Subraman must keep you up here. If he orders you to stay but everyone dies, he would claim Earth-bound radars did not match what ours did and he was being cautious of a unique event and so forth. He'll survive."

"If you disobey him and the sleds fail, it's your fault. Again, he survives."

"It's hopeless then. He survives no matter what."

"Not so. There's more. If he authorizes you to leave and the station survives, he is incompetent and you are a coward. If he authorizes you to leave and you burn up in the sleds, then again, he is incompetent and you are a fool. So he won't authorize you to leave under any circumstances.

"But the best thing for us is if he orders you to stay, you disobey him *and* you survive. Then you are a hero and he is a heartless bureaucrat thinking only of himself. Then he is finished." Roque leaned closer. "You must survive. Not only to get rid of Subraman. For Shep and Susan and Eddie. And for the rest of this crew."

Lisa cupped his chin with her graceful hand. "Roque, dear friend. I have every intention of surviving."

"Then you must do this Lisa." Roque turned away to a cabinet, withdrew two small flasks. "We must christen the sleds."

"Oh Roque, really?!" Lisa exclaimed, laughing.

"Absolutely. You are landing in the ocean, correct?"

"That's still the plan."

"No ship can sail the ocean unless it's christened. Bad luck! Would you allow your friend one last request?"

"Certainly!"

"One sled should be named Ted Reinhart, after the crewman who died, starting this whole chain of events. The second should be named after Jim Pruett."

"Who's Jim Pruett?" Lisa asked, puzzled.

"I love old movies, especially ones from the dawn of the Space Age. One movie was called 'Marooned.' Jim Pruett was one of the astronauts. I always liked his character."

Lisa was dubious. "Anything I should know about this character? Was he some kind of womanizer?"

"No no, my dear, he was a clean-cut, all-American guy. Please?"

Lisa agreed.

"Then let me give you one final hug and get down to the sled bays. I will announce from here."

Lisa floated into the first sled bay and got the up-check that all personnel were safely aboard. Soon after, the speakers sounded.

"Attention, all personnel. This is Roque Zacarías. I am not leaving. Commander Daniels does not agree with me but has granted my request to remain. However, you cannot leave until the sleds have been christened. Commander, if you will do the honors?"

Lisa moved to the hatch of the forward sled, grabbed a handhold, murmured to a waiting space hand and waited.

"Thirty years ago Ted Reinhart, one of our own, had a medical emergency we could not treat in orbit. There was no ship in dock and no way to send him home. At the end of the week, Ted was dead. As a result of his sacrifice, a long line of determined commanders ensured we have these lifeboats in our hour of need. This first sled therefore, is christened the ERV Ted Reinhart. Commander?"

With a strong swing, Lisa broke the first flask over the entry hatch. The space hand she had spoken with had a towel to catch the flying shards. Lisa moved through the corridor to the second sled.

"This next name will mean nothing to almost all of you. He was a character in a decades old movie about spaceflight. As a point of personal privilege, I christen this vehicle the ERV Jim Pruett. Commander?"

Again, the swing, the breakage, the glittering spheres of...what was it?

"Roque?"

"Yes, Commander?"

"What was in these flasks?"

"A gentle Muscat from old España. Champagne is traditional but alcohol is required."

"Thank you Roque."

"You should get going."

"Goodbye Roque. Goodbye Chaffee. You both have served us well."

"Goodbye, Commander."

Lisa closed the hatch on the *Pruett*, watched as it was dogged down. She then hurried back to the *Reinhart*. With a final look around the corridor, she ducked inside and closed the hatch firmly. Minutes later the ERVs undocked from the *Chaffee*. Short bursts of thrusters pushed the craft into the desired attitude for reentry. Lisa watched her command recede among the stars. She could not stop hurting for the gallant man she was forced to leave behind.

* * *

UNSOC Space Station Roger Chaffee, June 17 2082, 1430 EDT

Roque watched the ERVs recede with a sigh of regret. Deep in his heart, he knew he was doing the right thing. As a passenger in the ERV, he would be a liability. Instead, he was an asset in the *Chaffee*. One last act for the world and then he could relax with his Muscat, his music and his memories.

A loud bang interrupted his musings. A sand-sized grain of the Moon had impacted the *Chaffee*. It was just the harbinger of what was to come. Roque knew he was going to die quite soon in a hail of gravel travelling at thousands of kilometers per hour. Best to think of something else.

He had come to know Subraman intimately over the years and was confident in the analysis he had given Lisa Daniels. Any minute now, he wagered, Subraman would be calling to denounce Lisa as a coward.

Like magic, the radio came alive. Gayatri Vedya, the B Shift chief controller was calling on behalf of Subraman, asking for Commander Daniels. Roque rapidly made the cross-connect so the ERVs would be able to hear this transmission. A few deep breaths and he mentally took the stage for the last time.

Subraman's oily voice oozed over the speaker. "Ah, Mr. Zacarías, where is Commander Daniels? I wish to speak with her."

"Director Venderchanergee, how are you? It's been so long since you were up here. Fifteen years if I remember correctly. Her locator shows her in her room but she is not answering the Com. She may be taking a shower."

"Or maybe just crying in her bunk. Could you go and knock on her door for me, just to make sure? I have some questions for her."

"Well Director, I have to confess, when I heard it was you, I abandoned the board for a minute and went down myself. I definitely heard water running, so, yes; she's likely in the shower."

"Is that why it took you so long to answer?"

"Oh, I must apologize for that, sir. Running this board is not something I do all that often."

"Wait, why are you on the board at all? Where is—what's her name—that blonde woman who's so angry all the time?"

"Celine Greenfield?"

"Yes, that's the one. Isn't manning the board her job? I swear...the Chaffee seems like it's falling apart up there."

Roque winced slightly and muttered "Not yet, but soon."

"What's that? Your transmission was garbled."

"Her people were drafted into helping out at the aid station. We had some radiation cases here."

"Yes. I suspect that will be the new excuse for malingering. Radiation."

"Well sir, you know how it is. Say, did I ever tell you what happened up here during your last visit?"

They went on like that for twenty minutes. Roque would carefully deflect all of Subraman's questions with a glib response. In return, he told stories, remembered common acquaintances and generally chatted up Subraman.

Fred eventually realized Roque was stalling for time. He called Gus who was coordinating the ground and ocean response to the incoming ERVs.

"Gus, listen close, I don't have much time. Roque's giving Subby the old runaround. It is a thing of beauty. Lisa Daniels was able to send us an encrypted message. She kicked the sleds free of the station ten minutes ago and should be lighting up the retrorockets right about now. Entry Interface is in another forty minutes and landing is slated for 1640, somewhere on the East Coast, preferably New York/New Jersey. Get everyone on board, buddy. Coast Guard especially. Subby's got me stuck in here. Copy?"

"Got it, Fred. Roque's not coming back?"

"Doesn't look like it. I don't blame him either. There's nothing for him here."

"Still, seems a damned shame."

"We'll hoist a glass of port to him later. Gotta run. Out." Fred slapped his phone off and reentered the Control Center. Subraman glanced his way, his concentration still on Roque.

"And that's how I came into possession of an original mission patch from Apollo One." Roque finished the absolutely true story with a grand flourish.

"An amazing story, Mr. Zacarías. Commander Daniels must be out of the shower by now, please page her."

Roque was seen squinting at the screen, trying to see where the paging function was. "Nope, that's not it. No, I don't want to call the Collins…" He poked around for a few moments and then looked up, exasperated, to Subraman.

"Sir, I can't figure this darned thing out. It will be faster if I float down to her quarters myself. Be right back." He zipped out of frame before Subraman could countermand him.

Roque left the volume turned up and bobbed just out of the field of view of the camera. He was hoping he could stall Subby until Lisa finished the retrorocket burn.

"UNSOC Control, this is Commander Daniels on the ERV Reinhart, requesting terminal guidance control." Roque felt like cheering. He returned to his position in front of the camera. Now the ruse was over, he wanted to watch how it played out.

Subraman glared at the camera. For a moment, Roque felt the look was directed at him. He almost chuckled when he realized that Subby was glaring at Lisa, who was on an audio-only circuit.

Speaking slowly, as to a petulant child, Subraman said, "Commander Daniels, this is Director Venderchanergee. What is the meaning of this?"

"The Emergency Reentry Vehicles Tom Reinhart and Jim Pruett have completed retrofire and are inbound to Earth." A loud bang sounded over the speakers. "That was another piece of the moon hitting our shields, Director, in case you didn't know. Entry Interface will be in forty minutes. All of the crew are aboard, except for Roque Zacarías, who requested to stay on the Chaffee. We cannot go back. All we ask for now is terminal guidance to Earth."

"NO!" shouted Subraman in a rare loss of control. "You will proceed back to the Chaffee and return to your station."

"I told you before," came the voice, crackling now and then with static, "We don't have the delta V <wham> to make it back to the Chaffee, even if we wanted to. <bam> We do need your assistance once we break out of communications blackout."

Aboard the *Chaffee*, Roque distantly heard impacts as well but they were less important than the debris smashing into the shields on the ERVs. He watched the scene inside the Control Room with concern.

"Well, you won't get it," Subraman stated, striding over to the rear wall, behind the CAPCOMs. "You insisted on disobeying the direct orders of your superiors. Since you refused my orders, you can't ask for our help. I refuse to abet your criminal actions and will not allow my staff to help you, either." Flipping up the covers over the large red Emergency Power Off buttons, found in every data center, Subraman paused.

"Will you return to the Chaffee?" Subraman asked.

"We cannot," came the calm, but determined reply.

"Then you are on your own." Subraman rammed the EPO buttons home.

Roque stared with horror at the blank screen as the radio emitted continuous static.

* * *

UNSOC Space Station Roger Chaffee, June 17 2082, 1500 EDT

Roque did not even hear Commander Daniels radioing to the suddenly unresponsive Control Room. The decaying orbit of the ERVs had carried them beyond the orbit of the *Chaffee* and beyond the range of their radios.

He turned to the last bottle of Muscat and lovingly worked the cork out of the bottle. Fetching a clean beaker from the locker, he shook out a round ball of the fragrant wine and watched it infinitesimally settle into the beaker. Space was never zero-G, he had lectured countless visitors to his lab throughout the years. Hence, the preferred term *microgravity*. Left alone, the wine would eventually touch bottom in the beaker. Roque leaned forward and sucked a mouthful from the freely floating ball of rich amber fluid, then watched the wavelets chase each other around the remaining sphere.

"UNSOC to Commander Daniels," muttered the radio. Roque, surprised, turned up the volume. "Come in Commander Daniels, over." Roque chuckled at the anachronism. Nobody said *over* in UNSOC. Then he realized he did not hear the automatic *beep* normally signaling the end of transmission.

"<crrrk> here. <shwee> ing in brok<kkkkshhhhhhh>. Over."

"One minute to Entry Interface," said UNSOC. "Entry Interface in one minute. Over." Roque guessed it was Fred Palowicz on the radio. But from where?

"<Swheee>nute. Entry Interface in <zzz><snap>"

Roque waited until it was clear the ERVs were deep in reentry. Glancing out the window, he saw something that made his skin crawl. Rapidly aiming one of the station cameras on the sight, he keyed the radio.

"Roque to UNSOC. I have the reentry trails of the ERVs in sight."

"Roger, Chaffee. Roque, it was an honor knowing you." The voice was somber but professional. "Your sacrifice will not be forgotten."

"Fred, you better take care of Lisa and everyone else."

"We're working on it Roque. Godspeed."

"Thanks Fred. Say hello to Gus and a kiss for Gayatri. Roque Zacarías, listening, out." Roque knew they were killing themselves down there to bring the ERVs home. They didn't need to be reminded of the doomed spaceman circling above their heads.

The reentry occupied a portion of his mind. He had one final orbit before the big stuff would finally punch through the walls of the station. Ninety minutes to live, more or less. He patted the lock of hair in its bag. He would be with Lisa soon.

He carefully sipped more of the Muscat from the ball shimmering in the air. It had drifted closer to the beaker while he had been talking to Fred. *It was a real shame he couldn't swirl it in a thin crystal goblet*, he thought. Still, it was a symphony of taste on his tongue compared to the usual rations. Perhaps letting it air would make it too overwhelming. He sat back and thought of the España of his youth.

The reentry trails had stopped and Roque reported that fact to Fred. *The sleds should be out of communications blackout by now*, thought Roque.

"UNSOC, UNSOC, this is Commander Daniels aboard the ERV Reinhart. Come in, UNSOC."

Roque smiled. It was all over, almost. The impacts of the moon debris on the *Chaffee* stopped as it moved out of the debris plume. Another hour, more or less, before they were back in the thick of it. He selected his favorite music, queued it for play. As soon as the sleds landed he would fill the station with the sounds of the land of his birth.

He replenished the ball of Muscat. It was a shame to drink a wine so quickly, he mused. But the next pass would be his doom and it was a worse shame to let it be lost to space. Another sip of the ball and he was once again in the land of rolling hills and endless vineyards, under the warm Iberian sun.

Roque monitored the descent of the sleds. He laughed out-loud when the CAPCOMs revealed they were using a Shuttle landing simulator video game to assist in the energy management. He sat up a bit straighter as the terminal phase approached.

Here was the moment of truth. He had been able to fabricate nylon from the asteroid material found on the moon. Long experimenting taught him how to sew it into parachutes, now attached to the sleds. He sat, tense, praying they would work and not doom his friends to a watery grave.

In his mind's eye, he imagined the sequence. Any second now the first chute would fire. A simple ribbon chute, its primary purpose would be to orient the sled correctly as it provided some deceleration. Next, a drogue chute, larger, would be deployed. It was tightly reefed, its bottom tied together so it would not open all the way. Twice, the reefing lines would be cut, allowing the chute to open gradually. After a minute under drogue, the main show would begin.

He followed the ground chatter as the main chute spread its dirty white canopy above the sleds. Never before in the space program had square, ram-air parachutes been used for returning spacecraft. When he was certain both sleds were under full canopies, he sat back, content. It was his crowning achievement, the ERVs. From their very frame, through the heat shield, to the innovative parachutes, all had come from his talented hands.

His approaching death now meant very little he realized. All of his techniques had been transmitted to UNSOC; a copy was in Lisa's hands. When man went back into space, he would be using the same methods Roque had invented. His life was complete.

He listened with half an ear as the sleds drifted to a landing in the ocean. He was surprised when he heard his name on the radio.

"Roque, this is Lisa Daniels, over."

"Roque here, Lisa."

"We're down safe, thanks to you. I will never forget you." Her voice sounded peculiar, as if she was holding back some great emotion.

"I am glad I could help. This is, in a way, the best way to go. Out on top, not wasting away on a bed. I am content Lisa."

"I still wish you were here. The world owes you a debt of gratitude."

"Then tell my story, if you must. Please don't forget about Lynn's grave."

"I have your box right here Roque. Say hello to Lynn for me."

Roque smiled. "I will, my dear commander. Now, you have people that need your help. Goodbye Lisa Daniels." Taking a breath, he declared theatrically, "This is Roque Maximiano Zacarías, on board the UN Space Station Roger B. Chaffee, signing off," he turned off the radio and replaced the microphone in its clip for the last time.

Roque spent his last hour floating in the center of his lab. The lock of Lynn's hair was safely zipped into a pocket of his coveralls. He sipped his wine and idly began depressurizing the various compartments of the station. He knew the station would be punctured; he didn't want the reaction to the escaping atmosphere spinning the *Chaffee* around.

Roque listened without fear as the hailstorm of debris began smashing into the thin skin. His ears popped and he knew that his lab was holed. He sipped the last of the Muscat ball and fingered the lock of Lynn's hair in his pocket.

It was a small leak, from the sound of it. Roque was glad. He really didn't want to die from explosive decompression, nor did he want the agony from debris-punched holes in various non-fatal parts of his body. This way, he would slip away from hypoxia, before the really horrible stuff happened.

A figure coalesced in the air before him, her hair streaming away towards the hole in the lab's wall. She was graceful and smiling and looked quite young.

"Lynn," Roque breathed. He knew she had come for him at last. She held up her hand to grasp his. Roque smiled. He knew this may well be a hallucination from anoxia but he was well past caring. He let go of the empty wine bottle and grasped her hand. He felt her pull his teenage soul from his limp and unresisting body as they flew off, together again at last, in the everlasting dark.

* * *

New York Presbyterian Hospital, June 20 2082, 1000 EDT.

"That smooth-talking bastard!" cried Lisa Daniels. "He put one over on me!"

Shep stirred from his seat at the foot of her bed at New York's Presbyterian Hospital. "Which bastard is this, love?"

"Roque Zacarías, that's who. I can't believe I let him do this to me."

"Still in the dark here."

"Oh, Shep. Remember the Reinhart and Pruett?"

"I'll never forget them," he said. "They brought you safely home to me."

"You say the sweetest things. Well, the Reinhart was named for that space hand that died about thirty years ago."

"I remember you telling me about him. And the Pruett?"

"Roque asked me to let him name that sled. 'Point of personal privilege,' he said."

"So?" asked Shep, still mystified.

"So I looked up the reference. Jim Pruett was a character in a century-old movie at the dawn of the Space Age. Three men were in one of those old Apollo capsules which had just shoved away from a space station. Jim Pruett was the commander."

"Is this history, or fiction?"

"Oh, definitely fiction. Well, their retrorockets wouldn't fire and they couldn't get back to the space station. They were marooned in space and their oxygen was running out. The ground crew was frantically trying to get a rescue craft up there, when Jim Pruett decided to go outside to fix the engine."

"Sounds unlikely," said Shep.

"Well, the astronauts were all doped up so they wouldn't use so much oxygen and so forth, so they let him go. Once outside the capsule, he ripped his suit and died. I can't believe he did this to me!"

"Tricking you into naming the ERV after the gallant man who sacrificed himself to save the rest of the crew? I wish I had met him."

"Roque was such a charmer. You would have liked him. He asked me to do him a favor Shep. As soon as I get out of here, I want to go take care of it."

"After a little time in Ohio I hope," he said. "Eddie and Susan were really unhappy that Aunt Erin moved in to take care of them."

"Of course after Ohio! I'm sure I will be tied up here with all kinds of debriefings and what-not."

And in this, she was absolutely correct.

* * *

Dare County Cemetery, North Carolina, October 2, 2082, 1600 EDT.

The leaves on the occasional oak trees were changing glorious shades of red and yellow as Lisa made her way to the little cemetery on the eastern edge of North Carolina. It was a long drive from Ohio, after a much longer summer of meetings, press conferences and even harsher sessions behind the closed doors of the UN bureaucracy.

Over and over she told her story, until the details were graven deeply into her memory. She was accused of every kind of malfeasance, abandoning her station, incitement to mutiny and most cutting of all, deserting Roque Zacarías on the station to die a horrible death.

Without the solidarity of her fellow crew and most especially the testimony of Fred and Gayatri and Gus, Lisa was not sure she would have ever gotten out of the UN alive.

Now, this final request. Roque's instructions were clear, the grave was easily found with its simple headstone.

Lynn Caren Merriweather, born June 12th 2036, died August 29th, 2055. Beloved daughter.

So few words and yet, such an influential life. Without this woman, Roque would never have been in space. That meant no sleds, no tiles, no parachutes and a space station full of dead space hands.

The sandy soil loosened easily, Lisa pulled a flap of it free from the base of the headstone. She carefully dug out a hollow and lay Roque's box, with its nested tube of seawater from that long ago summer, next to the stone. Gently replacing the turf over the box, she gathered up the extra sand. Standing, she scattered it on the rest of the grave, speaking to the shade of the young woman buried beneath.

"He never forgot you Lynn. Even in death, he loved you and no other. He is orbiting up there now above us, grasping the lock of your hair. I know you and he are probably gazing down here, chuckling at me. But he asked me to come, so come to this place I did, to bring you a token of his fidelity and honor the woman I never met. Farewell."

Wiping her eyes, she saluted the grave and walked slowly away. As she turned to leave, she glanced to the sky, remembering Roque, and was the first to see the evening's fireballs of the moon, slicing their way across the lowering skies.

THE END

The Glade
(Fantasy)

By

Peter Orr

As they approached the forest, the horses slowed to a canter. Judging by the nervous whinnies, Jacob suspected they could sense something of what lay within the approaching expanse and wanted no part of it. Fortunately, they were well-trained, reliable mounts. They did not panic or struggle, simply coming to a calm halt just before the forest's boundary. Jacob sighed and dismounted, taking a moment to pat his horse reassuringly before making his way over to Cain. The older man was attempting to move the woman sitting slumped against his back.

"Throw her down," Jacob called up as he got into position. "I'll catch her."

Cain hesitated for a moment and then, apparently giving up on the careful approach, nodded his agreement and pushed her off. Jacob caught her roughly and started setting her to her feet as Cain leapt down to them, agile despite his age.

"Well, at least that was easier than getting her up there," he muttered gruffly.

With some effort Jacob got the woman upright and to his astonishment, she stayed in place without falling down.

"Those herbs you gave her are quite something," he stated, shaking his head. "I mean, drugging someone's easy, but this...."

"They're rather rare," Cain agreed. "They keep her in a kind of trance. As long as I pull her along, she'll keep walking without a thought in her head."

"And you've got enough to keep her like that?"

"No, but even when she wakes up she'll still be gagged and tied up with the cord."

Jacob glanced at the cord, wrapped repeatedly around her body to tie her arms to her sides. It looked innocuous enough, although a slight sheen distinguished it from any other piece of rope. Cain stepped over to her and detached the end of it, unwinding a few coils to give himself plenty of slack.

Jacob was skeptical. "And that cord really does everything you say it does?"

Cain smiled his not-quite smile. "Oh yes. I won't have any problem with her," he formed the end into a loop around his wrist, which seemed to fuse without him needing to tie any knot.

Jacob shrugged his shoulders but this kind of thing always made him feel uncomfortable. He had no doubts about the potency of Cain's collection of trinkets and artifacts, having seen the old man use them many times to defy death and destroy enemies. Nevertheless, and despite being a man of very few scruples, Jacob fastidiously avoided any involvement with the power Cain harnessed so readily.

He turned instead to their trussed up captive. Young, fair haired and pretty, he would readily have abused his position as captor, except that Cain had insisted he needed her undamaged. That also meant the headache of guarding the girl from any number of eager men back at their base. But Jacob would not have risen to his position in Cain's cadre without learning to follow the man's orders to the letter; he would almost certainly not have lived this long either. Every one of the bandits in Cain's employ knew the consequences of disobedience, something recently demonstrated yet again with the demise of Ethan, one of Cain's most trusted lieutenants.

It was thanks to Ethan that this woman had first come to Cain's attention. No one really understood the nature of the boss's interest in her and no one had questioned it. But the whole band was thrust into disarray the day after her arrival and then Ethan's outburst, when Cain made his unexpected announcement.

"Still can't believe you're retiring." Jacob shook his head now. "I didn't think anyone in this job got to retire."

"Well, I've lived longer than most."

Jacob paused. "Is there any chance of you telling me why?"

"No." Cain's expression was steady, giving nothing away. "You wouldn't understand, in any case."

"Okay," his lieutenant nodded, accepting this. "And would the answer be the same if I asked why you're taking her into this forest?"

"It would. I will just have to take my secrets with me," he paused for a second. "But there *is* something that I wish to tell you, Jacob."

Jacob met his gaze and furrowed his eyebrows in concentration. "Oh?"

"As you know, you have impressed me greatly over the years. I have decided to leave you as my heir, as leader of the whole operation."

Surprised, Jacob felt a thrill of victory wash over him and allowed it to register on his face. He had harboured desperate hopes for this, since Cain had picked him to help transport the girl. Now he would have the power he long craved.

Only one small concern marred his joy. "What about Gideon?" he chanced. Most of the lieutenants had marked *that* brute out as the natural successor.

"I've spoken to Gideon and he knows my choice. Don't let him say a word otherwise." Cain nodded. "Now, I will leave you. We have a long walk ahead of us."

Jacob nodded and coming down from his high, wondered vaguely whether to wish the old man goodbye. Expressions of sentiment were rare between them.

Instead, he asked a question. "Will we see you again?"

Cain stopped, looked back and smiled wanly. "It's possible. But I hope not."

And with that, the boss turned and set off into the mass of trees. Jacob frowned but recognized he deserved no better from the old man. He saw him pause just beyond the first row of trees, take something from his pouch and swallow it whole before continuing in. Jacob wondered, but dismissed the action as just another of the older man's little mysteries.

Now alone, he climbed into his saddle and prepared to take both horses back to the base but then paused and grinned. Dismounting, he strode instead to the slightly grander horse that had so recently been Cain's and mounted it instead. As he rode into the night, he reflected on this glorious turn of events. He decided he would be a leader no less successful and just as merciless as Cain himself had been.

Eleven days later, as a direct result of Cain's words to him, Jacob was killed in a particularly violent manner. No one mourned his passing.

* * *

It had been dusk when he left Jacob behind but soon moonlight illuminated the forest and only the sounds of chirping insects interrupted the windless calm. In such conditions, any forest in the world would feel otherworldly; but Cain knew this was *that* forest, the one about which stories are told. Raw power hung in the air like a heat haze.

His captive walked five steps behind, trudging soullessly along. At first, Cain found this pleasing but at length he came to wish the effect of the herbs would wear off so he could say his piece to her.

Just as he began to worry that he had given her too much; that she would be useless for the entire night, her footsteps grew halting. Finally he turned to see her desperately attempt to run away. The cord was taut but he felt barely a tug at his wrist. Realizing she was getting nowhere, she slowed to a halt and Cain took the opportunity to place thumb and forefinger on the cord and yank it. She flew towards him, falling to the ground.

"I'm afraid this cord is rather special," he explained as she tried to get to her feet, not an easy task with her arms bound. As soon as she succeeded he set off again and watched her struggle to keep up so she was not pulled over. He smiled, knowing if he wanted, he could quite easily drag her along the ground on her back. The cord had been a worthwhile investment.

He *could* have brought some men along to manhandle her but he was determined this should be an intimate affair, just the two of them.

She was making indignant noises through her gag and Cain briefly considered removing it, before thinking better of it. Instead, he retrieved his pouch and took from it another beetle, desperate and struggling. He held it between thumb and forefinger, making sure that she was watching as he pitched it into his mouth and swallowed it whole. He suppressed a shudder as its legs scratched at his gullet and saw his captive watching, entranced with disgust.

"They make me sensitive to the power," he explained. "That's how I know where we're going." The effects of the last one had not yet worn off but time was getting short and he wanted his sensitivity to be at its peak when they arrived at the Glade.

He turned and squinted at the moon. When he glanced down at her again, she had been struggling with her bindings. He regarded her critically. *About ninety minutes to live*, he thought. *I suppose it's time to start explaining things.*

"You're a rare woman Maria," he sighed. She ceased her struggle, eyeing him warily. "My men have been holding your village to ransom for close to a decade. Under my command, they've destroyed your houses, killed your friends and raped your neighbors. All quite deliberately. To keep you all terrified and delivering your goods and gold to us. You must hate us Maria." She refused even to nod in agreement and he found himself respecting her for that.

"So by rights, when you found one of my men wounded, you should have left him to die or even sped up the process. I would never have found out and you wouldn't be here now," he let that sink in and almost felt a pang at the cruelty of punishing her for her kindness. Almost.

"Instead, you saved Ethan's life and he told me all about you. He was in awe of you, in fact. He requested I leave your village alone. I considered killing him on the spot for his weakness but I didn't. I'm an old softie at heart, you see," he flashed a ruthless half-grin. "After all, he had a point. We didn't need your village anymore. It was just a relic of simpler times, when all I had were a few cut-price thugs. Now I run the largest, sleekest band of criminals this side of the world," he paused to take a mock bow.

He noticed she had ceased her futile resistance, appearing warily interested in what he had to say.

"So I decided to let your village go. In fact, I decided to retire. I know, it sounds unlikely, doesn't it? But I'd finally found what I'd been looking for and it was you."

He wasn't surprised to see her eyebrows furrow in confusion. "Yes, you. Before announcing my retirement, I had my men capture you and bring you to me. Of course Ethan protested. Between you and me, I think he'd grown rather fond of you. But he was starting to annoy me, so *then* I killed him. There's only so much insubordination I can take."

He heard Maria's forlorn groan through her gag and her eyes lowered. "Oh dear, were you fond of him too? That *is* a shame."

He was starting to feel the increased sensitivity the beetle had brought and his rather hazy awareness of the correct direction sharpened. Now he could feel how close their destination was. To his relief, they would reach it with time to spare.

"You have no idea where I'm taking you, do you?" he asked and she lifted her eyes to meet his again, resigned. "Have you ever heard of the Glade?" No glimmer of recognition appeared in her face. "Did your parents never tell you the stories? Maybe not."

He sighed happily. "This is a cursed forest; all manner of devilry is reputed to take place here. Don't worry; I have charms to ward away the worst of it. I've been here once before, to confirm the Glade really exists. I was only able to find it thanks to these damned beetles. I don't think the forest would have let me get there otherwise.

"The Glade is just as it's described in all the children's stories; I knew they were true as soon as I saw it. And so here I am, ready to offer the required sacrifice."

At this, Maria stiffened and stood stock-still. He played along, pausing his step. "Come now, what did you think this was about? Did you really think we would both be walking out of this forest?"

She began to whimper but her eyes remained defiant, the tears resolutely held back. He was impressed but having too much fun to give her a break.

"I needed you because you're special Maria. You saved Ethan's life even though you must have hated him. You're good, kind and pure. Exactly what I'd been looking for." Now tears were flowing down her face, although she was refusing to break down and weep. He drank it in, then tugged at the cord and set off again. She resisted initially, before recalling how pointless that was.

"You see," he explained, not bothering to turn around this time, "the stories say that with the right sacrifice at the right time, the Glade can do something extraordinary. They say it can bring back the dead," he allowed that to hang in the air for a while, as he felt that unfathomable place come closer and closer.

"The sacrifice must take place at the height of a bright blue moon," he continued and nodded upwards. "Not long now, not long at all." *Just over an hour left.*

"In order to bring someone back, you need a lock of their hair." Absently, he fumbled in the inner pocket of his coat, producing a tarnished tin case and flicking it open. Maria did not bother to look inside before he closed it again. "The catch is that it must have been cut off before their death. They are revived exactly as they were at the moment of its severance." Carefully he replaced it next to his heart.

"As a young boy, I saw people that I loved die and I was somewhat taken with this story," he was in full flow now, recollecting personal memories in a way he never could among his men. "I started collecting locks of hair from those I cared about, just in case. And then the war happened, I had to grow up quickly and I had no time for stories." He laughed quietly and shook his head. "But in the last few years, I had reason to think of it again, to use my considerable resources to locate this place. It's funny, of all of the locks of hair I collected; I never thought I'd use this one."

He realized the cord was taut and when he looked back at her, Maria was trying to run away again. He shook his head, allowing a little more slack on the leash to give the illusion of success before slowly reeling it back in. "I suppose you must struggle, even knowing it is pointless," he conceded. "Very well, we're nearly there."

It was true. It felt like a beacon of light, shining out from the foliage ahead. It was hard to believe she could not sense it too. In just a few moments more, they would be there, and he felt he should tell her the truth before they arrived, even though he was enjoying her misery.

"Other than the moon and the lock of hair, there is one other requirement for the resurrection to succeed," he explained. He stopped and looked back at her bloodshot gaze. "The sacrifice must go to their death entirely of their own free will."

There was a moment and as this sunk in he saw Maria's puzzlement. "No, it wouldn't work to force you with pain or threats to your loved ones. Believe me, if I could, I would. There is no way I could make you genuinely want to lay down your life, so your death would be pointless."

He sighed. "That's why you're not here to be sacrificed." Her frown returned; her hatred tempered with mistrust. "You're here to be a witness," he explained. "I will be the sacrifice."

And with that, giving her no time to comprehend, he pressed forward, dragging her through the last bushes and into the Glade.

* * *

Even without Cain's sensitivity to it, Maria could tell it was a place of great power. The clearing was perhaps the size of a village square but almost perfectly circular and totally enclosed. No gaps marred the perimeter of trees and ferns but the otherwise smooth ground was pocked with a handful of jutting rocks.

The canopies overhead stretched inwards, blocking out most of the moonlight and leaving only a single, wide shaft to illuminate the structure at the centre of the clearing. From this distance, she could not tell its exact nature; twisted and as tall as a man, she assumed it was a great stump but there was no sign of a fallen tree.

Most astonishing about this place was the lighting; the Glade was far too well illuminated for the meager shaft of moonlight. Her hairs slowly started to stand on end as she realized that the centerpiece itself seemed to glow.

Finally, she turned to her captor. To her disgust, he was already looking at her, drinking in her reaction. She suppressed a shudder.

"Now, I'm going to remove your gag," he explained. "I'm sure you're smart enough to understand screaming and shouting will achieve nothing. In fact, it would only result in the gag being reapplied," he tilted his head. "...*tighter.*"

She nodded slowly, aware that if he was telling the truth and she played along, she should come out of this alive. Of course, she had no reason to trust him.

As the gag fell away, she started panting, relishing the increased oxygen flow. Catching his eye, she saw he was expecting something of her. Probably gratitude.

Instead, she summoned up the foulest curse word she knew.

He looked stunned for a second and then a grin, almost genuine, broke out across his features before he burst into laughter.

"Wonderful," he exclaimed. "Good, kind, generous and utterly foul-mouthed. What fun my men would have had with you."

"You're disgusting," she shot back.

"I never denied it," he agreed. "Oh, he'll like you."

She frowned at the comment but refused to be thrown. "You made me fear for my life. Why? For fun?"

"Pretty much," he shrugged. "Come now. Would you deny me my last little pleasure in this life?" she answered him with a cold look. He sighed. "Well, you know the truth now."

He casually walked over to the nearest rock and leaned against it. Maria glanced again at the central structure and then back at him.

"And that's what I'm supposed to believe? That you're willingly going to sacrifice yourself to resurrect someone from the dead?"

He nodded. "That's basically it, yes."

She shook her head. "Who?" She considered the matter, "Someone you killed?"

He looked at her uneasily and shook his head. "Someone I lost."

She blew air from her nose. "Is that meant to make me feel sorry for you? I've lost a lot of people too. Mostly at the hands of your men."

"I know," he shrugged. "And I don't care."

She gave him the same hate-filled look as when she had been gagged, but kept her peace. "A lover?" she asked. For some reason he seemed to find that funny. "Family?"

"All you need to know is that it's someone I let down and a much better person than I am."

"And I'm here to witness this."

"More than that. Once he's back, he'll need you to look after him, to get him out of this forest and to help him find a life for himself."

She was taken aback. "And what makes you think that I'll do this little favor for you? What makes you think I won't just leave him to rot?"

He sighed. "Come on now Maria. You know the answer to that question."

When she thought about it, it was obvious. "Because I helped Ethan, even though he was one of your men."

"Precisely."

"But he hadn't done anything to me, not himself. Whereas you've kidnapped me, dragged me here, threatened my life, gloated...."

"I never actually threatened your life," he stated mildly. "I let you infer."

"I have every reason to leave this person, out of spite!"

"But you won't and I'll tell you why. He's an innocent, a mere child. If you were a bad person, a vindictive person, you might leave him here to spite me; but that's not you. You're a good, kind person, so you will help him, despite it being exactly what I want. That may infuriate you but you know it's the truth."

She shook in anger at his certainty, straining uselessly against her bonds but could only reluctantly acknowledge—he was right. She would not leave a child there, no matter how much she hated her captor. She slumped down.

"You could have brought one of your men. Even in your line of work you must have *someone* you can trust."

"Yes," he said slowly, considering Jacob. "But I don't want the boy to be raised with any attachment to the taint of my life. In fact, I wanted to entrust him to someone positively disgusted with me."

"Well, in that case you've certainly chosen well," she agreed, with an icy smile.

"It may be best that you not tell him about me. Make up whatever you need to. Just make sure he lives an honest life."

"I can't promise that," she stated honestly.

"I know. But I know that you will try."

Silence descended but now Maria was fiercely curious. "Alright, Cain," she demanded, relishing the chance to spit out his name. "I'll protect him. But I find it hard to believe that you—*you!*—possibly the most depraved bandit ever known, would lay down your life for anyone. Tell me *why*. You owe me that much."

He looked down, collecting his thoughts. She noticed his hand idly feeling the shape of the case in his coat pocket, reassuring himself it was still there. Finally, he looked up again.

"About a year ago," he explained, "I visited a medicine man that checked me over and told me I only had a few more years to live. He told me to expect certain pains and I have experienced them just as he described. I believe he was telling the truth."

He looked thoughtful. "I started to consider my legacy and I didn't like the way it looked."

She was amazed. "It took imminent death for you to realize the harm you were causing?"

"I never used to care. But when I thought about other people taking over the empire I built and doing the things I do...."

"It just seemed so much more grim when you wouldn't be the one to reap the benefits," she supplied.

"Exactly! And I decided, if I was to die, then it should mean something. You may have trouble believing this but after all of this time, I found that I wanted redemption."

She looked at him, uncomprehendingly, for a long time. "You want to be...redeemed?"

"I do."

"By saving one life?" she almost laughed and then started to get angry. "You think one life is enough to redeem you, for the countless innocents you've killed and had killed? For the brutality, the fear, the misery you've brought into our lives?" her voice grew louder.

He ignored her tone. "As I said, I grew up with those stories about the Glade. Some part of me always thought this would be how I should go; on my own terms, doing something noble."

She snorted. "So this is redemption? Sacrificing the few years you have left, to save someone you loved? That doesn't sound like balancing the scales; it sounds like holding them in place and hoping no one notices."

"Perhaps. We'll have to see. Maybe you'll change your mind about that."

Maria shook her head in despair. "If you'd really wanted to turn things around, you could have dismantled your *empire* and done the world a favor."

He smiled unpleasantly. "Oh, but I've done that too," he explained. "I had separate meetings with two of my most belligerent and ambitious lieutenants, telling each that they were my chosen replacement. Within days they will clash and start tearing apart everything I have worked for, each believing the other is a treacherous liar," he actually seemed pleased with himself.

Maria did not know how to react. "So you cheerfully betrayed everyone you've commanded and worked with?"

His grin faded, "Would you condemn me for that?"

"Well no, not in the circumstances. I suppose for a man like you, morally ambiguous is a step up."

He nodded and took a deep breath. "So you see...that might go part of the way. And while one life won't balance the scales, all of the good this boy goes on to do will also be to my credit."

She was not sure she agreed but she did not wish to argue details with him. She loathed to ask such a question but finally went ahead. "But are you sorry?"

"What do you mean?" he asked, interested.

"Do you regret how you've spent your life and the harm you've caused all of those people?"

He seemed to think about this for a long time. "No, I don't. I've lived well for the last twenty years. If I had stuck to what was right, I would probably have lived a life of suffering and died without making any impact on the world. No, I can't wish that I had chosen that path instead."

Maria went to speak but he cut her off, "But ask yourself which you would rather: that I was regretful or that I did something about it?"

"In theory, I think both are required." Now the adrenaline was wearing off, she could feel her exhaustion, the half-sleep of the drugs and the night's march through the forest catching up with her. "Look, is this going to happen any time soon?"

"Yes, it is. Don't worry, we won't miss it."

* * *

They settled into an uncomfortable silence. The height of the moon was fast approaching and Cain considered what still needed to be said. Reaching into his pockets, he started taking out a number of small bronze ornaments and putting them on the floor in a pile.

"Once it's over, you should take these with you; I'll leave some in my pockets and the boy can have my clothes. These are the charms that will protect you from some of the forest's less savory inhabitants. And these...."

He had retrieved his pouch and extracted a beetle from it. Maria grimaced as he showed it to her.

"Don't chew; swallow it whole. The longer it takes to die, the longer you'll be sensitive to its power. The whole forest is alive with it; just head for where there is none and you'll get to the edge."

He had not been paying attention while he talked to her and she saw the beetle wriggle from his fingers and fall to the ground. He looked down as it desperately scuttled for freedom, frowned, and then suddenly stepped forward onto it, grinding it with his foot. He looked back and caught Maria's expression. "Don't worry, you'll find plenty more in the pouch."

Maria shuddered. "I won't swallow any of those. I just won't."

"I suppose you may not need to," he conceded. "The forest may well let you leave without trouble. But just in case, take them," he put the pouch on the pile. "Between this and the charms you should be able to get back to the world outside without much trouble."

She warily looked over the pouch on the ground, checking that it was tightly sealed, before grimly nodding to him.

As he felt the power in the air start to increase, Cain's heart began to beat faster than he would admit. "Now, let's have a closer look, shall we?" he asked with false levity.

He did not need to use the cord's special power to bring Maria along with him. She was obviously curious to see the centerpiece, as curious as he had been the first time he had been here.

As they approached it, he looked over to see the glow it cast on her. Too pure to be eerie, it was still disconcerting. Not as strange as the object itself though.

From a distance, it might have appeared to be a twisted stump; up close, it looked like no vegetation on the planet. There was no line where a tree might have sheared off. The whole mass was smooth, dipping and bulging but unbroken. More importantly, it had entirely the wrong color and texture for wood: off-white and ungrained, admitting no flaw or crack, no vine or moss.

To Cain's new sense, it was almost overwhelming. The heat of its power burned angrily, emanating up from deep beneath the ground. Given its appearance, he caught himself starting to think of it as the exposed end of a bone, jutting right out of the earth itself. But that was of course ridiculous; nothing had bones that big. He swallowed, ignoring his nerves. "Quite something, isn't it?"

Maria said nothing, keeping as far away from the twisted fixture as the cord would allow. Cain nodded to himself, understanding. Out in the world this kind of power tended to be controlled, sanitized. Charms and potions kept it mostly predictable. But here was its wild edge, a channel to vast, terrible reserves. If it were to be released in the wrong way, there would be no telling what it could do to those in its path. If that happened, Cain would be lucky merely to die.

The air had a thickness to it, a power-tinge to the very shaft of light in which they bathed. The height of a bright blue moon was imminent and he needed to be ready. Carefully he took out the tin case, gingerly extracting the lock of hair within. Maria stepped closer, nervous interest in her gaze.

"That's old hair," she stated calmly. "It looks dull and brittle."

"It doesn't matter. As I said before, he should be revived exactly as he was when the hair was cut from him."

"After all of this time? How will he deal with losing those years?"

"I don't know," he admitted. "I hope you can make it better for him. Stop him from trying to seek out what he has lost, if you can," he felt suddenly sad but tried to hide it from his captive. He had no need for her pity.

Turning, he carefully placed the hair in a small alcove towards the top of the structure. "There," he whispered. "Now we just wait. Not long to go."

They stood in awkward silence, which Cain finally broke by fiddling with the end of the cord round his arm. After a few seconds, it came off and he let it fall to the ground. Maria looked up at him, startled.

"You look surprised. Don't be. The cord is attuned to me, so once I die it will fall off you and you'll be completely free. If you wanted you could run away now but I imagine you are curious enough to stay and watch what happens." It pleased him she no longer showed any signs of wanting to escape. "I would recommend taking the cord with you. You won't be able to use it without getting it attuned to you by a specialist but it should fetch a decent price. Same with the charms. Consider it payment for your services."

She flashed him an unfriendly look but relented. "I will."

"Right," he sighed. "I think it's just about time."

As if to confirm his words, the air shimmered. Maria took three long steps back.

"You should be fine out of the moonlight," Cain reassured her.

Then something occurred to him and he started taking off his boots. Without the slightest embarrassment, he swiftly stripped down, piling his clothes before him. He saw Maria conflicted between the urge to turn away for modesty's sake and the desire to keep him where she could see him. "Nothing you haven't seen before, I'm sure."

She refused to dignify that with an answer. Instead, she looked him firmly in the face. "I still hate you," she stated. Cain imagined she was emboldened by the fact he no longer had the cord to jerk her around.

"I would expect nothing less," he sneered. "I'm a thief, a murderer, a rapist. The world is better off without me." To his irritation, he realized he was stating this to reassure himself rather than her.

"I don't care about your redemption."

"That's fine. All I ask is that you care about the boy. And I know that you will."

"I think I might teach him to hate you."

It was clearly meant to sting but Cain allowed himself to take it seriously. "If you want to Maria, then that's fine. Just keep him good, remember."

Her defiant eyes softened. "I'll try."

And then the moon reached its height. Instantly the shaft of moonlight changed its nature, a powerful, watery blue mixed with streaks of white radiance. At the height of a bright blue moon, the whole world below is bathed in energy. In this place, that meant the conduit down into the planet was awakened. Cain's bare skin practically burned in the glow.

He saw Maria retreating, back to where they had left the charms, still watching the events unfold. He nodded to her but could not tell whether she had seen. He turned back to the structure, which seemed almost alive with the fluctuating illumination twisting before him. He knew this period of grace would last only a minute or so.

He reached the squirming mass, feeling it for the flaw, which must now be there. He found it, a jagged edge, grasped it and pulled. A shard came off in his hand, just as the tales had all said. He allowed himself to turn it once in his hands, admiring the beauty and then steeled himself, grasping it.

He thrust the sharp end into his heart.

Immediately blinding white light pulsed behind his eyes. He had a moment of visual clarity to observe the blood pumping out over his hands, and he reached to place them on the structure before falling forward into it. His blood smeared over the ivory surface, completing the connection. His vision gone, he felt his life judder to a halt.

* * *

Maria shuddered in horror as she saw Cain stab himself but refused to look away as he fell forward. As he connected with the structure the moonlight went crazy, streaks of power obscuring her view as the ivory turned brilliant white. Finally, too bright, she had to shield her eyes.

With no noise, no drama, the moon passed from the height of the sky and the shaft of light returned to normal, as it had been when they had first arrived at the Glade. Immediately her bindings fell from her, exactly as Cain had described. She stayed still, nerves still screaming, stretching her arms. Then she stepped forward softly, taking her time in case this was only a temporary reprieve. Soon enough she overcame her caution and, with a deep breath, stepped into the light.

Cain was gone, but there was the pile of his clothes, completely untouched. Beyond them was the structure, just as it had been before...except, *something* was different. She started to shake as she realized it had a new bulge to it, indistinguishable from the rest of the mass, exactly where Cain had come to rest. It had claimed its price.

She was still taking this in when a movement in the corner of her eye startled her. Her head shot up and she met the gaze of a face looking round the side of the structure. She took a breath.

"Hello there," she managed.

"Hello." A boy, pre-pubescent from the sound of it. Just as Cain had said. "Um, I don't have any clothes."

Maria laughed nervously. "Well, don't worry. There are some here for you."

Carefully she retrieved Cain's clothes and passed them round to the boy, making a show of looking the other way. *His* modesty she would respect.

A minute or so later the boy stepped out, his new tunic, trousers and coat comically big on him. She considered offering to swap with him; who was there in the forest to complain about him wearing women's clothes? Then she remembered Cain in his last moments and had no desire to strip anywhere near the Glade.

The boy was looking at the structure, some kind of awe on his face. "This must all be extremely strange," Maria started, wondering how to explain. "This place, well, it's...."

"This is the Glade," the boy whispered, almost reverently. He looked at her. "It really exists!" he shook his head. "Just now, just a minute ago, I cut a lock of my hair to save. But I didn't think...I didn't really think...."

He paused, so lost in thought that he didn't seem to notice Maria's eyes widening. "Can you tell me," he finally asked, "how I died?"

The curious pleading was so full of innocence. Maria sunk to the ground, exhausted and defeated. Cain's redemption was complete. It was written in his face.

THE END

Baby Girl
(Paranormal)

By

Nu Yang

Julia McKinley's night of studying demons was interrupted by a phone call from her father.

"Chicken or fish?" he asked.

"What?" she kept her attention on the illustration of the Pukwudgie troll on her MacBook screen instead of the brown leather-bound book next to her, which she should have been reading. A number eight on its side—the Egyptian symbol for infinity—was the only design on the large book's cover.

"I thought I'd pick you up some tacos from Willie's," her father said. "You must be hungry by now."

The time on her laptop told her it was almost nine. As soon as she realized how late in the night it was, her stomach growled, reminding her she had missed dinner. She leaned back in her chair at the kitchen table. "You buying?"

Her father chuckled. "Of course, Baby Girl."

"Then I want steak tacos."

Her father laughed.

It warmed her heart to hear the sound. Since her father left rehab two months ago, she believed he was heading in the right direction. He hadn't touched any alcohol in almost six months and he regularly attended his AA meetings and met with his sponsor, who had helped him get a job working maintenance at an apartment complex. Julia was proud of him for wanting to get better.

Her gaze drifted to the glossy photograph stuck on her refrigerator with a purple and gold L.A. Lakers magnet. Her father, with his black hair, mustache and dark eyes, smiled brightly at the camera. His arm wrapped around her mother, a petite woman with long black hair and smooth cocoa skin. Family members always told Julia she looked just like her mother. Maybe that's why after her mother died, her father had distanced himself from her. She could only watch helplessly as he turned to alcohol to make the pain go away. Now, she wanted to make sure whenever he had a problem, he would come to her instead.

"Are you watching TV?" her father asked.

"I'm working on a project for work," she clicked her mouse to navigate to another web page. "Someone came into the library today wanting to know about Native American trolls."

"Well, take a break and turn on your TV."

"Why? What's on?" Julia switched her iPhone to her other ear and moved from her kitchen to her living room. She plopped down on the couch next to her gray Siamese cat. Lulu lifted her blue eyes at Julia, as though annoyed her nap had been interrupted. Julia used the remote to turn on her flatscreen. "CNN, I assume." Her father tuned in daily to the twenty-four hour news outlet.

"That bastard Salazar is talking to Piers Morgan," her father said.

When Julia flipped to the channel, she saw Gideon Salazar sitting across from the interviewer, smiling with his teeth. Julia had only been a few months old when the supernatural *También* came out into the open thirty years ago. Named after the Spanish word for *also*, the *También* no longer wanted to hide, as though ashamed of their natures. They wanted peace, unity, freedom and a chance to prosper and raise their families like humans. Some of them stuck to that plan, working nine to five office jobs and settling in a nice house. But the majority of them kept on doing what they did best—cause chaos.

Salazar, the jaguar shapeshifter, had been one of the first supernatural beings to go public. He was also the first to use the phrase *También* during a press conference. The media used it so often it unofficially became the group's name. From what Julia saw from the interviews he gave, Salazar loved the spotlight. He was always handsomely dressed in a suit with his slicked-back hair, olive skin and soft brown eyes; but when he spoke, his stern voice commanded everyone's attention. There was talk he might run for Congress in the next election year.

Piers was asking Salazar about the recent riot at a demon-owned nightclub in Seattle, which had resulted in five dead demons.

"We do not condone this type of behavior," Salazar told Piers. "Hate crimes on demons have doubled this past year. Each unresolved case is a blemish in our justice system."

The screen cut to Al Sharpton, who in recent years had taken it upon himself to stand up for También rights.

"I don't know why anyone else can't see it," her father said. "Salazar is a phony."

"Like every other politician in this country," Julia added.

"You got a point there," she heard her father's keys jiggle. "Listen, I'll go grab some tacos from Willie's-"

"Remember—steak."

"Yeah, yeah...I'll go grab your *steak* tacos and come over to your place, all right?"

"Sounds good," she stretched her arms over her head. Forget studying. Spending the rest of the night with her dad, Willie's tacos and a bad sci-fi TV movie sounded much better.

"Okay Baby Girl, I'll see—hold on, someone's at the door," she heard the floorboards creak as her father crossed his wooden floor, then— "What the-" Her father cried out and there was a loud clang as he dropped his phone.

"Dad?" Julia jumped from the couch. A startled Lulu leapt with her. "Dad, what's going on?"

"Grab him." A man's deep voice came from the other line.

"Dad!" But the call ended. She quickly hit send to redial her father's number. No one picked up. "Shit!"

For a moment, she couldn't move inside her apartment. Four white walls closed in on her and Salazar's voice from the TV screen faded.

"Grab him."

The unknown voice sent a shiver down her back. Someone had taken her father. Someone, who sounded dangerous. Her hands curled into fists at her side. She raced back into her kitchen and grabbed her leather-bound book. For trouble like this, she needed something more old school. She ran to her door, stepped into a pair of tennis shoes and grabbed her car keys.

As she headed to her parked Honda Civic, she called a number. "Hey," she pleaded when the other person answered. "Can you meet me at my dad's place in ten minutes? Oh, and bring your book. "

* * *

Located in between Los Angeles and San Diego, Stockland was the typical Southern California city, with beaches, tourists and supernatural beings. It only took a couple of years before the También migrated from the big cities and began to populate suburbia.

Julia raced her Honda down the 405 with her windows open. The wind blowing at her face didn't help; her heart pounded, her palms sweated and her jumbled mind searched for answers. She needed a clear head, which was why she had called Sam Harper and told him what had happened. Sam was a librarian like her and he was a damned good one. He worked with the local police departments on solving cases involving the También, because he seemed to know everything about them. Julia wasn't sure if his fascination with them was professional or morbid but right now, she needed his brain.

When she arrived at her father's house Sam was already waiting for her. He got out of his black jeep dressed in sweats and a T-shirt, carrying his book. Standing more than six feet tall, he looked like a giant compared to her smaller frame. So maybe she needed him for his muscles too. She met Sam five years ago, after she graduated university and started her first job at Stockland's Public Library. She was surprised to find someone like Sam, with his dreadlocks and steel gray eyes, working as a librarian. She asked him once why he had become one. He simply said, "I like books." Just the plain, honest truth. From then on, she knew she could trust him.

"Thanks for coming," she said, approaching him with her book tucked under her arm.

His face softened. "We should go to the police, Jules."

"No offense Sam, but I don't have time to wait around for cops to dust for fingerprints."

She moved toward her father's house. It wasn't the same one where she had grown up with her parents but it was still a home to her. She loved coming over after work, for dinner and CNN. Her father's white Chevy pick-up truck sat in the driveway. She gestured to the front door and Sam followed cautiously. She didn't own a gun and the only self-defense moves she knew came from a class she took a year before, but she could recite a few spells from memory, including one that would make cockroaches crawl out of someone's mouth. That might come in handy.

Julia turned the knob and the door opened for her. She scanned the living room but only saw the second-hand furniture she and her father had picked out together after he returned home from rehab. Silver moonlight trickled in through the open blinds. She flipped on the switch and noticed her father's set of keys on the floor. She knelt down to pick them up. Her fingers traced over the photo keychain of her mother holding her as a baby.

"Do you smell that?" Sam asked behind her.

She sniffed. The air reeked of rotten eggs. "Sulfur," she rose and studied the room again. This time, she saw more than furniture; she saw a crime scene.

She walked over to the coffee table, clearing off her father's copy of the *Los Angeles Times*. "What do you know about retrieval spells?" she set her book on the table.

"I know whoever casts those spells is pretty damned crazy," Sam said. She ignored his comment and placed her hand on the infinity symbol on the book's cover.

When librarians received their books, they picked out their own symbol representing themselves, making each book unique. Her book's flap opened with her touch. Librarians had a blood-bond with their books, like a magical library card granting them access to the pages. For librarians who graduated from university, it was their way to safeguard their knowledge, so no one with the wrong intentions could get access to what was inside; they filled each book with their own studies.

Julia's hands hovered over the pages and they began to turn one by one. By using her bond, she didn't need a table of contents to find the spell she needed.

Sam sighed and sat beside her. "What kind of retrieval spell are you looking for?"

"A moment in time," she said, watching the pages turn.

He placed his hand on the Japanese character for "brave and valiant." His book opened and the pages flipped, searching for the spell.

The sound of turning pages echoed in the quiet house. Julia lowered her hands and waited.

Please. She closed her eyes and breathed in deep. *Please help me find what happened to my father.*

Silence filled the room. She opened her eyes to find both books open to a single page: "To Retrieve a Moment in Time."

She met Sam's steady gaze and together, they lowered their heads and read the spell.

* * *

Ten minutes later, Julia was prepared to find who had knocked on her father's door. She sat on the wooden floor in the front corridor and lit two candles with a lighter. She placed the keychain with the picture of her mother and herself as a baby next to the candles and placed her hands inches above the warm flames. The heat prickled the inside of her palms. Sam watched from a distance, tight-lipped with his arms crossed.

"We're librarians Jules. We find spells, not cast them," he said. "What makes you think this will work?"

"Because it has to."

Because she knew of no other way.

With a deep breath, she recited the spell. "Take these remnants from the past. Show us what was seen last. Ashes to ashes, dust to dust. Into your memory, I give you my trust." The candle flames turned bright blue and a chill shot down her back.

"Jules...." Sam took a step forward with his arms at his sides.

"It's okay," she said, catching her breath. "I'm okay." She wasn't sure if she was trying to convince Sam—or herself.

She kept her hands over the blue flames and repeated the words. This time, a blast of cold air slapped her in the face. Sam jumped back as the temperature dropped.

"You need to stop," he said.

Her heavy breathing echoed in the quiet room. Maybe Sam was right; she was just a librarian, not a spell caster.

She lowered her hands to her lap. "It didn't-" she hunched over as a sharp pain dug itself into the back of her head.

"Julia?" Sam rushed to her side.

She groaned as another painful jolt slammed in between her eyes. She convulsed in Sam's arms and her eyes rolled back until she saw the ceiling.

Grab him!

This time, it wasn't her memory speaking.

* * *

Julia stood in her father's front hallway. Her father was on his knees, holding his face. His car keys and his cell phone lay on the floor next to him.

"Dad, what's going on?" Her voice screamed from the other line.

Julia looked up to the doorway to see a large figure enter. He looked human with his blue jeans and hooded sweatshirt, but then she noticed the two black horns jutting out from his temples. She couldn't place his species but he had to belong to some kind of bull-spirit hybrid. He picked up her father's cell phone and flipped the cover closed, disconnecting the call. Then, his aqua blue eyes focused on her fallen father.

"Stay away from him," she hurried to her father's side, but when she tried to help him stand, her hands went right through his body as if it was a projection image. Trembling, she watched as the bull demon hoisted her father to his feet.

Her father's left cheek was red, as though he had just been punched. "What do you want?" he asked.

Another figure stepped into the doorway. Julia recognized the pale-faced demon right away from the local evening news. Trich was a fire spirit known for working in the criminal underworld. His explosive rage had a reputation on both sides of the law. Even though Trich wore an expensive suit and fedora hat, she could still smell the strong stench of sulfur on him.

"From you? Nothing." Trich said. His goon handed him her father's phone. "You're just bait," he pocketed the phone and motioned for the guard to take her father away.

Julia jumped to her feet. "Let him go!" Her pleas went nowhere.

The guard slammed a fist into her father's gut. Julia felt the wind sucked out of her as he groaned. The demon twisted her father's arms behind his back and led him out of his home. Trich lingered in the door, scanning the interior with a sneer. A flash of ruby glinted in his coal-black eyes.

"You bastard!" Julia tried to grab the demon but her hands went right through him. She let out a frustrated cry, upset she couldn't hurt him the way he was hurting her father. As he turned off the lights and exited the house, she raced after him. Her legs moved as if they were stuck in quicksand. She watched her father get stuffed into the backseat of a black van. "Dad!" But she wasn't fast enough. Everything became blurry as her vision narrowed. The pain between her eyes returned, but this time, it felt like hot lava poured into their sockets. She grabbed her head and screamed.

* * *

Something cool touched Julia's forehead. Her eyes flew open and she sat up, gasping for air.

"Take it easy." Sam pushed her back down to the ground. He wiped a damp towel across her sweaty forehead. "Just breathe."

She tried to inhale but each time she did, her chest ached, not just from the effects of the spell but also from what she had just witnessed. A demon had kidnapped her father! *You're just bait.* But for what and for who?

"I saw what happened Sam," she closed her eyes, but she could see her father's battered body. "I saw who took my dad. A demon named Trich. He works-"

Sam stopped wiping her face. "I know who *he* is." his voice grew cold. "The cops are always trying to bust him on something but the charges never stick. What does Trich want with your dad?"

"I don't know," she opened her eyes and slowly sat up. She was still in the corridor in front of the doorway. The two candles had gone cold.

"Here." Sam slipped her father's keychain into her hand.

She swallowed the lump in her throat as she looked at the photograph her father treasured so much. How could it be possible, that just an hour ago they were talking about dinner over the phone?

The phone.

"I need my phone," she said.

"It's on the counter." Sam left her to grab it. "You gonna call the police now?"

"Trich said my dad was bait. I don't want to put him in more danger by calling the police."

"Then, what are you going to do Jules? We've already cast a retrieval spell. How far are you going to take this on your own?" he stood over her with her phone in his hand. "Now that we know someone like Trich is involved, this is getting too dangerous."

She looked up at him without blinking. "You can leave if you want Sam, but this is my *father*."

He narrowed his gray eyes but handed her the phone.

"Thank you." she called her father's number. With each ring, her heart quickened. *Pick up. Please pick up!* The line clicked as someone answered. "Dad?"

"Hello Julia." Trich's velvety voice sent a shiver through her body. Her name must have shown up as the incoming call.

She pretended she didn't know whom she was talking to. "Who is this?" Sam crouched down beside her and she set the phone to speaker. "I'm looking for Leon McKinley."

"He's fine. I have one of my associates keeping him company." A muffled groan came from the background.

Julia struggled to keep her voice even. "What do you want?"

"Meet me at Mayhem in fifteen minutes and I can fill you in," Trich said.

Julia met Sam's hardened gaze. She knew if Trich were standing in front of Sam, her best friend would break the demon's nose.

"Willie's," she said.

Sam raised his brows and mouthed, "What?"

"If you want to fill me in, meet me at Willie's Tacos downtown," she told Trich. Willie's would be crowded with humans and También; if she had agreed to meet him at Mayhem, she knew they would outnumber her inside the popular demon nightclub.

"Fine," Trich said. "I could go for some fish tacos right now. I'll see you there and Julia, if you show up with any surprises, my associate has instructions on how to dispose of your father." With that, Trich ended the conversation.

She stared at the silent phone. Her stomach knotted, bile rising in her throat. She stood on shaky legs.

Sam put his hands on his hips. "Are we seriously going to meet Trich for tacos right now?"

"Not you," her voice sounded hollow, "just me."

"What are you talking about?"

"You heard him. No surprises," she walked over to the coffee table and picked up her book. "I can't risk it Sam, I'm sorry." She headed for the door when he grabbed her arm.

"And I can't risk you going after Trich alone. What if it's a trap? What if he knows you're a librarian and wants to use you for something?"

Everything inside her dropped into dead weight. "Then I guess it's my fault Trich took my dad." She felt as helpless as when her father's alcoholism took him away from her.

"Don't say that," Sam said with a shake of his head.

She pulled her arm from his hold, struggling to keep her tears from spilling. "Don't come with me Sam. I need to do this part on my own."

With a deep frown, he stepped back.

"I'll call you later," she raced into the darkness, clutching her book and father's keychain.

* * *

Julia turned down Main Street in her Honda. Downtown Stockland had a few skyscrapers that housed businesses, banks and hotels, but since it was a Saturday night, the streets filled with a younger crowd. Girls in short skirts and heels; guys roaring their engines down the street in their souped-up Civics. She drove past the long line in front of the popular Mayhem dance club. The También, with their human buddies, waited to cross the velvet rope to get into the exclusive venue, owned by millionaire and music producer Conrad Jones.

Conrad was already a famous Hollywood name before he came out as a werewolf ten years ago. She remembered nights during university when she stumbled into the club with her girlfriends, including one who was a fairy, dressed in bright colors with their hair and make-up done. Then, they danced with their bodies pressed against other bodies—some with heartbeats, and some without.

A handful of human protestors, across the street from Mayhem, raised their picket signs. GO BACK TO HELL. HUMANS ONLY. JUSTICE IN SEATTLE. If they weren't careful they *would* end up in a riot like at that Seattle club. Julia didn't know what it was like to live in a world without the También. Her father had told her stories about her grandparents not being able to sit in the front of a bus or drink from a water fountain just because of the color of their skin. Now instead of human rights, it was También rights that were the new movement.

But what right did Trich have in kidnapping her father?

She pulled into Willie's parking lot. The popular taco shop was usually filled with people coming from the beach and kids from her alma mater, UC-Stockland. She entered the restaurant and scanned the place. A group of elves, with their tall lean frames, pale skin, clear blue eyes and pointy ears, waited for their order. A Cyclops in a Hawaiian shirt eyeballed her as she walked past him. Loud laughter exploded from a table of college students, mixed with humans and También.

"Damn. You're a good-looking chocolate milkshake." Trich approached her with a grin. "You look just like the picture your daddy carries in his wallet. I'm Trich."

She cringed, not only from him being a creep but also from the overwhelming smell of sulfur filling her nostrils. The same expensive suit and fedora hat she had seen in her spell didn't do anything to mask his true nature.

"I got a table by the window," he said, "...and some tacos waiting for us. You like steak, right?" he winked.

She narrowed her eyes but followed him. Just as he said, there were two orders of tacos waiting for them. Despite her still-empty stomach, she didn't touch her food.

Trich took a large bite from his fish taco. "Delicious," he licked the salsa from his fingers.

She wanted to take the fork on the table and stab it through his hand. Instead, she sat back and crossed her arms. "Okay, I'm here. Fill me in."

"You want to get your dad back, right? All you have to do is a favor for me," he pointed to her plate. "Don't let that food go to waste darling."

"Why would I want to do a favor for you? I've heard the stories. Money laundering. Theft. Murder. What makes you think I won't go to the police?"

He finished his taco and wiped his thin lips with a napkin. "Because you're sitting right here across from me," he turned his head to the left, then to the right. "And I don't see any cops around, do you?"

He was calling her bluff but that didn't intimidate her. Maybe it was because they were talking in a crowded area or maybe it was because she didn't have time to be scared. She had to save her father—and if that included working for a demon, she would do it.

"What kind of favor do you want?" she asked.

"I have an associate who needs help reversing a spell. Last night, he went to collect a debt from a client—a gypsy—but when she couldn't pay up, he had no choice but to show her the consequences," he took another bite of his taco and slurped it down with a Coke. "You heard about the fire down here last night, at the bakery?"

Julia shook her head. She had worked late at the library and crashed right into bed when she got home and today, she had studied until her father's phone call.

"It was at Sweet Treats, just down the block. The gypsy was the owner," Trich said. "You see, she wasn't cooperating, so my associate had to teach her a lesson. He set the bakery on fire but before he did, the bitch put a curse on him. This morning, all his hair had fallen out."

"What happened to the owner?" Julia asked, even though she already knew the dreaded answer.

"She got what she deserved," Trich said, taking another sip of his Coke. "Bitch went up in flames with her cookies and cakes."

Julia felt lightheaded. She dug her nails in her palms to control herself from fleeing the table, because she couldn't stand to be around this monster for another minute.

"Her name was Emilie Balanescu and she was a member the Sinti Tribe," Trich said. "From what I gather, you know a great deal about the Romani people. I read your bio on the library's web page Julia. You studied the people and its language at university. As a *librarian*, it's your specialized department."

"So, this reversal spell is for your associate to get his hair back." Never mind that he had killed a woman and set her business on fire; all he cared about was his appearance. Now she felt like vomiting.

"Who knows what will fall off next?" Trich grabbed a steak taco from her plate. "This is a very important associate of mine. I gave him my word I would reverse the spell. If you do that for me, I give you my word your father will be returned to you."

"And I say your word means shit to me."

The ruby glint returned to his dark eyes. "Ah, *Baby Girl*, you should hear your father call out to you when he's in pain. It breaks my useless heart."

Anger electrified her body. She jumped to her feet, one hand on her fork. She was seconds from stabbing it into his neck.

"Careful Julia," Trich said. "You wouldn't want to draw any attention to us," he wrapped his hand around her wrist.

A moment later her entire arm felt like it was on fire. She let go of the fork but Trich kept his hold on her. The burning sensation traveled up and through her chest. She clenched her jaw to stop herself from screaming out in pain.

"I want to talk to my dad first," she hissed, sitting back down.

"He's fine."

Sweat trickled from her forehead. "I want to *talk to him.*"

He glared before releasing her. The pain vanished but the heat lingered. He took out his Blackberry and called a number. "Put Daddy on the phone," he handed the phone to Julia.

She put it to her ear. "Dad?"

"Baby Girl...." his voice sounded so weary.

"Don't worry. I'm going to get you out of there," she fought to keep her voice from cracking. "Just stay strong for me, okay?"

"You know how sorry I am about your mama, don't you? I never should have let your mother drive that night. She hated driving when it was dark out."

A knot formed in the middle of her chest. Unlike Trich, her heart could still feel. "Dad, don't—don't do that to yourself."

"I love you Baby Girl. Now go to the police. Tell them I can hear the ocean. I'm near the beach-"

"Gimme that." A gruff voice cut in before the call ended.

Julia sat dazed. She set the phone down and watched Trich finish his tacos as though this was a casual dinner meeting and not a matter of life and death.

"You have until midnight to reverse the spell," he said, finishing his Coke.

Midnight was only an hour and a half away. Ninety minutes to undo a gypsy's curse and save her father's life.

She got up and straightened her back "I'll find the spell for your associate and I'll find one for you too."

Trich raised a blond brow. "Is that a threat?" he asked in an amused tone.

Without saying anything else, she turned and left Willie's. The closer she got to her car, the more her legs wobbled. She swallowed the acidic taste in her mouth. When she slid into the driver's seat, she covered her face and gulped for air. Tears filled her eyes as her father's terrified voice flooded her mind.

Breathe, Julia, breathe.

She closed her eyes and wiped her wet cheeks. No more crying. Her time was precious now. She pulled out her iPhone and found Sam's name in her address book. Her finger paused over the number. This was her battle. She put the phone away and sped home.

* * *

When Julia returned to her apartment, it was 10:45. She rushed through her door with her book, ready to start her search for a reversal spell. From what Julia knew about the Sinti they kept to themselves, even among the tribe. Loners by nature, they had been reluctant to come out as spell casters thirty years ago but others, like Salazar, encouraged as many supernaturals to go public, in order to start a revolution. At times it felt like the revolution was still going.

Lulu greeted her in the living room with a soft meow. Her sleepy blue eyes looked up at Julia as though she could tell something was wrong.

"I can do this, right Lulu?" Julia said, sitting on the couch.

The cat jumped beside her and rubbed her soft fur against Julia's arm.

"Thanks." Julia stroked her companion behind the ear. She placed her left hand over the infinity symbol on the book cover and the pages came to life as it searched for something about the Sinti Tribe. Once again, her body lit up with pulsating energy. Lulu rubbed her head closer to Julia's warm skin.

The pages fluttered with each turn and came to a sudden stop. She lifted the book so she could see the picture, an illustration of a Sinti gypsy tribe member casting a spell on a person who had wronged her. According to the text, Sinti were known to use their enemy's weaknesses against them.

Julia narrowed her eyes. What did Trich's associate's hair have to do with his weakness?

As she contemplated the question, Lulu jerked her head up. She scurried off the couch and vanished into the kitchen. Julia lifted her head as well, listening for what had scared her cat. A large shadow passed outside her first-story window. She hurried to her front closet and grabbed the metal baseball bat her father had given her as a housewarming gift when she had moved out on her own. With the handle in her firm grasp, she opened the door, seconds away from swinging.

"Whoa!" Sam raised his arms to shield himself. "It's me Jules!"

Her heart pounded beneath her chest as she lowered her weapon. "What are you doing here?"

"You didn't call, so I got worried." his brows knitted. "What happened with Trich?"

She bit down on her bottom lip to stop it from shaking. She couldn't let her emotions take over again.

"You were right," she said, turning back into her apartment. "He wants to use me for something," she put the bat back in the closet.

Sam followed her in, closing the door behind him. "Like what?"

She showed him her book, the page still open on the picture of the Sinti woman cursing her enemy.

"He wants me to find a reversal spell on a gypsy curse," she said. "One that makes your hair fall out," she filled him in on Emilie Balanescu and her ninety-minute time limit as well.

Sam rubbed the back of his neck. "Jules, we can't do this alone."

"I know," she set the book back on the table and the pages turned at a rapid speed before settling on a spell.

Sam widened his eyes. "To conjure a spirit? What are you thinking?"

"The only person who can break this spell is Emilie Balanescu and she's dead."

"Fuck Jules, I watched you do a retrieval spell and go meet a demon but I'm not going to let you do *this*," he grabbed her book.

Julia gasped. "Sam, *don't!*"

His face tightened as the book emitted a blue light. Soon, the light flooded his body and the book's warding spell attacked him like a taser. He collapsed to the ground, shaking with each violent shock.

She yanked her book from his grasp. Back in its owner's possession, the blue light dissipated but the damage had already been done. She put her hands on Sam's chest to hold him down with each convulsion. Why would Sam do this to himself? Every librarian knew each book came with a protective warding spell.

"Sam?" It took all her strength to keep his strong frame from leaping off the floor. "Please, stop...."

He pursed his lips together. "Sp—spell-"

Julia shook her head. "What spell?"

Sam shut his eyes and he began to chant at a feverish pace. She leaned in and heard bits and pieces of Romani. She pulled back, her mouth open and eyes wide. He had taken her book in order to bond with the conjuring spell so he could perform it himself. He shuddered under her hands for another moment. Then, his body went still.

"Sam?" she held in her breath and pressed her knuckles against his hot forehead. "Can you hear me?"

His eyes fluttered open.

She finally exhaled and wrapped her arms around him. He lifted one arm to return the embrace. She pressed her face against his stubbly cheek, breathing in the salty scent of sweat and the faint smell of his woodsy cologne. When she lifted her head, Sam's soft gray eyes stared at her. Another surge of energy filled the space between them but it wasn't from either library book.

Sam's gaze drifted behind her. "Look."

She sat up and turned. A heavy-set woman wearing a long flowered dress and an apron stood in her living room. Her dark hair was pulled back in a loose bun and her brown eyes moved from Julia to Sam.

Julia stood to meet Emilie Balanescu. The air around the woman smelled like frosting and cinnamon.

"Emilie, my name is Julia McKinley," she said.

The other woman tilted her head.

"I need your help," she took another careful step toward the spirit. "A demon has taken my father. A demon named Trich-"

Emilie snarled. "Monster!"

Julia jumped back. "Yes, he's a monster, and I'm sorry for what happened to you but I need to know what kind of curse you put on Trich's associate. My father's life depends on it."

My life depends on it, she added in her thoughts.

"You wish to help the demon?" Emilie said.

"No, I wish to save my father."

Emilie looked her over and held out her closed fist. "Then let me show you what happened," she opened her hand to reveal a pile of gray ash. "Give me your hand."

Julia glanced at Sam, now propped up on his elbows. He gave her a quick nod. She turned back to Emilie and offered the woman her open palm. Emilie poured the ash into Julia's hand. It was still warm.

"Close your eyes and open your mind," Emilie said, enclosing the ash in Julia's hand.

Julia followed the instructions as Emilie began to speak in Romani. Soon, the words faded into English.

"Listen to me, gypsy!" Trich's angry voice broke through the darkness. "I will make your life a living hell if you don't give me the money you owe me."

An image played behind her closed eyes. She saw Trich, his fedora and his black-red eyes. He stood with Emilie in a large kitchen. Julia caught the familiar scent of cinnamon and sugar.

Trich grabbed Emile's arm. "Don't you remember who made this all possible? I can take it away just like that," he snapped his finger and a burst of fire appeared between his thumb and middle finger.

Emilie responded by spitting at Trich's sneer. She swore at him in her native language.

Trich removed a white handkerchief from the breast pocket of his suit jacket and wiped the saliva from his chin. "So, this is how you choose to repay me."

Julia watched the scene enfold like a horror movie; her stomach turned, even though she already knew the ending.

Trich wrapped his hands around Emilie's neck. She gasped and flailed, knocking the fedora from his head to reveal the uneven blond patches of hair. She grabbed a handful and pulled. He groaned and slapped her. "You bitch!"

With a bloody lip, Emilie raised the strands in her hand and started to chant in Romani. She grinned with each word.

"You won't be smiling for long." Trich flicked his wrist and the bottom of Emilie's dress caught fire.

Emilie clung to Trich's hair and lifted it over her head as the fire consumed her.

Everything around Julia burned.

She forced her eyes open, thankful to leave that horrible image. Shaking, she stared at Emilie's somber spirit. "I'm so sorry." The words came out in a hollow whisper.

"Now you know the truth," Emilie said.

She stepped to the side so she could see both Emilie and Sam. "Trich was the one who killed Emilie and set fire to her store."

Sam winced as he sat up, shaking his head. "That bastard."

Emilie pointed to Julia's hand. "Look inside."

She uncoiled her fist clutching the ash and gently picked out a blond lock of hair. She held it up into the light. It was such a small thing but it was the key to saving her father.

"I will help you Julia," Emilie said. "But you must also help me find vengeance," she glided across the floor until she stood inches from her and raised her hand, palm open. "I will give you all the power you need to stop Trich, so he will never harm another human or También again."

"You want to use me as a vessel," Julia said.

To bond with another form of magic was forbidden. If that happened, her connection with her book would be broken. She would no longer be a librarian.

"Jules." Sam's weak voice spoke up. "Think about it. Think about what you would be losing."

She looked at her book, flung to the floor after the warding spell attacked Sam. The infinity symbol called to her. Forever. Her bond was supposed to be forever.

So was her bond with her father. That was what she didn't want to lose.

Julia lifted her hand to meet Emilie's. Once their palms connected, Emilie stepped forward, dissolving into her. A rush of warm air coated her from the inside out. Her vision blurred like she was underwater. Her ears popped and her stomach lurched. She had to blink several times before her vision cleared. When it did, Sam was on his feet, one hand on the back of the couch to keep him steady, the other raised in case something had gone wrong.

"Sam." It was her voice, but the name rolled heavy off her tongue.

You trust him. It wasn't a question from Emilie, more like an observation.

I do, she answered.

Julia held out her hand for Sam. He hesitated, but then grabbed it. Relief broke out on his face when he realized she was still with him. "Jules," he pulled her into a tight hold. She buried her face into his chest, comforted with his presence. Then, she turned her head to check her wall clock. 11:30. Sam tensed too, when he followed her gaze.

She held up the lock of hair again. It was time to meet Trich.

* * *

Without the ability to use her book, Julia could only depend on the dead gypsy woman inhabiting her body and an injured librarian, as she met Trich at Stockland Beach. Standing in the empty parking lot in front of her Honda, Julia listened to the ocean waves roar as they tumbled to shore. She took a deep breath of fresh air, her lungs expanded and exhaled with a grateful sigh. For some reason she couldn't explain, she felt centered and at peace. Perhaps this was Emilie's spirit, knowing she would soon be able to confront the monster who killed her or the fact this would be over soon and Julia would be with her father.

Sam joined her at the hood of her car. He didn't say anything as he interlaced their fingers.

She kept her gaze straight ahead to the dark beach. "Whatever happens Sam, just—just let it happen."

He responded with silence.

A pair of headlights washed over them and a red convertible pulled up in front of her Honda. The driver—one of the guards with bullhorns on the sides of his head—stepped out and shot them a menacing look. From the backseat, Trich exited with another guard, this one holding her father. Her eyes narrowed when she saw her father's bruised face.

"Julia," his voice sounded raspy, as though he needed a glass of water.

She started toward him but Trich held up his hand.

"Not so fast," he glared at Sam. "Who are you?"

"I'm here to make sure you sons of bitches don't do anything stupid," Sam said.

Trich raised a brow, as he looked him over. Sam's size must have intimated him enough, since he stepped back. He returned his attention to Julia. "Show me what you got."

She felt Emilie stir inside her. "No problem."

Romani flowed from her lips. They moved at such a fast pace Julia couldn't decipher the words. She could only feel the charged emotion behind each syllable. Her head jerked up to the night sky as Emilie's power strengthened inside her. Energy coursed through every single pore, like rivers made of boiling water. The streams collided into a pool in the pit of her stomach. She removed the plastic baggie from her pocket that held the lock of Trich's hair and raised both arms over her head. Her voice grew louder.

A strong breeze knocked Trich's fedora off his head, revealing a pale, bald scalp.

"Jules." Sam's voice broke through the spell and blowing wind.

She wanted to call out to him and tell him she was fine but Emilie was in charge. The gypsy continued chanting, harnessing power into her hands until her chest ballooned. With one more shout, she lowered her arms and the wind died down. She opened her palm and the lock of hair was gone.

Trich touched his head, now thick with blond hair. "Excellent work Julia. My associate is very pleased." A grin broke out on his pale face. "Oh fuck it. I killed that gypsy and now I get to kill your daddy."

Julia's entire body went numb. The guard holding her father poured a bottle of whiskey over her father's head.

Trich snapped his finger and a small ball of fire formed over his index finger. One spark would set her father on fire in an instant.

"You see Baby Girl, I gave you my word I would return your dad but I never said he would be alive," he flicked the fiery ball toward her father's alcohol-soaked body.

"No!" she lifted her arm and an electric current surged from her chest to her fingertips. The ball of fire froze mid-air.

Trich's eyes bulged. "What the–"

Even she was surprised but Emilie knew what to do next. She slammed the ball of fire into the driver. His flailing body fell to its knees and quickly turned into a burning sack of bull.

"Shoot him!" Trich wailed to the guard holding her father.

The guard pulled a handgun from under his blazer. Sam charged forward, pushing him away and slamming the demon against the convertible. They wrestled for control of the gun.

Another whirlwind started beneath Julia's skin and a new string of Romani words flowed from her lips. With each one more blond hair sprouted from Trich. The hair on his head grew past his shoulders and down his back. Hair streamed out of his nostrils. His knuckles sprouted blond locks; hair appeared from under his nails.

Julia glared into his now hairy face. "So, this is how you chose to repay me."

Trich sneered as his own words were thrown back at him. "You bitch!" She wasn't sure if he was addressing her or Emilie but it didn't matter. He gagged on a very large hairball and soon, hair spilled out from his ears and his eyes.

"*Prender fuego,*" Julia said under her breath.

To catch fire.

She repeated the Spanish spell with no help from Emilie. This was the spell she had been saving for Trich. She had to fight fire with fire.

The edges of his pants burst into flames. He stomped his feet on the hard pavement and pulled at his hair but with each strand he removed, ten grew back. His muffled howls echoed in the parking lot as the fire engulfed him.

"Julia!" her father called out to her. He and Sam pinned the last guard against the convertible but the demon overpowered them both, tossing them aside. He picked up the gun from the ground, aiming it at her father.

"*Cucaracha explosión,*" she cried out.

Before he could pull the trigger, a hacking cough overcame him. He doubled-over and something black scurried from his mouth. Then another and another. Cockroaches scrambled across the cement. On his hands and knees, the demon's back arched and he fell over as lines of cockroaches poured from his gaping mouth.

Her father ran past Trich's charred body and into her arms. He pushed his hands through her hair. "Oh Baby Girl...."

Exhausted, she closed her eyes and let her father hold her.

"Are you okay?" he asked.

She nodded, blinking back the tears.

Her father cupped her face. "How did you do all that?"

She smiled at Sam. "I had a little help," she stepped away and a burning sensation formed in the middle of her chest as Emilie's spirit separated from her body.

"Thank you," the woman said. She headed toward the ocean and her image faded into the dark horizon.

Julia put her hand over her heart. Emilie had left behind one thing: that feeling of being centered and at peace.

* * *

Three weeks passed.

Julia was on her way to her father's place for dinner after work. She worked as a fourth grade teacher's aide now. She was still putting her knowledge to use answering questions from curious human and También children. *Why does Amy only have five fingers? Why doesn't Nathan have a belly button?*

After the library board found out what had happened to her book she was almost put on trial for breaking her bond but Sam's testimony saved her. Instead of being punished with jail time or a large fine, her book was burned. In her opinion, that punishment was worse. Sam didn't get off easy either. He was dismissed from the library for helping her but he still could use his book in his new consulting job with the Stockland Police Department.

A lot had changed over the past weeks but as she approached her father's door, she heard the familiar chatter from CNN coming through the open window. She took out her keys to find the copy to her father's house and smiled at the photograph dangling from the heart-shaped keychain. It was the picture of her young parents, which used to hang from her refrigerator. Now the L.A. Lakers magnet held up a photo of Lulu, which seemed to please the cat, since she purred at herself whenever she passed the fridge.

"Hey, Dad," she entered the house to find her father in his recliner in front of the television.

On the screen, Anderson Cooper was reporting on the latest scandal. Gideon Salazar, the Tambíen's beloved leader, had been caught tweeting shirtless pictures of himself to women who were not his wife. It was only a few months before that Salazar had been going off on human politicians for *their* infidelities.

"Look at this," her father gestured to the news. "I told you he was a phony."

Julia rested on the recliner's arm and leaned down to kiss his cheek. "I guess the more things change, the more they stay the same."

He patted her knee. "Not everything Baby Girl."

She smiled in return, just as a knock came from the door. She stood to answer it, narrowing her eyes at her father.

He gave her an innocent hug. "Must be dinner."

When she opened the door, she put a hand on her hip and cocked her head. "What are you doing here Sam?"

He leaned against the doorway with a crooked grin. His gray eyes twinkled as he held up two large paper bags from Willie's.

She stepped aside. "Well, come on in."

THE END

Uninvited

(Young Adult)

By

JG Faherty

It all started in Bev Pietro's garage, like so many other adventures. Except none of those ended in death.

"What the heck is that?" Kit Bannon reached out to touch the object in question on his best friend's work table.

"Don't touch it!" Bev Pietro leaned forward, blocking his outstretched hand.

"Geez, Bev. What's the big deal?" Kit walked around her so he could get a better look. He'd seen her build some odd things before but never anything like this.

From arm's length away, it looked like she'd created some type of computer-board club sandwich. Only, it was a monster; something Dagwood Bumstead might have made, if he worked with electronics instead of bread and meat.

Six circuit boards sat one over the other, tiny corner rods keeping each one about two inches from the next. A dizzying array of wafers, pronged chips and fans sat side-by-side with last-generation resistors, capacitors and transistors. Coiled wire and cordless phone batteries added to the forest of growths on both sides of each board. Thick globs of solder held everything together.

Completing the tower of confusion were two triangular antennae, which Kit recognized as normally used for pulling in hard-to-get FM signals on a home stereo. Five feet of speaker wire connected them to the top-level board. The antennae rested on the table behind a PC monitor, one of the old-fashioned kind from before flat screens became so popular.

"I don't know what it is but it works," Bev muttered, twisting a lock of hair between two fingers—a habit she'd had as long Kit had known her. It meant she was really concentrating.

He leaned closer. The monitor and the keyboard Bev currently cradled in her lap were both plugged into USB ports on one of the middle boards, which was connected by wires to something that looked like the inside of a cable receiver box. Knowing her habit for taking apart the family's appliances, he had a feeling they wouldn't be watching television in Bev's house anytime soon.

"What do you mean, it works?" he stuck a brick of grape bubble gum in his mouth and spoke around it as he chewed. "What does it do?"

"I'm not sure. I just finished putting it together. I hit the power switch and everything lit up."

"I don't see any lights." Kit bent down, peered at the underside of the boards. A power cord ran to an outlet under the bench.

"That's 'cause I turned it off, doofus. You can't plug a monitor or keyboard into a computer while it's running."

"I knew that."

"Yeah, right."

Kit blew a bubble; let it get almost as large as a softball before carefully sucking it back into his mouth. Bev would kill him if he got gum on any of her stuff.

"It's a computer?" he asked, wiping the sticky leftovers from his lips.

"It's got parts from one."

"What were you trying to build?"

"A satellite receiver but something else happened."

"Yeah? What?"

Kit pulled up a chair and sat down next to her. Some of his friends at school goofed on him for hanging out so much with a girl a year younger than him but he paid no attention to them. Let them dream about their pop stars. He had a real girl to spend time with.

And someday she'd realize they had something special and then they could date instead of being *just friends*.

Kit was nothing if not patient. You had to be if you wanted to hang out with Bev. She had a habit of getting lost in her hobbies and forgetting anyone else was there. Sometimes she drifted off in the middle of a conversation—like right now. Most people would think they needed to repeat their question but he knew Bev had heard him. She'd answer in her own time.

Meanwhile, he could sit and stare at her pretty blonde hair, her ocean-green eyes and her cute little nose. Since school let out for the summer and the weather had turned hot, he'd also taken to staring at other parts of her body, parts that had just recently started getting larger.

She touched a small button on the bottom board. A humming sound filled the air, followed by the whir of several computer fans all turning on. Her pale, lightly freckled hands sat poised over the keyboard, as if ready to start a typing competition.

Kit found himself waiting as anxiously as she did. He never doubted *something* would happen. *Everything* she built worked, although not always well…or the way she intended.

"Last time I got a picture. Something weird."

The monitor in question changed from black to sky blue, indicating it had power.

Before Kit could ask his next question, a swirling, twisting shape appeared on the screen. Colors danced within it, as if someone had poured colored dye into one of the miniature dust tornadoes you'd find whirling down the road in the hottest parts of an Oklahoma summer.

"Cool! How'd you do that?" he leaned in closer.

"I didn't. It just does it by itself. It's the same picture I got before. That's why I hooked up the keyboard. I want to see if I can change it."

"Change it how?" In Boy Scouts, he'd built a simple two-band radio and he could use a computer. But he knew he could no more build something like this than he could make one of his mom's triple layer fudge cakes. Bev was the engineering geek, not him.

"We'll see." she tapped some of the keys.

Nothing happened.

"It's not working," Kit said; his head close enough to hers to smell the fresh apple scent of her shampoo. He'd never known shampoo could make a person get all tingly inside.

"It might not do anything else."

She tapped out another sequence of keystrokes.

The rainbow wind-devil continued to perform its gyrations in the center of the screen.

"Let me try." Before Bev could object, he leaned over her and touched the Up arrow on the keyboard.

Instantly, the wind-devil got larger.

"Hey, it worked! I made it zoom in!" he tried to touch the key again but Bev smacked his hand.

"Stop it! You might break something. We'll try each key one at a time."

Bev tapped the Down arrow with a ragged, broken nail.

The image returned back to its original size.

"Try the Left and Right arrows next."

She hit the Left arrow and the image disappeared, replaced by a new, easily identifiable picture.

It was a field but unlike *any* field Kit had ever seen.

Black rocks lay scattered across ground the color of the funky brown mustard his dad used on hotdogs. No grass but several clumps of what looked like dead bushes, except instead of leaves these had wicked-looking thorns sticking out all over. Behind those, the cloudless sky was bright green.

"Are you sure your monitor's color is adjusted right?"

"Yes. I don't understand it. I'm not even using a video program."

"Hit another key, see what happens."

This time Bev touched the Page Up key.

The scene changed again. Now it showed something that might have been a tree, if the tree was made of wax and left out in the sun. Instead of bark, sagging ripples covered the dark-gray trunk. The branches drooped as if tired of fighting gravity anymore. A few orange-yellow leaves, large and round, fluttered in an invisible breeze.

From behind a cluster of leaves, a head peeked out.

"Do you see that?" Kit pointed at the two bright yellow eyes set in the brown fur.

"I see it. But what is it?" Bev moved forward until her face was almost pressed against the glass. One hand twisted in her hair.

"How should I know? Zoom in on it."

Bev hit the Up arrow and the picture grew larger but the animal, or bird, remained unidentifiable.

"Let's see what Enter does." Kit leaned across again and hit the key before Bev could say no.

A loud crackling noise sounded, like paper bags being lit on fire.

"I told you not to touch anything!" Bev pushed back from the workbench. A smell of overheating copper wire filled the garage.

"I'm sorry." Kit looked at the tower of circuit boards but no smoke or flames were visible.

"Oh, crap." Bev's voice sounded more surprised than angry.

One look told him why.

A yellow glow had built up between the two antennae. In the space of a few seconds, it went from the size of a walnut to somewhat larger than a softball.

"Kit!" She got up from her chair and backed away from the bench. He stayed right with her.

"Don't blame me, it's your machine."

They'd managed to put ten feet or so between themselves and the table when the amorphous, luminescent orb, now the size of a basketball and filling the entire space between the two antennae, turned black.

At the same moment, there was a *pop*, hardly louder than a cork pulled from a bottle.

Kit still jumped back another foot and felt Bev do the same.

From the center of the black circle came a screeching, flapping creature with yellow eyes. Kit had only seen something like it once before....

—On Bev's computer screen, hiding in the branches of a mutant tree—

"Look out!" Bev ducked and raised her arms over her head as the thing swept past.

Kit ran to the work table. Everything seemed back to normal; no mysterious glowing orbs, no black circles, no burning metal smell. On the monitor, the alien tree still fluttered in the breeze.

But no yellow eyes peeked out from among the leaves.

He turned back to where Bev sat curled up, her arms over her head. "Bev, it's gone. C'mon, we have to find it."

"Find it? How can it even be here?" she stood up slowly, eyes darting all around as if it might be waiting to pounce.

Maybe it is.

"I don't know but we can't let it run loose. Our parents will kill us."

They ran outside. The bright summer sun momentarily blinded Kit after the dimmer light of the garage and he pulled his Oklahoma State ball cap down low to shield his eyes.

Life on Glenmore Drive continued on as normal. Children rode their bikes; Mrs. Gartley watered her flower beds. Down the street, Andy Kilmer and one of his friends were washing their cars. Birds sang, bees flew and dogs barked.

No one screamed. No police sirens shattered the calm.

"Kit, it could be anywhere."

She was right. He didn't even know where to start looking. It could be in any one of a hundred trees, or in someone's attic, or ten miles away.

"Oh, man, I can't believe this."

"Did you get a good look at it?"

Kit thought for a minute. It had flown past so quickly that he'd only gotten an impression of it. Maybe the size of Chihuahua? Fluffy, dark fur, large, owlish yellow eyes, long arms and legs. A tail.

And of course, the *wings*.

"It was like a tiny, flying monkey." That didn't seem right but it was close enough.

"Yeah. It went right past my face. It didn't have a beak like a bird would. But I couldn't see a mouth or nose either. Just those big eyes."

"We better go back and turn that machine off before anything else comes through."

"Turn it off? I want to see what else is out there!"

"Are you crazy? You do realize you opened up some kind of black hole to another world, don't you?" Kit took off his hat and wiped a hand across his fresh crew-cut. He was slick with sweat and he didn't think it was from the heat.

"Well, *duh*. I think that's pretty obvious. And it can't be a black hole. It's more like a gateway or a wormhole."

"Whatever. I just don't think you should mess with it anymore."

She poked him in the chest. "I didn't mess with it! You did! You're the one who hit Enter. That's what opened the gate. As long as we just look, think about all the things we can discover. We'll be famous!"

Kit started to object but had a sudden picture of them, together on the cover of *People* magazine. 'Oklahoma Teens Discover First Life On Another Planet!' In his mind, he and Bev were posing before her machine, smiling.

And holding hands.

It could happen.

"All right but we only look," he followed her back to the workbench.

"Well...." Bev sat down and pulled the chair up to the table.

"Well what?"

She had that tone, the same one she'd used the day she talked him into helping her break open the bee's nest so she could photograph the hive's structure for a science report.

She still claimed she didn't know there were bees in it.

"It's just that, no one will believe us if we don't have any proof. So, maybe we could just bring some samples across, some leaves or dirt. Nothing alive," she was already busy using the arrow keys to zoom in on one leaf of the freaky tree.

"Bev, I don't think...."

Too late. She had the screen focused on a heavy, round leaf and she hit the Enter key.

The sharp odor of overheating transformers filled Kit's nose and once more the yellow orb started growing between the antennae.

Pop.

A moment later, the orangey-colored leaf fell to the tabletop. Kit reached out a tentative hand to touch it but she stopped him.

"Don't. It could be poisonous," she used a pair of needle nose pliers to pick up the thick frond. Unlike the tree leaves Kit was used to seeing, this one had no veins running through it. The top and bottom were the same shade.

Bev placed the alien plant sample into a plastic bag that had previously held her USB cables, folded the edge over and sealed it with a piece of tape.

A disquieting thought came to life in Kit's head. "Uh, what about bacteria or diseases?"

She looked at him and he'd never seen her eyes more serious, even when they'd been in the ambulance, on the way to the hospital for their bee stings.

"After the monkey-bird, if there're any viruses or bacteria in that world's atmosphere or on the animals that can hurt us, we're probably already infected. And so is the rest of the neighborhood."

Kit imagined everyone in a three block radius dropping dead from an alien disease. How would he explain *that* to his parents?

"So what's next?" he tried to banish the grim picture from his thoughts but although it moved away, it didn't disappear completely.

"We keep collecting samples until we have a good variety to bring to the authorities, like NASA." Bev played around with the Arrow, Page Up, and Page Down keys, changing the scene showing on the monitor. "I think I've got it now. Left and Right shift the view back and forth, Up and Down arrows are zoom in and out and the Page Up, Page Down keys move the view to another location entirely. I don't know if it's on the same world or another."

She tried each of the other keys on the board but none of them affected the picture.

After a few minutes of practice, Bev started focusing in on various rocks, soil and plant life. She figured out the zoom had to be relatively close up to an object, in order for it to be drawn through to the garage.

Kit busied himself with sample bagging. He snuck a box of zip lock bags, along with some Tupperware and a roll of kitchen garbage bags, from Bev's pantry.

As soon as she brought something over, Kit—now wearing a pair of gardening gloves—would bag it. Then he'd stick a Post-It note on it, as a makeshift label.

Thirty minutes later, they had a growing pile of samples on the table and floor. The garage smelled like an electrical fire and Bev's parents were due home from her brother's Little League game in a few minutes.

"I think we better stop now," Bev said. "We've had the machine on for almost ninety minutes and it's getting really hot. That must be its limit."

"What are you going to tell them?" he asked as she shut the machine off.

"My parents? Nothing." Bev laid a plastic tarp over her invention, and taped a piece of paper marked 'Do Not Touch!!' on it. "They'd freak. They'll find out when NASA comes knocking on the door. Then it'll be too late for me to get in trouble."

"You know, you can't just send a letter to NASA or call them," Kit said. The samples had been packed into two empty boxes, which they planned to store in Bev's closet.

"*No kidding.* But we can bring a couple to Mr. Sloan and have him contact NASA for us. Him they'll believe."

He figured she was right. They'd had Sloan for eighth-grade Biology this past year. Unlike most teachers, he was actually pretty cool and he didn't mind when students brought him dead bugs or snakes to identify.

Bev paused at her door. "You better not say anything either. Promise?"

"Cross my heart." He made the motion, held out both hands to show he hadn't crossed his fingers. "I can't wait to see everyone's faces when we're famous!"

* * *

Getting Mr. Sloan to believe their story had been harder than Kit had thought it would be. He'd figured they could just say they found these new plants and could Mr. Sloan please identify them? But the teacher had wanted to know where they found them. When they didn't have a believable story, they'd ended up showing him the machine and demonstrating it.

He'd wanted to tell their parents, tell the police, tell everyone but they'd finally convinced him to contact NASA or some similar agency. Of course, that was after Bev had threatened to hide the machine and tell everyone Sloan was a liar.

Sloan had brought one of the funny round leaves to the Botany department at Oklahoma State and they'd run tests on it. The results had been as crazy as Kit had expected. In addition to carbon, the cellular material contained silicon and gold, of all things. The cells themselves had three distinct walls or layers and fluids flowed through intracellular channels instead of xylem and phloem.

That had been enough for the university's botanist, Dr. Hez Ramzallah, to authorize sending a sample to NASA.

Three days later, a plain white van pulled up at the Pietro house.

* * *

"Kit, you've got to come right away!" Bev's voice was so loud Kit had to hold the phone away from his ear.

"What's wrong?"

"They're here. NASA!"

"What?"

"They want to see us use the machine, right now. Hurry!"

She didn't give him time to respond. He stared at the silent phone and tossed the book he'd been reading onto the bed and ran out of the house, stopping just long enough to grab his Whattaburger baseball cap from the floor.

Six strangers stood inside Bev's garage. With them were Mr. and Mrs. Pietro, Mr. Sloan and the botanist from the college, Dr. Ramzallah.

The three NASA scientists introduced themselves as Drs. Cooke, Tunney and Ching. They mentioned what they did; something with xenobiology in the title but Kit didn't listen. He was too busy trying not to stare at the other three men, the ones in the plain black suits and matching sunglasses who didn't introduce themselves. Stories about aliens always mentioned the *men in black*. He knew they weren't super-spies but they did look like the CIA or Secret Service agents he'd seen in movies and TV shows.

What if they're here to take away Bev's machine?

Or arrest us?

She didn't seem worried about them and neither did her parents, who were busy chastising her for not telling them what had been going on. Kit was glad his parents had gone to see his grandmother in the nursing home and wouldn't be back until that evening. He'd stayed home because he had a Little League game later in the afternoon.

When he'd first arrived, Bev had pulled him aside and told him how the scientists had originally exited the van in protective gear but they'd run tests on air samples from the garage, which came up negative for any unusual viruses or bacteria.

"They told me they didn't find anything on the leaf we sent them either but they were really mad. They lectured me and Mr. Sloan on how we could have contaminated the whole world. Mr. Sloan told them he hadn't worried about it, because by the time he saw the samples, we'd already been breathing around them and touching them for days and we were fine. Plus, by then we'd already spread any potential diseases too far to be controlled."

"Did you tell them about the monkey-bird?" Kit watched the scientists walk around the workbench, taking pictures of her invention but not touching anything.

"Are you crazy? They'd probably quarantine the city."

The scientists finished their examination and approached her.

"Please, Miss Pietro, can you show us exactly how you brought the samples over?" Dr. Cooke was the tallest of the scientists, an older man with white hair and eyebrows. Tiny glasses perched at the end of his long nose.

"Yes and also how you handled the samples?" Dr. Ching asked. Several inches shorter than Cooke or Tunney, he had shiny black hair and a chubby face.

Bev separated herself from her parents and turned the power on to her machine, which she and Kit had nicknamed the *transporter,* after the device on *Star Trek.* The various multi-colored lights winked on, accompanied by the muted sound of humming fans whirring to life.

She stationed herself at the keyboard, while Kit stood next to her, wearing his gloves. He had some of his zip-lock bags ready.

On the screen, the twirling, sparking light devil appeared.

"Is that apparition always there when you turn the monitor on?" Tunney asked as he took a picture of the rainbow dervish.

Bev nodded. "Yes. We don't know if it's actually some kind of storm or dust cloud or just the pattern on the monitor that indicates it's ready to use."

"We never tried to bring it across as a sample," Kit said.

They need to know we have some common sense.

"You shouldn't have used the machine at all," Ted Pietro said from the edge of the garage.

"Dad...." Bev rarely used her whiny voice, except with her parents. Kit always found it amazing how just a simple change in her inflection turned her from an overly-mature, serious science geek into a typical thirteen year-old girl, who'd just been told she couldn't buy the expensive jeans she wants.

"Don't *Dad* me young lady. Didn't you hear these people? You actually put the entire world in danger!"

"Geez, we didn't do it on purpose. We thought we were just looking at pictures and we tried to change them and then Kit hit the Enter button and the next thing we knew...."

"The leaf appeared on the table," Kit cut in; worried she might slip up and mention their first sample.

The one still running loose someplace—

She shot him a squinty-eyed glare and he shut up.

"Well, the harm, if any, has already been done." Cooke slid his glasses up. "We've conducted exhaustive tests on the plant material we received and it's our belief that because the life forms of our two worlds are so radically different, there's little chance of microorganisms from one place being harmful to the other."

"Can you show us how you bring forth a sample?" Tunney asked.

"Sure." Bev began working with the Arrows and other buttons, explaining how they'd figured out what each one did.

She located one of the round-leafed trees. "That's like the tree we got the leaf from."

She zoomed in on a branch and touched the Enter key. Tunney switched his camera for a digital camcorder and filmed the entire sequence of events, leading up to the appearance of the sample, from the initial yellowish glow to the final *Pop* as the luminescent orb changed into the black disk.

"We were always careful not to touch anything directly," Kit explained, as he picked up the leaf and dropped it into the plastic baggie.

"Really? So you didn't touch the gloves when you took them on and off? Did you place them on the table and then perhaps move them or rest a hand the table?" Ching asked as he drew on latex gloves and took the baggie from Kit. He dropped it into a larger sample bag, added his gloves, and sealed the bag.

"Well, uh...."

"We found lots of other stuff too. Do you want more soil or rocks?" Bev interrupted.

"Actually, we'd like to do some sample collecting ourselves, if that's all right," Cooke said.

"Just don't use it too long at a time."

"Yeah, the transporter starts making a funny, overheating kind of smell after about an hour or two," Kit said.

"Ninety minutes," Bev cut in, always precise when it came to her experiments.

"Transporter?" Ching asked.

"That's what we call it." Bev stood up and let Cooke take her chair.

Ching gently moved Kit out of the way and arranged a series of heavy-duty sample bags, along with a box of latex gloves, on the table. At his feet sat a large Styrofoam container to hold the bags.

Cooke shifted the view on the screen from one place to the next, stopping each time to bring across samples of dirt, rock and some small grass-like growths.

"Have you seen any animal life?" he asked at one point.

"Uh...." Kit didn't know what to say.

"Sort of. We saw something in a tree once but we didn't, um, want to transport anything alive, 'cause we wouldn't be able to do anything with it."

Bev's voice seemed to scream *"I'm lying!"* but Kit hoped the scientists wouldn't realize it. Ching and Tunney glanced at each other, giving Kit momentary heart failure.

"What did it look like?" Cooke asked.

"It was hard to see. It was behind some leaves. We know it had big yellow eyes and brownish fur."

"Hmmm." Cooke zoomed in on another tree, panned back and forth across the branches. No eyes peeked out at them.

"Nothing there. It would be interesting to see if it was something avian or primate in physiological appearance."

"Or both," Kit murmured under his breath. He winced but kept quiet when Bev ground her heel on his toes.

"Wait, what's that?" Ching pointed at the screen. It showed a clump of five long-leafed trees against a backdrop of naked rock outcroppings. Barren ground surrounded the trees.

Off in the distance, tiny, winged creatures swooped and darted against a burnt-ochre sky.

"Zoom in on those!" exclaimed Tunney.

Oh, no. Don't...

Against his will Kit found himself crowding forward with Bev and the scientists. Bodies pressed against him from behind as Sloan, Ramzallah and the Pietros moved closer. A glance backwards showed even the nameless, hulking guards had moved into the garage and were trying to peer over everyone's heads.

Cooke's fingers tap-tapped on the keys in rapid fashion as he desperately tried to zoom in and move sideways at the same time, keeping the flying creatures in view. The herky-jerky motion had Kit feeling ill until Cooke accidentally touched the Scroll Lock key and suddenly the movement smoothed out as the screen seemed to track the flight of one creature.

"Excellent! I've locked onto one of them," he said, as if he'd planned it that way.

He zoomed in again and now the details of the animal became distinct.

It was a monkey-bird. Now Kit had his first real look at the flying alien.

Its wings were membranous, like those of a bat. Bluish-green blood vessels stood out clearly against the grayish-brown skin. Long arms and legs, relative to its body size, were tucked against the chest but the black, curved claws were still visible.

Remembering Bev's previous comment about how the other one had no mouth or nose, he tried to study the face of the constantly darting and diving animal. Other than the eyes, no features were evident.

Until one of its flying partners swerved too close.

The monkey-bird drew back its fur-covered lips in a vicious snarl, and its lower jaw dropped down almost one hundred eighty degrees as the alien displayed overly-large jagged teeth. It lunged forward, snapping at the offending individual, which dodged to one side, just in time to avoid losing a chunk of flesh.

"I think it's safe to say the creatures are carnivorous," Tunney commented while he filmed the sequence.

"I'd like to bring one over but they appear too large to handle safely," Cooke said.

Kit heard the disappointment in his voice.

They're not so different from Bev and me—eager to grab proof of another world. I'll bet, if they'd been here that first day, they'd have done exactly the same thing we did.

Well, maybe.

"We should, however, try to find something smaller, more easily managed. If creatures this large exist, there must be smaller members of the local animal kingdom present. Regardless of the environment, a food chain would still work in essentially the same fashion."

Cooke nodded in response to Ching's statement and pulled back from the monkey-bird troop to begin scouring the landscape again. He panned to the left, continuing in one direction. Each touch of the Arrow key appeared to move the viewing area by several miles, if not more, as the scenery constantly changed.

The spindly scientist reached a grouping of dense trees, different from what they'd seen before. These were more like palm trees, with wide fronds at the top and no branches below the middle of the knobby, flesh-colored trunk. They were packed together like pines in a northern forest, so dense it was difficult to see between them.

"This would be an excellent location for arboreals, the local equivalents of squirrels perhaps, as well as whatever passes for birds."

Cooke zoomed in until a single tree filled the monitor and then began moving from one tree to the next. On the fourth tree, he hit paydirt.

"I saw something move!" Ching pointed at the screen.

Cooke nodded, already busy with the keypad. He narrowed the field of view to the lower fronds and waited. A moment later, one of the heavy, wide leaves jiggled and something crawled out onto it.

There was no way to tell how large the thing was but Kit had the impression it would have just fit inside his baseball glove.

"Ugh." Mrs. Pietro frowned and moved back a few steps.

Kit understood her reaction. The creature trudging across the sand-colored frond had twelve legs, six on each side and two bulbous eyes at one end. Each eye moved independently of the other, the same as a chameleon's, and had two pupils. One looked up while the other looked down.

"A perfect adaptation for arboreal life," Tunney stated. He leaned past Ching, capturing every detail in his camcorder.

The three-segmented body paused, giving everyone a good look at it. Below the eyes were two sets of mandibles, one vertical and one horizontal. They slowly opened and closed first one, and then the other. The two back segments expanded and contracted in regular motion. No antennae were visible but random patches of thick, stiff hairs sprouted from various locations on the body and multi-jointed legs.

"Amazing." Cooke tapped the Up Arrow once, increasing the magnification. Now a pattern of dark maroon blotches was visible against charcoal gray flesh.

"Is it too large?" Cooke asked.

"No." Ching lifted an empty Styrofoam cooler. "I'll position this so the creature drops into it. Once the lid is closed, we can bag the entire container."

"I don't want that thing in my garage," Mrs. Pietro stated.

The scientists ignored her. Ching placed the container between the two antennae of the transporter and nodded to Cooke. "Ready."

* * *

When he looked back on that moment, Kit often saw everything in slow motion. Cooke's finger lifting up—beginning its downward path towards the Enter key.

The sudden fuzziness on the screen as something interjected itself between their mystical camera and the life form on the frond.

An impression of an eye just as Cooke depressed the Enter key.

The beginning of the yellow glow.

* * *

"Stop! There's something in the way." Bev jumped forward and started smashing at the Down Arrow key.

It was too late. On the monitor, the view reversed, revealing first a face and then an entire body.

They'd been wrong in their estimation of size. Unless the alien planet was inhabited by a race of giants, the palm trees were only a couple of feet high and the spidery-thing barely two inches long.

"How do you stop this thing?" Now Cooke was hitting keys as well, smashing his entire hand down on the keyboard.

"I'm trying," Bev told him.

"Unplug it!" Kit heard his voice go up an octave but didn't care. *No way* he wanted that thing coming into the garage.

Not with those teeth.

Bev's mother screamed and the security team moved forward, pushing people out of the way. Bev reached out to hit the Off button but fell to the floor as Cooke slid back in the chair and hit her legs. Kit grabbed for the power cord but he missed. He found himself on the ground next to Bev as one of the security men shoved him away from the table.

Somehow, over the confusion of shouts and clatter, Kit heard the distinctive *Pop* that signaled something entering their world.

Bev's eyes widened and he knew she'd heard it too. He grabbed her hand.

"Hide!"

They crawled across the stained cement to Mr. Pietro's Jeep Liberty.

"Get inside." Kit opened one of the back doors and waited for Bev to jump in, then followed her, closing the door behind him. He prayed the darkly-tinted windows would hide them in the dim light of the garage.

Movement on the table caught his attention. The nightmarish creature from the other world had fallen through the black disk. It was even larger than he'd thought, easily six feet tall. Bev gasped and he pressed his hand against her mouth until she shook her head.

More than anything else, the life form resembled a skeleton with the barest amount of flesh still wrapped around the bones. Its flat, expressionless face turned this way and that as it fought for its balance on the table. A pair of black pupils floated in each sulfurous yellow, over-sized eyeball.

Its mouth opened and a high-pitched, keening cry echoed through the garage, painful even through the closed windows of the Jeep.

One of the security guards had hustled the scientists, teachers and Bev's parents out to the driveway but now he stopped and put his hands over his ears. The remaining two guards drew their guns and fired at the alien.

Several of the bullets scored direct hits, flinging the dark-brown visitor backwards off the table and into a metal rack of shelves. The alien crashed to the floor amidst a pile of cans and boxes.

The two guards moved slowly forward, alert for any movement.

It didn't help them.

The creature bounded up from behind the workbench and leaped onto one of the guards. It sank its inch-long, pointed teeth into the man's neck and tore out a lump of flesh. It didn't wait to see if the man was dead; it just jumped onto the second guard, who managed to fire two more shots before his arm was pulled from its socket. He tried to scream but the alien shoved a clawed hand into his mouth and tore off his lower jaw in one quick motion.

The third guard ran forward, gun out and firing. It seemed hard to believe he could miss at that range but not once did the monster flinch or fall backwards. Instead, it dove for the man's legs and tackled him. The two went down in a heap. The man, who looked to outweigh the alien by a good forty pounds, got on top and rammed his gun against the bulbous head.

Kit waited for the sound of the gun but it never came.

"Oh God," whispered Bev, as the last security guard leaned to the side. A long-fingered brown hand stuck out through his back. It clutched a section of red, glistening spine.

The man toppled over, a crimson pool spreading beneath him, blotting out the old oil stains on the cement.

Bev's parents stood frozen, their mouths hanging open, as the emaciated figure rose up and approached the end of the garage.

"No." Bev grabbed for the door handle but Kit pushed her down to the floor, held her there with his feet.

She didn't need to see this but he couldn't look away.

The alien reached up one skeletal arm and pulled the garage door down, cutting off the sight of the adults' shocked faces and thrusting the garage into semi-darkness.

Outside, shouts and banging sounded but the alien ignored them. From further away, police sirens howled to life.

Kit's blood turned colder than Miller's stream in November, as the alien stared at the computer keyboard and at the image of the trees on the monitor.

The air in the Jeep was stifling, sweat rolled down Kit's face, the tickle demanding immediate attention, but he steeled himself against any movement. He did remember to lift his feet and let Bev slide back up, onto the seat.

She clutched his hand as the intruder started tapping a long nail on the keys.

"That's more than just basic intelligence at work. It has knowledge of technology." Bev's whisper floated in the still air, barely audible.

How would I feel if something yanked me from my home to another world? Scared? Angry? For all we know, this thing was with its family, enjoying a nice walk in the park, when we stole it from everything it ever knew.

All I'd want to do, is go home.

It only took the creature a few minutes to figure out the keyboard controls. It wasted no time zooming in on another of its kind.

Instead of hitting the Enter key, the alien moved the two antennae to the floor and spaced them as far apart as their wires would allow, almost ten feet.

Then it held down Control-Alt-Delete.

The familiar yellow glow formed but it didn't stop when it reached softball size. By the time it was eight feet in diameter, the harsh tang of heated metal had filled the car almost to the choking point.

This time the *Pop* was more like a rifle report in the closed space of the garage.

From out of the black disk stepped another alien.

And another.

The disk didn't disappear, not even when the tenth one came out.

Or the twentieth.

Kit joined Bev on the floor of the Jeep when the invaders opened the garage door and the screaming started. He pressed his hands over his ears and leaned against Bev's shivering body.

Shadows continued to move past the truck's tinted windows as more and more aliens made their way through the gate and out into the world.

Kit wondered how long they had left before the transformer finally used up its ninety minutes of life.

Or before something looked into the Jeep.

THE END

Mack and Stretch
Save the Earth
(Young Adult)

By

David Perlmutter

Prospero was ready.

This unknown and unknowable planet from the quadrants beyond the system of Sol had been preparing to conquer what it considered to be the most life giving—and therefore the most obstinate—planet known to exist anywhere: the planet Earth. Conquering this planet would allow Prospero to seize all the available resources located there and take the people who had not died in its invasion into slavery.

This was something the envious world desperately needed. Its own resources were severely tapped and its own people on the cusp of revolution against the ruling classes. The army of Prospero, powered by a higher form of technology indistinguishable from magic, set off to conquer Earth, the only planet in its—or any nearby galaxy capable of sustaining life.

In spite of its preparations however, Prospero was to be surprised at the final results of its attack on Earth. For it seemed others were also practicing the art of magic on Earth, in spite of initial suspicions that that more ancient form of the art had died out hundreds of years ago.

And that was to be their undoing....

II.

Commander Hamlet, the leader of the expeditionary force designed to attack Earth, while examining the object of his imminent invasion through a *magic* device known simply as a Futuroscope, was interrupted by his adjutant Captain MacBeth with some pressing news that required his attention.

"I have the reports of the investigation into the presence of magic on the planet Earth, Sire," Captain MacBeth said, saluting.

"Very well," answered Hamlet. "What are the results?"

"There is very little presence of magic on the planet Earth at this moment," MacBeth responded. "We have, it seems, chosen the right moment in order to take over the planet. They have allowed science to conquer magic fairly easily, judging by the degree to which they allow science to control their industry and defense. Our magic is vastly superior to any level of science which they possess so our conquest seems evident."

"Seems?" Hamlet was suspicious regarding this last word. "Why this hesitation MacBeth?"

"Because, sir, there are two formidable practitioners of the white magic who live there, who can counter and defeat our black magic. Specifically, in the community of Grand Forks, North Dakota, in the United States of America, on the continent of...."

"Spare me the nomenclature man!" demanded Hamlet. "Who are these two fools who *might* pose a threat to us?"

"Their names, sir, are McKenna Mendelson and Melissa Cunningham, known to their close acquaintances as Mack and Stretch."

"Have you photographic evidence of their existence? If so, then produce it!"

MacBeth produced such a photograph. Upon seeing it, Hamlet roared with laughter.

In the photograph were two seemingly ordinary thirteen-year-old human girls. The first, McKenna, was short and chunky, with red hair cut with bangs, making a grotesque *funny face* by putting fingers at either side of her mouth; the other, Stretch, had blonde hair cut in a flat bob and was extremely tall and powerful in appearance. She was cradling a strong arm around her friend as she laughed at her antics.

Hamlet continued laughing for a few minutes before finally recovering. When he did, MacBeth approached him again.

"What do you consider so amusing, Sire?" he asked.

"You fool!" Hamlet chuckled. "Am I supposed to consider those two the *only possible obstacle* we have to conquering their worthless planet?"

"But Sire, I speak the truth," MacBeth protested. "Our records indicate they have performed countless secret acts of sorcery, to save themselves and their community since they became accredited sorcerers three Earth years ago. And they are not only magically gifted, they have physical and mental prowess unmatched among their peers. Ms. McKenna is said to possess the intelligence and cunning of a fox, while Ms. Stretch is said to possess the speed and strength of a dozen men...."

"Posh!" Hamlet cancelled MacBeth's concern. "Mere speculations! No human being matches our physical prowess; in spite of us all being short-bodied grey creatures with only one red eye in the center of our heads. Besides, no human being can possibly break the Prosperous chains, which we use to imprison our slaves. Go to this Grand Forks and capture them! Once there, we will liquidate them and our invasion can proceed! I want them captured and dead within ninety minutes! Do you hear me? NINETY MINUTES! Now *go!*"

MacBeth could do nothing except leave the room, while watching with some trepidation as his leader continued to laugh.

"The very idea!" he bellowed with glee. "Prospero conquered by Earthling teenagers! How naïve can you GET?"

III.

Hamlet's orders were carried out, as they always were. And so, the Earth had no idea what was going to hit it—until it was too late...

Meanwhile, our heroines, Mack and Stretch, were cheerfully giggling as they walked home from an invigorating workout session on the campus of the University of North Dakota. Dressed in matching blue track-suits and white sneakers and carrying heavy bags of gear along their shoulders, they might have been mistaken for sisters. For all intent and purpose, that was the case. Both being children of single parents whose jobs required considerable absence from home, Mack and Stretch had long leaned on one another for support. The taller and stronger girl protected her younger associate from attacks by bullies. The shorter and smarter one protected her friend from those who insulted Stretch's intelligence (which was far greater than her muscle-bound appearance might suggest). They had grown up sharing the same interests, which included both fitness and witchcraft and had become experts in both fields. This paid off in more than one respect.

Stretch was a phenomenal athlete, specializing in basketball, cross country running and field hockey. While Mack did not equal her in physical stature, she more than made up for it in enthusiasm and support for her friend at all times. Mack, in turn, was more than eager to help Stretch through her occasional scholastic emergencies, being as Mack was a regular resident of the Honor Roll. Yet Mack was still envious of Stretch in a way, since scholars rarely get the kind of attention or money given to athletes. But, for the sake of their friendship, she was willing to keep any resentments of that kind to herself.

In any event, Mack and Stretch were almost halfway home when Mack—heavily tired out by lugging her gear bag—stopped to rest on a nearby fire hydrant.

"Gee Mack," Stretch said. "We're not home yet!"

"I know that Stretch," replied Mack. "But, *as you well know*, I don't possess the kind of Herculean power you have!"

"Herculean?" Stretch asked. (She did possess physical power akin to that of the Greek hero, demonstrated by the fact that she could tote her heavy athletic gear bag around on her shoulder as if it were merely a purse.)

"Yeah. Like Hercules! Remember the Greek mythology unit we did in history?"

"Uh huh. But give me a break Mack! It's June, for crying out loud! Am I supposed to remember this stuff *all the time*?"

School being out for the summer, the dynamic duo were now free to concentrate—if only temporarily—on their two avocations. Stretch would have wanted to spend every day working out on the UND campus, as she was very much a health nut, concerned about maintaining her mighty musculature as much as possible. The very idea of becoming remotely fat or weak appalled her. Mack however, had different ideas. It was her interest in scholarly affairs that got them involved in witchcraft after all and her subsequent mighty prowess at that activity got them registered as members of the WWW (Witches, Wizards and Warlocks) of Grand Forks. Consequently, Mack was as avid about maintaining this end of her interests. She would have done so even more regularly, if Stretch had not *persuaded* her to join in her workouts for company. Stretch, for her part, felt she was only sub-par as a witch and felt the same envy for Mack's ability at the art that Mack felt for the size of Stretch's biceps and deltoids.

"Not *all* the time!" Mack said, as she started to get her breath back and leaned towards her friend. "But you gotta know something more than shoving a ball in a basket, if you're going to make it in life Stretch!"

"Don't I know it!" the taller girl replied. "But sometimes I think you rub that point in my face too hard Mack! Not everyone is born a genius like you!"

"Nor, for that matter, is everyone born an *athlete* my friend!" responded Mack. "You saw that personally today when I totally embarrassed myself doing your thing!"

"Don't be silly Mack! It's not like I meant to throw that basketball in your face—or you would fall down and trip on that gopher hole when we ran. Or even when we tried to lift weights...."

"Don't rub that in Ms. Showoff! You were practically balancing the heaviest weight on your *finger* and I could barely lift the *lightest* one!"

"There you go again, comparing me to...what's-his-name..."

"Hercules!"

"Right. But I'm not *that* strong Mack!"

"Oh, yeah? Well how come your dad always makes you move the furniture around...?"

"Because his back always goes out when *he* tries to do it! Besides, even though you're pretty smart, you aren't exactly Einstein either!"

"Are you *insulting* me?" Mack returned, enraged.

"No!" said Stretch. "*This* is an insult!"

She took her bag off her shoulder and dropped it on Mack's foot, who squealed in pain and threatened to throw a punch at her friend. But Stretch's mighty arm blocked Mack's feint easily. Suddenly they stopped, embraced, and laughed like the friends they truly were. That was how things worked out with them; even the best of friends fight once in a while, but they know how to make up in style too.

And then, the aliens arrived....

* * *

The arrival was unpleasant, as the Prosperian scout ship blocked the sun as soon as it entered Earth's atmosphere. And, as it was a clear, sunny day, it was something the two girls noticed immediately.

"Did it get cold all of a sudden?" Mack asked.

"Fraid so!" said Stretch. "And look what caused it!"

It was an enormous Frisbee-shaped disk, the kind of ship that caused alien vessels to be erroneously referred to as flying saucers by the media, many years ago. What was worse, it now descended abruptly down from the skies as soon as Mack and Stretch were spotted!

"Take cover!" Stretch ordered. Quickly the two of them stacked their athletic bags on top of one another in a crude attempt to make a fort, and hid behind them and the fire hydrant, as best they could. But it was hardly enough to fool the aliens.

When it landed across the street from where Mack and Stretch were hiding, the alien scouts emerged from the ship decked out in as much armored plated protection as they could manage. They found the crude hiding place, tore away the bags and unpleasantly hoisted Mack and Stretch to their feet.

"What the hell...." Mack protested. "What do you one-eyed, square-bodied idiots want with us?"

"We want you out of the way!" said the commander of the scout ship. "We were ordered to remove you from the face of existence and that is what we intend to do!"

"But why?" demanded Stretch.

"You two, Ms. Mendelson and Ms. Cunningham, are the only known practitioners of white magic on this planet! You are the only beings capable of destroying and defeating the forces of Prospero in battle with these abilities. Therefore, you must be eliminated!"

"Not on your *life* buddy!" growled Mack.

Together, at a nod from one another, each brought a foot down on the alien holding them prisoner, causing that captor to shout in pain and drop them to the ground. Using all their speed, the human duo ran off in the opposite direction from whence they had come, with the alien pursuers hot on their trail, laser blasters drawn and shooting.

"What do we do Mack?" Stretch gasped.

"We *are* doing it silly!" panted Mack. "We're running away. And the way we do it, they'll be tired out before long. So just keep going!"

But being able to keep going was something that was soon out of the question. They found their path blocked by a dead end street—and a wall!

"Damn!" cursed Mack. "Of all the....why did they have to build something like that *here*? And *now*?"

"Never mind. We still have options."

"Such as *what*?" asked Mack.

"We can FIGHT them!"

"You out of your *mind* Stretch? They're *aliens*...."

"But that doesn't mean they're tougher than *us* Mack! Nobody in this neighborhood is tougher than you and me."

"Yeah," Mack agreed. "Especially after the workout we just had today. Besides, I've been meaning to try out some of those karate moves I've been learning."

"Me too," Stretch agreed. "Don't forget we do that together."

"Yeah," replied Mack. "Like everything else we do!"

At that moment they were cornered by the alien forces but before the commander could raise his blaster to stun the duo—or any of the others could, either—Stretch's long leg came out, hit the commander's wrist, and kicked the blaster into a nearby clump of grass. While Mack didn't have her partner's length, she was able to connect with a couple of the others' bodies to make them do the same.

"Stupid females!" the commander cursed. "Do you not know who you are *dealing with here*?"

"No!" countered Mack. "And apparently *you* don't either! Let's get 'em, Stretch!"

"Right behind you buddy," responded the taller girl.

The next few minutes passed in a blur as the two Earth girls boxed, wrestled and karate kicked their way through the battle lines. Red wounds soon decorated the alien's bodies, as Mack and Stretch were their equals in size and strength, if not even their superiors. Of the nine aliens comprising the unit, only the commander ended up unscathed. Mack rushed in to a swarm of three of them, wrestling one into submission. She knocked another out with a stone-cold knockout punch and broke the third one's back with a kick directed firmly at his spinal column. Yet these achievements on her part were dwarfed by what Stretch was able to do to the others.

Given that, at six-foot-five, she was already considerably taller than the tallest Prosperian. She had that significant advantage but her great strength and keen athletic mind were two more attributes most of the alien race did not possess. She was able to stop the first, simply by throwing her mighty fist in his face, which caused him to fall down dead. Two others grabbed her arms to check her but she grabbed both of them by their wrists and threw them far away. The remaining alien was more successful in fighting her. He grabbed a stick, modified from a tree branch and knocked her to the ground when she was not looking. Though humbled by this, she was not wounded and proved this by grabbing him from behind and punching a hole directly through his stomach.

Finally, the commander, who had been knocked out earlier, ended the fracas by firing a beam of hot light directly at Stretch's back, which rendered her unconscious. Hearing Stretch's shriek of pain, Mack went to investigate and she too was incapacitated by a similar beam. The captain took their limp bodies and loaded Mack and Stretch back onto the ship for presentation to Commander Hamlet.

IV.

Gagged with silk handkerchiefs and bound in Prosperian chains, Mack and Stretch were awakened, stood up, and presented to the commander. When they had their gags removed, they angrily cursed their captors and all of their ancestors before Hamlet finally slapped them to get them to stop. They reeled from the blows, so weakened and humiliated were they from their recent ordeals.

"So," Hamlet scoffed, once they were alone together in the room, "you are the ones attempting to halt Prospero's conquest of your Earth, are you?"

"Yeah," said Mack, "only we don't know what you're *talking about!*"

"Then understand *this*, children." The irony of his having to look up to their taller bodies to say this was entirely lost on him. "We of the planet Prospero are in a difficult social and economic situation and we intend to use your Earth as a means of....replenishing the treasury, as it were."

"And you think we're gonna help you?...'cause we're sorcerers and we can fight off your men and we got strength and brains and all that?" argued Mack dismissively. "Well, forget it dumbass! Stretch and I don't work for no one except ourselves. Right Stretch?"

The taller girl grunted a non-verbal assent to her friend's claims.

"Oh, we do not require your *assistance!*" Hamlet said icily. "We merely want to destroy both of you, since you are the principal obstacles towards gaining our goal!"

"WHAT?" Mack and Stretch both shouted.

"Yes ladies!" Hamlet continued. "It would seem that your liquidation is now required. So you had best be saying your prayers—or whatever it is you Earthlings do before you meet your maker—since it will shortly be that time."

"The *hell* it will!" shouted Stretch, objecting violently, as were most of her objections. "I'm gonna bust these chains and free Mack and me. And then *you've had it!*"

"She's not lying!" Mack warned, as Stretch began straining every muscle of her body to achieve that superhuman feat. "I've seen her do stuff no other girl can ever do! Why, in only one minute, she can in two minutes…five minutes…ten…half an hour, for sure!" Then, in *sotto voce* to her partner, she pleaded: "Come on Stretch! Put it all in there! Show him what you can do!"

"I…can't Mack!" Stretch whined as her strength began to wane and the chains grew tighter. "This stuff is…unbreakable! *Nobody* can do it!"

"*What?*" Mack said out loud, angrily. Then to Hamlet: "How *dare* you! You humiliated her! *Nobody* does that to us and gets away with it, understand? *Nobody!*"

"She is far from the last strong person who has been humiliated by the chains of Prospero," Hamlet intoned. "You will find there are many more who tried resisting us by those means and found them difficult, if not impossible to resist."

He picked up a wand and a sugar bowl-shaped dish and uttered a short, inaudible chant as he tapped the wand against it.

"What the hell are you *doing*?" Mack demanded.

"You will find out soon enough!" Hamlet countered.

Indeed they did. Jets of blue flame covered Mack and Stretch's bodies and shook them around the room like rag dolls. Then, when they had seemingly survived this most violent and unladylike of treatments, both experienced severe pains in their abdomens which threw them firmly to the ground.

"What did you *do* to us?" Stretch demanded.

"I merely rendered you incapable of ever casting a spell again," Hamlet pronounced. "That is particularly true for Ms. Mendelson, seeing as it is she who is the more advanced in the sorcery department. And, now you are both powerless and robbed of your individual strengths. You pose no further threat to me and will now be terminated at my discretion, within ninety minutes of my command."

"You MONSTER!" Mack shouted. She attempted chanting to produce a demon, to free both of them but only succeeded in producing a fart, which reddened her cheeks and forced her to apologize. Like Stretch, she had been robbed of her greatest gift.

His patience with them now exhausted, Hamlet called for the guard and had the offending Earthlings removed from his presence.

V.

At blaster point, the two Earth girls, now helpless and nearly on the verge of tears, were sent off to the brig at the bottom of the ship. The chains were removed from their bodies but they were warned, viciously, in words that stung them as hard as metal fresh from the blacksmith's fire, that in the unlikely event they were to escape confinement, they would be placed in the chains again. Including on their necks; which as the consequence would cause them to die almost immediately. Having now said their piece, the guards left and harshly slammed the heavy wooden door behind them as a further warning. Mack and Stretch were completely helpless, weak and cowed in what was surely intended to be their home—at least until the ship returned to Prospero. And then who knew what would become of them?

Mack sat down on the reinforced stone floor while Stretch, who was on the verge of tears since being robbed of her strength, ran to a far corner of the room and began sobbing softly.

"Well," Mack said, as if it was only a matter of time before they were picked up to go home by their parents, "what now?"

Stretch, infuriated by what she thought was her friend's flippant response to the desperate situation they were both in, immediately stopped crying, her sadness replaced by a sudden, heated fury. Whirling around, she faced Mack with a burning intensity the latter had never seen upon her face—and which served the purpose of rendering Mack silent for once in her life.

"What now?" Stretch shouted as she advanced viciously towards her friend, completely altering the meaning of what had just been said. *"WHAT **NOW**? Is that all you can say? **WHAT NOW**?"*

"You keep a civil tongue in your mouth, Cunningham!" Mack sprung to her feet immediately and threatened her friend with her fists. "We may be pals and you may be stronger than me, but...."

"*SHUT UP!*"

The words exited from Stretch's lips as if they were a jet of flame from the largest and most fearsome dragon ever known to exist on planet Earth. As if she had been burned by this jet of flame, Mack fell to the ground, whimpering. She'd heard Stretch use this tone only—*only*—when either her honor, intelligence, or power, or Mack's—or indeed, Mack's body and life—was threatened by some capricious assailant at their middle school. At those times, Stretch had threatened the offender with a vicious beating that would leave him or her on the verge of death. Though Stretch was not of a nature that allowed her to actually *act* on many of these threats, would-be assailants were cowed enough by her size and implied strength alone that they immediately backed off.

But now it was *Mack* who was the butt of Stretch's purple-faced rage. Would *she* now be destroyed at her friend's hands?

"You listen to me, McKenna Mendelson, and you listen *good!*" Stretch growled viciously. "I am *tired* of being played for a chump! Do you hear me? TIRED! You and everybody else in our backwater hometown, and now everyone in the goddamned *universe* by the looks of it, but especially by YOU! You put me down constantly for being a stupid idiot but my brain's the only weak thing about me—or it was, *until now!* It was your goddamned fault we got caught in the first place!

"If you had only cast one of your precious spells when that bunch of no-brains that caught us had first come on the scene, then we'd be back home and enjoying ourselves! But NO! *You* had to go and show me up! You should have found some weak spot in those chains so I could break 'em but you wanted me to make a fool of myself in front of those aliens. Just like I supposedly made *you* look like a fool in front of my cool athlete friends at UND! That was the only reason we got caught and *you know it!* Well, this is the end for me with you, get it? I will find some dark spot in this rusted metal crap-hole, lock you inside it and *sit on it* until you *die* for all the crap you put me through today! YOU UNDERSTAND THAT, MACK?"

Mack *did* understand. Fearlessly and as menacingly as she could appear under the circumstances—and given her short stature—she walked forward and began using the same low, almost masculine tone her friend had just used, in order to countermand her.

"All right *Melissa*! You've *had* your chance to insult my integrity and character—now I'm gonna insult *yours*!"

Stretch hated being addressed by her given name (except by her beloved father of course) and this did the trick, as Mack had expected, of refueling her angry fire. Stretch bared her lips back in a snarl, giving her the appearance of an enraged or spooked horse but otherwise did nothing for the time being as Mack spoke back to her in the same manner she had just used.

"You've had enough of *my* crap, have you?" Mack blazed. "The pot can't call the kettle black, Cunningham! You've annoyed *me* as much as I apparently have *you*! THANKS FOR *TELLING ME HOW YOU FEEL ABOUT ME, BY THE WAY*! Do you know how much trouble I've gotten in because of you? How they tried to drum you out of the Triple W for being such an incompetent witch that I had to threaten to *resign* in order to keep you in? Know how many guys won't ask me out because they're afraid Stretch the Giant Killer will smash them into the Earth with her thumbs if they do? No, you don't!

"You don't know much of *anything* do you? Except where it happens to be stuff that involves bouncing and throwing and hitting things! You think, now we got female leagues and tourneys for every sport imaginable you can get away with being the dumb jock huh? Well, you can't! Don't forget who the *brains* in this relationship is, Stretch old girl.

"And especially don't forget I helped you pass tests that you *needed to pass* in order to get to the next grade! Plus making sure that you could do those basic spells to pass the Triple W examination. You have speed and brawn aplenty Stretch—but you're not smart enough to realize you need your grey matter to help you out in this world. But I am smart enough, so if you listen to me we'll get out of this! If you don't want to, then you're dooming yourself to changing the light bulbs of every Prosperian chandelier for the rest of your life. Is that what you want Stretch? Seriously? Or do you still want to stay a *loser* without my help?"

"You *bitch*!" Stretch shouted. "You goddamned little *bitch*!"

"Well, we're even then," retorted Mack, "'cause you're a goddamn *big bitch*!"

"*I'll kill you*!" Stretch screamed.

"Not if I kill *you first*!" shouted Mack.

They bellowed and screeched like the wild animals they were descended from, launching themselves at one another.

VI.

The fight raged for several minutes and, by the end, the sparsely furnished room was a complete shambles. The two friends knew each other well, and so, fought in a manner designed to take advantage of each other's weaknesses. Knowing she was not in any way equal to her friend in size and strength, Mack concentrated her efforts on her gymnastic skills. She rolled and tumbled away from Stretch, as the latter foamed at the mouth in frustration. Her efforts to injure Mack with her fists became futile.

They stalemated at opposite ends of a wooden table and chair set in the center of the room, leering threateningly at one another other as they gripped either end of it. Mack acted fast and upended the table so that it fell legs first on top of Stretch. She then added the chairs as a form of counterbalance to weaken Stretch further, while she searched for an exit.

This search did not last long, as Stretch promptly regained her formidable strength and reduced the pile of wood on top of her to useless kindling. Mack, witnessing the explosion of the wood, tried to get away, only to have Stretch abruptly corner her and stomp a giant foot on top of her own. Using this time to her advantage, Stretch painfully ripped a lock of hair out of Mack's head and waved it under her nose. Mack, sensitive to anything in her nasal cavity, sneezed and fell back against the wall.

"Stretch, please!" Mack cried, knowing full well she was doomed, as the bigger girl prepared to throw one of her powerful arms in her face, while continuing to grind into Mack's foot with her heel. "I'm sorry! Everything just came out of me at once after you blew up at me...."

"It's *too late* for that Mack!" Stretch snapped. "Now I'm gonna do to you what I used to threaten to do to everyone who tried to hurt you when I wasn't looking. And believe me; you're *not* going to like it!"

Stretch threw Mack into the wall again with her leg and prepared to advance on her, the heavyweight champion mercilessly confronting a cornered opponent who was smaller and weaker. But when Stretch's super-powered fist finally connected, it wasn't with Mack's face....

VII.

"Holy cow, Stretch! Look at that!"

Mack had managed to duck Stretch's blow just in time, so when the taller girl's fist hit something solid, it was, in fact, the wall that she drove through. Though made of seemingly impenetrable steel (as their captors had boasted), the shock of connecting with Stretch's muscles caused the wall to come tumbling down—and expose a previously unknown avenue of escape for the girls! They gaped in astonishment as soon as that realization came to them.

"Geez!" Stretch exclaimed as she held her fist, showing signs of injury from the impact, but not an awful lot. "That *hurt!*"

"It hurt the wall more than it did you!" Mack pointed out. "The thing fell like it was made out of paper! Now we can hopefully find some way to get out of here, and back home."

"No," said Stretch, backing away as Mack tried to grasp her other hand.

"What gives Stretch?" Mack asked concerned.

"We can't be friends anymore now Mack," said Stretch. "I mean, I nearly *killed* you! Can you still *trust* me after that?"

"Are you *kidding*?" Mack answered, embracing her. "I need your help now more than ever, pal!"

"But after what I said to you…and what you said to me…."

"*That* only happened because there were quite a few things we clammed up about regarding each other, because we didn't want to hurt each other's feelings. We need to do that more Stretch. You know—let each other know there's some stuff we gotta work on as people. I know we spend a lot of time together but we still can't possibly know everything about each other, any more than we can our alien buddies. You gotta understand that I can take criticism, just like I expect you can too. Just like your games, you know—they throw you out if you won't play by the rules. Remember that?"

"Yeah," Stretch agreed. "I need to be more open with you I guess," she held up a hand like a Girl Scout reciting a pledge. "Look, Mack—if you can forgive me, I can forgive you and then I promise I won't *ever* try to kill you again…."

"You don't need to say all of that, Stretch," Mack said simply. "I know. And you do, too."

They hugged and then, walking proudly together, went off to explore what was in that hole created by Stretch's feat of strength.

VIII.

The hole, it turned out, was actually a crude, forced entranceway into the ship's ventilation system—which was not unlike those of the buildings of Earth, but, as the Prosperians were always facetiously putting it, theirs were *better*. From their understanding of how the things worked (Mack's more than Stretch's obviously) they determined that, if they crawled through the ventilation system, they would likely find some way to escape the confines of the ship. If the ship had taken off, it was simply a matter of stealing a small, portable vessel to return to Earth. If not, they could just escape by running away, if, by the smallest miracle, they ended up being undetected when they quit the scene.

Mack served as the advance trooper for the march through the ventilation shaft, being that she was the smaller and more mobile of the two of them in the confined spaces. Stretch, for once, was the one at a disadvantage, for her massive frame could barely be contained by the system's narrow causeways. Consequently, she either got stuck for long periods of time or got her head stuck in holes it had been responsible for creating. In both cases it was only through an assertion of her power, and the occasional assist from Mack, that Stretch was able to break this confinement and follow Mack through the limited space of the ventilation tunnels. As she had earlier, Stretch endured these indignities stoically, certain she and Mack would find a way out of their difficult predicament.

Finally, Mack came to a stop, rather abruptly, causing Stretch to create yet another hole in the pipe with her head while trying to prevent herself from running into Mack.

"Ssh!" Mack said to her friend, when Stretch got her head out of the next hole she had inadvertently created.

"What is it Mack?" Stretch whispered.

"There's a grate in front of me!" Mack said. "If we both get on it together it won't support us and we'll fall down onto whatever's below us."

"What's down there?" asked Stretch.

Mack went forward slightly and examined the contents of the room below. She backed up into the tunnel and reported.

"Looks like it's the laundry," she said. "All I could hear and see were the machines running." Then abruptly, she got an idea. "I think we're in luck Stretch."

"How so?" Stretch asked.

"Well, we need to get out of here and get our magic mojo back, don't we?"

"Uh huh."

"So, we're beneath the laundry room aren't we?"

"Yeah?"

"And what do they keep in the laundry room?"

"Washing machines?"

"Besides that!"

"Dryers?"

"Well, *obviously*! But this is a *military* vessel Stretch! The laundry room is where they clean the *uniforms*!"

"Okay. But what has that got to with *us*?"

Mack felt a burst of rage coming forward, as she sometimes failed to see how Stretch—or anyone else for that matter—could be as *stupid* as she was. But this feeling quickly passed and Mack continued.

"We can drop down through the gap in this pipe and snatch a couple of the uniforms," Mack explained. "Then we fall in with the others. Sooner or later we'll get a chance to present ourselves in Hamlet's chambers. When that time comes, we steal that little vessel he's using to keep our magical powers in and we get 'em back. Then we threaten to turn him into a toad or something unless he releases us and then we get to go home."

"That sounds good, Mack," Stretch said. "But how are we going to get out of here, first?"

"I got that covered," Mack answered. "I'm small enough to fit through that grating. I'll get the cover off of it and then I'll swing down and hang onto the edge with one hand. The other one I give to you and then we just start tugging until we get loose and fall down to the floor."

"You sure it's going to work?" Stretch asked.

"And I suppose *you* have a *better* idea?" Mack challenged. Silence was the response. "I *thought* so," said Mack.

She went to the edge of the vent and began pulling at the handles and locks holding the grate in place over the gap in the pipe. Had the material been sturdier, Mack would not have been able to get it as open as quickly as she did, with a speed that impressed Stretch. Once the panel was removed, Mack quickly got her body down into the gap. With one hand, she held onto the edge, with the other she gestured to Stretch.

"Now!" Mack commanded. "Give me your hand!"

"I...can't, Mack! I'm stuck here!"

"Well, I can't hold on like this all day you know. Never mind. I'll come over and...."

"NO!" Stretch suddenly screamed.

Mack suddenly let go of the edge with her other hand while she spoke. Now it appeared she would be doomed to fall to the ground!

Fortunately Stretch, with her athletic timing, asserted herself enough to send her right hand zooming out and catch Mack's hair just before she disappeared through the hole. Stretch tried to pull Mack back in but she didn't have enough of a grip to make her strength count. Her assertions of strength were enough however, to make the tunnel shake in response. Soon a gaping hole emerged beneath where Stretch was writhing and, before either she or Mack could do anything about it, they were falling...!

IX.

Mack and Stretch plummeted down to the ground, screaming as they fell, for they knew full well what waited for them below. Injury certainly, perhaps even death, if the injuries were severe enough. However, they were fortunate enough to hit two objects before they reached the floor. It was unfortunate for the two Prosperian soldiers who broke their fall—they were knocked out cold, as were the girls.

Stretch was the first to regain consciousness and when she did, she screamed loud enough to wake Mack—and everyone else on the ship that was asleep, seeing how far her voice could carry itself.

"What the hell...?" Mack said, as she revived herself and got up off the soldier who broke her fall. "What are you panicking about Stretch?"

"They're *dead*!" Stretch moaned. "We *killed* them! And when they find out about it, they'll kill *us*!"

Mack could not reach Stretch's face to slap her, which would have been the customary procedure to cure this oh-so-obvious case of hysterics on Stretch's part. So Mack did what she could do—she stomped hard on Stretch's foot.

"*Ow!*" Stretch shouted as she grabbed her injured foot. "Cut that out Mack! My feet are my fortune!"

"Shut up and stay calm!" Mack barked and when Stretch had acquiesced and restored the traditional stoic impression on her visage, Mack continued.

"We didn't kill these guys—we knocked them out is all. It'd take somebody even bigger than you to kill a guy if they fell on him. They're just out cold and they're in the perfect position for us to strip them and take what's theirs!"

"Mack!" Stretch was appalled. "We're virgins, remember? And I don't know how experienced they are but, with us being only thirteen, I think that would constitute rape, wouldn't it?"

"Their uniforms dummy!" Mack snapped. "We take their uniforms, pretend to be part of the team for a bit and then we find a vessel to get us back home. Is that clear enough for you?"

"Yeah," Stretch apologized. "Sorry, Mack. But you know how I feel about that kind of stuff...."

"You and your purity pledge!" said Mack affectionately. "I know. Come on. Let's get ourselves ready."

X.

Soon afterwards, two new Prosperian soldiers were unexpectedly added to the rolls. One was only slightly bigger than the average Prosperian. The older incredibly more so. Still, in the regulation helmet, gloves, boots, sunglasses, flak jackets and pants, they looked like they belonged. So, if anyone was initially suspicious of them, they eased their minds by chalking the appearance of the two new *men* up to the genetic abnormalities that occasionally occurred on Prospero, through the breeding of the native race with alien organisms.

As it turned out, these two new soldiers had joined at an opportune time. For, as soon as they exited the laundry room, a commandment was issued on the loudspeaker requesting (read: demanding) the presence of all available soldiers to present themselves in the presence of Commander Hamlet in the his chambers or instantly face charges of insubordination and therefore a speedy death. Thus, these two new entries in the Prosperian soldier sweepstakes were carried along a tide of troops to the chambers of Commander Hamlet. It was exactly where they wanted to be.

Hamlet was waiting for them. And he spoke to them nonstop for nearly three hours. About anything and everything they would need to know about the people and terrain of Earth, the planet they were about to invade. Everyone paid close attention as always, for they knew Hamlet disliked the idea that his speeches could be remotely considered a substitute for NyQuil—even if sometimes that actually was the case. The chief exceptions were the two larger-than-normal recruits plunked against the chamber walls. Those two had to be hissed at or violently coaxed into restoring their attention and senses when they began violently snoring in the midst of the oratory.

At the conclusion of the speech making, Hamlet and everyone else left the chamber. Save for those two.

"Boy!" Mack said as soon as they were gone and she had removed the helmet and glasses from her disguise. "What a windbag that Hamlet is, huh, Stretch? Stretch?"

Her companion was sound asleep; having been driven to that condition some time ago by Hamlet's wandering words. Mack was forced to clout her on the head to get her to wake up, which immediately did the trick.

"You sure hit hard Mack!" Stretch observed, removing her helmet and glasses and rubbing a pained spot on her head. "Even with the helmet on I felt it!"

"Who do you think I learned how to do it from?" Mack asked rhetorically. "Look! There's the thing with our magic in it!"

She had indeed spotted the sugar bowl-like container where Hamlet had contained the magical powers. The powers they had earned from long practice and skill development as witches, only to have him drain those powers from them and leave them helpless. But not for long.

Mack took the lid off the device and shined it in the direction of herself and Stretch, just as Hamlet had done earlier. Immediately their magical abilities—the skills that had made them qualified witches—were absorbed back into their bodies. As they did, Mack and Stretch found a renewed sense of vigor build inside of them.

"Have we got them back now?" Stretch asked.

"Only one way to find out. Let's do the fire spell and see if it works."

"Right," said Stretch.

They each said a low oath and sent an arm in the direction of the area they wanted fire to be created. In an instant the room was ablaze and filling with smoke.

"We got it back all right!" Mack coughed. "Let's get the hell out of here!"

"I'm with you!" Stretch agreed. Hastily putting their helmets and glasses on again, they left.

XI.

They were cornered immediately by a superior officer. Fortunately, there was no time for questioning anyone about tardiness or where they had been, for the invasion had begun! Mack and Stretch were simply hustled—bodily—to a two-person spaceport in a shuttle bay. They were told to report immediately as soon as they arrived at the intended destination—Grand Forks, North Dakota— within ninety minutes. Or else they risked disciplinary actions—such as death. What they were *not* told, was how to operate said spaceport, so they were left looking at it for a minute and wondering what to do. At least Stretch was.

"Mack!" she whimpered finally. "What are we gonna do? They're gonna destroy our hometown and we're letting them get away with it!"

"No we're not!" Mack growled in response. "Stop being a whiny little kid about this Stretch! We're going to get out of here and stop them, and that's that!"

"But how?" Stretch questioned. "We don't know how to fly this thing...or drive anything else for that matter!"

"We don't need to!" Mack said. "Get on!"

Once they were safely on board, Mack took the glove off of her right hand and waved it. A flash of light was directed at the spaceport's instrument panel, a short explosion occurred. A mechanical voice asked what was required, *"Sir?"*

"FLY!" Mack commanded. "To Grand Forks, North Dakota damn it and fast! And if you so much as *try* to drop us at Grand Forks, British Columbia, Stretch and I will take you apart and sell you for a considerable fortune in scrap metal! Got it?"

The message was received and understood. *"Sir"*. And abruptly, the pair found themselves hurtling through space....

XII.

The trip was fast and speedy and it was only through some of Mack's additional spells that they managed to hold on to the device for the descent downwards to Earth and Grand Forks. However, they got there as soon as possible and without a scratch on them. Such would not be the case for the following assault on the Prosperians but, by this time, Mack and Stretch no longer cared. Newly re-empowered with their magical skills—which served the purpose of compensating their physical abilities—they were determined to rid themselves of the alien menace to Earth, once and for all.

Mack ordered the machine to stop flying after she spotted the Prosperian troops massing alongside the Red River, in Riverside Park. It dropped down behind one of the stone walls the city had erected to keep the river at bay following the Flood of 1997. The young sorceresses shed their outer disguises and made their way down to where Commander Hamlet was addressing the troops, as he had before. He did not notice them, until he turned around and spotted them standing right behind him, (although most of the soldiers had already seen them and started quaking in fear in response).

"*You!*" he shouted angrily.

"Yeah!" Mack answered. "Us!"

"How did you escape...?" he began to demand, before Stretch cut him off by cuffing her hand around his neck.

"Shut up and listen!" Stretch growled. "We want you *out of here*...and not even in your precious *ninety minutes* either! We mean *now!*"

"You don't even want to *know* what we'll do to you if you don't!" added Mack. She tossed a beam of light on the ground to get their attention while Stretch, harshly and in a most undignified manner, threw Hamlet on the ground. He convulsed with rage in response.

"*Macbeth!*" he demanded of his subordinate. "You were supposed to have *restrained* them, remember?"

"Yes sir," said MacBeth. "But they escaped...."

"Escaped? How?"

"Like *this!*" said Stretch. She picked him up, punched him hard, and sent him flying into the nearest bush. He emerged even more disheveled than before and even more enraged.

"We *were* prepared to negotiate peacefully with your race, had you admitted the inadequacy of your firepower against ours," screamed Hamlet. "But now, *to hell with that!* ATTACK THEM! And KILL THEM!"

"Just *try* it!" Mack and Stretch snarled in unison.

Immediately, they were surrounded by the grey bodied, red-eyed Prosperians, who outnumbered them five to one. The pair were, however, up for the challenge. Just as before, they punched, kicked, wrestled, tackled and mercilessly beat up any Prosperian in their path. And, for extra emphasis, they made them magically disappear once they had defeated them, which reduced the size of the force they were fighting almost immediately and made the edge increasingly within their grasp. Yet it was at that moment the tide began turning.

One alien soldier remembered how Stretch had been humbled by the chains of Prospero earlier. Sensing how to control her, he taunted her as she fought off several of his fellows at once. His taunts enraged her enough to get her to chase him and then tricked her into sticking her hands out so he could stick the chains on her arms. He tightened them and she was weak once again. As she struggled in vain to free herself, a fresh corps of recently landed Prosperian soldiers arrived and forcefully pushed her to the ground and began attacking her.

"MACK!" Stretch bellowed at this point. "HELP ME! They got the chains on me again!"

Mack, in the midst of fighting off a larger than average size Prosperian as big as her, turned in the direction of Stretch once she heard her companion's cry. She ran to aid Stretch but her opponent, disregarding any rules of honor, on his or any other planet, literally stabbed her in the back!

"STRETCH!" Mack called out to her friend. "I've been HIT! I haven't got long!"

"NO!" Stretch shouted. She tried to rise but too many Prosperians held her in check.

"Don't worry!" Mack said. "I know what to do—the time reversal spell!"

"Are you *sure*?" asked Stretch. "That's kind of dangerous…"

"WE DON'T HAVE A CHOICE!" said Mack.

With her last remaining breaths, Mack uttered a series of archaic Latin words as loudly as she could. Then the entire park was surrounded by a dense, inky-black fog….

XIII.

"So that's it so far," Mack said. "What do you think?"

They were in Mack's room at home. She was seated at her desk as she read aloud the manuscript of her recently completed story to Stretch, who bent down by Mack's shoulder as she read.

"It's fine, by my standards anyway," the taller girl admitted as she stood to her full height. "But what do I know about writing? You said in there that I was just a dumb jock!"

"I had to exaggerate a bit Stretch," Mack admitted as she turned her chair around to face Stretch. "Our lives are *boring*. Publishers need things jazzed up if they're gonna read it, let alone *publish* it!"

"Yeah, but I'm not that dumb!" said Stretch. "You know that. And plus, I'm not that strong either."

"You can bench-press twice my weight! I saw you do that today!"

"Sure, but I can't punch my way through a wall. And you have me punching through a *metal* one, yet!"

"Like I said—exaggeration! That's what sells stories Stretch. You just don't understand the way the writing game works."

"Well, you got some things right. Our appearances, my height, our friendship. Except that bit about us fighting each other—we'd never *really* do that, right?"

"Sure we wouldn't. But the story needed conflict..."

"Never mind the writer jargon Mack—it only confuses me. I'm used to normal stories and magic and aliens and unbreakable chains and all that stuff you have us go through just isn't normal."

"Writers write what they know Stretch," Mack insisted. "I know you and me and what we do. All I did was put us into a fairly fantastic setting and let us loose. No harm in that, right?"

"No," Stretch admitted. "But just don't push the fantasy bit too far. *Or* share this piece of whimsy with anybody who could use it against me. If I hear anybody start calling me "Stretch The Giant Killer," I'll come down here and beat you up *so hard...*"

"Okay Stretch!" Mack answered. "I'll lay off on it for a bit. But it takes the stress off me, you know? Just like you on the court."

"Yeah," said Stretch. "Never thought of it like that," she flexed one muscled arm for them both to see. "But still, my guns may be big but *nobody* is the kind of strong you made me in your little fairy tale. If I didn't actually *have* a brain in my head, I might really believe that and I'd get myself into trouble."

"That's the last thing I wanted buddy," Mack said as she and Stretch firmly embraced.

"Well, I gotta go," Stretch said as she broke their clinch. "See you later Mack. And be careful about what you write about!"

"I will. So long Stretch."

When her friend had left the room, Mack thoughtfully considered the manuscript she had written for a moment. Then she dropped it on the floor and waved her hands above it and toward her desk. In moments, the bottom drawer of the desk opened, the manuscript floated into it and then the drawer closed.

THE END

In the Shadow
of the Banyan Tree
(Honorable Mention)

By

Jennifer Phillips

Concentrating on an itch that cannot be scratched is a certain path to insanity.

Although my muscles are paralyzed, I can still feel everything. Some assume that the paralysis extends to my nerves but this is not the case. I can feel everything—every bedsore, every fly that walks upon my arm, every piercing jab of a mosquito and every tingle that becomes an itch. I feel it all; I just cannot do anything about it. The fly has free reign to march up and down my torso until he becomes bored and leaves. The mosquito feeds on me until sated, flying away heavy and full of my blood. The itching develops and builds. Like an orchestra settling into a movement, it starts and swells; it expands and reaches a crescendo before it finally passes. I say it again: *Concentrating on an itch that cannot be scratched is a certain path to insanity.*

Indonesia has been my home for many years but I have been in Denpasar for only three of those years. More precisely, three years, six months and four days, which means I have called this place—the Denpasar Nursing and Aging Care Facility—home for three years, six months and one day. It took three days for doctors to determine that although I was alive, no one was coming to claim me. I was far from my home and the company, scouting for locations. No one missed me and no one would ask for me. Others had been lost at sea with little notice; anonymity has its price.

Someone has left the television on and because no one has thought to set me upright today, I can only listen. My understanding of Bahasa, the official language of Indonesia, is enough that I can discern from the disembodied voices on the newscast I hear that I have ninety minutes left to live.

My name is Jonah Ripert but no one here knows this. When I was found on the beach, breathing but immobile, I carried no identification or any of my work permit papers per the unwritten and unspoken company policy for those who do my job.

My room is at the end of the ward and outside my window stands an ancient banyan tree. Twisted and dense, with contorted branches growing back, around, and down to the ground as though they are reaching for something unattainable, the tree occupies many of my days and many of my thoughts. Geckos and birds move in and out of the deep hollows created by the tree's structure and at times the tree appears to move, so active are its residents. The massive tree is the living subject of the only picture in my room. The window that frames the picture is warped by heat and humidity has blistered and cracked the paint. This is the image that occupies my days when someone is kind enough to prop me upright.

Members of the staff say the tree is haunted. A small boy (his age, like much of time in Indonesia, is indeterminate—some say he was four, others say six) fell to his death after climbing the tree to get a better look at the ocean just beyond. He was trying to see if he could locate his father's fishing boat but his foot became tangled in part of the trunk causing him to lose his balance. His spirit is said to inhabit the tree, and the branches that reach the ground and become part of the trunk are his arms, stretching to find his father. Local parents tell the story as a cautionary tale, suggesting to misbehaving offspring that the tree took the boy's life and kept his spirit because he was not obedient.

I sometimes hear the staff conversing in Bahasa. They call me *orang asing*, foreigner, or sometimes *raksasa*, giant. These are the same words they use to describe the banyan tree. Yet it is the word *haunted* that describes me and the tree best.

I can smell the salt air that drifts through the open window, which means the wind is blowing directly off the sea. It mixes with the lingering scent of chemicals used to clean and disinfect the room, a nostril-burning mixture of lemon and ammonia. Rooms are cleaned every day with the same citrus solution, washing away the hints of death that are deposited slowly by the residents. The ward is largely silent; most of my neighbors are now gone. As soon as the warning sirens sounded some rickety busses, discovered too late to be too small, carted away those who retained the small dim light of cognizance. I have had no visitors and no inquiries since I arrived here and am therefore expendable. A few others are left behind. I can hear a woman screaming now, down the hall. She is crying for her mother but this is a trick of the madwoman's imagination; her mother is long departed. I am the youngest person in this nursing home. It was the only place equipped to handle my condition.

My thoughts wander down the abandoned hallways of the place I have called home, rendering pictures of rooms and views of the center courtyard I can now see only through my mind's eye. I see the kitchen, ill-equipped by Western standards but nonetheless capable of preparing spare but adequate meals for those who can still eat. Although my eating regimen consists of intravenous feedings, the smells from the kitchen help me create in my mind the island meals that once were part of my daily diet. My meals' simplicity hid their daily magic—combinations of chili and garlic and *ketjap*, that evoked memories of its lesser descendant ketchup—combined with fish so fresh it twitched until it was cooked. What I would give for another dish of *bami goreng*, with its steaming stir-fried noodles, or a platter of *krupuks*, the addictive shrimp chips that if they ever caught on in America would give tasteless cardboard potato chips a run for their money.

I have much time to think as I lie here in Denpasar. The stroke that hit me as I was piloting a small boat, scouting new ocean locations for my employer, rendered me completely immobile. I do not recognize the medical terms the doctors and staff use. Medical terms in Bahasa are beyond my comprehension. In the chemically induced medical hazy days after I was rescued, there was but one phrase uttered in English for some inexplicable reason: locked-in syndrome. This phrase I understand. I can move my eyelids but that is all. When you cannot move and cannot communicate, you are left with your thoughts and sometimes being alone with your thoughts is the most painful torture of all. My thoughts skip and jump, like the small lizards called *chechucks* that defy gravity and run up the egg-yolk yellow walls throughout the ward. I think back to what brought me here: my divorce, the job, Indonesia, the smell and taste of food—here, there, jump jump jump, my mind tries to fill my days with thoughts, a thin substitute for human connection.

I will not say that our divorce was easy or painless; all divorces are painful in some way. But ours was not one of those bitter, protracted battles that pull all involved down in wave after wave of suffocating anger. What played out before us was not a battle but an evaporation, ending not with a grand flourish of attorneys and judges. Instead it dispelled, like the mist on a hot road following a summer rain. After a few hours in the midday sun the only evidence that the road had ever been wet is a few dank puddles of stagnant water. All that remained after the meager possessions and sizeable debt were divided was a thin file of fragile paper documents, one page noting the union, another sealing its dissolution. They are like the leaves on the banyan tree, easily rustled by the wind. Of the two events codified in the documents it is the divorce, not the marriage, which has proved to be as solid as the tree's trunk. The banyan tree does not bend and neither do I.

Why did someone choose to paint these walls yellow? I have had time to reflect on this and it is my guess that this was an attempt to impart a sunny, cheerful air to the rooms. Instead they cast a jaundiced light on everyone, giving even the healthiest staff members a sickly pallor. The nursing home, painted attempts at cheer aside, is one of the saddest places in this town. It is an underfunded home for the destitute aging and those whose problems are beyond the capacity of their families to care for them emotionally or financially. It is a dumping ground for the crazy and ill— and, apparently, the best option for unidentifiable quadriplegic expatriates. Even my favorite nurse, a young woman named Siri whose hair smelled like lychees and fresh cream when she leaned over me to expertly make the bed with me still in it, had a sickly pallor in these rooms. Her smile and sunny disposition countered the effect of the yellow walls. She chattered away in a dialect I did not know and did not need to know. I wonder where she is now and hope that she is safe.

I can hear others moving in the hall now. We were left here in haste and some are wondering where their midday meals are. "*Nasi, nasi;*" a man calls out for rice. He begins to bang on the wall with a rhythmic beat, calling for food that has no chance of materializing. I envy the others who do not understand their fate; the end will come quickly and unexpectedly for them. I am alone in my understanding of what soon will happen. Many of them could escape if they knew. I know, but can do nothing.

I have tried to teach myself to shift my thoughts elsewhere.

When I shift my thoughts, I think of the ocean. The same water that is outside my window now was at one time my job. I worked for a chemical company in the States and after the divorce I wanted to leave, escape to somewhere else. The position in Jakarta had no U.S. equivalent but my transfer request was approved. I knew little about Indonesia. Some travel shows on Bali were the extent of my introduction to my new home. Everyone who describes arriving in a Third-World country seems to use the same phrase: "an assault on the senses." The acrid smell of garbage hangs in the air, held in place by humidity so high it traps odors close, low to the ground. Roads have lanes helpfully painted but routinely ignored and instructions for the flow of traffic are considered little more than a quaint suggestion. Traffic consists of an improbable mix of cars, trucks, motorcycles and scooters, busses, *becaks* (modified bicycles with a driver on back and passengers in front) and the occasional donkey, all moving at the maximum possible speed that conditions allow, starting and stopping without warning. There is little that can prepare you for Jakarta traffic but I credit a series of successive summers at the local amusement park with considerable time dedicated to the thrill rides.

* * *

It did not take me long to love Indonesia. Living in Florida prepared me for the heat, humidity and the sudden afternoon showers that washed the streets and rooftops during the rainy season, leaving them wet and clean, if only for a short time. The people are wonderful. Small, smiling and patient, they surprised me with their warmth and acceptance. It made for a sharp contrast to my daily work life at the facility.

My first job was in the lab, a medium-sized detached building in the company's complex, separated from the manufacturing area by a footpath lined with crushed shells. Entering the lab was another dose of culture shock. This was not the pristine and sterile image of a scientific lab shown in movies and on television. The lighting was adequate but flickered with the inconsistency characteristic of unreliable power backed up by generators. The desks and furniture were a mish-mash of what looked to be discarded office equipment from the mid-'80s. Walls were lined with cages of animals, used to test responses to the chemicals the company was manufacturing. My job was to clean and dispose of the testing waste, verifying the volume against the day's experimentation schedule and transporting this hazardous cargo to the incinerator. The cages contained a nightmare of balding and burned cats and dogs, skin blistered and peeling, with sores oozing red and yellow and green. Glass slides captured pus and blood for examination by detached and seemingly robotic scientists. After two days working in the lab, I turned to chemicals of a different sort. The local pharmacists asked no questions when I begged for something to help me sleep.

One day a gray kitten was brought in. After three days of testing he still showed no signs of any reaction to the chemicals they had pasted on a shaved spot on his left side. They painted the poisonous sludge on him with a cotton swab, demented artists working on a living canvas. Late that night, on the kitten's third day, I was cleaning the lab when an earthquake rattled the building. It was enough to spring the latches on many of the cages but the tortured residents didn't have the capacity to exploit their sudden fortune. I quickly tucked the gray kitten into an inside pocket of my shirt, well underneath the work-issued coveralls. He seemed to understand and signified his willing complicity in his kidnapping by remaining completely silent until I got him home. He lived with me for nine months. His fur grew back and he was a happy and playful cat, showing gratitude in the way that only rescued animals can convey. Late in his eighth month with me, he developed a cancerous tumor that grew with such ferocity I would have sworn I could see it pulsing and growing if I stared at him long enough. He did not suffer for long; the cancer moved very quickly. The tumor was on his left side.

Eventually I was reassigned to another part of the disposal process. After some reflection, I believe it was my size that condemned me to the reassignment. I am six feet tall—not that large by American standards but I stand a full head above most of my Indonesian coworkers. My height provided the perfect leverage for the job at hand. The company was limited in the amount of waste that could be incinerated—not by the volume going in but by the emissions coming out. In some months the volume to be incinerated exceeded the allowed limits. My boss in Maintenance and Disposal was a stocky, red-faced Australian who looked like a hairy and unkempt version of the short balding guy from the television show *Seinfeld*. Jeremy Brechtel was vile in manner and he never met a rule he intended to follow. This disdain for rules and the reasons behind them is why I found myself on the deck of a boat, rolling heavy yellow drums of chemical waste into the ocean.

"How deep is it here—are these barrels going to wash up on shore?" I asked.

"It's plentay deep," his Australian accent lengthening the word.

"But what happens if the salt water corrodes the barrels?"

"Dilution is the solution," he said with a wide grin, rubbing a sweaty forearm across his forehead as he lifted the Gunung Api Chemicals-logoed baseball cap off his sunburned head. "We're pretty far out here," he continued. He winked at me and smiled, putting his cap back on, setting it straight and low across his brow. Salt water stung my eyes as I rolled the next barrel in and watched it sink, thinking of the walls of the lab lined with the ramifications of the barrel's contents and my happy gray kitten, which I had named Fred. I do not remember if it was the sea or sweat or tears that stung my eyes.

* * *

The activity on the television sends a flickering light through my room. My time is running short now and the sirens outside are piercing the air. I have between fifteen and twenty minutes left. Speed, gravity, and water depth—I am guessing at all of these but know that the combination of these components is my death warrant. The low rumble that is the instigating cause of my pending death was barely felt here on land. This is not how I would have chosen to die. Of course I have thought of death, longed for it even. The inability to move after years of travel and exploration is a prison; the term locked-in is apt. The irony of locked-in syndrome is that you can think of many ways to take your own life, all of which involve the need for you to be able to do something. You must move an arm to use a gun. You must be able to swallow to take pills. Yet if I could do these things—move my arms, swallow on my own—that alone would remove the impetus to end my life. It is precisely because I cannot do these things for myself that I am compelled to think of ways to take my own life. I suppose I am as prepared as anyone could be and yet it is the fact that this end is not of my choosing that makes it unbearable.

If I could run again, I would. I have run from many things. I ran from my role as a husband. I ran from my home and all of the things that reminded me I was not who I wanted to be. I ran from the familiar and then I ran from the unknown. I ran from my responsibility to report the chemical dumping because I needed my job, then I ran from that job because the nightmares of burned and scarred creatures invaded my dreams every night. So I ran to pills and sleep agents because I could. I ran until a stroke stopped me. Now only my thoughts run; my mind races. By forming no bonds, I grew no roots. The freedom was a prison itself though and my condition, while in captivity, has allowed my mind to form the bonds my soul could not bear to establish.

* * *

She is coming for me, the angry sea. Full of chemicals I dumped, creating a toxic cauldron of the next decade's industrial solvents. A sudden gust of wind pushes into the room and is sucked out just as quickly, a deep exhale and inhale on the shore. The wind has dislodged a curl and the lock of hair hangs loosely across my forehead. A maddening tickle stretches across my face, causing so much sensation that it hurts, and I can feel a bead of sweat form and trace a path from my temple to my cheek.

I am crying as the waves crash into the building. The water is cold and murky as the tsunami swallows me whole. The last thing I see is the banyan tree, reaching for me as I breathe in the ocean, my body unable to release the scream inside.

THE END